# TIMED OUT

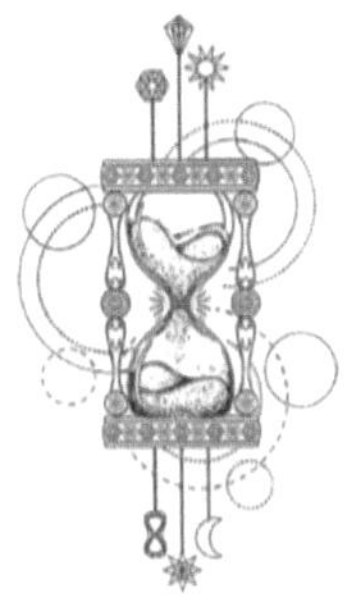

Micky O'Brady

Timed Out
Copyright © 2024 Micky O'Brady
Cover Design: www.KimG-Design.com
Interior Format: Dorothy Dreyer

Published by Snowy Wings Publishing
PO Box 1035, Turner, OR 97392

Paperback ISBN: 978-1-958051-50-4
eBook ISBN: 978-1-958051-49-8

# Table of Contents

# Chapter One –

# Bubbled Up

Somewhere, Somewhen

My pillow moves.

Up and down. Up and down. Up and down.

Ow. Not good for my headache.

I force my heavy eyelids open, only to be assaulted by blinding whiteness. *Whoa.* Too bright. Squinting, I reopen my burning eyes, this time slower. More carefully. Still, everything is white, the super-pure kind, illuminated, and yes, blinding, like I was swallowed by an immaculate cloud too close to the sun. I blink. Then blink again. No change. Everything stays white. Maybe something is wrong with my eyes. I lift a hand to rub them, then drop it, when the spike in blood pressure cranks up the headache by the nth degree.

A raspy, pitiful groan leaves my throat.

"Shh," somebody whispers, voice rough. "Take it easy. That stuff had a good bite to it." My pillow moves—and sits up from under me.

What the—

I jackknife up to sitting, only to be rewarded by a rush of nausea and the sensation of an axe splitting my head in two. "Ngh."

"Told you to take it easy." A cool hand is pressed against my neck. "Give it a minute, it'll get better."

*Kieran?* Ignoring the advice, I whip my head around, elation flooding me and washing away the nausea when my gaze falls on the person sitting behind me in this all-white room. "Kieran!"

He looks worse for the wear, still in his captain's uniform, only it would be a violation of USEF dress code if he ever showed up for duty in a uniform as dirty and tattered as this one. Or the way he looks in general: his black hair disheveled, dark circles under his eyes. Still, he gives me a wry smile, wiggling his fingers as a greeting. "Hi."

I'm about to lean forward and throw myself around his neck, when my brain catches up with my surroundings—and no, not this featureless, white room of nothingness, rather, my situation and the last thing I remember. And that's not a pleasant memory. At all. It brings the nausea right back up to full force.

"That guy," I whisper. "We were on the *Hope*. The war was about to flare up. Your appeal to the fleet… and then in your quarters, that guy." I swallow hard as the memory resurfaces, but it doesn't keep the rising anger at bay. I've done the whole 'being kidnapped' thing. I've been there, done that, got the t-shirt, or rather the bionic leg. I really, *really* didn't need to repeat the experience.

Kieran presses his lips into a thin line. "That guy, whoever he was, shot us with whatever it was. And brought us here, to wherever this is." He makes a swiping gesture with his left hand. "For whatever reason."

I huff. I can wager a guess. Lifting both hands, I put the next words into air quotes. "Because we violated the one major timeline." What BS—we didn't do anything! My First Sense is clear, leaving no room for doubt: Kieran needed to come out of the Essken Realm. I know that. Meaning, that can't be it; can't be the *major violation of the timeline*. There's nothing else though that would be a violation—strong word to begin with—of the timeline. I should know, shouldn't I? First Sense and all?

Kieran harrumphs. "Violating the timeline. Quite ironic, given that until a few hours ago, I was stuck in a place where time works differently. I literally haven't had the time to do anything. I was considered dead for close to four decades."

His words trigger a memory. Blame it on whatever the guy shot us with, but I'm definitely slower than usual. The Taro's message I received during Kieran's speech and only a few minutes before we were taken against our will, is not something I'd usually forget:

*Something is off. Lieutenant Thorburn, do not trust anybody. Stay alert. Listen to your First Sense. The Temporal War isn't over.*

I close my eyes and groan.

"What?"

While my mind might be slow today, my emotions have no problem rising to the challenge. Biting down onto my cheek to ground myself, I count to three before I trust myself to speak without screaming in frustration. And I shouldn't be screaming. I need to break news to Kieran I wouldn't consider easy to digest. Would I have preferred to talk about the Temporal War and how it messed us up at home, over a nice cup of tea, after Kieran has had time to come to terms with what has happened to him? For sure. Do we always get what we want? Apparently not.

I sigh. "You know, maybe that guy was right, or maybe he wasn't. I do know there's a third option." I pause, chewing on my lower lip. "The FBTI knows about a temporal war being fought upstream from my time, from the future. We don't know why—who started it, who the players are, and what the reason for it is, but we do know it comes from the—my—future and aims to change something in the—my—past." Given the Taro's warning, it's not too tough to add one and one and arrive at two, meaning, the guy could have something to do with the Temporal War. And therefore, so could his statement that we violated the timeline. Someone could be manipulating him—or us.

Kieran's alert gaze stays focused on me as he narrows his eyes, digesting the news. "A temporal war. A *temporal* war. You think— You think we were taken because of this war?"

"It's possible. They've tried to intervene at many points in time, most of them in the past, why not in our *now?*" My headache pounds, which doesn't make thinking any easier.

Cocking his head, he whistles through his teeth. "At many points in time—is that why you were in the past, with us, so much?"

"Yes." I nod. "After the Battle of Balthar when I returned to my time, the Taro, Zio, and I all felt a shift in the timeline. Our First Sense alerted us something had changed, something was trying to alter the past. To make a long story short, somebody in the future put one of our admirals under their influence and sent him back in time to—" I shift my weight. This is awkward.

"To what?"

"To kill you." There, I said it.

"To kill *me.*" Kieran takes the news cool as a cucumber with one eyebrow raised. "Why would anybody go through such effort to get rid of me?"

"That's a very good question. Mashaule—"

"Mashaule? Mashey?" Kieran jerks his head back, eyebrows pinched together. "My former *Captain* Mashaule?"

I grimace. "Yeah. Yes. Admiral Mashaule. He had... issues. He claimed killing you would save billions of lives." I know the moment the words leave my mouth, I shouldn't have spoken them. Kieran pales and drops his gaze. What a beginner's mistake on my part. I knew the loss of life during the war troubled him greatly, and that wasn't his fault to begin with. The way he looked before he went into that nebula where he got swallowed by the Realm... I wouldn't say he was broken, but he wasn't whole either. Chocho losing Suzie under his command didn't make it any better. Actually, it might've been what pushed him over the edge, another loss close to home. His guilt was almost palpable. Me telling him his death could've saved billions? Yeah. Not helping, Thorburn. Not helping.

I clear my throat and scramble to save what I messed up. "Obviously they were—are—wrong. All of our First Senses—"

"But what if they were right?" Kieran's voice is so low I'd have a hard time hearing him if it wasn't so unnaturally dead quiet in here. Giving me a challenging look, he repeats himself. "What if they were right? If they're from the future, they must know more than we do."

Nu-uh, I refuse to believe that. "Why? History swallows details all the time. And they weren't right," I say with conviction. "If I had to pick one person who always fought for peace, it was—is—you, Kieran. If anything, killing you would have made the war worse. I'm sure of it." I know it from the bottom of my heart and within the depth of my soul. Call it my First Sense, sure, but I *know* the war would have been worse without Kieran.

He holds my gaze for a long three seconds, then lowers his chin in a nod. "Okay. I'm really hoping that shoe won't fit. And to get back to matters at hand, if we were taken from the *Hope* because of this Temporal War, they're clearly not in a hurry. I've been awake for about half an hour. Nothing has happened."

I blow out a puff of air through pursed lips. One crisis narrowly averted. "That's... good, I would say."

Kieran shrugs. "Good or bad, no idea. From a tactical point of view, I like being left in peace. The longer we have to recover, the stronger we get and the more information we can collect. Which unfortunately leads me to the bad part of this."

"Which is what?" I repeat my earlier attempt to rub my eyes, and this time the headache is merciful enough to not try to kill me.

"There's nothing here that would help us in any way." He gestures to the all-white area around us, frustration creeping into his words. "This is a prison. Brig. Whatever you want to call it."

Not that I expected otherwise. You get shot at and abducted—and put in a five-star accommodation? Unlikely. Still. I raise an eyebrow. "This looks way too nice." Roomy, bright, no bars... okay, also no windows. No door within view either. No furniture at all either. Only this endless bright white all around us.

"Don't let that fool you. Look around. What do you see?"

I turn my head from left to right, checking out my surroundings.

"It looks like a really big room. At least fifty by fifty meters, tough to say, because of all the bright white light. I'd say the walls are also white, but they're somehow glowing? It's weird for sure." I mean, after a few meters, everything turns milky-foggy. Plus, even the floor is white, but comfy and cushioned, as if a thick, plush carpet covered it, only it looks like white concrete. Feels rough, yet cushy. Definitely weird, and the ceiling no less. I look up, narrowing my eyes. "Is that… a dome?" The lack of contrast or anything other than this endless perfect white makes it impossible to determine if this is a flat ceiling about four or five meters above us, or a dome.

"Good question. I think it is, but I also think we shouldn't trust that."

Uh-oh. "Why?"

He sighs. "Before you woke up, I had a look around. This room is maybe four by four meters, if at all."

"What?" I turn my head so fast from left to right, a wave of dizziness crashes over me. "It looks so much bigger—"

"It must be that foggy milky white messing with our eyes. But once you walk, you walk right into a wall, there, there, and there." He points in three directions.

Out of habit, I feel for PADdy on my wrist to confirm with a scan—and find nothing. For one short second, I allow myself disappointment. Of course, whoever abducted us would've taken my wrist PAD. Not a surprise. Just very, very annoying.

Dropping my hand from my wrist, I focus on our priorities. "What about there?" I nod in the direction of the only location Kieran didn't mention.

"Funny you should ask. Once you reach that corner, a toilet becomes visible. A sink. They just appear. From where? Don't ask me. You step back, they're gone. Get closer, they're back."

I snap my mouth closed. Right. Sorting my sore limbs, I work myself up to standing, my biosynthetic left knee doing most of the work. Curious, I walk several large steps to the left—and like Kieran said, a toilet appears out of thin air. I kick it. "Solid." Backing up, I keep my eye on it until it dissolves, for a lack of a better word. I whistle through my teeth as the nausea inside my stomach changes into something else, more of a bitter, acidic feeling as I ask the one question I've learned to prioritize: "When do you think we are?" And speaking of… I push one hand into my pocket. Also, no SED, no Setayashi-emitting device. Of course not. Didn't really expect it to be there, but one can always hope.

A muscle in Kieran's jaw twitches as he stands up. "When we are? Definitely not in my time, not that I expected that anymore after you mentioned a temporal war. I can't speak for you, but given that you also seem surprised by the vanishing toilet act, I assume it's not yours, either." He shakes his head and balls his fists at his side. "I don't know. Somewhen in the future, so much is sure, but why? Because of crimes against the timeline we supposedly committed? Or because of a war we're no part of? What the absolute—!" I jerk as he slams one palm into the wall behind him. It wafts and fluctuates, like it was made out of a mix of cloud and waterbed. When he speaks again, his voice is rough, barely controlled. "I just spent thirty-five years in the Essken Realm. Thirty-five years in a place my mind couldn't make sense of. I came out, the world was still at war with the Essken, nothing had changed. *This* doesn't help." He rams his palm once more into the wall, a desperate grunt tearing from his throat, so full of misery and despair, it hurts.

My heart goes out to him. "Kieran, I—"

Like a switch flipped, a strong tingling runs down my whole body, head to toes and back again. Energy ripples through the air, bringing goosebumps and every hair on my body to rise. For one tiny, short, minuscule moment I feel dizzy, confused, disoriented—

Kieran drops his hand with a deflated sigh. "I just came home, Nonie. I haven't eve—" Gasping mid-word, he wraps both arms around his midsection, eyes wide. "Holy—! What the—?" He sucks in a sharp breath through his teeth, but before I can even react, another wave of overwhelming dizziness hits so bad, I have to close my eyes or I'd fall over. When I open them again, everything is blurry, like something is wrong with my eyes. I blink and rub them, but still, everything's as blurry as before.

A pained grunt comes from Kieran, tearing me out of my half-frozen state. He doubles over, wrapping his arms around his body, his teeth clenched.

"Kieran!" I dart forward—and stop dead after half a step like I ran into a wall. Something is pushing on me, even though nothing's there, but I feel a weight on me, or rather, around me. My whole body is being squished as if the air is hugging me too tightly, making breathing difficult. A weird buzzing sensation hums in my veins, making the tips of my fingers tingle.

Kieran stiffens and gasps, his grimace becoming more harrowed, and with another suppressed grunt, he sinks down to one knee, unsteady. Finally, I snap out of it, reflex taking over. I grab him by the hand—

*Zzzing!*

I might as well have touched a live wire. The moment my skin touches his, a surge shoots through me, igniting me from the inside. A strangulated groan breaks from my throat as I double over, my body on fire. I grunt and grit my teeth, panting hard. My insides burn, *everything* burns, but I can't let go. My muscles won't obey my commands, and the onslaught of cutting pain makes my knees buckle.

I choke on a choppy inhale. Something pulses inside my body in a desperate way, each pulse sharp as knives, cutting deep, and with it comes an instinctual urge to… To do what? Can't think clearly, and it's not like I could stop this, whatever it is.

Kieran's breaths come out in short puffs, his body rigid. Whatever is happening to us, it's scary. My core aches more and more with every second, pushing me closer to the limit of what I can tolerate—

Until something snaps on my inside—and everything changes. Euphoria floods me, together with a whole-body tingle and a tsunami of endorphins, soothing my aching core. Instead of a burning inferno it feels more like a warm, wholesome churning, something I could rather get used to. The whole-body prickle increases and shifts away from my center into my arms, bringing the tingle in my hands to a whole new level. For about three whole seconds, utter blissful relief floods me, then, as if that same switch turned it off, everything is over.

A sigh of relief breaks from Kieran's throat, followed by a hoarse inhale.

Neither of us moves, only the sound of our ragged breathing filling the room.

Then, Kieran blows out one long, wheezing exhale. "Are you okay?" His gaze finds mine, wide and wary at the same time.

I shake my head and let go of him. "No. Yes. I— I guess so. It felt nauseous and dizzy at first, but when I touched you… it hurt." I shake out my hands to get rid of the residual weird sensation.

The apple in his throat moves up and down. "No nausea for me. Only a blast of cold air, and then, well, it hurt, like something was tearing me apart on the inside. Acid running through my veins would feel similar." He tries to shrug it off, like it wasn't a big deal, but his pallor is calling him a liar. "What was that?"

"I have no idea." I never felt anything like it before. "But it affected both of us."

Chewing on his lower lip, Kieran leans his head from the left to the right. "Could it have been an invasive scan? Or a weapon?" He motions around us. "We know nothing about where or when we are. Who knows what technology these people use, and for what reason."

"I don't know. I would say if this was a scan, I don't want to know what type of weapons they have. Maybe it was a defensive mechanism because you punched the wall. Maybe a deterrent from breaking out?" I wrap my arms around his torso. What a weird and scary episode, but weird and scary have been our middle names for quite a while at this point. I'm learning not to freak out, unless there's a very good reason for it, and right now, we're not there. Yet, maybe, but still. "Either way, since I am very unfortunately PADdy-less, there's nothing I can do to find out. Though, maybe don't punch the wall, in case that triggered it." I stick my tongue out at him.

Kieran chuckles and relaxes into me. He snuggles his nose into my neck, the warmth of his breath calming me, despite the crappy situation we're in. "Good plan, Lieutenant. And… well, I'm sorry for losing it and punching said wall. I just… I just feel like I haven't even taken a breath since I got sucked into the Realm. Heck, since the war started. And you know me, I hate not having all the information."

"Like now."

"Like now. It's in my job description as a USEF captain to be proactive. To know the game being played. But how can I, when the advantage is so clearly on the attacker's side?"

Determination floods my system. "We're going to find out where we are, when we are, and how we can get back home." And I mean it. Less than two months ago, I was flung into the past, kept the timeline intact, made it back home, took down a madman—okay, granted, said madman escaped—but I followed him, tracked him through time and space, watched my boyfriend die, found out he didn't, rescued him from the Essken Realm, and watched him potentially avert war between the Essken and humanity—and now we're here. Kidnapped.

As ridiculous as it sounds, I've been through worse than being abducted to the future.

And so has Kieran.

I pull away from him and squeeze his arms. Part of me notices he hasn't lost any muscle mass when he was in the Realm. He's really the Kieran who quote-unquote just left the *Pioneer* to fly into that nebula. "We got this, Kieran. It's the famous Captain Wildason and the youngest academy graduate in the history of the academy." Well, up to *that* point in time, but still. "Whoever got us here, we'll find a way to go back home and everything will be fine." I ball my fists at my side.

"Of course, it will," Kieran whispers hoarsely, and when I look up at him, he smiles. If I didn't know him so well, if I wasn't so obsessed with everything Kieran, I might not have seen the dullness in his eyes. Or heard the undertone in his voice.

But I do, and I did.

And it scares me.

It scares me, because it doesn't sound like Kieran believes what he just said.

It scares me.

# TIMED OUT

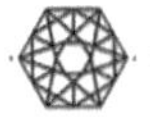

## *Somewhere Inside That Bubble-Thing, Somewhen*

For the next two or maybe three hours, nothing happens. After a while, both of us drift off to sleep, cuddled into each other. It could be ten minutes or ten hours later, when I jerk awake from an ear-piercing, shrill alarm sound.

"What the—!"

Kieran and I jump to our feet, in our fighting stance. My heart races, but at least adrenaline has chased away the cobwebs of sleep enough to complete a sentence. "What the heck is going on?"

The light of our prison changes: No more uber-white, bright light, but instead an intense, all-encompassing red floods the room. The alarm cranks up the volume and rhythm, from a whining, two-second spanning howl down to short bursts of screeching beeps—and then stops at the same time as part of the wall to our left disappears, leaving a rectangular opening, about door-sized.

USEF training takes over in an instant. Kieran moves forward in his fighting stance, cautious but determined, and I follow. An open door is an invitation until proven otherwise, right?

*"Prisoners, stop."*

The voice comes out of nowhere, surrounds us and echoes through the room as *something* changes in the floors. One second, they're squishy and soft, the next—not. Like strong and unyielding instant magnetism, my feet are glued to the surface.

I grunt as velocity and inertia carry me forward over my feet cemented to the ground. Stretching my arms out, I catch my balance before falling forward. Kieran isn't doing any better than me; we both look like first-time ice skaters who hit a snag in the ice, trying to not fall forward. I give each of my feet a good yank, but to no avail. "I'm stuck!"

"Me too." Kieran squats down, examining his shoes and trying to pry the soles off the ground. "There's nothing between my shoe and the ground, and I can't even lift my foot inside the—"

"Quite the useless exercise you're engaging in." This time the voice is coming from the door, loud, clear, and a tad arrogant. We both snap our heads up. The sticky floors can wait.

The man standing in the entrance to our... *room* is the same man I saw last before blacking out on board the *Hope*: mid-thirties, I would guess. Brown, buzzcut hair combined with his square, wide shoulders and broad chin, he looks military, for a lack of a better word. The whole vibe he gives off feels aggressive and angry. Can't say it makes me feel all warm and fuzzy.

Kieran pulls up to his full height, shoulders pulled back. Anger flares in his eyes and colors his voice. "It's you again."

"Indeed, it's me." The man smiles, but it does nothing to reassure me, not when his gaze stays cold and hard. "I wish we had met under different circumstances, but your actions have made it impossible not to intervene." He moves closer, like a panther, with soft, almost gliding steps. Like a man who's used to watching his back and being attacked at any moment. Coming to a stop in front of Kieran, he looks him over, head to toe. "I thought you were taller."

Kieran raises an eyebrow, unimpressed. "A hundred and ninety-two centimeters. Beats the number you got on your IQ by over a hundred."

The other guy blinks, then grins, and this time for real. "They warned me you're a smart ass. Seems like history got that part right."

*History.* I try to move my legs, but my feet won't budge, so I lift a hand to catch the man's attention. "When are we?"

He keeps his gaze locked with Kieran for another second, then cocks his head and turns toward me. "On the other hand, it's rather disturbing to see that history got you correct as well."

Not quite sure whether that's a compliment or not. Judging from about a combined whole minute of interaction, I'd probably go with *not.* "Why would that be disturbing?"

Within a second, he's in front of me, fast, quiet, and so close, I feel his breath on my face when he speaks. "Because your obsession and addiction to meddling with time is what brought us into this mess in the first place."

I jerk back, part from the words, part from the sensation of his exhale brushing over my face. "I—"

"Never mind, save your words for the court." He looks down his nose at me. "Quite disappointing. All this damage. And in the end, you're nothing but a stupid little gir—"

"Yeah, hold it right there." Hell to the no! Like Kieran, I stand straighter, pulling my shoulders back. I've been bullied all my life as the daughter of a pro-Magellan USEF-officer, I won't just stand here and take what he dishes out. Giving him the fakest smile ever, I put my hands on my hips. "I know you're feeling all strong and superior right now, but I'll let you in on a secret." I lower my voice to a whisper. "Only my feet are locked up." Lightning fast, I shoot my hands forward and wrap them around his throat. Surprise flashes across his face—

A slap a sensation of doom hits me, one split-second of just knowing this man is trouble, and will be trouble.

As fast as it came, the feeling is gone as his hands come up to mine, desperately pulling, yanking, clawing at them.

I shake off that weird sensation and widen my smile, while keeping my fingers relaxed around his throat, and I'm using that term loosely here. "Now, this is me *not* choking you. Why, you ask? Because I'd like to make a good impression, despite your less than stellar manners."

Kieran gives a soft little chuckle, so soft, I doubt the man could hear it. Plus, he's busy pulling on my wrists, to no avail: Magellan strength. Okay, half-Magellan strength, but still better than his. And I take it back: there's no way he's military or trained to fight, even though he looks the part. He'd know how to defend against a simple choke from the front. Heck, the way I'm standing, I'm wide open. One good kick to the groin and I'd let go for sure, yet all he does is pry at my fingers.

I let go with an exaggerated drop of my hands. "Okay then. Let's pretend the last few minutes didn't happen and start over. Hi, I'm Lieutenant Nonie Thorburn, and this is Captain Kieran Wildason. I think you know that, but still. What's your name?" Commence exaggerated fake-smiling.

The man scoots two steps back, out of my reach, massaging his throat. Wimp. I didn't even squeeze it. Much.

He presses his lips into a thin line. "Cormac Sheridan, First Executioner of the FBTI."

I suppress a flinch. None of that sounded good. I'm part of the FBTI, and granted, I know next to nothing about our FBTI, since I was kind of kept busy since my recruitment, but one should hope they'd treat one of their own a tad nicer. Plus, excuse me, *Executioner*? That sounds cheerful. Can't imagine Taro Magona being okay with that wording.

Still, I keep my expression carefully neutral. "Thank you, Mister Sheridan. Now, if you wouldn't mind telling us when and where we are…?"

Sheridan drops his hands from his neck, still glaring at me. Guess he's a sore loser when he isn't in control. "You're at the Confederation's headquarters. The year is 2399."

Holy—! The sound of my pulse swells in my ears. 2399. That's a hundred years from when we were, a whole century! My stomach drops as I look over at Kieran, catching his eye. He doesn't like the news any more than I do.

Sheridan clears his throat and cranks his neck. "If that comes as a surprise, it shouldn't. You should've known that somebody would catch up with you. And by the way, thank you." Anger tightens his features. "I won't underestimate you again, Thorburn. Unbelievable that people thought you two were on the right side of history." The last words come out hissed, and they slice like a knife. A self-indulgent, nasty smile tugs on the corners of his lips. "I'm so glad I'm getting the chance to remove your impact on the timeline for the rest of your lives."

# Chapter Two –

# Change of Scenery

S heridan walks toward the door. "Come," he says, without looking back, and continues to walk, turning to the right after he exits.

And yet, I don't move.

*Remove your impact on the timeline.* He said it with such hate in his voice, such… disgust, it feels like he punched me in the stomach. It feels *real.* And it feels uncalled for, maybe that's what's stunning me the most. All that hate—why? I don't get it. We haven't done anything!

"Nonie, hey." Kieran nudges me and jerks his chin in the direction Sheridan vanished in, the muscles in his jaw working overtime. "In the interest of cooperation, we should probably do as he says."

"What— Uhh, yeah. Yeah, you're right." I shake my head once, twice, then try to lift my foot— And it works. Not stuck. With a small, faint smile, I look at Kieran. "Guess we have no excuse to not go with him, huh?"

He lowers his gaze and shakes his head once. "Unfortunately, we don't. But it might be helpful. We need to find out as much as possible besides our location and the time we're in," he murmurs to me, his hard gaze trained on the door Sheridan vanished through. "Could you jump us back home, under the right circumstances?"

"You mean, if I had a Setayashi-emitting device? Sure, that shouldn't be a problem. But—"

*"Prisoners, follow."* The same voice that told us to stop a few minutes earlier echoes through the room.

Kieran frowns and pinches the bridge of his nose. "Let's comply for now. Who knows what other tricks they have up their sleeves. Keep your eyes and ears open, Lieutenant."

I nod and fall into step next to him. No need to remind me. "Always."

"By the way," he adds under his breath, a bit of his usual playfulness returning to his tone, "the way you choked him? Badass. I like it." A much more Kieran-like mischievous smile plays around his lips, making him look way more like the man I knew back in his own time.

My cheeks warm, I shrug. "I can't say I appreciated his way of talking to us." Or how he brought us here. Or how we were treated so far. And while old me from a few months ago would not have choked somebody to prove a point, new me has been through a few rough spots. I've lost my innocence and definitely my fear of confrontation, of fighting. One could say I had a pretty intense desensitization happen lately. Not sure if that's a good thing, but it for sure comes in handy in my line of work.

Kieran huffs. "I'm with you on that one. I hope he learned some manners." He walks past me and leads the way, following Sheridan.

As soon as we leave our room, the light behind us turns back to bright white. I wonder if that's—

Kieran comes to a dead stop so suddenly I ram my shoulder into his back. "Sorry, I—" And then I see why he stopped so abruptly. "Sun and Stars." The view punches a puff of air out of my lungs. When we thought we might be under a dome, we were right. We were.

And we were not the only ones.

Dozens and dozens of these things block my view. I can't see anything but them. I let my gaze drift from one white, milky dome to the next, then look back to ours. They're all the same, about four meters high, about four in diameter, lined up neatly in rows, from what I can see. What I can't see is where they stop, or a ceiling above us, even though this is clearly an indoor space. There could be hundreds on this floor, no idea. I can't make out any overhead lights, and they don't need them: All illumination comes from the domes around us. It's quite the eerie sight, like we were ants sitting on a large sheet of illuminated bubble wrap.

"Do I need to make you move?" Sheridan waits for us about five meters ahead.

Ignoring him, Kieran lowers his head to mine. "What is this place?"

"Not their guest quarters," I reply. "There must be over a hundred of these—"

"We have one thousand Sensory Deprivation-chambers in this location, if you must know. And now move, or again, I'm going to make you and it will be my pleasure." This time, Sheridan sounds even more grumpy, if that's possible. Definitely not a cheerful guy.

Kieran and I exchange a look and catch up with him. He leads us past another of these bubble-chamber things, and—

I gasp. "They're transparent!" There, in the middle of the bubble next to ours, stands a man, his back to us, head bowed, hands in his pockets. He sways his upper body left and right in a rhythmic fashion. To be honest… it looks like he's lost his mind.

Sheridan throws a dismissive glance over his shoulder. "Of course, they are. We like to keep track of our prisoners."

My mouth drops open. No kidding—we couldn't see a thing from the inside, but apparently that's not true from the outside.

Kieran pokes me into the ribs. "Look at that one." He points to the bubble on our left. A woman, in her fifties, maybe, limps over to the wall closer to us. It looks like she was coming for us, but even though she's technically looking in our direction, I doubt she sees us. I doubt she *can* see us.

When she's close to the wall next to us though… It turns milky, just like it was for us on the inside.

"Did you see that?" I look over at Kieran, trying my best not to stumble over my feet while keeping up with Sheridan. Being on display is not my preferred way to spend the day, but if there's a way to change that…

He nods. "I did. I wonder—"

"Nu-uh." Without looking back, Sheridan lifts his index finger and wiggles it. "Don't even think about it. It's the privacy function for the bathroom. You have ninety seconds to complete whatever you don't want others to see. You need more time, tough luck."

Oh. Okay. Be thankful for small favors, right?

Sheridan leads us past several more of these bubbles, most of them inhabited—occupied?—with only one person in them. How lonely must it be in there, all by yourself, surrounded by nothing but seemingly endless white? Do they know their every move is visible from the outside? And who's watching? I crane my neck, looking for cameras, for anything that could be used for observation, but don't see anything. Doesn't mean it's not there though. Our technology is bound to change within a century.

After about two minutes, we reach a clearing of sorts, a circular area without any bubble-thingies, maybe the diameter of three of them combined.

"Stop." Sheridan lifts a hand and—

"Ngh!" Both of us grunt when our feet lock with the floors as inertia tries to continue its job and carries our bodies forward. Sheesh! That's bound to throw out somebody's knee at one point.

With a smug look on his face, the executioner faces us, but if he wanted us to show our annoyance, it's not happening. Both Kieran and I are carrying a neutral expression. Neither of us is going to give him the satisfaction of a reaction.

Sheridan raises his voice. "Sheridan plus two, main court."

Is he dematting us? Kieran and I exchange a glance—

—and within an instant our surroundings have changed. Gone is the darkness with the bubbles, and here we are, in a large, sun-flooded room with floor-to-ceiling windows on three sides. No transition, no tingling, no slow loss of perception and gradual return of it. Just the strangest sensation of disorientation with the change of surroundings. Here one second—there the next.

"Holy Sun and Stars!" I wheeze. That was… within the blink of an eye. Whoa.

"The accused, Your Honor." Sheridan steps back, leaving us to face a large wooden podium and a woman sitting behind it, neither of which I had really noticed in the two seconds since dematting here. I was kind of busy recovering from… positional displacement. But it's not the woman who gives my heart a little pause. Neither is it the other male human to her left side, seated about half a meter farther back. Or the large FBTI-symbol on the wall behind her. Nope. That little skipped beat to my heart would be courtesy of the person seated to her right: The person in Essken armor. An *Essken*. Here. With us. *Not* in their realm.

As if it needed to make up for the delay, my heart beats twice as fast. An Essken! If that means humans and Essken learned to get along, it makes me happy despite the predicament Kieran and I are currently in. Could he be Lorr? But it's a hundred years later, so probably not? Or, how old do Essken get? It could be him, but then, they all look the same in their armor, no offense.

Kieran sucks in a sharp gasp, drowned out by the judge's words. "Thank you, First Executioner," says the woman. "Are these the two accused?"

"Yes, Your Honor. I apprehended them myself, minutes after the uprising of '95."

"Very good, indeed. Optimal timing." The judge nods, her brown curly hair bouncing around her head. Her age is tough to guess. On the one hand her hair shows some streaks of grey, but on the other, her skin is tight and without any wrinkles. She could be thirty, or she could be fifty. Judging by the authority in her voice, I'm guessing closer to fifty.

She raises one hand. "Identity check!"

For one short, yet incredibly long second *something* moves over and through me, like… a warm sensation bringing tingling and the slightest bit of dizziness and disorientation. As soon as the sensation is gone, a voice comes from somewhere: *"Scan completed. Nonie Thorburn, age 18. Kieran Wildason, age 23. Temporal displacement of 104 years noted in both specimens."*

Excuse me, *specimens*? Really? And also, I'm not eightee— Oops. Maybe I am eighteen. When I returned home with Mashaule on September 14ᵗʰ, it was after my birthday, so yes: I was eighteen years old. *Am* eighteen years old. Weird disappointment washes over me: I missed my birthday! I missed becoming an official adult! It's something so completely mundane in the great scheme of things it shouldn't matter, yet it does.

I missed becoming an adult.

But while I missed one single, albeit important, birthday, Kieran seems to officially have missed several while in the Realm. That scan still labeled him as twenty-three, not… sixty-two. *Ouch.* I suppress a grimace thinking that number as the judge leans forward to get a better look at us. I'm sure we're making a splendid first impression, Kieran in his uniform he donned about 140 years in the past, me in mine I put on before getting him out of the Realm. Neither of us looks presentable, really.

"Captain Kieran Wildason and Lieutenant Nonie Thorburn."

"That would be correct," Kieran says, stepping forward in what I call his captain's pose: shoulders straight, chin up, eye contact with the other party. "And you are?"

"Judge Naila Alberti, First Judge of the FBTI's High Court." She inclines her head in greeting, showing some more silver strands on her head. "These are my Second Judges, Ivan Gudino, and Tinn." She gestures first at the human, then at the Essken. "I apologize for the way you were brought here, which I imagine must've been somewhat distressing, but we had no other choice."

Kieran raises a brow. "No other choice—why? Why did you bring us here in the first place, lack of options or not?" Despite keeping his voice level, the irritation in it is clear. He opens his palms to the ceiling. "An explanation of why we were torn from our time and held captive here would be appreciated."

That's definitely more politely said than I would've phrased it.

Judge Alberti folds her hands in front of her. "I understand your frustration, Captain. Let me counter your question with one of mine. What is your understanding of time? How does it work?"

Kieran narrows his brows. "I'm not an expert in time—"

"But you are. Your ship, the *Pioneer*, gave shelter to a stranded time traveler." She points at me, then back at Kieran. "You yourself spent many years in the Essken Realm, not aging, before you were brought out of it by Lieutenant Thorburn. For somebody who claims to not be an expert, you have seen and experienced more peculiarities of time than ninety-nine point nine-nine percent of humanity ever have or will. Please answer the question. What is your understanding of time?" Her gaze hardens with the last words, and Kieran tenses even more than he did with her mentioning the Realm.

"My understanding of time is that it flows in one direction, and we travel it in one direction from birth to death as we age. Usually, at least." He gives me the same pointed look the judge gave me a minute earlier. "Obviously, that is an incomplete picture, given that time worked differently in the Essken Realm and that I'm not a temporal scientist, but that's my understanding. But please, enlighten me." He looks first at the judge, then the Essken, who inclines his head, the only visible reaction to Kieran's words.

I'm not hearing a voice inside my head, like in the Realm—and Lorr had said they couldn't communicate with us in ours, hence, all our issues and the decades-long war. So, how do we talk to him? Does he understand us? I mean, Tinn's an appointed judge, so I would hope so.

Alberti raises one eyebrow but ignores Kieran's little barb. "Then you do understand that changes will ripple through the stream of time, correct? What happens in the past, affects the future."

Well, duh. That's why I was always so very careful when in the past. Changing the-slash-my future I wanted to return to wasn't really high on my list of priorities.

Kieran's expression says he's thinking about the same, yet he stays polite. "Yes, Your Honor. That's the theory as I understand it."

She nods. "Then you will also understand that we must take all precautions possible to secure the timeline as it is intended to progress, as inconvenient as they may seem. It is our responsibility."

Okay, is it just me or was that directed at, or rather, against me? Feels like it, and boy, does it go against the grain. All I have been doing since I was thrown into the whole time-travel adventure is pay attention to my actions and their potential effect to minimize interference. And to have her insinuate I did something wrong… Not cool.

I lift my chin up high. "Excuse me, everything I did, I did in alignment with my First Sense. I—"

Sheridan snaps at me. "*Your* First Sense, Lieutenant? That, if historic records are correct, you barely found out about a few weeks ago, from your point of view? Are we really to trust our future on *that*?"

I jerk back. Whoa. Uncalled for. "I've been getting better—"

"But obviously not good enough." Sheridan takes me by the upper arm and yanks me around. "We're lucky I could take you two from where you were easy to access before you could commit your crimes." He growls, anger flaring in his eyes.

"Executioner!" There's warning in Alberti's voice, but Sheridan doesn't let go.

Okay then. I twist and pull my arm free, *this* close to hitting him in the face for manhandling me like that. Alas, I have bigger fish to fry, because: *before* Kieran and I could commit our *crimes*? *Before*? And plural?

Giving Sheridan a warning glance to better not touch me again, I address the judge. "Your Honor, if the captain and I haven't committed whatever crime you're accusing us of, we shouldn't be here. You cannot judge us by something we haven't even done yet."

"Thank you so much for that, Executioner." Alberti doesn't even so much as move a facial muscle, even though her voice drips with sarcasm. She directs her attention to us, the sarcasm gone. "Lieutenant, it is well within the FBTI's authorization to intervene whenever it is necessary. Literally *whenever* it is necessary. We adhere to our guidelines. To data. I can highly suggest reading the temporal research by K. Okata et al, if you're confused. In your case—"

Sheridan makes a slashing motion with his hand. "In your case, the evidence is clear. We need to act to protect ourselves—"

"Executioner!" Alberti slams a palm down onto the desk before her, and both other judges jerk back. For once, she glares at the FBTI agent instead of us. "Do not disrespect the court again, or I will have you removed from the proceedings. No matter you report directly to the Taro, you do not and will not speak for me, is that understood?"

It takes Sheridan a good three seconds before he can unclench his jaw and bite out a reply. "Yes, Your Honor."

"Good. And to be clear, I agreed with the Taro and consented to the *capture* of these two, but they have *not* been found guilty yet."

We haven't? Because it surely sounds like it.

"But—" Sheridan snaps his mouth shut with Alberti's angry glance.

"As discussed with Taro Izola, we will review the evidence he provided and then decide on a course of action."

The muscles in Sheridan's jaw pop, that's how hard he's biting down. Alberti takes a slow, deep breath and exhales it over several seconds. Now, I'm not saying the enemy of my enemy is my friend, but right now, Sheridan is less my friend than the judge. Which means, she is the person to convince how ridiculous this all is.

Putting on my best I'm-very-harmless-and-also-confused-face I raise my hand. "I need a clarification, please. Whatever we did in the past has served as the basis upon which your time developed, so if you keep us from doing whatever you accuse us of, wouldn't that alter the course of the timeline and erase your time as you know it?" Please, let's clarify. Because as she had us explain like school children, changes travel into the future: We do something to mess up Sheridan's family, he never is born, ergo, the timeline is changed. For the better maybe, but I don't want to be mean.

As if he had read my thoughts, Sheridan hisses out a reply. "Your actions build the foundation upon which we exist—"

Hah! I knew it! "Thank you for pointing that out and—"

"—and we're making sure it stays that way, no thanks to either of you!" He glares at me as if I was his personal enemy number one.

Wow. Dramatic much? "I appreciate that you're looking out for the timeline, I really do, but what does that even mean? Whatever happened, happened, and here we—you—are." It's about the principle first and foremost: "I guess I'm asking if the future can dictate to the past what it's supposed to do?"

Sheridan huffs out loud. "You're looking for loopholes? Unbelie—"

"Executioner Sheridan, impulse control, please. I'm growing impatient with you. For many reasons. I understand your point of view might be different due to the Taro's and your line of work, but this is my courtroom, and you will act accordingly." Judge Alberti raises her voice only the slightest, but it shuts him up on the spot. "Lieutenant, you are allowed to make your own decisions. In fact, heeding my own advice, looking at the temporal research by K. Okata et al, it is encouraged. But in your case, the situation is more complicated." She sighs. "Since the executioner barged ahead, I guess an explanation is in order. See, the sum of all your actions developed the timeline. We're here because of what you and the people of your time did or didn't do, and there's no judgement in that statement. That's all fair game. But the problem is that we have evidence our intervention is needed to secure the unchanged flow of time."

"Excuse me?" Kieran shakes his head. "You need to interfere? But that would change—"

"Not if we have already done it."

I groan. "A predestination paradox? You are where you are and exist because of the intervention, now you have to go back and make sure it happens?" If that doesn't sound like my life, I don't know what does.

"Correct. But mind you, I haven't made up my mind yet whether the data supports that theory. We got you here because it seems to be part of the expected flow of time. What comes next, I will have to carefully evaluate. Clearly, the timeline progresses to where we are right now, or we wouldn't be here, you are correct. The question becomes, does it so without our intervention, or because of it?"

"And—" Sheridan snaps his mouth shut when he catches the judge's glance, and so do I. Now is not the moment to antagonize her, no matter what my First Sense says—and no, it's not happy. I have about a hundred comments and as many questions, but only one is truly urgent. "So, what is it that has you all so nervous? What is it you're trying to prevent from changing?"

Kieran lifts a hand, catching the judge's attention. "And if you're worried about us doing something that would alter the timeline, maybe give us a pointer so we can avoid that action."

"I appreciate the input, Captain, but unfortunately it's not that easy." Alberti gives Kieran a small smile, the first since we've met her. "I will need some time, ironically, to come to a conclusion. We will gather more data, but keep you in our custody in the meantime. Also, I intend to talk to both of you to come up with a better-informed opinion after I've looked at all the evidence." She holds up a wrist-PAD—that's PADdy, that's mine!

"Oh," Sheridan says, stepping forward. "Speaking of. Taro Izola requested the accused's PAD for further evaluation." He holds his hand up and out for her to drop the device in it, but Alberti only gives him a dismissive glance.

"I will personally carry this piece of evidence with me, Executioner. Please inform the Taro I don't just trust anybody with it."

As if slapped, Sheridan flinches. "But—"

"Again, Captain, Lieutenant," the judge addresses us, ignoring Sheridan, "I apologize for uprooting your lives, but I'd rather have history judge me for interrupting yours than for destroying billions of others."

"Destroying billions—" Kieran takes sharp intake of air with those words.

"Unfortunately, yes. From the data the Taro provided me, it is quite clear that without our intervention *you*, Captain, will be responsible for the death of billions, a mass-murder not possible without *your* help, Lieutenant. If not prevented, Earth would lose ninety percent of its population because of the two of you."

## Confederation Headquarters, 2399

As Sheridan escorts us back, the judge's last sentence keeps on playing over and over inside my head. … *Earth would lose ninety percent of its population because of the two of you.* It sounds unfathomable. Impossible. I can't imagine any scenario where Kieran and I would let this happen.

But then, sometimes things happen, whether we want them to or not.

I steal a glance over at him. He didn't even flinch with the demat back to that bubble field. Hasn't even looked left or right, just stared ahead, unblinking, face an unreadable mask as Sheridan escorts us to our bubble-prison.

Prison. To prevent the death of billions.

Is that what they're going to do? Lock us away? They can't. Not that I'm thinking the world revolves around us, but I'd imagine us missing would change things, which would then affect their now, unless of course we both die in whatever it is Kieran does—with my help—that kills billions.

If that isn't a sobering and depressing thought, I don't know what is.

So, what are they going to do about it, assuming they can't and won't imprison us here? Send us home with a list of dos and don'ts? But isn't that going to affect our actions—because that's the point of telling us? Isn't that going to alter the timeline then as well, us knowing? Or is that what the judge hinted at, them telling us is what keeps us from going down that road?

A bitter taste lingers in the back of my throat. None of what I heard sounds right. None of it feels right, and that would be my First Sense recognizing that, thank you very much.

Sheridan leads us back to our bubble and leaves us alone, the opening closing behind him without a sound. It's as white, milky, and empty in here as before. One could think the last thirty minutes didn't happen, but they did. And boy, did they change things.

"Hey." I wrap my arms around Kieran and pull him into me. "You're taking what they said with a grain of salt, right?" I bury my face in his shirt. His scent does wonders to my endorphins. It's like a cure-all for everything and anything. Sad? Angry? Frustrated? Take a sniff of Kieran. Huh. Okay, that sounded weird, but it does help.

Taking another deep inhale, I lift my head when he doesn't respond. "I don't believe they've got everything figured out."

"I'm not so sure, Nonie. Not so sure." He draws me into his chest tighter, making it impossible for me to crane my neck even more to keep looking at him.

Sighing, I cuddle into his shoulder, willing him to feel how much I'm on his side. "They're judging us by something we haven't done, and something we may never do, now that we're warned. Besides that, I'm feeling they shouldn't be meddling with time, even though in this case I do understand the reason for it, my First Sense doesn't like what it's been hearing. What if it's all just a load of BS?"

Kieran huffs, the sound rumbling through his chest. "Again, not so sure. You told me Mashey has been trying to kill me to save billions of lives. Well. I do see a pattern here. Can I even fault them for abducting us knowing what I do now? Maybe the Temporal War is all about that, trying to keep billions of people from being killed. Trying to *keep me* from killing billions of people. I—"

Excuse me, what? I jerk back and place both my hands on his cheeks. "No. No, no, no. Don't even go there. You are not responsible for anything like that. You are not killing billions of people, Kieran!"

The muscles in his jaw harden under my palms. "Their Taro seems to think differently."

"Why do you assume just because they're from the future they know better?" I throw my hands in the air, then wrap my arms around him again as Kieran leans back to give me a look that says, *duh*.

"Because they've seen how history played out?"

I shake my head. "And they're giving us their version, Kieran! Their filtered, biased version of something that hasn't happened yet. We have no overview of the whole history and have to go by their word and against what my First Sense tells me is right!"

He focuses his gaze on somewhere behind my left ear. "I can't risk billions of lives on your First Sense. Who knows if it's even right—"

I suck in a sharp breath. "Ouch, Kieran. Ouch." Do I know I'm a newbie with everything Magellan and time-travel? Uh, yes. But that doesn't mean I couldn't trust my First Sense. I always did, my whole life, only I didn't know what that sensation in the pit of my stomach was. Still, it's never led me astray.

He grimaces. "I'm sorry. That was uncalled for. I'm sorry."

I get it. He doesn't have a First Sense to put the judge's words into perspective. Of course he's frustrated, shocked, and probably terrified by what Alberti said. None of it is easy to digest. I can't say I'm happy about it either, but at least I do have my First Sense backing me up.

I lay one palm against his cheek, gentler this time, and turn his face toward me. "Hey. I understand. You hear me? I understand. But I'm not ready to risk your life or mine on two people's statements. Snap out of it, Kieran. We've got to get more data. There's a mystery event caused by us supposedly wiping out ninety percent of people on Earth? How do they know? Where's the junction where we made a decision that led to that disaster? We've got to know what we're dealing with. We've got to get out of *here*, or we're always only going to get a one-sided opinion."

For the longest moment, Kieran holds my gaze, not a muscle twitching in his face. Just when I'm about to wave a hand in front of his eyes to check if he's in there, he pulls me closer and lowers his head so his breath brushes across my ear. With one hand, he slides the hairband off my ponytail so my hair falls down the length of my back. Dropping his voice to a mere whisper, his lips brush my ear. "They can see us from the outside. I'm sure they have surveillance equipment in here, video, audio, whatever. We need to be more than careful what we talk about."

The relief of hearing him talk like a USEF captain is immense. I let go of a slow exhale. Hiding his words behind my hair is a good idea. I nod and move my arms around his neck, so I can conceal my mouth behind them. "Agree."

His chest expands and he holds a breath before speaking again. "You're right. I'm sorry. Again. I know better than to blindly trust them, especially after you told me about that Temporal War."

My pulse kicks up a notch. "Exactly! I can't help but wonder if somebody from the future is trying to make us do whatever the judge is trying to prevent. Could be. Or could be the opposite. They're not giving us much to go by."

"No, but I doubt we're going to get anything useful out of those two."

The way he emphasizes *those two* speaks volumes. I crank my head to look up at him while keeping my lips hidden. "You're hoping somebody else will give us more information."

"I'm counting on it. You are, as I said, correct. We've got to get more data. Problem is—and you're right there as well—a second opinion is hard to come by in these accommodations. Getting out of here should be our main objective, but obviously that's not going to be easy. We know next to nothing about their time and technology. Our best bet may be whenever we're taken somewhere else. We need to be ready to act within a moment's notice."

I lower my head against his shoulder again, glad Kieran is back to more his normal self. Or, at least pretending to be more his normal self. "Agree. Once we're out, we hide and work on a plan to get back to our time. And to find out what it is we're supposed to do, or not supposed to do." Because I couldn't live my life watching out for abductions from the future or double-guessing every step I take, afraid it might be the one to destroy billions of others, and I know neither could Kieran.

Kieran lowers one hand and twirls a strand of hair around his fingers, silent for now. Not difficult to figure out what's running through his head.

I squeeze him harder. "We'll figure this out, Kieran. I—"

For the shortest, most dizzying moment, the ground shifts under our feet, like we stepped on quicksand. The sensation is gone as fast as it came, but both of us felt it. We both twitch at the same time.

Kieran stiffens. "Did you feel—"

*"Please do not move or respond."*

Holy Sun and Stars! That voice is directly inside my head, like when I was in the R—

*"If you can hear me, both of you clear your throat."*

TBH, my first reflex is to not comply. But, you sneak communication in here and make it secretive, I get the feeling you're on our side. Or, at least not on *theirs*.

Kieran must've come to the same conclusion. We both clear our throats.

*"Wonderful. A heads up: We have a way of dematting you out of there, but it won't be pretty. You have to stay as close together as possible, so right now is fine. Do not move, or we cannot guarantee a trauma-free rematerialization. Clear your throat if you understand."*

This time we're both faster in complying. My heart speeds up, but so does Kieran's. We're more than close enough for me to feel it like my own.

*"Get ready in three… two… one—"*

The ground under my feet turns into quicksand and pain hits me like a truck on a highway. Holy Universe! My whole body feels like I'm being squished through a pinhole. The oddest sensation of stretching, stretching, *streetchiiiing* tears on my insides far beyond what a human, or half-Magellan body should be able to endure. For the shortest moment, I think I see a purple tree, a sparkling river, like in the Essken Realm, then everything turns black around me, but black with streaks, somehow. I can't breathe, I can't move. All that's keeping me together is the sensation of being torn apart, ironically.

For the longest few seconds of my life I'm convinced this is it—

And then my feet hit slippery ground with a *bam* like I jumped off a roof. My knees buckle, the impact forcing me down into a crouch. I lose hold of Kieran and thrust out my hands, barely catching myself without face-planting, palms sliding over the cold, wet floor. Rain hits me, hard and ice cold. I look up and around, but it's so dark, I only see an outline of Kieran next to me, on one knee, head bent down, one hand pressed to his stomach as the ground sways up and down, left and right.

"What the absolute—" He grunts, most of the words swallowed by—

Somebody grabs me by the arms and pulls me up hard—no, *two* people grab me, one on my left, one on my right. My first instinct is to fight, to pull away—

"Run, if you want to live! Come on, come on, move, *move*! We gotta get inside!" The woman to my left yells so loud against the wind, her voice breaks at the end. She tightens her grip around my arm, pulling harder. Something of what little I can see in her expression, maybe the wide eyes, the open mouth, and short little breaths she's taking, maybe that she sounds so young, but whatever it is, it shuts my fight response down. For now.

I fall into a sprint through the darkness with the woman and the other person holding on to my arms. A gust of wind hits me in the face, bringing not just more rain, but also the scent of… salt. The ocean. My brain needed a minute to process the shift in location and make sense of my surroundings. It finally catches me up. We're at sea. *Definitely* at sea, if the rocking and swaying of the ground under my feet is any indication. It's too dark to make out details, but given that we've been running fast for a few seconds already, this isn't just a small sailboat. If I'm not mistaken, thick, white lines are drawn onto the surface we sprint across, but I can't be sure.

The ship bucks up and rolls to the left, throwing us into a stumble my biosynthetic left leg has a hard time compensating for. Another spray of cold, salty water hits my face. My feet slip while running, but so do everybody else's. I suck in a surprised breath, cool air tickling the back of my throat, and catch my footing before sliding into a forced splits.

"Move, move!" The woman holding on to me screams on top of her lungs. A male voice grunts and yelps behind us—must be Kieran and whoever is quote-unquote escorting him.

My face is wet from the ocean's spray and rain, my clothing feels damp, as a door opens seemingly out of nowhere, soft yellow light reaching out into the darkness. A woman waves from the inside, frantically. "Faster, guys, ten seconds! *Ten seconds!*"

Ten seconds—to what? My heart skips a beat with the urge in her voice and announcement of a countdown. I hate countdowns.

Just before we burst through the hatch, the outline of a high wall, tower, or whatever, becomes visible, the door being the only structure of it I can make out clearly. The two people holding on to me shove me through first, but press after me, forcing me several meters into the ship before they hold me back and we stop. Kieran, flanked by two young men, crashes through the entrance a mere second after us.

As soon as the last person has entered, the woman yanks the hatch closed with a resounding bang. For a moment, silence hovers in this narrow hallway. Gone are the howling of the wind and the noise of the sea, our fast breathing the only disruptions cutting through the silence.

Then, the woman laughs under her breath. "That was close."

The other people let go of Kieran and me. One wipes a forearm across their face, grinning. Another one bends forward, supporting his weight on his knees, shaking his head in disbelief. The other two just grin and high five each other.

Right.

Kieran and I lock gazes over the heads of everybody else. He looks as wet as everybody else, hair dripping. One slight raise of his eyebrow, and I know what he's thinking. This is nice, being freed and all, but the enemy of our enemy isn't automatically our friend. Tactically, we exchanged one nightmare for another, the current one not much better for us than the bubble-thing. We've been dematted to a ship, potentially smack in the middle of some ocean, with little to no means of escape. They led us into a narrow hallway and locked the hatch behind us. We know nothing about them, their time, their reasoning behind their actions, or how many other people are on board, or what kind of weapons they might have on us, but we do know they have the ability to get us out of a highly-secured prison.

Add the threat of Sheridan possibly popping up out of nowhere like he did on the *Hope*, and to say we're at a disadvantage would be an understatement.

Kieran's gaze pointedly drifts over to the woman next to me, the one who held on to my left side, then over to a guy next to him, and back to me.

Welcome to Multi-Attacker-Scenarios 1-0-1, and while they seem nice and not threatening, there's a reason why the academy is big on teaching situation control. We prefer our officers to take charge and assess the situation from a position of dominance.

Let's just say experience has shown things tend to go south if we don't.

Like we rehearsed it, Kieran and I dart forward at the same time. No signal needed. Out of the corner of my eye I register him going for the guy next to him, but I'm too busy with my own gal. Keeping my hand close to her skin I slide my arm around her throat from behind, pulling her off balance and into a headlock. She squeaks, throws her hands up to her throat—but too late. I've cinched it in before she even realizes what's going on. Definitely not a trained fighter either. Seems to be a common thing in this century, or maybe I'm biased, having dealt with academy-trained people most of my life.

"Everybody, freeze!" Kieran's voice booms through the narrow hallway. Like me, he's got the person on his heels in a tight headlock from behind. Ah, the joys of a common academy education. It's not that the headlock was such a devastating attack, not at all, but these two people serve as shields for us. As a statement as well.

The remaining three people freeze. Nobody draws a weapon on us, nobody moves. The elation of the last moments is replaced by an expression of absolute shock on their faces. Especially with the woman who just closed the door. Her face displays absolute disbelief over what's happening.

"But—" she whispers, shaking her head.

Kieran ignores her. "First, I'd like to get some answers. We don't mean to harm anybody, but I'm sure you know you have us at a disadvantage. Basics first. Where are we, who are you?"

If we had any doubts who the boss was, we'd know the moment everybody looks at the woman at the door. She's not much older than me, maybe Kieran's age, early twenties. About my height, so moderately tall, with a slender build. Her curly brown hair is cut to chin level. It does hold a bit of a shimmer, maybe not noticeable to anybody else, but to me, as a half-Magellan, it is. Could totally be coincidence or an awesome conditioner she's using, but could also be that somewhere in her ancestry there's a Magellan. Times have hopefully changed, after all.

The woman blushes, swallowing hard. "Uhh, well, yes. Sorry. I— We—" She closes her eyes and shakes her head, then starts over. "Sorry. We usually don't do this."

"Do what?" I ask, holding on to my hostage tightly, not that she was struggling, but still. Playing possum fooled me once. My chest still hurts with a deep inhale from when I learned my lesson, courtesy of the knife Mashaule rammed in there.

The woman's eyes widen when she looks at me, like, *really* looks at me, the color of her cheeks darkening. "Uhh, well, break people out of FBTI-secured facilities."

"And we appreciate that you did. Again, we don't mean to hurt anybody, but I'm sure you understand why we do feel a bit uncomfortable in this situation." Kieran inclines his head toward the locked hatch, and all I can think is, *he's good.* I mean, I knew that, but it's good to know the effect of the judge's revelation didn't influence his skills. Whoever taught situation control in his time would get a thrill out of Kieran's implementation. His intonation is exactly right. He sounds strong, yet added enough of an apology in his tone to not come across as aggressive. Perfect to build trust, despite us holding two of their people in headlocks. Which, again, isn't such a biggie—unless you're untrained in self-defense or tactics.

"No no, I totally see that, I do." The woman waves both hands in front of her, like apologetic jazz hands. "The guy you're holding on to is Carlos. That one over there, Marty, and the one you're holding"—

she points at me—"is Zael. My name is Kaytee Dub."

"Thank you, and nice to meet you, Kaytee," Kieran says, inclining his head once more. "I'm sure you know who we are, since from what I hear you don't seem to be in the habit of breaking random people out of the FBTI's hold?" He gives her the smallest uptick of his lips.

Her cheeks are beet red at this point. "Yes. Yes, of course we know who you are. Captain Kieran Wildason. Lieutenant Nonie Thorburn."

One of the guys, Marty, chuckles.

"Shut it, Marty," Kaytee hisses.

I raise an eyebrow at her. "Well, it's nice to meet you, but tell us one good reason why we shouldn't use these two as shields and hostages and go looking for an escape pod—life boat." It's a ship on the water, not in space, Thorburn!

Kaytee shakes her head frantically. "Not a good idea. We're in the middle of the Pacific, way too far for any life boat to make. And I can't guarantee they'll even work," she adds sheepishly. "But, I completely understand. I promise—and I realize you don't know me, so my word holds no value to you—but I promise you're amongst friends."

My good old human sixth sense tells me she's right, but still. "That's good to hear, but I wouldn't mind something more convincing."

Kaytee drops her gaze to the ground, then sighs once and shrugs. "Oh well. It's gonna be fine." She raises both hands to stomach level—

"Kaytee, don't!" Marty calls out, the sudden outburst causing Kieran and myself to tighten our grip on our hostages.

"Out of options, Marty," Kaytee replies, and slides her right palm over the back of her left hand, as if she was brushing off a bug sitting there. The image of an ID card pops up about thirty centimeters in front of her hand, about the size of a paper folder.

"There you go," she says. "You don't need to worry about me. Or the others, for that matter. We're on your side."

For a long moment I don't get it. Don't understand why her ID, so niftily projected into the air, would change anything. But then I read it. Like, *really* read it.

First Name:        Kayla
Middle Name:       Thorburn
Last Name:         Wildason

Holy Sun and Stars! Kayla Thorburn Wildason? *Thorburn Wildason?*

"Well, that was unexpected," Kieran says, surprise in his voice.

Kaytee gives a sheepish grin and shrug. "Kaytee is a mix of my first name and middle initial. Kay-T. The Dub… well, I'm sure you can figure it out." She makes another swiping gesture, and the ID vanishes. "Anyway, welcome to the *USS Achievement*. It's an honor to have my great-grandparents on board."

# Chapter Three -

# Achievement

*USS Achievement, 2399*

Kaytee leads us through the ship's bowels, deeper and deeper. Everything is tight. Much tighter than on a starship. Everything also looks more… used. Older as well, even though I could bet this ship wasn't even built yet during my time. It smells musky and moldy, not to the degree of being a problem, just so that it barely registers as unpleasant.

"The *Achievement* was one of the last aircraft carriers commissioned by the US Navy," Kaytee says, as she leads us down a narrow flight of stairs. "A few years into its service, Earth— Never mind." She flinches and looks forward.

Earth-what? "Are you trying not to spoil the past by telling us about the future?" I appreciate the effort. Kaytee Dub—one point. FBTI— zero.

She shoots me an apologetic glance over her shoulder. "I'm trying, yes. But as you can tell, it's not so easy."

"No kidding," I murmur. Welcome to my life. I sigh and get a good grip on the railing while following Kaytee. These stairs are steep.

"We discussed what we can tell you and what we shouldn't tell you, and I guess I screwed up once already, so I better watch my mouth. Careful, don't hit your head." She slaps her hand against a protruding edge that could've caused a headache.

I look back at Kieran, after evading the obstacle. We've exchanged about a million glances since we found out our, uhh, great-grand daughter was the one to break us out of the FBTI-hold. Wouldn't even know where to begin naming the emotions coursing through me. I definitely feel old all of a sudden. Happens when you become a great-grandma overnight. That's not the biggest emotion though, that honor goes to confusion. I don't know what to make of the obvious proof that Kieran and I... well, that we had—will have—kids. Or at least one kid. It seems way too personal for everybody to know, and such a big step for us. Up to a few days ago, I thought we could never be together, because we lived in different times. Oh, and, minor obstacle, because Kieran was assumed dead. A future together wasn't really in the cards for us. That changed after Kieran came back from the Essken Realm, but since then, it's also only been a few hours, max—and Sheridan kidnapped us from our time a mere minute or two after we decided to keep our relationship going. Everything was—is—so new, and now... now we've been promoted to great-grandparents.

Well, if nothing else, it's good to know we'll apparently work out.

Kaytee enters a room, the holo-sign next to the entrance hatch reading *Mess Hall.* "And voila, meet the rest of the team. May I present, the Unexpected Overachievers." She bows and steps aside, revealing a group of five humans... and one Essken. Two Essken in as many locations, maybe humanity did learn something.

As we enter, the sound of our steps echoes through the huge, industrial-looking room. The ceiling hangs low, some thick pipes running under it in certain areas. The lights are off for most of the room, leaving only the first ten rows of tables or so bathed in cool white light—that being said, the lights are odd. I wasn't quite sure if I was seeing things—or rather, not seeing things—on the way over, but just like in all the hallways, it seems the ceiling itself was emitting light. There's no bulb or actual lamp that I can make out as a source. It provides a very even illumination up to a few rows of tables into the room, and still is enough to get an impression of the mess hall's size until the shadows take over and swallow all the remaining rays of light.

As I would expect on a seafaring ship, the tables are bolted to the floor and mostly blue, and when I say mostly, I mean besides an about PAD-sized, smooth, black rectangle slightly to the left of every seat in front of the tables. I'm missing the typical silverware-holders and batches of napkins on the tables, like in any other mess hall I've been to, but otherwise, everything else looks like I would expect, from the shiny dark cobalt blue floors to the one-legged blue chairs in front of the tables, which are also bolted into the floor. I mean, makes sense on a ship without grav-stabilization. If sailors from this time are anything like the one in mine, they want to feel the ship move under their feet, which is exactly what I don't want in space. Too many axes to roll around.

The people Kaytee gestured at get up from the chairs and tables they'd been sitting on. They all look young, like early twenties, and have this excitement written onto their faces. Several exchange glances and grin, or poke the other person in the side with their elbow.

"Everybody, obviously you all did well and we were successful, thank you, thank you, and here we go. Meet Captain Kieran Wildason and Lieutenant Nonie Thorburn." Kaytee gestures at each of us and bows again, exaggerating the movement. "Kieran, Nonie, those guys there are Rocky, Isa, Sterling, Kairo, and Jaasu."

At the mentioning of their names everybody raises a hand and waves or nods. I'm just happy she called us by our first names, and not great-grandma and great-grandpa. Shudder.

"And last, but not least, Koll." Kaytee points at the Essken. "We thought about hiding him so you wouldn't know humans and Essken coexist in our time, but figured you'd see Tinn at the FBTI court anyway, so…" She shrugs as a sly grin slips over her face. "To celebrate the occasion, we asked him to put on his fancy environmental suit for you, but he preferred to stay in his sweats, metaphorically speaking. He—"

"I literally smell your lie, Kaytee. You love my environmental sweat suit."

Both Kieran and me jerk our heads over to the source of the voice: The Essken. Koll.

"Holy Sun and Stars," I whisper, then speak up louder. "You understand us? We can talk?" Because I heard his voice through my good old ears, not inside my head like I had with Lorr in the Realm. And there was *humor* laced with it. Lorr sounded more robotic to me, but this Essken? Not at all.

Koll nods and flattens his palm against the chest plate of his armor. "Your words are captured and translated into electrical impulses inside my suit. The reverse is happening for my response. It's quite effective, especially when used in combination with our sense of smell. It helps us interpret your words."

"Fascinating," Kieran murmurs. He shakes his head, a look of guarded wonder in his eyes. "I'm happy to see your species and ours cooperating. Being on the same page. It surely didn't look like that during my time."

"We've had a complicated relationship after the war, but our species understand each other better now," Koll replies. A little bit of an artificial roughness swings in his voice, but otherwise I wouldn't be able to tell it wasn't vocal cords producing the sound. I wonder... did he choose his voice based on his gender? How many genders do they have? Man, so much I don't know...

"I can see about a million questions on your face." One of the women, Isa, I think, slides back onto the table behind her. Like everybody else here, she is young. Her brown skin contrasts nicely with her pale blue eyes and the bright yellow onesie-outfit. It's quite the remarkable look. "Sorry we can't give you more."

I lift both hands, palms out. "Hey, no worries. Am I curious? Heck, yes. Do I like the timeline in one piece? Also yes. And while—" I suck in my lower lip and focus on my First Sense, probably looking as spaced out as Zio always did to me when he was still my mentor and I had no idea what was going on. Like him, I only need a second or two to be sure. My First Sense is quiet. I nod. "And while my First Sense is quiet and not up in arms, I know too much already. I mean, I wasn't even sure I wanted kids, and now look at you." I shoot a glance at Kaytee. "Looks like it's not a choice anymore—no offense."

"None taken." She slides into one of the chairs behind a table. "And believe me, I wasn't going to come out to you as your great-granddaughter, but if you remember correctly, the circumstances required some improv on my behalf." She taps the chair next to her. "Come on, sit down, this is going to take longer. Rocky, you mind bringing us some water?"

Rocky, a Caucasian guy with a blond buzzcut, nods and walks off to somewhere in the dark area behind us. Kieran's gaze follows him, then swings over the ceiling and to the computer access panels integrated into the tables. Inconspicuously, he lays a palm on it as if he was leaning onto the table for support. Nothing happens. Either the panel is programmed to respond to registered individuals only, or the panel is dead.

Either way, it won't work for us.

Kaytee sighs. "Look, I know this is a lot. You were thrown into the future, and life as you know it is no more."

"Good start with the pep talk." Kieran's dry comment draws a chuckle from several of the crew as he sits down next to me. "But don't underestimate us. We're used to dealing with unusual situations."

"We know. Which is why we chose this approach." She folds her hands on the table in front of her. "Look, I know where you're coming from, not just literally, but also proverbially. I got my First Sense from you—granted, it's watered down, but it has served me well."

My mouth forms a little *o*. It's so weird hearing her talk about what she got from me.

"And," Kaytee continues, "that's exactly the reason why you're here. With us. Okay, here we go. You're going to need *some* information, and we're going to keep it as generic as possible, but without it... It's imperative you understand the situation you're in." She taps her index finger onto the table. "If your First Sense kicks in, let me know, okay?"

I sit up straighter. "Sure." That I can do. Easily. The judge's comment still irks me, though. *Are we really to trust our future on* that? I cross my arms over my chest. First Sense-shaming. Boo.

Kaytee folds her hands on the table. "Okay, so the FBTI just started patrolling the timeline a few months ago—"

"Excuse me? We're actively *patrolling* the timeline?" I shake my head as if that would clarify what she just said.

"Yup, you heard me right. Taro Izola has come up with technology that allows for travel through time, if one is genetically able to do so. Meaning, there's only a few people with the abilities and even fewer on their employee roster they trust to do that job. Like, one."

And we had the pleasure already, it seems. "Sheridan."

Isa makes a gagging noise. "Yeah, Sheridan. He's our only executioner protecting the timeline. He's the sharpest, yet also stupidest tool they have. One of the last with a bit of a higher percentage of Magellan blood who didn't—"

"Isa!" Kaytee hisses.

"Oops." Isa flinches and waves a hand. "Never mind. 'Pologies."

Kieran looks from one to another. "Nobody is going to tell us what that comment meant, I assume?"

Rolling her eyes Kaytee takes in a slow, controlled breath. "Unfortunately not." She swipes her hair behind her right ear, her fingers brushing over some round, metallic structure on her mastoid bone. A muscle in her jaw tics, and she shakes her head twice, until the hair has fallen forward again, hiding whatever that was. Some kind of jewelry?

"Anyway, long story short. When we got the briefing our timeline needed saving and that you two would destroy your-slash-our future… It didn't feel right. I knew then and am still sure the FBTI is wrong. Which, by the way, is something you should never, ever say out loud. I learned that the hard way." She grimaces. "Forget I said that. Anyway. Back to the topic and *only* the topic. I'm telling you all of this because you need to know what is expected of you. Or is your First Sense protesting?" She gives me a questioning glance, one eyebrow raised.

I sigh. "Not at all. It just feels very odd to throw out caution." In the grand scheme of things, I'm still a newbie to time-travel, but I have enough experience to be PTSD'ed from my fear of accidentally changing the timeline.

Kieran taps his fingers together, his focus on Kaytee. "You got us out of the FBTI-hold, but if the same had happened in my time, or Nonie's, I bet you the authorities would move heaven and earth to find us again. What makes you think we can continue hiding from them? And more importantly, how do you propose we get back to our time?"

"Got one more," I say, and that's the real biggie. "What will keep them from trying again? They could kidnap us again the moment we return. Or a day later. A day sooner. If you want to protect your future and therefore us, our plan—whatever we do—needs to be watertight." Mashaule jumped back and forth to points in time he or the downstream power considered for easier attacks on Kieran's life. The FBTI could be doing the same thing, since they have the ability to do controlled jumps. And I really don't want a repeat of Sheridan getting the upper hand on us.

Kaytee grimaces. "No kidding it needs to be watertight. Okay, here's the rundown, bear with me. One, I don't think they'll find you here." She taps her index finger onto the table. "The *USS Achievement* is a decommissioned and officially sunken ship. Nobody knows she's here, afloat, not on the bottom of the sea. And we only know, because..." She nods her head at Isa.

"Because I work for Historic Preservation, and we were supposed to sink it," Isa says. "Only it was a fail. We sank every other old warship, worldwide, just not this one. The explosives didn't go off, and instead of fixing it, they swept it under the rug. Too expensive to fix, and from their point of view, the ship would sink soon anyway from old age and decay." She shrugs, the tight brown curls on her head dancing from the movement.

Sinking all old war ships? "Why would you do that instead of dismantling them and using the resources? Sinking the ships, I mean?" I ask.

"Because we have enough resources that we can use the ships to provide new structures for corals to grow on and marine life to find shelter. After a few decades, it's fantastic for a new generation of demat-divers to explore and take in the beauty of the ocean and the past in one dive. Oh, and, you know, because that's important, all toxic material has been removed prior, obviously."

"That's good to know." Kieran clears his throat and shoots me a look that says *stay on topic*. "And it explains why they won't have the *Achievement* on their proverbial radar, but it doesn't explain why they won't have us on their literal radar. In my time, we'd be scanning the planet with all we got. Nonie and my bio-signatures could be found like that. I'm assuming technology has rather improved in that regard."

Kaytee gives him a bland look. "Without giving too much away, it has, but to answer your question, we're safe here." She drops her hand again. "That's why we chose the *Achievement*. She is one of the last stealth ships, and by stealth, I mean off the radar. Really off the radar. Can't be found, unless you have the coordinates. She's also equipped with DP, demat-protection. You can't demat *into* the ship, only *onto* the surface, and only to a small area there, if you have the exact current coordinates. That's why we chose this ship, and that's why we had to get you off the deck as quickly as we did, to avoid our bio-signatures popping up on their world-wide scans. If you stay below deck, nobody will find you here."

I nod. "I like that part, but what's to keep Sheridan from jumping back in time and preventing you from getting us out of their hold? Would he dare change the past?" I wouldn't put it past him. He didn't really make a stellar first impression.

Kaytee points her index finger at me and clicks her tongue. "Good thinking, but that's a no. Like I said, we barely started patrolling the timeline, and that was a tough sell. Every temporal jump needs to be okay'ed by the Taro and Judge Alberti, and while the Taro is very much supportive of time travel, the judge is not. She wouldn't allow

Sheridan to go back and change our past in this kind of manner. I mean, I can't promise she won't be swayed, but I'm ninety-nine percent sure she's going to wait this situation out. If she isn't..." She shrugs and opens her palms to the ceiling. "I guess we'll never know if they decide to go back and prevent us from breaking you out."

"Yay," I mumble. Because then we'd just be stuck in that stupid cell not knowing any better. I want to believe this century's FBTI has enough decency to not jump through time and change what they feel needs changing, but so far I can't say I trust much in their common—or rather, temporal—sense.

Rocky comes back with a black gym bag and drops it on the empty table to our left. "Water for everybody. I set the FDs to start on dinner, but just FYI, Koll should have a look at them, something's off."

"Technical support. On it." The Essken slides out of his seat and vanishes into the dark.

"Thanks, guys." Kaytee nods at them and takes a water from Rocky's hands, passing it down the line.

I crack mine open and take a deep swig of it. Feels like I haven't had anything for at least a century. Harr harr. After setting it down, I wipe my mouth with my sleeve. "Don't take this the wrong way, but how does a bunch of youngsters and yes, I get you're all older than me, but still—how does a bunch of youngsters have access to a decommissioned Navy ship? To demat technology? Or, how were you guys able to break us out of FBTI jail? How could you get that done? Again, I mean that as a praise of your abilities; I doubt it was easy. How could you pull that off?" Clearly, they're not professionals. They're motivated for sure, but I'm about ninety-nine percent sure they're not a special ops unit trained by USEF, unless times have really changed.

Kaytee takes a sip of her water and wiggles her eyebrows. "No offense taken. Impressive, right? We're quite proud of ourselves as well. Like I said, we usually don't do any of that. In fact, let me tell you what we usually do, and that'll lead to the answers to your question. Me, I work for the FBTI. The path was clear from birth when my aptitude test came back positive for time-jump abilities. Got the implant, and then it was clear I'd be working for them. I could have worked somewhere else, but the FBTI is the leader of our free world, so duh, it's not a career you throw away lightly." She takes another sip, then points at Marty and Jaasu. "Marty, Jaasu, and I work together. Marty takes care of the temporal tech, well, he's a junior operator, but still, Jaasu works in ops. We all were together in that big meeting I mentioned, together with Sheridan. Even the Taro was there, which, like, never happens. That's when they told us about the need to fix the timeline in the past before it veered off, and it didn't feel right to us. It *isn't* right. We just started sending out Sheridan to patrol the timeline, and all of a sudden, they discover something is wrong. Really? *I* didn't feel it. *Jaasu* here didn't feel it, and his grandpa was half-Magellan. *My mom*—your granddaughter—didn't feel it, and her First Sense is stronger than mine, obviously. Not a huge leap to deduct they might be wrong. What if Sheridan misinterpreted something? And I don't even mean that in an accusing way, just..." She lifts and drops her shoulders. "Time is complicated. He's new at it. Not hard to conclude he can make mistakes."

I point at her. "I agree. If it veered off, you'd never know. The past would have changed, and therefore the outcome, you, would have changed."

She lifts both hands and shakes her head. "Hey, I said the same thing and *boom*, suspended by Sheridan for disrespecting the Taro. It's weird, believe me, which is why I couldn't let it rest. So, anyway, Marty and I contacted Zael. Known her forever, went to FBTI boot camp with her, so we trust each other. She's in FBTI-processing and found out when Sheridan was going to jump, and where you were going to be held. Then we recruited Rocky, who's our FBTI-tech-guy, since he could give us a tiny pinhole to slip through the security system to get you out, but—"

"We needed Koll for communication with you and his Essken technology to get you out," Marty finishes the sentence for her. "I know Koll from when I was little. My mom worked with his people."

I facepalm. "That's why we heard a voice in our head. Should've added one and one, because I thought to myself it sounded like in the

Realm, right, Kieran." I nudge him with my elbow.

"Well. I wish I had heard their voices that clear when I was in the Realm." Kieran says it completely calm, and only a person knowing him well would pick up on the slight pallor of his face, or the tightness of his lips. He glides one hand through his hair, stopping his motion half-way through, eyes taking on a glassy, far-away quality. "During my time in the Realm, I couldn't hear the Essken talk like I heard Koll. I could feel, or sense, what they wanted to get across, but I still felt trapped. Helpless. Can't say communicating through dreams and mental images is my strong side." His lips curl into a defiant half-smile.

Empathy shines from Kaytee's eyes. "That must've been—"

The hair on my arms and neck rises as if a lightning storm's rolling in overhead. First, I think it's from Kieran's words, the suffering they're laced with, but no… a wave of dizziness hits me like a sledgehammer, turning my vision blurry. That's when recognition hits. It's the same thing that happened in the cell.

My next breath comes in shallow and wheezy as Kieran gasps and stiffens, a look of shock on his face. Nausea rises, the imperative kind that makes me want to vomit on the spot.

"—difficult," Kaytee finishes her sentence, and Holy Universe, I can't even focus on her, I don't see double, I see triple-quadruple and more, like there were dozens of layers of Kaytee. I blink, but the images stay.

With a groan, Kieran arches his back, then deflates and leans forward, forearms on the table, fists balled, head bowed, each breath shuddered.

"Uhh, Kieran? Are you okay?" Kaytee twists in her seat toward him, her voice sounding like far, far away to me. "Do we need to get—"

Pressure weighs on me, making breathing hard, like something was wrapping itself around me. Out of nowhere, a yearning so deep, so all-encompassing fills me up it cancels out all higher thoughts and lets instinct take over. I obey its command, reaching out and wrapping my fingers around Kieran's balled, tight fist.

*Zzing!*

Holy—! My back buckles, then bows back, controlled by forces stronger than my will. Not a good idea. *So* not a good idea! I feel like I've been hit by lightning, if lightning also was acidic, but then—

Something happens.

Like the last time, the pain changes to more of a euphoric feeling as my body begins to tingle, especially my hands. The storm, the chaos inside of me, calms down, becoming soothing, instead of stinging, and—

And like that, it's over.

Kieran deflates, dropping his head onto the table, while I slump forward, the hand not holding on to Kieran's shaking. The dizziness is gone, so is the quadruple-blurry vision. My heart beats like it just powered me through a marathon, fast and hard.

"Geez, guys!" Kaytee jumps up. "Are you okay? What's going on?" Her wild gaze darts from Kieran to me and back.

I hold up a finger to buy myself a moment. Kieran's chest is heaving up and down in an irregular rhythm. I bend forward, closing the distance between us. "You okay?" I whisper into his ear, my other hand pressed into his back.

He nods, then pushes himself upright, slow inch by slow inch. "Like the last time," he says matter-of-factly, and I nod, rubbing my hand over the one that touched Kieran. I didn't even make the decision to touch him. It just happened, as if my body was acting on its own account.

Freaky.

"Right?" Kieran turns toward me. "Like last time."

"Y-yeah," I say. "So, not likely to be a defensive mechanism by the FBTI then."

"Guys, what's going on?" Kaytee has both hands firmly planted on the table, her brows scrunched together. "You're kind of freaking me out."

"Me, too," Isa says, a statement the others agree to with nods.

"Sorry." Kieran gives her a half smile, which looks weird in his pale face. "Just an odd episode."

"That I can tell." Kaytee crosses her arms in front of her chest and sits down again. "Care to elaborate?"

I shake out my arms, then pull myself together and nod. This is their time, maybe they'll know what those events are. "Sure. This was the second time we had this attack, for a lack of a better word. First time was at the FBTI jail, and then right now. There's some blurry vision and nausea for me that Kieran doesn't experience." I give him a questioning look, since this time it could've been different.

"I had none of that. Only this sensation of being assaulted out of nowhere, like somebody injected acid into my veins, which isn't what I would call pleasant," he adds.

"I felt the same after I touched your hand, and no, definitely not pleasant." This whole episode lasted what, three seconds? Four? Now that it's over, all that's left is a weird metallic taste in my mouth. "Please tell me you know what it is, because if something happens once, it's coincidence. It happens twice, it isn't."

Kieran looks from one of our new friends to the next, as Koll is sliding back into his seat. "My main concern is whether this is a weapon used against us. Could the FBTI have done something to us, to... I don't know, maybe control us through pain? I'm not quite sure how or to what purpose, but warfare isn't always logical."

The others exchange glances amongst themselves. "I don't think we've ever heard about anything like that," Kaytee says eventually. "I didn't feel or see anything." The others shake their heads. "And for the FBTI to attack specifically the two of you without knowing where you are? Too big for them to pull off. Too targeted. Maybe it has to do with your temporal displacement? Like, a reaction to our time? Maybe people aren't made to visit the future?"

I shrug, then fake a smile. "Definitely a possibility. And just because it happened twice, doesn't mean it's going to happen again. Even though two occurrences make coincidence less likely, they also don't make a pattern yet, I get it. Probably just the transition." I don't want to make a big deal out of those events, especially because nobody else was affected, but... it does leave a weird taste in my mouth, literally and proverbially. Nothing about those two episodes feels right, pain and discomfort aside. If it was from the transition, why did I never experience anything like it when I jumped through time before? Could it really be just because we jumped into the future? Is the future rejecting us to protect the timeline?

Out of the corner of my eye, I pick up on Kieran's critical expression. He's not convinced, and I can't blame him. Neither am I. It feels too… big for just a side effect of sorts.

Kaytee's features soften. "Maybe. Just let us know if it happens again. Nobody here's a real doctor, but we all had field medic training. Okay?"

"Okay." I return her smile. Not sure if any field medic training would help us, and even though it happened twice, right now, it doesn't matter. It's not our most pressing issue at the moment. As long as those episodes stay self-contained and don't worsen, I won't give them any more brain space than I have to, until I have to. "We'll keep an eye on things, right?" I nudge Kieran with my shoulder.

"We will." Kieran lays a hand on my thigh. "And to go back to— what were we talking about…?" His face is still tight, and the hand on my thigh shaking. I take it back. These episodes aren't my main concern, but I'm not dismissing them either. While I'm sure I don't look unaffected either, Kieran looks like crap.

"We were talking about the Essken Realm." Rocky turns to Koll and whispers something to him.

Koll listens, then bows his head. "Kieran, in the name of my people I apologize for keeping you with us for so many years. Reality works differently in the Realm, as you know, and we hadn't understood that difference when you found us."

A bit of color returns to Kieran's cheeks. "No apology needed. I know your people didn't intend to harm me."

"Not at all. You still are the only full human we could ever communicate with, to this day." He taps his skull, as if to say in our minds.

Kaytee rolls her eyes. "Koll, careful what you say—"

"Really?" Surprise flares in Kieran's eyes. "That makes me feel special, don't get me wrong, but why?"

Koll addresses Kaytee. "This is non-essential information, Kaytee." When Kaytee rolls her eyes once more, but doesn't protest, he carries on. "That's what we asked ourselves as well. We tried to communicate with humans and many other species, but it never worked. Until you— and you." He nods at me. "In fact, as you know, nobody who entered the Realm survived. And," his tone turns sheepish, "no human did well with our communication attempts within your realm either."

"The Mind Crucification," I whisper. I got Kieran out of it, and he survived. Even at my time, he was the only one who had come out with his mind intact and not driven to insanity.

"Correct. Again, my apologies. But, we assume that the unique genome Nonie has, her sensitivity to the timeline and other realms, enables her to communicate with us and exist in our realm. And since the two of you are bonded, some of her abilities leak through the connection and protect you, Kieran."

Kieran and I exchange a glance. Some of my abilities… "So, you're saying, if we hadn't been bonded, Kieran would've died in your realm, like everybody else?"

"I don't think I even would've entered," Kieran answers my question, tone flat. "Without the protection through the Bond, the crucification would've rendered me unable to function, if not dead."

Now that's a sobering thought if I ever heard one.

"*Anyway*, let's get off that cheerful topic and back to the who-is-who." Kaytee counts off her fingers: "Me and Zael as the instigators and mission leaders, Rocky to open the door, Koll to notify you and get you out, and Isa here had the idea with the *Achievement*. We actually went to high school together, and both got stuck dealing with time, me at the FBTI, her in Historic Preservation, which is how she knew about this beauty here, as she said. The other guys and gals," she makes a swiping gesture with her hands, "we approached because we knew them, could trust them, and we needed more help. I've never partially powered up an old Navy ship, but Carlos has. Sterling works in security, and we felt it might be prudent to have somebody watch out for us. Kairo is

Sterling's boyfriend and a man of all trades. So yeah, that's how we all ended up together." She shrugs.

I whistle through my teeth. "Impressive." Our break-out wasn't a coordinated, well thought-through military or para-military operation. It was a bunch of young adults with a common goal. Somewhere some high-ranking FBTI officer is having a heart attack over us vanishing. And being demoted, probably.

Kieran's thoughts are going the same way. "I agree with Nonie. Your problem-solving skills and dedication are commendable, I must say."

Everybody—literally, everybody—blushes. Some of them mumble a few words, like, *wasn't a big deal, anybody would've done this,* or *our pleasure,* but most of them just look… happy. Satisfied, to a degree.

After taking another sip of water, Kieran addresses Kaytee again. "All right, so, I understand how everybody, including us, got to the point where we currently are. What's the next step?"

That… that wipes the smiles off everybody's face in no time.

Uh-oh.

Kaytee brushes a strand of hair behind her ear, the metallic thing behind it reflecting some of the artificial light. "So, the thing is there is no plan yet." She sits up straight and looks us in the eye.

"No plan yet?" I echo. *Uh-oh* indeed.

"Nope. None whatsoever. We're lucky everything went as smoothly as it did, and without Koll and his tech, we couldn't have done it at all. And as it is, now we're looking at an empty slate. We have no access to Setayashi-radiation like Sheridan does. All devices and materials to synthesize emitters are heavily controlled."

My stomach drops. "No Setayashi source?" That means we're stuck in this time, despite having been unstuck from the FBTI jail.

She shakes her head. "I wish we did, but no chance."

A muscle tightens in Kieran's jaw. "We can figure out a way. Right, Nonie?"

It takes me a second too long to be truly convincing, but I nod. "Yeah, sure. Little hiccup, but manageable." As long as I don't need to blow up another planet with a Marmelite core to get that Setayashi spike. Been there, done that, didn't want the t-shirt the first time around.

"I apologize, but look, all this"—Kaytee gestures around the table—"was a last minute scramble. Our priority was to get you guys out before—" She sucks in a harsh breath through her teeth and drops her gaze to the table.

"Before what?" I ask, a weird feeling spreading in the pit of my stomach. "Why don't I like the way you stopped yourself?"

Kaytee tentatively releases the breath she held. "You know—"

"Kay," Zael says, warning in her voice.

The two women look at each other.

"They gotta know, Zae."

"No, they don't."

"They're already asking the right questions. We can't keep it quiet. The judge would've told them eventually. They have a right to know."

Zael shakes her head. "Maybe, maybe not. I'm not letting you make that decision alone. Jaasu?"

Jaasu pinches his eyes shut and sucks in his lower lip. "I think we're okay. Kaytee is okay."

"You *think*." Skepticism radiates form Zael's tone.

"Well, sue me, but I have a fraction of a First Sense compared to others." Jaasu points at me, which hello, brings everybody's attention to me.

I wiggle my fingers at everyone. "Anything I can do?"

Jaasu nods. "What does your First Sense say?"

"About Kaytee telling us what we supposedly have a right to know about? You do realize I might be biased and give you the answer serving me best, right?"

Shaking his head, Jaasu crosses his arms in front of his chest. He might be a year or two older than Kieran, maybe even the oldest of this group, but it's tough to say. His hair is multi-colored, which makes him look younger. The coloring is amazing, by the way. Not in streaks or highlights, but his hair shimmers, like an iridescent rainbow of colors, depending on the angle the light hits it.

But anyway.

Jasuu raises an eyebrow. "Everything I read about you emphasizes your integrity. You're not going to lie if it goes against the timeline."

Touché. And happy to hear there must be information out there other than what Sheridan claims he read about me. That being said, I sigh. "I don't like that you read about me, or rather, that there is stuff to read about me, but I guess I can't change that. Also, can't forget that." I give him a pointed glance, then take a deep, calming breath and turn inwards to listen. Recognizing my First Sense acting up is different from asking it for directions, so to speak. When it isn't happy, I feel it: Nausea, this odd feeling in the pit of my stomach, and the sensation of *nope*. It's clear what it is, at least now that I know how to interpret it. But asking it… It's more like trying to feel my way through a maze with my eyes closed, having to use my other senses and intuition. Somehow, all of that input together forms my First Sense, like I was reaching out into time and… feeling it, for a lack of a better term. It sounds weird, and it's definitely weird getting used to it, but it does work well, screw the judge's pessimism. When I first got thrown back to the *Pioneer* and met Kieran, I obviously had no idea. Yet there was this sensation that guided me, that feeling in the pit of my stomach I responded to without knowing I catered to my First Sense. Then lately, when I chased Mashaule, my use of it became more natural and instinctive, like jumping through time became more of a second-nature kind of thing, too. Maybe my skills are going to develop further, who knows. I mean, they all here probably do know, but I'm not going to ask.

That thought alone, potentially asking about the extent my skills are going to develop to, brings a sharp, cutting sensation to rise in my center. It comes together with a feeling of resistance, as if the path in that direction was blocked. A small smile spreads over my lips. Guess my First Sense agrees with my assessment: don't ask that question.

Instead, I focus on Kaytee and her telling us whatever it is she's holding off on. No resistance, only the soft flow of time, accompanied by a peaceful feeling.

I'll take that as a yes.

Opening my eyes, I nod. "My First Sense is okay with you telling us what you were about to."

Kaytee huffs. "Well, your First Sense might be okay with it, but I promise, you will not be once you hear it."

Kieran holds on tighter to my thigh, as if he was securing us against what Kaytee is about to say.

She smacks her lips twice. "Okay, here we go. The reason why we had to prioritize to get you out above all else and asap is because… They were planning to send you home again, because duh, they can't just remove you from your time without it causing a major change in the timeline. But you weren't going to be sent home in the way you think. Since they can't risk you knowing too much about the future the plan was to… to use brain programming on you." Her throat works on a hard swallow. She looks us straight in the eye. "Yes, the judge is still looking into the Taro's data, but either way, if they get their hands on you again, they will need to make sure you act the way they want you to once they send you back to your time. They will set up parameters for your brain to perform within. No free will. Every step predetermined as per our historic records. You won't be the same anymore, but a pre-programmed mind in a life no longer yours to live."

# Chapter Four –

# Time-Tohuwabohu

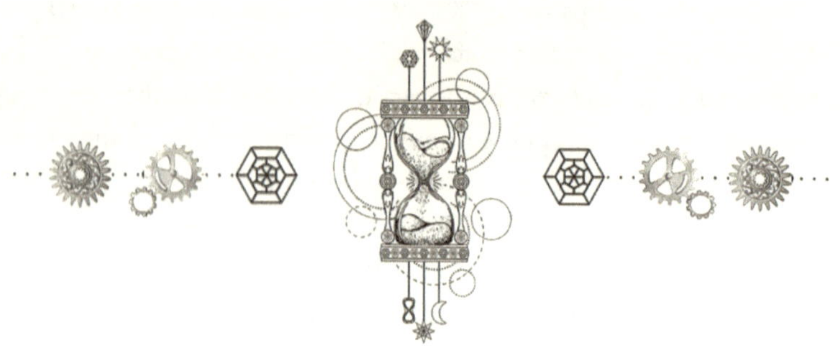

**_USS Achievement, 2399_**

Koll leads us through the *Achievement*'s hallways toward our quarters.

Since Kaytee dropped that bomb on us, I haven't been able to focus. Altering our minds—programming us, free will gone… Unfathomable. It sounds like humanity took a century-spanning step backwards, not forwards. Taking our free will… barbaric.

My First Sense screams in protest when I think about that potential future—or rather, past—and it makes me mad. Clearly, there's a disconnect between what my First Sense perceives as correct and what the FBTI believes. Who is correct?

To be fair, we're a hundred years behind the times and accused by the *FBTI,* not some no-name-no-clue organization. They should know what they're doing, they should have a valid reason to warrant such an invasive step. And, to not be too biased for obvious reasons, while I don't like the action they were going to take, maybe they were still correct in their assessment of me. Maybe it's me who is wrong, not them.

Problem is, I don't think I'm wrong. Is that an inflated ego talking? Self-preservation? My First Sense? Or maybe a combination of all three? Who knows, but in the end, I can only work with the limited facts I have and trust in my First Sense like I trust in Kieran's innate goodness and will to do no harm.

We turn around another corner, the illuminated part of the ceiling moving with us, like we carried a tiny sun over our heads. It's a bit weird, because I still don't see any lightbulbs or any medium that could be used as such, only a normal, off-white steel ceiling that happens to light up wherever we go. Welcome to the future.

That being said, when they told us the ship was decommissioned, they weren't lying. On second glance, it only has minimal function. I don't think the air is working everywhere, or maybe it's just going stronger in some areas than others. Explains the musky smell. None of the control panels we pass seem functional either, they're all dark and covered with a layer of dust.

"I apologize, but we only have limited resources and accommodations," Koll says. "We were able to route power to one officers' room for you, but it might be tight."

"No problem. We don't mind that." Kieran replies, gliding a finger over another unused and powered-down console on our left. He's been studying every square-inch of this ship on the way over to the quarters from the mess hall like it was the most fascinating thing he'd ever seen. And it is, somewhat, at least. The weirdest disconnect though is that it clearly is more modern than what I'm used to—not that I was an expert on naval vessels, but still—it looks old and out of shape, somehow. Time jumps are sometimes plain mind-boggling.

Eventually, Koll stops in front of a hatch no different from any of the others we passed. "You have time to rest. It's late. A pleasure meeting you." He lowers his head once, and turns to leave.

"Koll," I say, "do you mind if I ask you something?" Something that's been on my mind since I left the Essken Realm—granted, it had moved to the back burner as priorities shifted since then, but still.

He stops and faces us. "Not at all. I was wondering if you were going to ask me what's been troubling you." When he sees my puzzled expression, he taps one finger to the middle of face. "I could smell the curiosity. Some worry. Concern."

I whistle. Spot on. "Must be convenient to have another sense help you out with communication."

"Very much so, especially with humans. Magellans smell different to us, less aggressive, and with less nuances. You could say they're more quiet compared to humans. But with your people, it helps to interpret the subtleties and meaning behind words. Pure verbal communication otherwise lacks precision. It's tricky."

Huffing with a little laugh, I put my hands on my hips. "No kidding. I kind of envy you for having another sense to help you. Humans could use that— Wait. The Essken I met before you, they all had different scents, strong ones, and you—"

"I don't. We're using odor suppressants when in your realm. We've found it to be easier for humans to deal with us this way."

"But doesn't that mess with your communication then?" As if we humans were only speaking in whispers, and part of the information could be missed or overheard.

"It does, but not to the degree that it would cause problems. A small price to pay to improve interactions between our two peoples. So, what's on your mind?"

Right. I squirm, stepping from one foot onto the other. "I hope it isn't giving away too much, but I'd really like to know if you were able to repair the damage to your realm." He's here, and so was the other Essken at court. Everything I heard suggests things are going well between humans and Essken and that we work together, in harmony, apparently. Wouldn't be so harmonious if we kept on destroying their home. Or—a rush of heat shoots through my body. What if we ended up destroying it, and that's why the Essken are here? Because their home is gone?

"The damage by your colonized worlds and the Tau-radiation?" He pauses, then shakes his head in such a human way, it hurts to think our people were once enemies. "The damage is gone. It's been fixed. I appreciate you asking."

Relief floods me. It's fixed. Maybe humanity can change and learn after all. "Thank you for that, Koll. I needed a bit of good news today. And by the way, I'm really happy to see you *here*." I emphasize my words by pointing at him, then the ship. An Essken in our realm. Former enemies, now friends. "You are kind of my beacon of hope the future is going to work out well." I give him a smile, and he bows in return.

"Honored to be your beacon of hope. And the pleasure is all mine. I'll see you in the morning. Rest well."

"You, too. And thank you." I wave.

Kieran lifts a hand in a short goodbye gesture, and drops it like it weighed a ton once Koll has turned away from us.

For a few seconds, silence hovers, the overwhelmed kind.

After a while, I blow out a puff of air. "What a day."

Kieran harrumphs. "I still feel like I was put through the wringer from that… attack earlier."

I rub my palm over his upper arm. "You look better though." Not as pale anymore. More like himself.

"I'd feel and look even better if I knew what those episodes were. Or why it's only us, and nobody else." He pauses sucking in his lower lip. "I'm still not discarding the idea of a weapon, of some kind of way to control us. Humanity has used biological warfare before to blackmail others to surrender if they wanted the antidote. This could be similar."

A shudder runs down my back. "If that's our future…"

"We've taken a huge step back, agreed." Kieran sighs. "I don't want to be too pessimistic, but I'm having a hard time with optimism right now. Or do you think the attacks are from the jump to the future, like Kaytee speculated? Why would we be affected at the same time then? Two people can have seizures, doesn't mean they're going to seize at the same time—unless there's a trigger, which brings me right back to my theory that the episodes are man-made. Somehow, at least." He leans against the wall, using one hand to support his weight.

"Can't argue against that. We'll add it to the list of things to figure out, which seems to be growing by the minute." If I still had PADdy, I'd so have started said list already.

Kieran narrows his eyes at me. "Speaking of things to figure out, I wanted to ask you something, and I didn't get to it earlier. During both episodes, you took my hand. Why? And please don't get me wrong, you may touch my hand or any other body part of mine any time you'd like, but I was curious why you did. Because I for sure was busy trying to not fall over."

I shift my weight from one foot to the other. Good observation, only I don't have a good answer. At least not one that makes a whole lot of sense. "I dunno. The first time you were actually going down on one knee, so I was trying to catch you, but…"

"But?"

"But if I'm honest, I don't think that's the only reason. I…" I chew on the inside of my cheek. So much is going on it's tough to take it all in and figure out what's important and what isn't. And I still don't know if it is, but it could be worth mentioning. "Both times I felt… Never mind, it sounds weird."

"Please. Weird is our daily routine."

I snort. "True. Okay then. Both times I felt a pull, like, an instinct, that I needed to touch you."

Kudos to Kieran for not making my admission awkward or cracking a joke. He lifts one eyebrow instead. "An instinct?"

"Well, yes, like my body knew more than me. It's hard to describe. First, I feel pressure all around me, then I get this gnawing sensation on the inside, a hunger that's driving me to touch you." I shrug, like it was no big deal. Happens every day, right?

"And when you touch me? Does it get better?"

That's a tricky question. "That hunger? Yes. But when I touch you, I feel exactly what you described, the acid in my veins, or electricity shooting through me."

He cocks his head to the side and pushes off the wall. "Wait. You didn't feel that from the beginning?"

"Not at all. Just nausea and dizziness, that's it."

"But then whatever happens to me, transfers to you."

I nod. "Seems like it."

For three long seconds Kieran looks me in the eye, not saying a word. I can all but see the thoughts racing through his head. "One, now I'm even more confused as to the origin of these events. Two, then please don't touch me, Nonie—in this circumstance, I mean," he tries to joke. "It's bad enough I'm hurting, I don't need you to do the same." Laying one hand over my deltoid, he squeezes once before he drops his hand again, a look of concern on his face.

I shrug. "I can try. And maybe I can get my hands on a PAD or something and do a scan to see what's going on."

"Good plan, Lieutenant. I really would feel much better at least knowing what's going on."

"You and me both, Captain. You and me both. To repeat our earlier statement: what a day."

Rolling his eyes, Kieran reaches for the doorknob. "Mine has lasted decades. Still feels like only hours ago that I was in my time on the *Pioneer,* saw you, and left for the nebula. Then there was the Realm, which felt like forever, but also like no time passed, then you get me out, we keep our USEF-fleet from blowing each other up, and with a snap of Sheridan's fingers, here we are, ready for a good night's sleep."

Kieran opens the hatch to the quarters Koll assigned us. It swings aside, revealing a small room, but not as small as I had feared after the disclaimer we'd been given. A desk and chair combo are mounted to the floor to the right, screens and control panels integrated into its surface dark. Somebody put two piles of fresh clothing on the bed on the left side of the room, and my heart makes a little excited leap. The bed takes up all the space from wall to wall on that side, and it's not very wide either, which… well, shouldn't be a problem. Overall, the room looks nice compared to how bare this ship is when it comes to comfort. It reminds me much more of a lower decks' starship cabin than I thought, only the floors aren't carpeted, but some hard surface with a good grip under our soles.

I look back at Kieran. "If we had a competition about the

weirdest day, you'd win." Even though mine wasn't uneventful either.

He raises an eyebrow at me as he steps through the door, humor playing in his eyes. "You conceding?"

I punch him in the arm as I follow him inside. "No, I said *if* we had a competition, which we don't, so there's nothing to win." And I'm not conceding. Tah-tah. "The weirdness of the last hours is mainly due to all the secret-keeping. I wish they could tell us more about everything. I understand why they don't of course, but I can't say I especially like it."

Kieran glides a hand over the control panel in the desk. It stays dark. "You're not used to the other side, Nonie. I get it, took me a while to be even close to comfortable with it. In the beginning, I used to lie awake many a night thinking about what the future would hold. Or where— when—you might be at that very moment in your time. How different life might be for you compared to mine. Over the years, I've been imagining every possible future for you, for me, for us. Or so I thought. Turns out real life beats my imagination." He crosses the room toward the bed and pushes one palm into the mattress, testing its firmness, before he sits down on it.

"Ouch." I close the heavy door behind me, then sit next to him, resting my forearms on my knees. "Sometimes I forget what it must've been like for you. When you knew you could ask me, but I wouldn't give you a reply that was helpful in any way."

"It wasn't easy, but you know what? I learned I needed to trust you. That I *could* trust you. Maybe we should give Kaytee and the others the benefit of the doubt and let them take the lead."

I cock my head back to look at him. "That's coming from you? Giving up control?"

Kieran grins. "Better them than the judge. Plus, I'm able to adjust to the situation's needs."

A small laugh leaves my throat before I turn serious again. "That I know, but..."

"But what?"

I look down at my folded hands. "You know, I've been thinking..."

"Oh, dear," Kieran interrupts and chuckles when I elbow him into the side.

"*Anyway,* I want to know how our abduction plays into the Temporal War. Why are we here? And no, don't say so you-slash-we don't kill most of Earth's population, I swear to you that's not it." I slap his thigh, gently.

Kieran snaps his mouth shut again. He swallows once, then sighs, the playfulness gone from his voice. "I hope with all my fiber you're right with that. But to play devil's advocate, you told me Mashey was trying to kill me to prevent me from killing—"

"And Taro Magona knew that was wrong, just like I did. Zio knew as well." I cross my arms in front of my chest. "That's not it, Kieran. Trust our combined First Senses. But *something* is brewing around us, around you and me. I agree with that. I can't imagine our abduction to here is completely independent from that Temporal War, especially since both you and I have already been targets of somebody from the future. You, when Mashaule tried to kill you, and me, when I was kidnapped as a child." A moment passes, and even without seeing his eyes, I know his gaze is on me.

"You're saying your kidnapping was also an attempt to change the timeline?"

Nodding, I rub a hand over my bionic leg out of reflex. Yet another update for Kieran. Should be common courtesy to not abduct anybody before the debrief. *Har-har.* "At this point, I *know* it was. I told you the kidnappers vanished from USEF jail, right?" I opened up to him about that traumatic day when I was on the *Pioneer* for the first time. Kieran had offered to help me look into the circumstances when he still thought I was a regular civilian, a sweet, albeit an unnecessary offer—but still appreciated.

"And you think that's because—"

"I know they had means to contact the future via a disk that also emits Satayashi radiation, which one would need to initiate a time-jump. They were tasked to change *something* in the flow of time that was related to me—change my path, kill me, who knows. In your case, we know Mashaule was ordered to try and kill you. Two interventions to change the flow of time. It must be more than a coincidence, especially if you take into consideration that we're here now, in the future. Together."

Understanding flashes in his eyes. "You're thinking whoever gave orders to have me killed or to kidnap you might have given the order to kidnap us to here and now, or at least manipulated enough people for that to happen? Maybe even with the goal to have our brains reprogrammed and neutralizing us that way instead of killing us."

Lifting and dropping my shoulders, I kick my boots off and draw both legs onto the bed, sitting criss-cross applesauce. "Fair assumption, isn't it? In general, I trust authority, and I would trust the FBTI and the judge, but what if they have been given false information?"

"By Sheridan?"

"For example. Or by somebody deeper into the future, wherever the Temporal War is starting from. But—"

"But what?"

I weigh my head left to right. "First, I would really like to know where and when the Temporal War originates. Mashaule once said something about 250 years in the future, Magona sensed something about 200 years downstream, and here we are, a hundred years into the future, and we still have no idea. Doesn't mean it's *not* starting here, because I doubt somebody evil enough to recruit Mashaule to change the flow of time would always tell the truth, or that Magona's First Sense is so honed, she can tell these things. But even more vexing is my second problem: why is nobody intervening from the future-future? Is that because the Temporal War is originating there and what they're doing to us *is* their intervention? Why else is nobody helping us, if the integrity of the timeline is at stake?" That thought has been nagging me for a while, since I was chasing Mashaule. Now it begs for even more attention.

"You're saying some kind of future FBTI should be realizing somebody is messing with time and help us?" Kieran wraps one arm around my shoulders, and I swear that simple gesture has a weight drop from said shoulders, as if he'd pushed it off.

"Yes. If the technology exists now where Sheridan can travel through time easily, why is there nobody from, say, fifty years, or a hundred or so further ahead, coming here to fix whatever needs fixing? Even if this is part of the Temporal War, somebody from even further up could be on our side and helping us." I protected my past from Mashaule, and yes, I understand that, all annoyance and risk to myself aside, this FBTI here is trying to do the same with their past—my present. But therefore, it's also not hard to deduct sometime downstream somebody else is trying to protect *their* past. But where are they?

Kieran purses his lips, lost in thought. I blow a raspberry and roll my eyes. "I mean, unless of course they don't need to intervene, because everything is happening according to their plans. Which could be good or bad."

Kieran huffs. "Right. Because if the future knows everything will play out the way it should, it could mean we get out of here and stay safe, good for us, or it could mean the FBTI gets their way and we go back with altered minds, bad for us." He huffs again. "Thinking this through, I'm not sure I like the other option for the lack of intervention much more either. Maybe there is nobody left anymore to travel back in time."

Silence hovers as we look at each other, my stomach twisting into a figure eight.

The apple in his throat moves up and down. "You know… It's quite the effort to go through if they're wrong. The admiral trying to kill me by jumping through time. Your kidnapping. Now our abduction to here. This isn't just a spur of the moment thing. This is well planned and executed."

I hear what he's saying. A shudder runs down my spine. "You think they might be doing the right thing."

Kieran's only response is a lift and drop of his shoulders.

I lean my head against his shoulder. It's not as if I hadn't thought about that possibility, but I'm still not on board with it. "I understand what you're saying. They could be trying to do the right thing by removing us from the timeline. But also, how can we know this isn't a ploy in the Temporal War?" I whisper. It must be. Thinking about being responsible for the death of that many people… it brings nausea to a boil inside of me, just like when I thought I had blown up a whole planet full of Quaneez, even when they were still considered the enemy. Imagining a scenario where both of us make so many mistakes or wrong decisions to add up to the near annihilation of the human race… unimaginable.

A cold shudder runs down my spine. "I can't believe we'd be able to cause death on such great a scale."

Kieran stays silent for a moment, chewing on his lower lip. "Not you. I am."

"With my help." I wiggle my hands. Yay.

"Apparently." Raking his fingers through his hair, he takes a deep breath in and holds it. "I don't know what to believe, Nonie. In the end, we're new here. We don't know how the game is played, who all the moving pieces are—or *when* they are. What their motivation may be. Or, like you said, what potentially wrong information they might've been fed. That being said and all potential repercussions aside, I do lean toward trusting your First Sense and Kaytee more than the judge, so there's that."

I lean back and let my head fall against the cold metal wall behind us. "Because she's our…" Our great-granddaughter? Can't even get that to cross my lips. Way too weird.

A smile tugs on Kieran's lips as he turns to me, drawing one knee up onto the bed. "Yes. That, and she's genuine."

"You do know you basically just knighted her by saying you trust her, right?" All I heard from my *mentors* Chase and Zio is that Kieran didn't trust easily. I experienced gaining his trust, then losing it when he realized Nonie Magnetta wasn't whom he expected her to be. Kieran has trust issues, period. Can't fault him for that, having been shot by his nanny, but he has them.

A soft laugh leaves his throat. "I have high hopes for her. By the way, she has your nose." He taps a finger to the tip of my nose.

Warmth invades my cheeks. "That's so, so weird," I murmur. "I feel though she has your eyes. Can that even be, two generations removed?"

He shrugs. "Sure. Would even be more when it comes to my eyes, because my dad insists I got them from his dad."

"It's still so weird. Seeing Kaytee as the proof that you and I…" I suck in my lower lip, feeling my cheeks heat. "That we're going to have kids."

He takes my hand and plays with the rainbow-ring on my finger. "Before I was in the Realm, I always wanted kids." The words come out so casually, so calm, they strike a chord in me.

Twisting so I can get a better look at him, I draw one leg closer, not sure which part of the sentence to focus on. Before the Realm—so not anymore? He had actively thought about having kids? Deciding to let the first part of his statement go, I raise one eyebrow. "You did? I never knew that."

"Well, it's not as if we'd had the time to talk about our future—or if there'd been a chance for a future to happen until literally a few hours ago. Give or take a century, apparently."

A dry huff leaves my throat. "I hear you there." Great minds think alike.

Still makes me feel a tad inadequate that I, au contraire to Kieran, don't have an outline of my life ready. I always knew the Academy was my goal. Graduating well, if not best of my class. Get into D-2— Yeah. That was my idea of planning my life. I literally had nothing else on my to-do-list after I made D-2. Nothing. No schedule for promotions, no other plans, be that for work, or for my private life.

I drop my gaze to the mattress. "See, I'm not sure what I want. I mean, clearly I'll be having kids, but it's not a decision I made before meeting Kaytee." And I somehow feel cheated out of my decision-making process. I don't mind it that much but doesn't change that I do feel cheated.

"And nobody would have expected you to," Kieran adds, kicking off his boots. "You're young."

"So are you, and you just said you always wanted kids."

"But it's not a decision I consciously made, just something that always felt right, like it was a given, yeah, one day I'd have kids. Maybe like some people know they want to become a doctor, or a teacher, or a captain with the USEF." He sits back and rocks his shoulder into mine.

"Well, I knew I wanted to join D-2, and look how that turned out. Instead, I'm a time-traveling FBTI-officer trapped in the future." I frown and pause for a second. "Didn't really expect that."

Kieran looks at me from below his lashes, like, *really?*

I chuckle. "All right, I see your point. You didn't expect any of this."

"No, I didn't, but… I'm dealing with it."

Right. Glancing at him sideways, I ask the one-million-dollar question. "But are you? When you said your day had lasted forever, you were right. To put it into a different light, the last time you went to bed you did so about a hundred and forty years ago, before you spent decades in the Essken Realm, got abducted from my time, then accused of killing billions, and to top it off, abducted again by your great-grand child. One hit kept making room for the next and then the next. Heck, you are still in your captain's uniform from the *Pioneer*." I push my fist against his chin, like a slow-motion punch, for emphasis. "So, excuse me for wondering if you're really dealing with everything."

Several long moments pass before his shoulders slump forward. "I don't know, Nonie. I mean, I do know I haven't even begun to process any of it. My only hope is that I can compartmentalize and get through everything. To be honest, so far, I don't like this time. What has become of us—of humanity? The domed prison we were in, the few things we've learned about this time… Not a fan. My biggest hope is that we're going to make it back home. To your time, I mean. I know I can't return to mine or I'd change yours, but I want to at least be somewhat close to the period I lived in. To Chase, Zio… you know. To somebody I haven't *outlived*." He puts the last word in air-quotes. "And while I'm truly concerned about the judge's accusations, I'd like to not get my brain fried by the FBTI but return home in full possession of my mental decision-making capacities, if that was ever in doubt." Tension eases out of his muscles. "Happy with that?"

"Considering what we've got to work with, yes. By the way, I can guarantee you we'll make it home. Can't predict our mental state, but we're going to get home, that's for sure." I take his hand and place a kiss onto the knuckles.

"Oh, really?" He lifts his head, looking at me with skepticism. "You sound so sure about it."

I blow on my cuticles and rub them over my shirt. Can't say I hadn't learned from my mistakes, or rather, from my lack of deduction. "I give you one word: Kaytee."

Kieran narrows his eyes a split second before they widen. "Oh. Oh! Okay. Got it. We will make it back somehow, through the FBTI or ourselves, and altered minds or not, or else no Kaytee. No us one hundred years ago, no babies to eventually spawn little Kaytee Dub." He accentuates his conclusion with little waves of his index finger, and I roll my eyes.

"You really have a way with words, you know that, right?"

"I've been told that a few times here and there, yes." A hint of humor colors his voice as a small smile tugs on the corners of his lips. "But anyway, since we do seem to get back somehow, we should talk about our next steps. I don't like not having a plan in place."

"Well," I draw the word out, "I have an idea." A slightly crazy and not completely thought-through idea, but at least an idea. Sitting up straighter, I twist to face Kieran. "Look, there must be a way to jump. Somehow, somewhere, there must be a Setayashi trigger for me to use, even if this century restricts the material for them. So, I say we find one. Once we do, we jump. But, we can't go home. They'd come after us, and we couldn't say we didn't see them coming. No, we're only safe if we can convince the FBTI we're not the threat here, but whoever is causing the Temporal War is."

"Assuming us being here and potentially ending up mind-controlled is part of the Temporal War."

"Consider it my working theory. Like we said, you were a victim of attempted temporal assassination, for a lack of a better word, and so was

I. Now we're here. I refuse to see that as a coincidence."

Nodding twice, Kieran chews on his lower lip. "Agreed. So, your plan is to exonerate us."

"Exonerate us *and* find out who is behind the Temporal War, which will help us find out if the accusations against us are based in truth or just part of the game. We have to stop it, or else they'll just keep coming, and we'll never be safe." We are neither going to spend our whole life on the run, nor are we going to endanger the people helping us along the way. Not our style.

Kieran nods. "Following. So, where do we go, if not home?"

A smile spreads across my face. "I was lying. We *are* going home—somewhat, but not the way you think. We're going to the *Pioneer*."

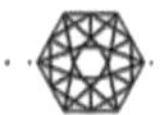

### Mess Hall, USS Achievement, 2399, four a.m.

Kaytee wrinkles her nose. "And you truly think that disc will contain enough evidence of this Temporal War? Because, none of us have ever heard about it. There's nothing in the history books I ever read."

Shaking my head, I pull my black shirt straight and scoot forward at the table. We didn't have much sleep, but wearing fresh clothing makes me feel like a whole new person. "In which history books, considering time travel isn't really common knowledge for people outside the FBTI, even in your time, I assume? Doesn't mean the Temporal War doesn't exist. And yes, the disk contains data that should help us pinpoint the source, be that a time period or even a person." That's why I'm so hopeful. The judge seems to be somebody who listens to data, facts, and evidence. If we bring evidence, how can she ignore it?

Frowning, Kaytee sighs. "Okay. But is it even still there? On the *Pioneer*? It's been… what, like, a hundred and fifty years?"

Well, when she puts it like that, it sounds much less likely, but I refuse to let that diffuse my optimism. "Why shouldn't it? It's hidden in a secret compartment, and if the *Pioneer* has been removed from active duty and converted into a museum, the likelihood for people to discover it is quite low." Apparently, the *Pioneer* was decommissioned about eighty years ago, I deduced from comments here and there. While they're not giving us details, we do get the gist of things without them being spoken out loud. Implications can be information, too. My First Sense hasn't acted up, and neither has Kaytee's or Jaasu's, apparently.

I'll take it.

Kaytee frowns. "Yes, she's a museum. Fixed orbit around the moon together with five other ships. It's a fun trip for kids or history-obsessed people."

To be honest, I find the idea of the *Pioneer* as a museum quite amusing, because it supposedly was that in my time already, only in reality, she served the FBTI and Taro Magona. Now, apparently, she has caught up to her former alibi.

"Okay." I give her thumbs up. "That should make it easier—"

"Easier, but nonetheless risky," Kaytee says. "Every second spent topside on the *Achievement* increases the likelihood they'll find us. And we have to do it twice, dematting out from here and then in again. Then the same on the *Pioneer*—who says they won't be looking off-world as well? Unlikely, but possible."

"But it's a risk worth taking," Kieran says. He looks kind of badass in his black tactical outfit, courtesy of the Unexpected Overachievers. "We need to convince the FBTI to stop hunting us down, and we need them to see that somebody is trying to manipulate time and that they might be a target, just as we are."

"Kind of like, the enemy of my enemy is my friend?" Zael adds air quotes to her question, and Kieran smiles.

"Seems to be our motto here, but yes, more like, a common enemy unites. One should hope the FBTI's common sense prevails when presented with evidence of temporal interference."

Kaytee blows out a puff of air through pursed lips. "Man, I can't believe that's happening. The timeline could have changed already to where we are now. What a crazy thought things could have gone differently!"

But is it? Is it really such a crazy thought? Her words trigger a memory: Other-me. Old-Kieran. The way they looked at each other. So close, yet so far apart. Other-Nonie thought she was in the main timeline, but I'm still here, so clearly I am. But… would I know if I wasn't in the main strand? We think off-branches stop existing after a while, like they faded out. But everything in that universe where I met another version of myself and saw Old-Kieran, everything felt real. Solid. Like it had been there forever and would be there forever. My First Sense liked it.

It's hard to believe that all might have already fizzed out or will soon stop to exist. Since Kieran was still alive in that reality, the divergence of our two timelines could have happened forty years earlier, when my Kieran went into the nebula, and Old-Kieran didn't. Meaning, that strand existed for forty long years without fizzing out. Is that normal? Is that long? Probably not, in the grand scheme of time, but it seems like a lot to me.

I rub a palm across my eyes. And it doesn't matter now. "So, either way, since you were talking about risks, once we're on the *Pioneer*, we access Kieran's quarters. Now, you tell me how easy or not easy that's going to be. It's your time, not mine." Plus, it's not as if I could get us tickets or whatever we need to get there.

"Isa, that's you," Kaytee says.

The other woman grabs a mug with coffee from the tray Rocky brought over to our tables in the front part of the mess hall and sits down across from Kieran and me, next to Kaytee. Only a few of the others are around: Kairo, Koll, Zael, and Rocky. The rest are still asleep. Granted, none of the people present look what I would call fresh besides Koll, but here they are. Not a bad showing for a 4:00 a.m. meeting, but also not bad what we came up with after our brainstorming-session and on only a few hours of sleep. Not that Kieran looked well-rested, but at least he slept—and without the nightmares that plagued him before he entered the Realm, courtesy of the Essken trying to communicate with him. I know, because he didn't thrash around in the middle of the night, didn't scream, didn't panic. While our situation isn't exactly ideal at the moment, being trapped in the future and hunted by an opponent with a huge advantage over us, seeing Kieran find some peace in sleep is a blessing I intend to count.

"The *Pioneer* isn't part of my department, just FYI, but I know enough about her to be of help. I think." Isa takes a slurping sip of coffee, then curses once and smacks her lips. "Geez, that's hot. Anyway, you might be lucky in one regard. None of the ships' interiors have been touched. All we do to museum ships is lock doors in the open position and protect the rooms behind them with a forcefield. That way visitors can see what the living situations were during those times, but they can't touch anything. Touching is bad."

Kieran and I exchange a glance before I nod at her. "That sounds good. I know my time kept everything the way it was in Kieran's quarters, so it stands to hope the generations after us preserved them as well." Maybe Taro Magona's First Sense gave her a hint which role Kieran's quarters would play, or maybe she was just respectful of Kieran and his memory in general, but when I had come back to the *Pioneer* after being thrown into the past the very first time, it had felt like I never left. Like Kieran never left. Nothing was changed and everything preserved the way he left it.

Scratching his neck, Kieran sighs. "Hearing that makes me slightly uncomfortable. I hope somebody picked up whatever clothing I threw on the floor. No need for generations to see when I was messy, but to be fair, I didn't know I wasn't going to return to my quarters."

Something in his last sentence brings goosebumps to a rise. No, you never know when it'll be the last time. In our line of work, the last time can be much more unpredictable and come much sooner than for others. It's obviously a fact of life I and everybody else who enlisted with USEF have accepted. Especially during my time, when the Quaneez-War was going on and so, so many died at their hands, but… But it's so abstract. Yes, it's dangerous. Yes, you could die. But I don't think I had drawn the correct conclusions from those threats.

I never left my quarters like I'd never see them again.

Never said goodbye to Dad thinking it might be the last time, besides once, before my secret mission which got me stranded in the past.

I didn't—and neither did Kieran.

Not that untidy quarters are the worst if you die, but other loose ends might be. Family. Friends. Words that should have been spoken, but never were.

I swallow hard, then force those thoughts away and a smile on my face. "Well, I can attest that when I was in your quarters in my time, they looked passable."

"You were in my quarters? Then?" Surprise colors his tone as he tilts his head at me.

I nod. "Yes. Right after the Battle of Balthar. The disruption of the Bond… I didn't feel good, but I also felt I needed to go to your quarters, and…" I shrug in an apologetic manner, then meet his gaze. "I found the letter." The letter speaking of his nightmares, his trauma, his fears, but also of his love for me.

Kieran's cheeks take on a reddish hue. "You… did." The apple in his throat moves up and down. "I… I wasn't in a good place when I wrote it."

"I know." And I'm not sure he's in a much better place right now. He's just hiding it well. I cover his hand on the table with mine. "Come to think of it, maybe it was my First Sense guiding me there. What you wrote, it eventually helped me add one and one and start looking for you in that nebula." Maybe that imperative need to check his quarters was born from the timeline trying to make sure I got Kieran out of the Realm again.

Kieran wraps his fingers around mine as I squeeze his hand. "Then I'm glad I wrote it."

Isa clears her throat. "Well, anyway, going back to the *Pioneer*, pun intended, literally going back isn't the problem. Here are the easy parts: The museum doesn't operate on Terran Standard Time, but is open twenty-four hours a day, seven days a week. Tickets never sell out, so we can purchase some under a fake account, no problem." She pauses. "And that was the easy part."

I grimace. "Oh. Okay. What is so difficult about the rest? Once we're there, isn't there a way to turn off the forcefield blocking entrance to Kieran's quarters? There must be an override or something." There's always an override.

Looking like she bit into something sour, Isa clicks her tongue. "You're about two problems ahead already. The issue is we can demat in and out, but only to the demat room. There are demat blockers in place for the rest of the ship for security reasons as well as to make the visit there historically accurate. You dematted from a demat area to another demat area. Your guys' time was still not good at dematting to other locations in a moving spaceship."

True. Even though she roped Kieran's and my time together, she's right. We can demat to a planet or non-moving surface, even while we're moving, as long we're in a stable distance to it, but from a moving ship to a moving target not on a locked-in course, anything where we can't keep a fixed distance… not so much.

Kieran drums his fingers on the table. "That doesn't sound like a huge downfall. I do remember the way from the demat room to my quarters." He draws his index finger in a line over the metal surface. "Once we're there, we break in, get what we need, and then get out. That's where I can see problems happening, agreed. If we set off an alarm, we might have to speed it up to get off the ship."

"There you go, that's *part one* of the problem." Isa wraps both hands around her mug and scoots forward to the edge of her seat. "You missed the part where it gets more annoying once we arrive."

"Security?" Kieran purses his lips and stops his drumming.

"Kind of. Overall security is lax. It's a museum ship, weapons inactive, drive only sufficient to keep a stable orbit. It's an old ship—no offense. But once we demat on, the ship's AIvatar will know we're there. And that's going to be a problem." She exchanges a worried glance with Kaytee.

"AIvatar?" I ask.

"The Artificial Intelligence Avatar. Cheaper to have interactive holograms give the guided tours than staffing those museums with live people around the clock. They get triggered by demats or life signs. Very annoying for us, because they'll stick to us like glue."

Ugh. "Witnesses." That's quite inconvenient, I must say. "Can they keep us from doing what we want to?"

"Heck, yeah they can," Kaytee chimes in. "They're fully corporeal. They can wrestle you down in no time, while you can't do a thing to them. Ever tried to choke out a hologram?"

While I can't say I have, I'm hung up on the first part of that explanation. Corporeal. Like… the hologram that I saw young Mashaule interacting with on board the *Eclipse*. That one even had a freakin' shadow. I suck in my lower lip. If the bad guy from the future had the technology to appear corporeal, he must have been from this time or later. Keeping my face as neutral as possible, I turn to Kaytee. "Is that new? Corporeal holograms?"

"It's pretty— Heck no, Nonie!" Kaytee grins and wiggles her pointer finger. "No fishing for information. You're learning more than I was planning to give you already."

"Can't blame a girl for trying," I mutter and shrug. What did she want to say? It's pretty new? It's pretty old? It can't be that old, we only jumped a hundred years into the future. Got to admit I'd be surprised if whoever was waging that Temporal War was from a time between mine and the one we're in now, but that's more a feeling than anything else. Could they be here? Sure. Further up in the future from here? Also a possibility.

I file that information for later and focus on Isa. Priorities. "So, what can we do about the Alvatars? I imagine they won't be happy if we try to force our way into an area where we're not supposed to be."

"No, they absolutely won't. They'll restrain you until police arrives, and no matter how skilled a fighter you are, they'll outsmart you. You can't win against an opponent who can't tire or get hurt."

"Ugh." I grunt. That doesn't sound thrilling, or like a walk in the park, not that I expected the latter. I wish there was an easier way to get in—

An idea pops up. There might be! "What about Koll?" I lean forward to look at the Essken. "Why not avoid the AIvatars and take the direct route? I assume the FBTI-cell had demat blockers, and you got us out despite them. Can't you get us into Kieran's quarters like that?" *Snip*, and we're there?

Koll nods. "I could. That being said, I need to step through the Realm to do so, which I would like to avoid for obvious reasons." He gestures at Kieran, who lowers his chin in a nod.

"Appreciate that." A muscle in his jaw tics.

"Also, if I dropped you off in Kieran's quarters, or anywhere, the sensors would obviously react to your presence. You'd have less than a tenth of a second until intruder alert and the appearance of about twenty very unhappy AIvatars. So, Isa is right, we have to demat in the old-fashioned way."

"And hope that Rocky can come up with something." Isa points her thumb at the Caucasian blond guy.

"I was just about to say to leave that part to me," Rocky says, looking awake for the first time since our impromptu early morning meeting started. Until now, he'd been sitting next to Kaytee with his eyes half closed most of the time. Now he looks like we plugged his mental battery pack into an outlet of sorts, hyperalert with an excited gleam in his eyes. "While I can't keep the emergency intruder program from executing, I have other weapons at my disposal." He cracks his knuckles then lifts up one palm. "Kieran's quarters are secured with a forcefield, and no, unfortunately you can't shut it down with your palm print and walk right in. The security features added to *Pioneer* override regular access, which I think is hilarious. I like that they're thorough, but time travelers aside, nobody from the old crew is still alive, so why bother?"

I grimace. Yikes. When he says it like that…

"Anyway. We can force our way into the quarters once we get you there, and we will. To make it short and sweet, I should be able to hack the *Pioneer's* systems, access the added security features, and block the AIvatars from sending information off-ship without triggering the *Pioneer's* original security alerts, because guess what, those they left in place." He rolls his eyes then holds up all ten fingers. "And that all translates to: I can give you about ten minutes before somebody will realize something is off with the *Pioneer*'s AIvatars and security arrives."

Kieran and I exchange a glance before he nods. "Ten minutes should be sufficient for the trip from the demat room to my quarters and back, but time won't help us fight off these invincible AIvatars."

"No, time won't help you." Rocky cracks his knuckles. "But I will."

# Chapter Five – 

# Museum

"Okay. We're still sure this is a good idea?" Kaytee holds her hand hovering above the touchpad to open the door to the flight deck. Scanning over our assembled crew, she draws in a deep breath. "Because as soon as I open the door, we are *on*, people. Time's working against us, no pun intended. So, one last time, are we sure that disk is worth it?"

I give a curt nod. "Yes. One hundred and ten percent. It has proof of the Temporal War, and maybe even enough data that can help your FBTI analyze the origin of the interference. It can clear us and help to hopefully end this mess." Because at some point, I'd really like to be done with war, for good. Quaneez-slash-Essken, temporal, doesn't matter.

"That's what I figured you'd say. Allrighty then, everybody's in place, we talked it through like twenty times. Now is as good a time as any. Kieran, Nonie, you ready?"

Both of us nod. "Always," says Kieran, as he cranks his neck.

Kaytee chuckles. "That's what history tells us. Didn't expect anything else. Remember, don't engage with the AIvatars any more than necessary to keep them happy. Whenever they go back online, Rocky should have scrambled the video so they won't know scrap when they run your image against a database, but I'd rather be safe than sorry. Plus, I'm also one hundred and ten percent sure the FBTI will have bots searching for you. Duh, right?"

Right. Probably not only bots, and that's the part that makes me nervous. It's one thing trying to pull off a difficult plan, but a completely other if you're partially operating in the dark, like Kieran and I. We know the *Pioneer*, but we don't know squat about these AIvatars or what else might've changed up there. We don't know the details of this time at all. It feels way too much like going in unprepared, but complaining isn't going to help. We're not going to get a crash course in last century's history, and I understand that.

I just don't like it.

Zael taps Kaytee's shoulder. "You sure you want to go? If the FBTI makes the connection between them and you—"

"The FBTI has made the connection already, I'm sure of that. And still, they haven't found us yet, have they?"

"No, but…" She brushes her hair back and taps the bone behind her ear.

Harrumphing, Kaytee rolls her eyes. "I'm as secure as Kieran and Nonie are. I can't expect them to risk being caught and not be able to expose myself to the same risk. Don't sweat it, Zael. I'm going. Somebody who knows this time needs to be present."

Since we came up with this plan, they have been going back and forth on that. Actually, the others have. Kaytee said from the very beginning she's going to come with us. Everybody else tried to convince her to guide us via comm, but she wouldn't have it. *My idea to break them out of the FBTI, my responsibility,* she kept saying. I respect that. A lot. I wonder if at some point in my future that respect will change into something more akin to pride, along the lines of *look at my descendant, how awesome she is. Got that from me, probably.*

Yikes. I cringe internally. So, so weird.

That being said though, we *all* have that in common, her, Kieran, and me. Neither of us is going to step back and let others take a risk that's ours to take. Non-negotiable. If anything goes wrong, we at least know the *Pioneer*. Yes, there's new tech on it, but it's still our *Pioneer*. That should count for something, right?

Zael lifts her other hand in a defeated gesture. "Okay, okay. Just making sure. We should be fine. Rocky's been down in tech and glued to his interface for the last two hours; he's got the algorithm in place, demat's ready, and we'll keep a continuous comm-lock on you as much as we can."

"'Preciate it." Kaytee raises her voice the slightest bit: "Rocky?"

"Ready when you are," his voice comes through my earpiece, loud and clear. "Once you open that hatch, the countdown's on. Ten minutes, that's all I can guarantee."

"Got it." She checks in once more with Kieran and me. "Ready?"

"So ready," I reply, my heart speeding up.

"Okay then. Three, two, one—now!" She rams her palm against the emergency opening sensor and the hatch bursts open to the outside. Bright, sunny daylight floods the dark hallway, stinging in my eyes, but no time to dwell on that, because yup, we are *on*.

Kaytee sprints ahead, closely followed by Kieran and myself. Pumping our arms and legs, we give it all we have, meaning Kieran is leading our pack within two seconds. Not one to be beaten that easily, I speed up as well, passing Kaytee with a few longer strides. Pays to be tall and *half*-Magellan, great-granddaughter!

The ship sways slightly under our feet, but it's nothing in comparison to the storm rocking it back and forth during our arrival yesterday. This is nice. Sunny, warm, smelling of the ocean and freedom. If I could, I'd enjoy it.

Kieran skids to a stop at the far end of the flight deck. I was right when we arrived last night. The thick white and yellow lines crossing the surface are all markings for the planes, I presume. Stopping right next to Kieran, I don't even breathe heavy. Too short a sprint for that.

Kaytee all but crashes into us. "*Now*, Rocky!"

Somewhere below deck Rocky must be pushing his buttons—

From one heartbeat to the next, the sea, the *Achievement*, and the wide-open skies are gone and replaced by cool, processed air and white walls around us.

Holy Sun and Stars! I press my palm against my temple. These demats are... quite something. Immediate. Disorienting. Blinking twice, I look around until the room stops swaying.

Kieran takes a small stumbling step backwards on the *Pioneer's* demat-platform before he catches himself. "Home," he whispers, and a small smile tugs on the corners of my lips. It's home, all right. If I didn't know we were a century in the future I wouldn't see it. The *Pioneer's* demat room looks like, well, yesterday to me. Its bright white walls haven't lost their shine, haven't dulled a bit. Everything looks just as spiffy as when I last set foot on board.

I glance over my shoulder at Kieran. He has this nostalgic expression on his face, this look of longing as if only now he understood this wasn't anymore what he called it: home.

Before I can say anything, a small flash of light distracts me—and out of nowhere a person appears in front of us, about my height, maybe late twenties, male, with dark olive skin and warm brown eyes. His hair is swept back in an elaborate, wavy style, looking a tad ridiculous with the blue uniform both Kieran and I only know too well. The guy smiles the most welcoming open smile I've ever seen, seriously.

"Welcome to the *USEF Pioneer*. I'm so happy you came to visit. Would one tour guide be sufficient for you, or would you prefer to split up and each have your personal guide? Judging by your matching outfits, I assume you're visiting as one party?" The Alvatar gestures up and down our black-clad bodies, courtesy of Kaytee's all-encompassing planning.

"*Working on shutting that annoying fella down,*" Rocky says through the com. "*I'll let you know as soon as the road is cleared.*"

Stepping off the demat platform, Kaytee takes charge. "One guide is perfect, thank you. We won't be long." She jerks her head for us to follow, then walks right past the AIvatar toward the door.

"Fantastic," he replies. "My name is Art, and I'll be happy to help you with everything about this ship. Did you know, the last mission the *Pioneer* flew was—"

Kaytee passes the doors into the *Pioneer*'s hallways and stops dead in her tracks. "Huh. Which way to the captain's quarters?"

"To the left," Kieran, me, and Art respond at the same time.

Kaytee grunts and speed walks ahead, followed by us and Art.

"Excuse me, gentlepeople, I didn't catch your names. I'm having difficulties connecting at the moment, but it shouldn't interfere with my guidance skills."

Rocky snickers in my ear, and well, I for one hope Art's difficulties will interfere with a lot of things. He's a marvelous piece of engineering though. Like Kaytee said, he looks real. Corporeal. His steps make sounds on the floors. But that also means I really don't want to fight him or more of his friends, who, I'm sure, can pop out of nowhere at any time if needed be.

"I'm Mina," Kaytee says in response, "my friends are Wesley and Sunday."

"So very nice to meet you three," Art says. "Oh, you're walking right past the conference room. Did you know that during the years of—"

"Thank you, Art, but we really want to focus on the captain's quarters first." Kaytee says it with an apology in her tone. I wonder how much the AIvatars can pick up on deviations from the norm. When will they get suspicious? What's the baseline they're running their observations against? And if they're disconnected, how much can they really act on their own? A bead of sweat runs down my neck. Maybe if I knew more about them, I wouldn't be so nervous. Of course, Kaytee does, which is why she is cool as a cucumber as she smiles at Art.

The AIvatar returns her smile, and boy, does it look real. "No problem at all, Mina. Many guests want to start with the captain's quarters or the bridge. They are the highlights, after all. Did you know the captain's quarters remained untouched since the *Pioneer*'s first captain, Captain Kieran Wildason, left them? Even though the *Pioneer* had been in duty for many more years, that was never changed."

"That's, uhh, interesting," Kieran says, the tightness in his voice a hinting at his discomfort with exactly that.

I could swear Art adds a spring to his step. "It is, isn't it? Even back then, people recognized the importance to preserve history, and now we have the pleasure to present it to you." He bows while walking. Somehow, he makes it look graceful.

One more turn, and we're right there. After all, the important areas were all close together: Bridge, captain's quarters, conference room, demat room. Mess hall? You can change decks for that.

Kaytee stops in front of the open doors to Kieran's quarters. "Captain's quarters," she says, more for updating Rocky than for our benefit.

*"Almost there,"* Rocky mumbles. *"Almost. And we're good in time."*

"I love that," I say, meaning that we're this close to taking out Art through Rocky's programming back door, but of course to Art it sounded like a comment about the tour.

"Most people do," he chirps. My, he is a happy camper. Obnoxiously so.

Kieran's gaze scans over the open door and the room behind it. "Feels exposing having m— the room so open." The forcefield slightly distorts the view toward the frame, but overall, it's like looking through an open door, as if one could walk right through.

I touch one finger to the field. It buzzes and sparks but doesn't hurt. Feels though as if I was pushing into a spongy mass, like thick, bouncy Jello. Pretty weird.

"Please do not touch the forcefield," Art says. "It responds with reciprocal counter-pressure. I wouldn't want you to hurt yourself, Sunday."

"Thank you, Art." I withdraw my finger and wipe it on my pants. So polite.

"You're welcome. And to let you know, during active duty, the quarters would of course have been locked and only accessible via palm print. In later ships—"

*"Get ready,"* Rocky says, and Kaytee throws a warning glance at Kieran, then me.

"—updates were installed to recognize bio signnnnn—" Art freezes, and I mean, he *freezes.* As if we had paused a video stream, he stays in the same position, eyes narrowed, unblinking, staring ahead unseeing. His mouth is half open and his lips half pursed, from the last word he spoke. He looks like he had a stroke in mid-sentence. It's a tad freaky.

*"And boom, call me the king of hacking, thank you very much!"* The sound of Rocky smacking or hitting something, comes over the comm. Did he give Koll a metallic high-five?

"Let's move," Kieran claps his hands twice, then fishes for one of the small, rectangular devices in his black cargo pants' pocket Rocky gave to each of us. Kaytee and I dig in our pockets as well, retrieving the grey little plastic pieces. Curiosity spikes. Supposedly these things can break through the forcefield, and I say supposedly, because alone they're *nothing,* as Rocky said, but together they act… as what? Explosives?

"Put them on the floor, faster, faster!" Kaytee throws hers close to the force field, and so do we. To be honest, it looks a bit like kids playing breaking and entering with imaginary—

Oh.

Never mind. The three pieces, each looking like nothing more than a boring grey plastic cuboid about PADdy's size, shimmer and flicker, then open up. As though they pulled material from an unknown dimension, thin sheets of metal, circuits and… *stuff* unfold and build up into a knee-high pyramid of sorts. One side of it, the one toward the force field, starts glowing red.

O-kay. Now I see what Rocky meant.

"Step back, guys!" Spreading out her arms, Kaytee moves us back. "There might be shrapnel—"

*"Shit,"* Rocky curses.

"—gnatures and make entrance into limited-access quarters more—" Art finishes half his sentence with a little swiping gesture of his forearm, then freezes again.

Only problem is, he isn't freezing like last time. This time he's processing.

"Shit," Kaytee echoes Rocky. We were supposed to have minutes! Minutes!

"*Crap, crap, crap!*" Frantic typing comes through the earpiece. "*They've logged me out! No idea how they found me so fast or—*"

The pyramid glows redder—and Art jerks up straight, like snapping to attention. His voice stays level, like he continued to narrate interesting facts about the *Pioneer,* and it makes what he says especially creepy. "Security breech. Blackout of twenty point one-two seconds noted."

For one teeny-tiny moment, nothing happens. We look at Art, Art looks at the pyramid, and the pyramid begins to emit a high-pitched whine.

As if that was the trigger, Art darts forward and at the pyramid. "You are attempting to obtain unauthorized access to these quarters. I cannot permit the destruction that will come from using such a dev—"

Kieran tackles him. Like, legit tackles him, forcing him back and into the opposite wall. "Keep that thing working," he calls over his shoulder. "I'll take care—Ugh!"

As if Kieran weighed nothing, Art throws him off to the side.

"Hey!" I jump at Art, trying to drive him back and away from that pyramid thing, our key to Kieran's quarters and only hope to get that disk. The impact against his surprisingly hard chest drives the air out of my lung—

And the next moment I find myself hitting the floor in an epic face plant, coming eye to eye with the skid mark I gave the wall on the day I let Kieran enter the nebula. What the—

"Stay away, or I'll make you," Kaytee screams. "And *King of Hacking*, do freakin' something!"

Well, at least she keeps her cool enough to not use his real name. Not sure it matters at this point, but we're not exposing anybody else if we can help it.

Rocky curses under his breath, typing furiously. I snap into a ground fighting position—and there's Art, facing off with Kaytee. She has her hands up, her eyes are spitting fire—

And *pop, pop, pop,* out of literally nowhere, more AIvatars pop up, all looking like Art. Somebody took the easy way out in programming, it appears. Lazy for sure, pure copy-paste. They couldn't even be bothered to randomize the face.

"Initiating combative lockdown protocol," one of them says, and I don't like any of that. Getting up from the ground, I throw myself at the AIvatar closest to me, and so does Kieran.

"Mina," he yells, "keep him from—ngh!" A pained grunt breaks from his throat as his AIvatar picks him up and throws him into a wall.

Repeat: *picks him up and throws him into a wall.* As if Kieran freakin' weighed nothing.

"Crap." I wheeze—and change my attack. In the very last moment before colliding with the AIvatar in front of me, I duck under his arm and get to his back. He didn't expect that, which is good, but doesn't react at all to my kick right up his A-frame between his legs, which is bad.

Kaytee cries out in frustration. "No, don't touch that, don't— Shit!"

A crunching, metallic sound makes it unnecessary to look to know what happened. That, plus the sudden stop of the high-pitched whine, and it's clear we're in deep doo-doo, for more than one reason.

Kaytee hits the ground hard somewhere to the left, skidding across the sparkling floors for a meter or two before coming to a stop. Art is on her right away, ignoring the smoking heap of bent metal in front of Kieran's quarters.

Disappointment and anger hit hard. Our only chance to enter the quarters, to get the disk. It's gone, and there's nothing we can do, that I can do.

*"I can't break through their walls, people! You gotta get back to the demat room!"*

Yeah. Our luck ran out half-way, and going back to the demat room sounds about as successful as walking in space without a suit.

My AIvatar spins around toward me, face contorted into an

aggressive mask. He throws his arms forward to grab me—

A familiar wave of dizziness crashes over me for one long second while something tugs on me, adding weight and pressure to my shoulders, my chest, like on the *Achievement*, like in the FBTI bubble-cell. My heart skips a beat, because Holy Universe, it feels the same, yet it isn't.

Not by a long shot.

Yes, like on the *Achievement*, I'm seeing double-quadruple again, but not like before, at least I don't think so, I might've not paid enough attention last time, in retrospect. Everybody here has a ghostly shadow, or two, or three, behind them or around them, but none of them are exact copies. Subtle differences set the shadows apart from the originals. Hair. Clothing. The position they're in.

And not only that, other ghostly outlines, like translucent people, are everywhere, walking right through us in either direction, some run, and while that's creepy and freaky, it's got nothing on the real kicker: Time around us has slowed down to a crawl, like somebody had turned a dial to slow motion. Kaytee, trying to pick herself up, one centimeter at a time, Art, reaching for her, fingers bent to claws, face contorted into a silent snarl.

Everything is slowed down, but so clear, it makes those ghosts walking through us seem even blurrier.

"What the—?"

Hearing Kieran's whispered words, I turn toward him, the nausea churning faster from the movement. Kieran lowers his arm, initially raised to block the AIvatar's punch, which is now coming down in super slow-motion. Dropping his defense, he steps back and looks around, meeting my gaze. "What's happening? Are you oka—"

He sucks in a sharp breath as he twitches like somebody shot him in the gut, wrapping both hands around his midsection and doubling over. His eyes widen in understanding and frustration as he grunts, and my body reacts. A need flares up inside my core, greater than the need to breathe. Instinct wants me closer to Kieran, to—

"Don't. Think. About. It. Get. The. Disk." He pushes the words out through clenched teeth as he bends over, supporting himself with one hand on the wall. A lock of hair falls into Kieran's face, covering a small bruise courtesy of the AIvatar.

Resisting that pull goes against everything my body wants. It's humming in anticipation, like an addict's anticipating a fix, and if that isn't scary, I don't know what is.

As if on autopilot I take a step toward Kieran, stretch out my hand—

Kieran twists away from me. "Get. The. Disk," he grunts.

I jerk my hand back with a little yelp, heart hammering from the effort, but hey, his words brought at least some of my higher brain functions back online. Against the pull of want and need, against this deep-rooted hunger, I clasp my hands together in front of my chest, then force myself to look away.

The disk. Yes. The disk is still behind the forcefield we can't overcome. My gaze darts to the broken pyramid. I need to come up with a plan, with *something*. Think, Nonie, think! Fate has granted us a reprieve, I can't waste it, Kieran is right. I can see the desk from here, if only entering the quarters was as easy as when—

An idea strikes.

Panting from the effort of not running straight to Kieran and touching him, of not giving in to the siren calls of an instinct I don't understand, I duck under the AIvatar's snail-paced attack, move out to the side, then spin around. With two lightning-fast steps, I'm at the door, right next to Kieran.

Being so close to him is like denying my body the right to breathe. I want to touch him, *need* to touch—

But I won't.

Priorities, because *this*, this could work.

His breath comes out in irregular puffs, his face contorted into a grimace of pain. I want to take whoever or whatever is responsible for causing him to hurt like this and do something really not nice as payback. Alas, that's not on the menu for today.

Getting the disk, is.

Neither my nor Kieran's AIvatar have even yet registered I moved, and that alone should freak me out majorly but alas, like I said, priorities.

Panting, I throw a half-panicked glance at Kieran. "Kieran! Initiate Code Magenta!"

For the longest moment he just looks at me as if my words wouldn't penetrate the pain, but then his eyes pop wide with understanding. "*Pioneer*, initiate Code Magenta!"

And Pioneer responds, stretching the words out, as if her processing was slowed. *"Coooode Maaaageeeentaaaaa. Coooode Maaaageeeentaaaaa. Aaaall non-eeesseeentiiiaal peeersooonneeeel pleeeease reeeetuuuurn—"*

Part one of my idea: Working. In regards to part two… Here goes nothing. I ram my palm against the reader so hard, I fear I cracked it.

*"Nooooniiiiie Maaaaagneeettaaa, aaaaaccccessss graaaantedddd."*

And *poof*, the forcefield snuffs out with a little pop.

I pump one fist up and down. "Yes!" A grin spreads over my face. What did Rocky say? The security features added to *Pioneer* override her regular access, but then, under Code Magenta different rules apply. After all, it was made to make life easier for *me* and always designed to supersede *Pioneer*'s original programming.

And to think I was annoyed when my palm print was saved as I arrived in Kieran's time. Now it's saving our butt!

I— Holy Universe!

I suck in a gasp as the yearning pulling me toward Kieran cranks it up to the nth degree, like he was a magnet and me the purest metal. A distorted low, guttural sound with a choked croak at the end breaks from his throat, and the pull on my body becomes unbearable, an eleven on a scale to ten.

I twist around, only to see what I suspected already: Kieran looks way worse. He shifts his weight, like he was trying to evade invisible attacks, sweat dotting his forehead, eyes closed and face scrunched into a mask of pain.

Instinct takes over without me having a say in it, as if my decision to stay away from Kieran didn't count. Adrenaline spikes, at least bringing a nice serving of euphoria with it when I step closer and grab Kieran's other hand.

*Zzing!*

I gasp as both, sweet relief from giving in and fiery heat from turning into a conduit, shoot through my veins. No matter I expected that, the pain still makes me stumble. This time, I feel it much clearer than before. How it enters, how it rips me apart and puts me together again on its way through my arm and into my core, how it fills my center up, up, *up* until it turns warm and fuzzy, *wholesome*, spills to my other arm, and—

And chaos breaks loose.

Within the blink of an eye everything is back to normal. The pressure on my chest is gone, the sensation of nausea, of hunger, of need—and the yells and noises of several people fighting are back, as if I hit the unmute button.

Kieran grunts as the AIvatar finally executes his strike, but luckily only hammer-fisting Kieran onto his bowed back instead of over the head. He rips his hand free from mine, whirls around, and blocks the next punch. His motions are slower than normal, more sluggish, but still fast enough to counter and keep the AIvatar's back to me.

I don't waste the opportunity.

At the academy, they train us to respond to the situation, and even though I was always good at these kinds of drills, this one is next level. Time slowing down, then speeding up, while fighting AIvatars in the future? I guess I was out sick when this scenario was on the curriculum.

Ignoring the lingering slight discomfort tingling through my body, I burst through the doorway and into Kieran's quarters, gulping in air to combat the lingering dizziness. Every second counts, I cannot *not* be at my best.

"Nonie, run! I got you! Run!" Kieran's yell is undistorted and followed by first the sound of a body crashing into another body, then by chairs toppling over behind me.

I suck in another sharp breath and ignore them. One problem at a time. The disk can get us out of here; I need that first. My mad dash through the quarters brings me to the desk within two seconds. Gliding my thumb over the hidden spot, I find the indentation I knew was going to be there. "Come on, come on…!" The drawer pops open—

No.

No, no, no.

Panic rises. It can't be. It can't be empty.

Blood drains from my face as I feel around the drawer, tracing every corner, covering every square inch with my palm and fingers.

Nothing.

I close my mouth without a sound.

I was so sure.

So, so sure.

Bending down as I rattle the drawer, I look into it, but it doesn't change a thing. The drawer is empty.

And I don't know where to go from here. I have no backup idea, no way to fix this—

Kieran comes flying through the door, crashing onto the dining table and sliding over it. Art—or one of his buddies—hot on his heels.

"Do not damage the furniture of this protected place," the AIvatar growls.

Kieran groans as he picks himself up and slides off the table, careful to keep it between himself and the AIvatar. "You threw me in here, mate. Wasn't me."

Art ignores the comment. "This area is off limits to the public. You have broken several laws, including attacking a government-sanctioned AIvatar. I urge you to—"

"*Oh, hell. Guys, I'm sorry, they're—*" A loud, surprised yelp drowns out Rocky's voice.

"Guys! Watch out!" The end of Kaytee's last word is swallowed by gurgling sound and a large *thump* about a second before three people barge into Kieran's quarters—three *people*, not three AIvatars, all in FBTI-uniforms, with rifles up and aimed into the room, aimed at *us.*

"Hands up! Hands up! Get them high where I can see them," yells one of them as a fourth person walks in, unarmed, a smug smile on his annoying face.

Double-crap.

A sensation of doom, of things going wrong, of having gone wrong, rises in my chest, not unlike what I felt when choking Sheridan in FBTI jail. Look at me, becoming clairvoyant at my old age. I wish I'd been wrong.

Sheridan snaps his fingers. "Stand down, Alvatar." Art relaxes, and the executioner shakes his head, smacking his lips. "Tah-tah. Figured you'd make a mistake eventually. Only a matter of time. Literally."

"So much for demat blockers," Kieran mumbles under his breath, moving back step by step, his hands in the air, until he stands next to me at the desk.

"There are no demat blockers holding against the FBTI's systems, but nice thought." Sheridan rocks back on his heels, then nods his chin in our direction. "That being said, the whole *Pioneer* is on lockdown. There's no way out for you. Team, take them in."

Kieran grabs me by the arm. "Now, Nonie," he hiss-whispers.

Now—?

Oh! Failure hits me like a punch to the gut. "I don't have it, it's not here." The stupid disk isn't where it's supposed to be!

"Wha—" The look on Kieran's face when he gets it, when he understands we're trapped here, we're about to end up in the same prison we started out in, is not one I ever want to see again. It makes me feel inadequate on a whole new level.

Two of the armed men prowl toward us, their knees bent, their steps careful, their aim never wavering. "Keep your hands where we can see them. Do *not* move," one of them orders us, not in the most friendly voice.

Kieran's gaze meets mine, the frustration I'm feeling clearly mirrored in them.

"I'm sorry," I whisper. So sorry. I should've had a backup plan, I should've—

"No talking!" The FBTI-agent closest to us snarls. "On your knees! Move!"

Is there anything else we can do but comply?

No.

Not with two rifles aimed at us and a third armed person standing farther back, as backup.

Not without a way out of here if we made it past them.

I lower myself to one knee, careful to keep my hands up, so disappointed in myself. So unbelievably disappoin—

Adrenaline rushes me, powered by a wild thought. Wait a second. What if—

Kieran steps in front of me, blocking me from the agents.

"Hey! Freeze!" The high-pitched whine of a weapon charging cuts through the air. "Hands up! *Up!*"

But Kieran doesn't comply. He balls his fists, takes one large step forward—

"Kieran!" I hiss, fear for him spiking up and jabbing at my core. "What the heck!" I grab his shirt and yank on him, to no avail. He twists, releasing my hold.

"Wildason, stand down!" Sheridan barks. "These guys are firing live ammo, you don't want to—"

"You have no idea what I want," Kieran growls, taking yet another step forward and raising his hands. What's he gonna do, punch their weapon's fire?

I curse under my breath when the armed men lift their line of fire to make Kieran their target.

Dammit, there's no time! No time to think, no time to explain. Only time to hope *he* gets me. "Beacon of hope! Bring us to your home! Now!" I yell.

Sheridan and the men look at me like I'm crazy, and even Kieran stops in his tracks for a split second, and it's that split second that saves us.

For one short, fleeting moment, the air wafts in front of us. An Essken appears out of thin air, right between us. He grabs Kieran from behind by his right arm, me by the left and before I can as much as blink, everything turns black.

# Chapter Six -

# Out

*Somewhere, Somewhen*

There's no transition.

One moment, we're in Kieran's quarters, the next we're in the Realm—not an ounce of doubt about it. Before my brain has even caught up with the change in location, my First Sense does a weird somersault as if it rejoiced being back. My body knows it, too, maybe because gravity isn't quite right, like the last time I visited, or maybe because the ground I'm kneeling on is, like last time, squishy and soft.

"Holy Universe." I wheeze. The Realm. Not the *Pioneer* anymore. Unlike last time, I'm not welcomed by near-perfect darkness, but the same landscape I saw before, only finally, nature has made up its mind. Somewhat, at least. The large tree in the distance isn't turning topsy-turvy anymore but properly rooted to the ground. Granted, its leaves are purple, but… it suits the tree. The river flowing close to it is sticking to one direction this time, but to make up for the lack of variation its water sparkles in iridescent colors, sometimes more reddish, then more blue or more golden.

Yeah. It's most definitely the Realm and not an FBTI prison cell. Relief washes over me. That could've been—

Kieran grunts and falls forward, barely stretching out a hand and catching himself on all fours.

"Kieran!" I whirl around to my left as fast as I can while on my knees and grab him by the biceps, stabilizing him. His whole body is stiff, so rigid I can't hold him in this position. Scrambling to my feet, I use both hands and my body to pull him up. Rarely have I been happier about my Magellan genes, because Kieran isn't helping. It's like pulling dead weight from the ground, but once I get him to stand up, at least he stands by himself, stiff like a log, swaying, eyes wide and unseeing.

Guilt slams into me. "I'm sorry, Kieran, I'm sorry, I'm sorry, I'm so, so sorry! It was the only way out." I cup his cheek with my palm, searching his face for any indication of how bad it is, how much the Realm is affecting him. "I'm sorry."

For the longest moment of my life, I'm afraid I lost him again, and that this time I'm responsible for his suffering. He looks like he did when I found him in the Realm, like in a coma, unresponsive. Fear cramps inside my stomach—but then, like he was coming out of a deep sleep, his breathing picks up and his eyes begin to focus.

A boulder the size of a class-two-meteorite falls off my shoulders. I keep brushing my thumbs over his cheeks so hard I'm probably bruising him. "Kieran! Hey, come on, come on, you can do it! Wake up!"

His gaze darts left, right, then straight at me—and sharpens. He blinks once, twice, then grimaces. "N-nonie." His breath comes out in short bursts through clenched teeth, while his body is tense from head to toe, coiled and stiff.

"His reaction to the Realm is improving."

The unexpected voice from behind me makes me jerk and hit myself in the forehead with my hand. "Holy Sun!"

"I apologize, I didn't mean to startle you." The Essken's voice is audible and not inside my head this time. It sounds familiar—not that I heard that many Essken before, but still. Plus, logic dictates it would be him.

"Koll? Is that you?"

He nods. "It is."

He must've been in stealth mode. I neither heard nor saw him, but also, I didn't smell him, probably because of that full-body deodorant. Either way, thanks are in order. "Koll, you are the very best. Thank you for getting what I was going for. You were our only hope."

"It's my pleasure to be of help. And I apologize for taking a moment to figure out what you meant, that you wanted *me*, your beacon of hope, to bring you to *my* home, our realm. A good move."

I blush. "Thank you for that, but it was a move born out of desperation. The only safe place I could think of was the Realm, no matter the risk." I stroke Kieran's cheek. "I'm sorry about that."

He reaches up to my hand. "T's all 'ight. I'm okay. And we got 'way fr'm Sh'ridan."

Hearing him speak in his normal voice, the words only slightly slurred, soothes my stressed-out soul. I brush my thumb over the back of his hand. That moment when I thought he was back to comatose because of me… Not one I want to relive ever again.

"You are indeed tolerating our realm much better than before," Koll says.

Kieran's lips kick up in a faint smile, and while he's swaying the slightest bit, he looks normal. Awake, alert—like himself. "Ev'rything feels a bit off, but it's no comparison to how it felt b'fore. Is this… is this what your home looks like?" He gestures at the topsy-turvy tree.

"It is not. Our home does not need air nor light. We have sensitive visual organs. Too much light hurts us, but we have adapted." He taps the front of his helmet. "What you see here is what we designed to facilitate communication with humans and to sustain your physiology. Your body isn't made to tolerate our realm, and neither is your mind. And while the last time your mind was trapped, for a lack of a better word, and you couldn't make sense of our home, you're now communicating like the only person we know who ever could." He turns his head and gives me the Essken-equivalent of a pointed glance.

"Guess we're special, Kieran." I nudge him with my shoulder. "But why? You thought it was my genome enabling me, and the Bond protecting Kieran. Nothing has changed though." He was comatose the last time, and now he isn't. Not that I'm complaining.

"It might be an accumulative effect. It might be his body building something akin to an immunity to the effects of our home. Mind you, time works differently in here, so, as a linear being, he could not have built it while here, just as he didn't age. Time didn't affect your body whatsoever while in here, but once you left the Realm, Kieran, your body developed the skills to keep you awake. Again, only a theory, but one our scientists have been working on."

Kieran squeezes his grip into my fingers and rakes his other hand through his hair, his words clear when he replies. "Either way, I'm thankful you got us out of that situation and to the Realm. Even if I had been back to the same state of mind, getting away from Sheridan is more important than my mental state."

Even though he says it in a casual way, the relief in his voice makes me really happy he adjusted to the Realm. I know he wouldn't have held it against me, but I would've felt quite bad for making him repeat his trauma. The decades Kieran spent in the here were difficult for him. He suffered what he called a never-ending nightmare, caused by the Essken trying to communicate with him, showing him their worlds exploding from our attacks, their homes being destroyed by our colonies. *A never-ending nightmare of pain and suffering,* he said. Not something one gets over in a minute or two, and he's had no time to process any of it. I can read between the lines, and I know Kieran. There's no denying it affected him greatly. He never wanted to fight this war. Being shown what we did to them over and over, not being in control, being left with no way to communicate… So yeah, not getting re-traumatized by another stint to the Realm is definitely the way to go.

"Agreed," Koll says. "If Sheridan had taken you back, I doubt I would've been able to get you freed once again. You would've been in deep trouble."

Oh, speaking of. I swing my head toward Kieran and glare at him.

"Deep trouble, huh? Definitely, especially with someone throwing all caution and common sense overboard. What in the name of the universe was that, Kieran? Ignoring the demands of an armed agent while being outnumbered and without a weapon to call your own or backup?" That's suicidal!

Kieran presses his lips into a thin line and drops his gaze to the ground. "I… I had a plan."

A plan. Sure. Raising my eyebrows, I give him my best spill-it glance. "A plan."

Kieran exhales harshly. "Yeah, but… Anyway. Koll. Thank you again." He slips his fingers in-between mine, squeezing tight, stabilizing himself on me, and I… I let it go.

"Just please don't just watch out for me, but also for yourself, okay?" I whisper at him, squeezing his fingers back. That was one scary moment for sure.

He lowers his chin in a close to imperceivable nod, keeping his focus on the Essken as Koll bows and then gestures at Kieran. "Maybe—"

A tsunami-wave of nausea rolls over me, drowning me in dizziness. I gasp. From one blink of the eye to the next, everything feels different. Kieran's next breath gets cut short as… reality warps and distorts, elongating some parts and squishing others, like in a carnival mirror.

"Another one," Kieran rasps, stating the obvious.

No more than a half second after he says it that same instinct to be close to Kieran kicks in, and even though I'm holding onto his hand already, I squeeze it tighter. The need to do so, to not let go, is overwhelmingly strong.

"Oh," Koll says, amusement in his voice. "You get to see some K'zees. A sign of good luck."

K'zees—?

The air around us… *ripples* and shimmers, like hot air rising from a street in summer. Koll chuckles, poking into the air with a finger into nothingness— No, wait. I blink. Not nothingness, but… As if my eyes and brain needed time to adjust, dozens and dozens of golden, sparkling… energy coils, for a lack of a better term, appear from the blurred areas. First small, earthworm-size, then growing as they wiggle their way toward us, getting bigger to the size of a forearm and tearing out of the blurry haze surrounding us, like soda bubbles rising from the bottom of a glass and popping out on the surface, joining others.

They're everywhere, swarming me, swarming Kieran, pushing into me and tugging on my clothing like dogs nipping at ankles.

Holy Universe!

"Are you seeing that?" Kieran's grip on my hand equals mine, strong as a bench vise. "That's new."

"Definitely seeing that." I swallow, trying to rid myself of the ball of anticipation and simultaneous trepidation lodged in my throat.

Koll looks around, lifts his hand to another energy coil, and pops it like a bubble, dispersing into a myriad of sparks, like a miniature firework. "So beautiful." He reaches far for another one, and the more he moves, the more these K'zees evade him, wiggling over to Kieran and me instead. They wrap themselves around me, joining the ones already close, bringing on a now familiar pressure and weight to settle over me.

In awe, I look down my body. Koll is right, everything about the K'zees is beyond beautiful, how they shine and glitter, how they move along me—so beautiful, it hurts. My body reacts to them on a cellular level, as though they activated the ultimate magnetism within me. There's a hum and buzz taking a hold of me, a yearning to touch them, to feel them. I lift my shaking hand to one of the glittery coils slithering around my body. It comes closer, touches me—and then jerks back, repelled.

Disappointment hits hard, like I was denied a life-saving breath of air. I reach for another one fluttering through the air, but it darts past me and—

Straight into Kieran.

Kieran stiffens and gasps as if stabbed, and so do I.

Holy—! I felt that—*zzing*, a shot of electricity right through our connected hands.

Another coil shoots into him and through to me, we both twitch, me a split second later than him.

Another one. *Another* one.

Every single new K'zee appearing around us goes straight for Kieran, as if they had figured out who the easier target was. Maybe one in every ten or twenty tries me, bounces off, then darts to Kieran, shooting through him and into me. The burning inside my core doubles, then triples, while Kieran's grimace becomes more harrowed. The K'zees are giving him an ethereal golden glow similar to mine, but I have no eye for the beauty they bring anymore. The more of these things assault Kieran, the more they set me on fire through him. My back buckles, then arches, controlled by forces stronger than my will. The acidic lightning burns through me, but also somehow makes me feel good, gives me a fix. My body likes it. *Wants* it. The part of my mind still lucid enough to think recognizes the flaw in my experience, because whatever these things are, whatever they're doing to Kieran, it can't be good.

Kieran trembles under the assault of coil after coil. "We need to— Need to stop it. Need to—"

I'd love to right about now, but I have no idea how. Blood swooshes in my ears like crashing waves, my head pounds, and my body feels as if I've been thrown into the sun. Unrelenting scorching hot pain shoots through my right hand connected to Kieran up into my center. Part of me realizes I need to pull away and break the connection, because this *hurts*, but the part of my body in control of my muscles doesn't obey. Quite the opposite, it feels like it opens up and invites those coils in, soaking them up like a flower put in water, an ultimate conduit. K'zees are everywhere, only sparing Koll. Where he stands, not a single K'zee is visible. Desperately, I catch his gaze. "H-hel-l—" Unable to complete the word my mouth drops open as the pain travels through my body, whirls around my core, then spreads to the periphery, my arm, my hand—

Koll steps closer, grabbing and supporting me by the biceps. "How can I help you?"

The instant he touches me, an avalanche of energy is released inside my body, numbing the pain and fixing what felt broken. A burst of power ripples through me as the coils align, all at once, responding to an invisible drill sergeant, heating up my core, my arm, my hand, as reality stretches out around us for the same infinite, yet short moment. My First Sense flares up brighter and more powerful than ever before, taking over, the sensation both a relief and a shock to my system, and—*snap!*—like a rubber band snapping back into place, everything is back to normal.

No more coils. K'zees. Whatever.

No more pain.

Just, *poof,* the K'zees are gone, as if nothing happened.

"Holy Sun and Stars," I wheeze, bending forward and supporting my weight with one hand on my knee, the other holding on to Kieran's so tight, I might bruise him. "That was… intense." I blink and shake my head, chasing away the last of the thrumming and dizziness, even though that hollow feeling in my stomach stays, an odd sensation, like my First Sense was throbbing.

"The worst so far," Kieran croaks. "It's becoming a very annoying habit."

"It is?" Koll lets go of my arm when I'm back to standing straight. He makes a motion with his hand, and a chair pops up behind Kieran and me. "This was the first time I have seen K'zees react to somebody. They avoid us, which is a pity, given how beautiful they are."

Letting myself fall into the chair, I let go of Kieran's hand and rub both of mine over my eyes, a feeling of desperation filling the hollow the pain just left. We have enough going on in our lives right now. These K'zees attacking us isn't helping.

At all.

A low, residual hum keeps reverberating through me, as if my body hadn't rid itself of all these weird energy coils yet. I huff. Now I know why it felt like electricity the last couple of times, because that's what's been shooting into us, coiled-up lightning.

I wipe my palms over my thighs, then look at Koll. "It was the first time we actually saw them. But those K'zees… they've been attacking us."

"If I hadn't seen them cause you pain, I wouldn't have believed it."

Koll shakes his head. "We assumed them to be harmless. A natural occurrence of no significance."

"Harmless to you," Kieran adds. "This might've been the first time we saw these things, but they've struck at us three times before, like hot skewers or lightning bolts. Not exactly pleasant." He sways a bit, face still paler than normal.

Koll points at the chair he manifested behind Kieran, then does the Essken-equivalent of a shrug. "I have to admit, I'm perplexed. I saw them go straight for you, while for us they dissolve when we touch them. Also, they've been nothing but infrequent occurrences without any pattern, regularity, or specific movement, like they've shown right now." Koll makes a wave motion with his hand, pointing it at Kieran. "I don't understand how they can cause you pain."

Kieran finally takes a seat, resting his head against the chair's back, closing his eyes. "Maybe they can't penetrate your suit."

"There's no difference to when we are in our natural form."

Opening his eyes, Kieran frowns. "Odd. All of it. It's been different basically every time, for example when— Wait, you were there when one of these episodes happened, on the *Achievement*! When we were in the mess hall—"

I sit up straighter, then deflate when I remember. "No, Koll wasn't there when the episode hit, he was doing something-something that needed fixing." Something about dinner, if I recall correctly, not that it mattered. I direct my gaze at the Essken. "Did you see any K'zees then, by any chance?"

Koll manifests a chair for himself, so now all three of us are sitting in comfy armchairs in the middle of a field of crazy colors and crazier physics. Also, a first for me.

Leaning forward, Koll shakes his head. "No, I didn't. Maybe they didn't cause what you felt before."

Kieran leans his head from left to right. "You might be right, but… I don't know. It felt eerily similar, almost too much so to just be coincidence."

"Agreed. The dizziness first, nausea, then the sensation of hot knives cutting my insides." But also, some kind of warmth and intense flare-up of my First Sense, which is weird. I cut Kieran a glance. "And by the way, I tried not touching you during the episode on board the *Pioneer*, and I can tell you that my body might be reacting without my say in it." That part has also stayed the same, this call, or instinct, taking over. I brush my sweaty palms over my thighs once more. This time, Kieran and I were holding hands already, but similar as before, I couldn't pull away. Like my body was addicted and thought it the most ridiculous idea to not get my fix.

I shudder. Not a big fan of my body acting without my consent.

"To play devil's advocate once again though, the episode on board the *Pioneer* was different." Kieran says. "It wasn't just me, right? I mean, I saw everything slow down around us, why and how would those K'zees be able to do that? What are we thinking? Less likely to be FBTI-made, more likely to be some kind of temporal distortion?" He looks at me, one brow raised.

I shrug. "It would make sense, given that time slowed down, but why did it not affect us? If it was a temporal distortion of sorts, shouldn't it not play favorites?" Sure, let's set time into slow motion, but keep Nonie and Kieran going at real speed. I don't think I'm that much of a special little snowflake, unfortunately.

"But slow-motion didn't happen this time, or did I miss something?" Kieran gives me a questioning glance.

I cringe. "Well… not exactly. Yes? Maybe? Nothing slowed down, as far as I remember, but… I saw everything stretch out, like on a bungee cord, distorted for a bit, and then everything snapped back together."

"That's the first time our perception differs then," Kieran says, brows pulled low. "But I don't know where that leaves us."

I swallow hard, then look at him. "Neither do I, but I have a feeling whenever we find out what's going on, we're not going to like it."

# Chapter Seven – 

# Realm

*The Realm, Somewhen*

Kieran holds my gaze for a solid three or four seconds before he nods. "Agreed. We should expect a worst-case scenario, but on the other hand, right now, in this very moment, I don't think we're going to come up with a solution."

I see where he's coming from. "We have too many balls in the air and only two hands to catch them." I allow myself one big sigh. "You're right. We could talk about these attacks, events, K'Zees, etc, forever, but we don't have that luxury, and we need to focus on—imagine that—even more pressing matters."

"Like our next steps." Kieran takes one big breath and exhales with a sigh at the end. "Koll, while we appreciate you bringing us here, what now?"

Very good question. I have no idea how the transition between realms works. Last time I entered via the Maelstrom and with the help of Tau-radiation, but coming here this time was instantaneous. No

Maelstrom. Maybe if there's no Tau-radiation, there's no connection between here and the Maelstrom, but we've got to start somewhere.

An idea pops up. "Could you get us back home to our time before Sheridan took us, or right after?" That would give us the most options, and hopefully a chance to at least inform Chase and the others. Maybe we can play it smart, somehow. Excitement rises. It could work: "When I met with Lorr, he showed me events that had already happened. He took me to those events." Like the Battle of Balthar. I stood there and saw the Quaneez cruiser rush toward the colony. Quite the memorable and frightening experience. And while I don't know quite yet how exactly to keep Sheridan away from us, we've got to start somewhere, and I would love to cross his plans. Somehow.

"Unfortunately, I can't help you go back in time. The events of that time period have happened already, as you know. We are unable to re-live past events."

Okay, that's confusing. I shake my head. "But why could Lorr—"

"He *showed* you—but he didn't interact or change anything, did he?"

Huh. "N-no, he didn't."

"And that's the difference. Re-experiencing is easy. Re-living isn't."

Sounds like a rule to live by. I file the one hundred new questions about the workings and details of the Realm for later, and sigh. "Well, that leaves us trapped in a way."

Koll spreads his arms out wide. "But it doesn't. You have all the options from our realm, Nonie. That is another reason why I decided to bring you here once we realized you were in trouble on the *Pioneer*."

"All the options? What do you mean by that?" Last time I was in the Realm, there were no options, only one way. I got in via my shuttle and the Tau-radiation, and that's how I got out about thirty minutes later.

"You can enter the realm-inbetween from here without any Tau-radiation. The choice when and where to go is yours."

Hope sparks. "The realm-inbetween? Do you mean the Maelstrom? The place I travelled through to visit the Realm last time?"

"That's the realm-inbetween. Correct. You can access it from here. I've seen you do so many times."

Excuse me? That's a bomb he just dropped on me. "Wait, what? Many times—you've *seen me?*"

"Of course, I have. Keep in mind, this is my Batch's Loch'rm. We have been following your realm in a linear matter for decades now."

I hold both palms out. "Whoa, easy there. Your what's what did what?"

Koll laughs, making it the first time I've ever heard an Essken do that. It sounds... genuine. "Now I know why we never had this conversation in the decades passed. Ah, linear time is so full of surprises."

Yeah, fun ride. Try skipping ahead some time. Gets even more surprising then.

Kieran leans forward. "*Linear* time?" The way he says it brings a shudder to run down my back. "And you called me a linear being earlier. I thought it meant I was straight forward, but..." He looks at me, then at Koll. "I don't think that's what it means."

I grimace. "No, it doesn't." This one's on me, I guess. Again, in a perfect world, abductions shouldn't happen before debriefings, if for no other reason than for the sake of bringing everybody up to speed prior to the unpleasantness of a kidnapping. But maybe then, in a perfect world we wouldn't have been taken against our will and brought to the future, how about that?

Anyway. Giving Kieran an apologetic shrug, I sigh. "Lorr, the Essken I met when I found you in the Realm, mentioned they were not used to linear time, but... there was too much going on to even bring it up. I simply forgot." To everybody else finding out a species wasn't linear would be the discovery of the century, but in our life, it ranks under *oops, too much more important stuff is happening, I didn't get to it.* I don't think I even mentioned it to Chase, Zio, or Dad—because there was no freakin' time. In my defense, we came back from the Realm, kept the fleet from attacking each other, and were kidnapped. In a normal life we, would've gotten debriefed, and I would've had time to tell my story.

Worst running gag of the century: the time-traveler has no time.

Kieran shakes his head in disbelief. "I... I don't know what to say. Non-linear?"

Trying to override the awkwardness of the moment, of me somewhat messing up, I nod. "But to be totally honest, I didn't really understand the whole non-linear time-thing. Lorr really didn't explain it well—or, at all." I purse my lips. "Is he still alive, by the way?" I ask Koll. It is a hundred years later, I have no idea how old Essken can get.

Koll hesitates. "My usual response to a human would be that he was a great leader."

"Wait...*was*?"

"Was. And then the human would draw the conclusion that he died because of my use of past tense. Most humans are tactful to not ask further questions."

Apparently, I don't fall into that category. "So, he hasn't died."

The Essken sighs a very human sigh. "We do not end, Nonie. Once we come in to existence, we do not end."

Kieran exhales softly. "Is that what not linear means?" he asks. "Not just how you experience time, but you... don't die? You live forever? Is that what you're saying?"

I look from Kieran to Koll and back. No, that's not it. He misunderstood that. That can't be it. Or... Something Lorr said comes back to me, and all of a sudden it makes a whole lot more sense. "When we destroy your ships, your worlds, Lorr said they transferred back here, to the Realm, to heal. I think it means they can't die in our realm, right?"

"And even here, we do not end," Koll says, in exactly the same words I remember Lorr using. Only now I understand. I think I really, *truly* understand.

"You really don't die." I whisper the words more than I say them. "I thought... I mean... I didn't think it meant you didn't die *at all*. When I talked to Lorr I understood that when we thought we killed you it only brought you back to the Realm... But no. It means you really don't die. You don't end. In *either* realm." Boy, did I misinterpret Lorr.

"That's correct." Koll lowers his head in a slow nod.

"Holy Sun and Stars," I breathe. Clearly, I didn't grasp the extent of what Lorr was trying to explain. As a disclaimer, a lot of concepts I had taken for granted were thrown ad absurdum when I talked to Lorr: A different realm. Communication via telepathy. And not to forget, finding Kieran alive, well—and at the same age he entered the Realm in. I assumed and understood time worked differently in the Realm for many a reason, but I clearly didn't arrive at two when I tried to add one and one.

Kieran's voice shakes with his next words, the faintest trace of hope swinging in them. "No matter what we did, you didn't die? The ships I—we destroyed… None of the Essken died?"

"None ended, but they all went through a very long and painful Rek'cha, a healing process. It involves a reconstruction of their bodies and mind on a cellular level, an experience that ranks as the most painful and challenging an Essken can go through. Many have lost their minds as they were rebuilt. For some, the reparation process has halted, leaving them stuck in an unfinished state, and—"

"And?" My voice is hoarse.

Koll takes a moment before he answers. "And we have to keep them in a separated area, for their own protection and the protection of the healthy. The… the screams." He taps his head. "The screams of the healing have driven some of my people insane. It is… a nightmare."

Kieran opens his mouth, then closes it, his eyes wide and unseeing. He blinks, then forces his lids closed, pinching them together, as he buries his face in his hands and leans forward. "A nightmare," he whispers.

A nightmare. *A never-ending nightmare of pain and suffering.*

He heard the tortured screams of Essken torn apart by our action at night, heard screams so horrific they drove the Essken mad, and it nearly broke him, even before he entered the Realm.

"Thirty-five years," he whispers, the trace of hope now gone, replaced by bone-deep sorrow. "That's what I felt for thirty-five years. I saw your ships explode, I felt your pain, your agony… Thirty-five years…"

I rub a hand over his back as he stands up. "Kieran…" I can't imagine bearing witness to such a magnitude of suffering and staying sane.

Keeping his eyes pinched shut, Kieran swallows, then rasps, "I thought we killed you. We didn't, and I want to be happy about it, but it seems we did something worse."

My heart seizes and then shatters hearing the guilt in his words, not just his own, but for us, for humanity. For what we did to them. Can I even imagine what he lived with, seeing humanity cause so much pain and presumed death over and over again? *A never-ending nightmare of pain and suffering.*

Koll leans forward, closer to Kieran, and lays one hand onto the other man's knee. "Both our peoples have made mistakes and operated under wrong assumptions. You didn't kill us, Kieran. None of you did. Your use of Tau-radiation threatened our existence, but once you stopped using it, the Realm recovered and our risk was gone. We survived as a people, because the Realm survived, even though some of us never were the same. In return, we deeply regret what we did to humans. We didn't know. We didn't understand. You didn't end us, but we ended many of you."

"We let this war go on too long." Kieran swallows so hard, I can hear it.

"But it ended because of you," Koll says, keeping his hand on Kieran's knee. "Because of your presence in the Realm, we began to understand humans. We only defended and tried to minimize casualties, because we began to understand from listening to you. Other peoples have not been as lucky before you. We… we have caused great harm." He straightens himself up. "But we have also learned from our mistakes—and eventually humanity did, too, and peace prevailed. And at this time, we're still trying to make amends to the human people by offering our friendship and sharing our technology. Lorr's Batch had to learn about your realm, and humans paid the price—*you* paid the price when we tried to communicate with you."

*A never-ending nightmare of pain and suffering.*

Nodding slowly, Kieran lets his hands sink down. They shake as he clasps them together. He clears his throat and looks up at Koll, sincerity in his expression. "If that's the price we pay for peace, the price *I* pay for peace, then so be it."

An ache opens up in my chest. USEF doesn't even know what they have with Kieran. Or, maybe they do now, or will know soon, but they surely didn't know during his time. Pride fills me, pride for the man who survived thirty-five years in the Essken Realm, being subjected to his version of hell, and here he is, accepting it and putting a positive spin on it. Or, trying to, at least.

I do see that shake of his hands, pick up on the cracking of his voice.

But, all things considered, it's progress.

Kieran draws in a long, unsteady breath and holds it. "It makes it more bearable, knowing I made a difference. That it helped. I— I'm glad we didn't kill you, but I'm so very sorry we… disabled so many Essken. I'm not sure if that fate is better than death."

After a short pause, Koll inclines his head. "I'm not sure either, but I also know that if it hadn't been for you, the cost of war would have been higher. On both sides."

As hard as it is to imagine a higher number of casualties, he might be right. Something comes to my mind though, something I hope I'm misinterpreting. "I once met an Essken kid and helped him against some kind of predator. When the adult Essken came for him, they… Well, I thought they killed him, but they brought him back to the Realm. Are you telling me that kid also needed to go through all the pain healing?" Because that doesn't sound right, or good, in any way.

Koll nods. "Kids' armor isn't made for your realm. If his suit was compromised in any way it was better to get him back home fast rather than wait. Either or, his self would've been damaged by exposure to your realm. I understand that is troubling for you, but it was the best option out of two bad choices."

My throat constricts. I should've been faster— But it's not as if I dragged my feet. Maybe the suit got damaged when he broke into that hole. I rub my forehead with my palm, then drop that hand to lay on

Kieran's sloped-forward shoulders. So much to unpack, so little time. I look at Koll. "Do… do the humans of this time know Essken don't die?"

Koll leans back into his chair. "No. We keep three facts about our species to ourselves, since we have found humans don't react well to either or. One, we don't tell you we are non-linear, and two, that also means we don't tell you we don't die. You feel threatened."

Probably. Knowing us, we'd worry that they'd start another war and decimate us while we'd have no way of permanently harming them.

"Finally, we don't mention the destructive effect of Tau-radiation on our realm. It would be a bad tactical decision on our part to advertise what truly kills us. All your people know is that it destroys our home, but you're unaware of the true implications."

And yet there are many who'd be happy to use it. "Yeah," I whisper. "I see why that's loaded. Did Lorr get in trouble for telling me? Is he okay?" Even though I didn't understand the full meaning behind his words, he might've told others, judging by what Koll said. I wouldn't want him in trouble—like us, he only did what he thought best for his people.

"I wouldn't know. Lorr's Loch'rm isn't in contact with this time period. It's mine."

There's that word again. "That doesn't really clarify it," I say, checking in with Kieran. He's more the expert than I am.

"For me neither." Kieran takes my hand from his shoulder and squeezes it, a look of gratitude on his face as he drops a tiny kiss onto my knuckles.

The Essken makes a gesture with his hands, like framing a ball. "Then let me explain. A Batch is a group of Essken dedicated to existing within the same Loch'rm." It sounds like *lock-room* when Koll says it. "Numbers are in the billions for a single Batch. A Loch'rm is a part of our realm attached to a different one, like yours, to allow for exploration and interaction. Where we intersect, some of your laws of nature bleed through. With your realm, we follow linear time while connected. With other realms, other rules might apply."

I don't even know what to latch on more but decide to go for the obvious. "*Other* realms?" As in plural?

"There are countless levels of reality our Batches interact with. And after Lorr's Loch'rm ended, we updated our protocol when it comes to first contact with new species and realms. We do not want to make the same mistakes again we did with yours."

Holy everything…! My mind was blown discovering the Quaneez-Essken Realm, but *countless* others? "And you've been to all of them?"

"I personally haven't. My people overall have visited quite many. We can't exist in all of them, mind you. Some are too harsh for us. In some we can be ourselves. In others, like yours, we need our suits. In none of the others it took us so long to figure out the physics. We couldn't understand you were auditory for the longest time." He twirls a finger where humans would have ears. "We assumed your hails were attacks, and yours hurt us more than the Magellans' for example. We had so much to learn."

So do we, apparently. That feeling when the world you thought you knew suddenly expands by the nth degree. Whoa. I swallow dry. "Can other people from other realms cross as well? Like you?" Like me?

Koll shakes his head. "As far as we know, crossings are extremely limited. We seem to be the most adaptable species when it comes to viability in other realms. But despite the impossibility of an exchange, many other realms are quite welcoming to us."

"Then why even deal with ours?" Kieran swallows hard. Good question, because I wouldn't call us welcoming. Maybe now, but not a hundred and fifty years ago. Not when Kieran was ordered to fight the Essken tooth and nail, against his will.

"Don't sell yourselves short. My Batch actually chose your realm for our current Loch'rm on purpose."

I blink. "On purpose? You chose us? I have so many questions about that!"

"That I believe. Exploring other realms is what we do, it is our nature and gives our being purpose. Every Batch chooses a realm for their Loch'rm. We set certain parameters to keep the two close, and once we do, their laws of physics tether us together."

My head is spinning. "That sounds complicated."

"It is for some, less for others. For the connection between your and our worlds, think of an area of our realm sticking to your timeline, like pinecones stuck to their branch. The pinecone only adheres to a small part of the branch, and that's the part, or rather, the time period, we interact with. Lorr, the Essken you met when you came here the first time, was the first leader to suggest your realm for a Loch'rm. His was the first Batch to connect to a time period and to experience your world and linear time. We have learned a lot about life in your realm since you met Lorr."

So have we. Eventually, I'll have to look into the history books, but I would credit Lorr for peace between our two people. And now I get it. "So, you were saying the Batch Lorr belonged to, their Loch'rm, is not in contact with *this* time period." I point down, like I needed to specify which time period I meant. Technically not helpful, but Koll gets it. "Or to stick to your analogy, your Loch'rm is the pinecone farther down on the branch." A new part of Essken Realm connected to ours further down the time stream, complete with billions of new Essken.

"Correct. When our Loch'rm is over and we return into the Realm's collective, we'll exchange information. I'll tell him you said hi."

"That would be nice, thank you." I smile, but it fades within a second or so. Batches, Loch'rms, non-linear Essken… My mind is blown. Or rather, fried. Being attacked by K'Zees seems to do that. Add the constant serving of elevated adrenaline, and no wonder I feel the way I do: sore, tired, and headachy. Closing my eyes, I let myself sink deeper into the chair, exhaling slowly.

In this very moment, life feels like a lot.

A lot of risk.

A lot of danger, uncertainty, and never enough moments to recharge.

A lot of not knowing what to do.

Yeah.

Keeping my eyes closed, I lift a hand. "Gentlemen, I could sit here and learn about the Essken for a long time, but I'm afraid we have to focus on the matters at hand. What's our next step? We're here, not captured by Sheridan, but what now? And I'm really relying on your input here, because I have no idea." I doubt going back to the *Achievement* is safe at this point, and it's not as if we had tons of friends in the future we can enlist in helping us.

Kieran tugs on my hand. "I got you, Nonie. Our next step's easy. We head back to the *Pioneer*."

I pop my eyes open and gape at him. "The *Pioneer*?"

"Correct." A smug, teasing smile tugs on his lips.

Back to the *Pioneer*. Huh. "Getting Kaytee out?" I'd like that—more than my earlier idea to go straight back to the *Hope* after our abduction. Leaving Kaytee with Sheridan and the AIvatars didn't feel good. I know we didn't have a choice, but it's not exactly nice to leave your great-granddaughter in peril and arrested by the FBTI.

"Well—"

I sit up straighter. Koll said I could access the Maelstrom from here, so I should be able to bring us back somewhat at the right time. "Okay, if we went back to the *Pioneer* now—"

"Nuh-uh. That's not it." Kieran taps his finger onto the back of my hand. "You're too eager, Lieutenant. Take a breath. I got this. We can't help Kaytee right now, we've got bigger fish to fry. Hence, we're not going back to the time we just came from. We go back to my *Pioneer*."

To the past? "Why would we go to your *Pioneer*? That's asking for trouble. Two of you, potentially two of me—"

"Not if we time it right," Kieran says, wiggling his eyebrows like an evil mastermind. "We'll drop out of the Realm and into time a few minutes *after* you hid the disk."

One-Mississippi, Two-Mississipp—

"Holy Universe, yes!" I facepalm myself. "Of course! You're a genius, Kieran! I hid the disk right after you went into the nebula, and it was gone when we tried to find it right now, and—okay, now it's all coming together—it was already gone when I found your letter! That means somebody must have taken the disk in-between me leaving it there and me finding the letter! That could have been us! Brilliant!"

Seriously: Brilliant!

Me on the other hand… "I'm still not thinking like a time-traveler." Disappointment washes over me. I have to start thinking more of the effect events have on and within time, not just the event itself. To put it into a metaphor, I'm good at knowing where or when I threw my stone into the water, but I'm not good at keeping track of the ripples it caused. I shake my head, then look at the Essken. "Just to clarify again, I can access the Maelstrom from here. Even without a Setayashi- or Tau-device." Because, as usual, I'm fresh out of those.

Koll laughs again, softer this time. "Yes. And I'll be happy to be of assistance with that." He snaps his fingers, and a rift opens next to us, like somebody took a scalpel and cut through the fabric of reality. Chaos swirls on the other side, a myriad of colors and events. The Maelstrom. It calls to me and pulls on me, as if it couldn't wait for me to dive in.

"Your people are nothing short of amazing," Kieran says, eyeing the Maelstrom and the Realm. "Is that… is that how you would cross to our realm as well?"

Koll shakes his head. "No. There are areas of reduced resistance when it comes to crossing for us, usually around nebula in your realm. We cross through those."

"And that would explain why we never sensed you before you popped up in a nebula behind us," Kieran says, huffing out in amazement. "Or why our terraformed colonies close to any nebula wreaked more havoc on the Realm, and you attacked them. Now it all makes sense." He huffs once more. "Not a silent propulsion drive that jumped you to right under our noses but transitioning from another realm. I didn't see that coming, I must say."

I don't think anybody did, really.

"And we didn't see the difference in physics coming," Koll replies. "Our ships were not made for your realm. A lot has changed since."

Kieran tugs on my hand, a small mischievous smile on his face. "Isn't that what Trip always said? Their ships weren't made for actual space flight. Guess he was right."

"Let's not tell him," I deadpan. We'd never hear the end of it.

"The Conolly-theory on FTL drive has—" Koll stops himself. "Never mind. You will find out eventually." Koll lowers his head, then motions at the rift. "Please. You know how to travel the realm-inbetween. I hope to see you both again, and unharmed."

Kieran stands and extends a hand. "So do we, Koll. Thank you again for helping us. I cannot wait for our people to finally become friends in my time."

"And while I wasn't able to be there for that occasion, I'm very happy it came to that. My Batch is enjoying their Loch'rm with your world a lot." He takes Kieran's hand and shakes it. Somehow, this little moment here, the shaking of hands between Kieran and an Essken, gives me hope we're going to fix all of this mess. We're going to take care of the Temporal War and we're going to take care of the Quaneez War. We can make it work and ensure a safe future.

I fold my fingers together and crack my knuckles. "Alright. I'm having a rare moment of I-got-this thanks to our teamwork. You opened a way to the Maelstrom, I jump us back in time. Once we have the disk, we have both a means to jump back to the future without any help and a way to prove the existence of interference with the timeline." I hold out my hand for Kieran, and he takes it, inhaling a deep breath.

"So, you're going to jump us through time. Do I... do I need to do anything?"

"Nope. Maybe enjoy the ride?"

He laughs, then chuckles. "I'll try. I don't remember any of the other jumps, so no idea what to expect."

Me neither. Mashaule screamed like a banshee when I took him back to our now, even though he had been jumping with the help of the disk. But then, Kieran and I are bonded, and he did well here, in the Realm. I squeeze his hand. "You'll be fine."

He squeezes it back. "With you, always."

Before I can get all gooey about the meaning behind his words, I nod one more time at Koll, then step us out of the Realm and into the Maelstrom of time.

# Chapter Eight -
# Grief

**The Maelstrom**

The moment I step us through the rift, Kieran chokes on his next breath. Surprise and wonder flicker across his face. "Wow…! This… this is what it's like?" He turns his head left and right, eyes wide, taking in the beauty of the Maelstrom.

Digging my heels in so we don't drift past where I want to go, I slow us down and pull Kieran closer by his hand. "It's a sight to behold, isn't it?"

He looks at me with awe in his eyes, mouth slightly agape. "I can't put it into words." He reaches for my other hand and holds on to that as well. The apple in his throat moves up and down as he looks around, taking in the swirling Maelstrom of colors around us, brushing past us and in-between us. "It's breathtaking."

An odd sense of pride washes over me. It's not like either of us did anything on purpose to make Kieran tolerate the Maelstrom, but it's still a stark contrast to Mashaule. To me, too. The first time I traveled, I blacked out. Second time, the same. It took me several jumps to really take in what's going on around me, like my senses had to develop to understand my surroundings. Last time I jumped together with Mashaule, I recognized events inside the Maelstrom I hadn't before. Now I know what's passing around us, and it's still getting clearer every time. It used to be big events of my life, then big events in general. Then I began to see more and more details, like zooming into a calendar from year-view to daily view. Now, if I focus, I can feel events down to the hour.

Maybe it's really all about practice making perfect and every jump helping my mind to make sense of what it saw. Okay, granted, seeing is exaggerating it. It's more a feeling, like my First Sense combined with my eyes getting the job done. I think. It's not really an exact science and I'm still waiting for the manual on time jumps.

"What do you see?" I ask, making a hand motion at our surroundings.

"Swirling colors in glittery clouds. It's mesmerizing."

"Do you see anything in those clouds? Or feel it? Events?" I wouldn't expect him to, but he's already a step ahead of me at that stage. I'm thinking it's the benefit of the Bond bleeding through.

"No. There's nothing in those clouds." Kieran shakes his head, then squints. "I mean, maybe? I thought I just saw an image of Pioneer there on the left, but it's more a feeling than that I'm sure."

Interesting. "Guess that's coming through from the Bond. Or you're growing yourself a First Sense, who knows." I grin at him and squeeze his hand. "Hey, maybe us being together is the key. I've never just chilled in the Maelstrom as we do now." I give a pointed look at our feet, floating free in the Maelstrom, tendrils of time evading the obstacles and reuniting once they've passed.

He raises both eyebrows. "Never?"

"Never ever. In the beginning, the jump just happened to me. It took me a while to control it. Couldn't even think straight at first. Guess I'm getting better."

"So, you can bring us to Pioneer at the time after I went into the nebula?"

"Shouldn't be a problem." Famous last words, but I should be able to find the event. My last jump I focused on where I wanted to go and felt the *pull. It should work.*

*Twisting by the hip, I look over my shoulder. Funny. Everything seemed so chaotic during my first jumps, and now… It feels organized. I can tell we drifted back in time and past my birth, without having to look for events or other hints. That's definitively progress. Taking a deep breath, I focus on the day we thought Kieran died, and specifically on the time after I dropped off the disk. Would be inconvenient running into myself. Again.*

*The Maelstrom picks up speed, or maybe we do. A sharp gasp leaves Kieran's throat—*

*"There. I got." I let go of one of his hands. "Get ready to feel ground under your feet in three, two—"*

With a bang, we hit carpeted floor, soft and cushioned. The impact drives me to one knee as Kieran stumbles forward, catching himself on our entwined fingers and before he falls over—

"My bed?" He lets go of my hand and touches the bed. "My bed!" Spinning on his heels, he takes in the rest of the surroundings. "My quarters! Holy Sun and Stars, Nonie! It's the correct location!" A laugh breaks free, one that says he wasn't quite sure I could deliver what I promised.

"Hey!" I get up and brush off my knee. "Doubt sucks!"

Kieran whirls around and rushes me. I'm swept up in his embrace, feet off the ground, the whole shebang. "I didn't doubt you, Nonie. Never. This is amazing. *You* are amazing." He kisses the spot behind my ear and squeezes me hard. "Hearing you talk about traveling through time and seeing you do it, being part of it… Wow. Just wow." He sets me back on the ground. "I got the coolest girlfriend in the universe. Heck, in *time.*" He gives my nose a little peck.

"Cheesy," I mumble under my breath, fighting to hide a smile.

"Cheesy, but you like it." He winks at me.

Aw shucks. Well, he got me there.

"Do you know which exact date you landed us here? It doesn't matter as long as the disk is here. I'm just curious." Kieran walks around the bed toward the desk, and boy, does it look right. It fits, seeing him back in his quarters.

I shrug. "I aimed for—"

A beep comes from the door and both of us freeze.

"Shit," Kieran hiss whispers. "Somebody's coming!"

I drop to my belly and roll myself under the bed. Crap, crap—what did I do wrong? Did I bring us in too early? Is that me dropping off the disk? Or worse, has Kieran not gone to the nebula? If it's him and he's getting ready for bed, we're in deep doo-doo.

I roll to my stomach, bumping into Kieran scooting under from the other side, on his back. His alert gaze meets mine as the door hisses open.

From down here, the couch and dining table are blocking my view of the entrance, but I do hear the steps though. Slow. Hesitant. Two people, I would say?

The door closes, and silence hovers.

And hovers.

And hovers.

After maybe twenty or thirty seconds, a small eternity, somebody takes in a ragged breath and releases it in an unsteady rush. "Tell me the last three hours haven't happened, Zee. Please."

"I'd like nothing more than that, Trip, but I'm afraid that is a miracle I cannot provide."

Oh crap. Chase and Zio, my future mentors and Kieran's best friends.

Chase sniffs once, then clears his throat. Still his voice breaks. "He can't be gone. He can't have died in that nebula."

Ouch. That explains when we are.

His last word lingers before Zio speaks again, even slower and softer than normal. "I'm trying to tell myself to accept what happened, but it's difficult. Coming here…" He sighs, and somebody takes a few more steps into the room. "In this very room it feels like he's here."

Uh-oh… Because of the memories or because of his First Sense alerting him to our presence? Job well done landing us exactly at this very moment, Lieutenant. There's only one other person in USEF with a First Sense, and that person is currently in the room with us.

Somebody pulls out a chair from behind the table and sits down.

"What do we tell Nonie when—if—she comes by again?"

"She knows, Chase. This is her history." Zio takes out a chair I have in my line of sight and sits down. "She always did, I suppose."

"I figured. On the bridge..." He blows out a controlled breath through pursed lips. Another one, before he trusts himself to speak. "On the bridge, the way she looked when Kieran... died... She knew, and that's when *I* knew." He huffs with a small laugh. "I guess I was just hoping that if she was surprised by the events maybe something changed and this is a new timeline where Kieran died, while he was—is—still alive in the main one. Or vice versa, that we're a new branch and he'll come out alive again. I guess I just want him to still be there. Somewhere, at least."

"You know there is only one timeline, Chase, and if we were in a branch that split off—"

"Yeah, yeah, I know, we'd stop existing. But hey, we wouldn't know it. And I wouldn't have to live with the knowledge that I let him enter that nebula. I'm his first officer, I live and breathe security, I'm his best friend—together with you, of course—but my point is that *I let him enter that nebula*. I didn't see any sense in it, but I let him go to humor him. Whatever happened in there, I missed it. And now... now, he's gone."

The pain in his voice is raw. Potent. I work on a dry swallow. I know they loved Kieran. They never stopped. It was clear with every conversation we had during my time at the Academy, but hearing them grieve gives their loss another dimension.

A faint choked sound breaks free from Kieran. I look over to him and immediately wish I'd paid more attention to him than to the two men at the dining table. He's staring up at the bed only a few inches above his head, eyes wide, biting into his left fist he brought to his mouth, chest rising and falling out of rhythm.

It's one thing to get lost in the nebula.

It's another to hear your friends mourn you.

My heart stutters seeing him suffer a consequence of his action he never intended.

Stretching out my right hand, I fish for his by his side. The moment our fingers touch, he works his between mine and holds on to me as if his life depended on it, as if I grounded him.

Zio is the next to break the silence. "Have you spoken to his father already?"

Chase sighs. "Yeah. Yes. It was… intense."

"The admiral is an intense man."

"As a baseline, agreed. Telling him what happened might have been the most difficult conversation I've ever had in my adult life. I've given the news before. I'm always empathetic, you know that, but this time I cried. Not ashamed to admit it. I couldn't keep my professionalism up. When his dad understood, *truly* understood what I was telling him, when he started crying… I couldn't hold it in." He sniffs.

Kieran slowly shakes his head left to right, eyes now squeezed shut, as if he could un-hear what Chase said.

"You know, Zee, I've known Kieran's dad for a long time. Since the first winter break at the academy, when I went home with Kieran. That man has been through the death of his wife, the fear of almost losing Kieran as a kid, and now he's lost him for good." He pauses. "He asked me for access to our sensor logs to look at what happened."

"He needs closure. We all do."

"True."

Silence falls again, heavy. I brush my thumb over the back of Kieran's hand until the death grip he has on mine relaxes a bit. "Dad," he whispers low, under his breath.

Somebody, probably Chase, given that he's the more antsy of the two, drums his fingers onto the table, then stops. "Do you think he was depressed? And I know this falls under doctor-patient confidentiality, but I was wondering… He changed over the last months. The war, everything. It took a toll on him."

"That it did. You know I can't talk about details, but as his friend,

I shared your concerns. That's all I'm going to say."

Chase blows out another puff of air, then gets up and takes a few steps in our direction. My heart speeds up. Don't come over here, please. Just don't.

He stops a few feet away—and turns around.

I barely hold in a sigh of relief. Thank the Universe for small favors.

"Zee?" Chase's voice is low, and off-pitch. "Where do we go from here? Without Kieran. Where do we go?"

Zio gets up and sets the chair back under the table. "We carry on his legacy. We make sure we meet Nonie at the academy. We teach her how to save him from the Quaneez. His life may have been cut short, but it is our responsibility to assure it's lived happily and with love for the time granted to him. That's our future. And, while we are at it, we find a way to stop this war."

Both men are standing in front of the window, looking out. If I crank my neck and angle my head, I can see them both next to each other. Chase lays a hand onto Zio's shoulder and squeezes it.

"I don't think we're ever going to be whole again."

Zio gives a slow shake of his head. "No. I don't think so either."

They fall silent, looking out into the nebula that claimed their friend. After a minute or two, Chase claps Zio's shoulder twice, and both men walk toward the door. It opens, but before they leave, they both stop.

"Goodbye, Kieran," Chase whispers.

One more heavy sigh, and the doors close behind them.

Silence stays in their wake as I let go of a breath of air I didn't know I held. Kieran lets go of my hand and inches himself out from under the bed. I follow.

That was intense, to parrot Chase's expression. My emotions are on a rollercoaster. Before my two mentors came in, Kieran and I were so happy everything worked out. Now all the positivity is sucked out of the air and replaced with thick, potent grief.

Kieran stays hunched over, hands on his knees, shoulders heaving up and down.

"Hey." With three quick strides, I'm at his side, taking him by the upper arms and helping him up. "Wasn't quite what we came here for, huh?" I wrap him into a tight hug he returns.

"No. Not really. I… I hate to admit it, but I don't think I've processed what happened very well."

No kidding he hasn't. "Don't forget there was no time."

"I know. I'm beginning to think recovering from the Realm and coming to terms with the implications it has on my life will take me a while." A stuttering breath leaves his body. "Sometimes, I think I'm my old self, from before I went into the nebula. I wasn't in a good place when I did, you know that. *They* know that. But since you got me out, I've had moments where I forgot about that weight on my shoulders. And sometimes I feel as sad and hopeless as I did that day, only for different reasons."

"You telling me being kidnapped by the future and accused of having a hand in the death of billions isn't improving your mood?" I kiss his neck.

He chuckles. "No, it isn't. But believe it or not, visiting the Realm with you helped. The fact that I wasn't as powerless as last time, as trapped as last time, *helped*. That I now know the Essken didn't die, even though some might wish they did, it helped. The biggest help though is this. You. Me. Being a team." Nuzzling himself closer into the embrace, his eyelashes brush over the sensitive skin on my neck as he closes his eyes. "Thank you."

"No need to thank me, Kieran. I'm always here for you. I got your back, just like you'd have mine."

We stay like this for a while, as if the outside world wasn't there to threaten us, as if we had all the time in the world. And maybe we do.

I slowly release him from my hug. "Check the desk?" Anxiety rises together with my words. If the disk isn't there, we have no means to leave this time. Or this ship. That's going to be an awkward discussion when they find us here, and not one I'd like to have. Buzzwords *keeping the timeline intact.*

Kieran nods and walks over to the desk, opening the secret drawer.

"Here goes nothing." He reaches inside, frowns—and pulls out a grey oval disk. "This what you're looking for?"

"Yes!" I shoot one fist up in the air. "That's it!" For once something is going the way it should, and it feels fantastic!

Kieran wraps his fingers around it and closes the drawer with his other hand, a pensive expression on his face. "You know… I could stay. Space is an odd place, I could come up with a story why I'm suddenly back here, alive. I could spare them the sorrow. Spare my dad." He turns the disk in his hand, slowly.

A knotty, twisty ache opens in my chest. Not sure whether that's only from my First Sense protesting the idea of Kieran staying in this time, or from the sadness threaded in his voice. Maybe both.

I step next to him, wrap one arm around his back and lean my head against his shoulder. "You—"

"I can't stay. I know. Changing the timeline isn't going to happen. I know that very well. And don't get me wrong. I also don't want to stay. Fate served me a second chance, and one with you, so I'm not stupid enough to not appreciate that, *but*…" He closes his fist over the disk. "Fate is also dangling the chance for a do-over in front of my nose right now. And rubbing it in, by showing me Zee and Trip."

"Haven't we already established fate is a bit sadistic when it comes to us?"

He huff-laughs once. "That we have. Which is why I'm being mature and doing the right thing." Kieran holds the disk out to me. "Bring us back to the future, Nonie. Let's end that Temporal War and then get on with our lives."

# Chapter Nine -

# No Prank

## The Maelstrom

The moment I press the button on the disk, the Setayashi-radiation lights me up. It doesn't take any conscious thought or effort for me to slip us into the Maelstrom.

"It worked." Kieran still sounds way too surprised for my taste.

"Told you." I hold on to him tighter. Don't want to find out what happens if we got separated. Could I find him? Probably. Do I want to risk it and find out? Nope.

I focus on the future, the FBTI-court, maybe a few minutes after Sheridan brought us back to the white bubble-thingy. That should work.

Time swirls around us, faster. I catch a glimpse of my dad and mom together, then my birth, then—

Kieran gasps, yanks on my hand to stop me, reaches out for something, our fingers still entwined—

I pull on his arm as my knuckles graze a time swirl. "No, don't touch—"

*Too late.*

With a *bang* we hit grassy ground in a tumble of arms and legs. Kieran's knee hits me in the gut, but I think I elbow him smack in his face.

"Ow!" I pull myself out from halfway under Kieran. "What the hell was—"

"Hands up and keep them up!" somebody commands behind us. "This is a private property, and one where the owner is armed. Don't turn around or make any sudden moves!"

Kieran gulps in air and freezes halfway off me, which, apparently is not what the person wanted.

"Move, I said." The words are emphasized by the high-pitched whine of a weapon charging.

Aww, crap. When are we? Where are we? What are we breaking by being here? My First Sense brings up some nausea. Just fantastic. The disk—? My gaze darts around. There. The disk is on the ground, amidst some roses.

Roses?

I do a quick scan of our surroundings. A garden. We landed in a beautiful garden, of all places. Flower beds are everywhere, some filled with roses, others with tulips, and others with flowers I can't name. Not an outdoor person. Big trees throw their shadows onto the perfectly manicured lawn we landed on.

"And when I said move, I meant *now*."

I throw one more longing look at the disk. Alas, at the moment there's nothing left to do but to comply. Kieran and I detangle our remaining limbs and stand up, hands raised, still facing the direction we were told to.

"I'm sorry," Kieran whispers. "I didn't mean to."

I look over at him. "Sorry for—"

"All right, now keep your hands up and slowly turn around so I can see who decided to ruin my morning's work."

Doing as I'm told, I turn to face a vaguely familiar older man in USEF leisure attire aiming a rifle at us. Great.

"Hm," he grunts. "The last students deciding I was a good victim during prank week flooded my basement. Accidentally, supposedly, but we're not going to have a repeat performance of that."

Huh? Prank? Students? Is he an instructor at the academy, and that's why he looks familiar? Would explain the USEF-leisure outfit.

The old man narrows his brows. He really looks familiar now. "You, the guy! I'm still waiting, and I'm getting impatient." He aims his weapon at Kieran, who still hasn't turned.

I kick the back of his leg with mine. Dude! This is neither the time nor the place to play hero, or to get shot for trespassing. We can deal with the implications for the timeline better when we're alive than if we're dead.

Kieran sighs like the weight of the world was on his shoulders.

Then, he turns around.

The man in front of us startles. Within half a second or less his face loses all color, like all his blood drained. His mouth opens and closes, but no sounds make it out besides a little gurgle. Slowly, he lowers the rifle, or maybe he doesn't do it on purpose, I'm not sure. He shakes his head, blinks several times, then rubs a palm over his eyes. "K-Kieran?"

Okay, theory half confirmed. They know each other. Maybe an older instructor, who retired before I started?

Kieran chews on his lower lip, then raises a hand, a small, shy smile on his lips. "Hi, Dad."

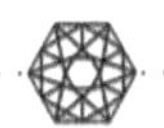

### Admiral Wildason's Backyard, Somewhen

*Dad?* My gaze darts from one man to the other. Heck, that's why he looked familiar! Not an old instructor, but Admiral Niall Wildason, Kieran's dad! Now that I know what I'm looking for, I could punch myself for not coming to the correct conclusion right away. They have the same eyes, the same body type, even though Admiral Wildason is at least in his mid-eighties. I should've seen it.

Admiral Wildason drops his weapon and takes one staggering step toward his son. "A-are you real? Because, if this is a prank—"

"The day Mom died, you took the tickets to the opera you wanted to gift her when she came back and you put them in her jewelry box. You kept them, but you have never listened to opera since then. In fact, you hate it." Kieran lets his hands sink down. "It's me, Dad. I'm real."

The moment his dad accepts it, he opens his arms. "Son."

They both dart forward, Kieran faster and less unsteady than his father, and crash into each other, embracing the other in a fierce hug.

Emotion clogs my throat. If it wasn't for the birds singing and the soft breeze rustling the leaves on the trees and flowers, time could've stopped. Kieran and his dad appear frozen in their embrace, holding on so tight to each other, Kieran's biceps threaten to rip his shirt. It takes a good minute before they pull apart, even though his dad keeps a tight grip on Kieran's forearm, as if he feared he could pop out of existence as quickly as he entered it.

Careful not to interrupt their moment, I sneak to the bed of roses and grab the disk. I'm not going to leave our only way out to be eaten by slugs or something.

"Kieran." Admiral Wildason lays a hand on his son's cheek in such a tender gesture, I'm not the only one tearing up. "You look just like I remember you." He drops his hand and his gaze, then shakes his head. "Explain to me what happened. Why you're here. How you're here. How you're looking so young. If I'm dying and you're welcoming me to the afterlife, I'd like to know."

"You're not dying, Dad. You're way too— Wait. How old are you now?" Kieran furrows his brows.

"Eighty-six." The admiral flexes his biceps of the arm not holding on to his son.

"Eighty-six. It's been—"

"Twenty-three years since you died."

Kieran swallows hard, then fakes a smile. "Well, about that. It wasn't really as dramatic as it sounded."

"I beg to differ if you're here, twenty-three years later, looking not a day older than when I saw you last. So, spill it, Son."

Grimacing, Kieran looks over his shoulder at me.

Cue taken, because this is where it gets complicated. Messy. Well, *even more* complicated and messy. I step forward, my First Sense slightly apprehensive, but not full-out protesting. "Admiral Wildason, hi. Maybe I can help lift the mystery a bit."

His gaze flicks over to me. "I think that sounds fantastic. And you are?"

Uh. My smile withers away. Good question. Who am I? My last name should ring a bell, so—

"This is my girlfriend. Nonie," Kieran says, grabbing me by the arm and pulling me into his side.

"Hi," I squeak, because *girlfriend!* I don't think Kieran has labelled me his girlfriend in front of somebody else before—not that we've had many opportunities there.

Admiral Wildason's eyes widen. "Your girlfriend? That's new."

Kieran grins. "Actually, quite old, if we're being technical."

I elbow him in the side and give him *the* look, like, *maybe let me do the talking?*

Kieran chuckles. "Dad, everything is complicated. I don't think we should be here, if I'm honest, but… since we're here already I feel we might as well…?" Now he gives me *the* look, the one that speaks of love and loss, of the need to spend some time here, with his dad.

I hold up one finger. "Excuse us for a sec." Taking Kieran by the elbow, I turn us both around and take a few steps away from the admiral, then whisper under my breath at him. "You can't touch things when we jump. Like, you really can't."

"I didn't do it on purpose, okay? I… I saw something when we were traveling, well, I saw Dad, and… I guess I threw us off course." He grimaces. "Sorry. I'm sorry. I just—" He doesn't finish the sentence, and he doesn't have to.

My anger melts like ice cream in the sun. "I know. I know. I get it." I know what it feels like to want to see your parent so badly you're willing to re-prioritize. After all, I chose to wait and listen in on my dad and mom back in the hut on Alpha Rubrum. It turned out in favor for me, but even if it hadn't, I probably wouldn't regret it.

"So, what does that mean?" He gives me a sheepish look from under his lashes. "Can we… can we stay just for a minute or so?"

I sigh. No kidding *we shouldn't even be here*, as Kieran said. But we are, and the question becomes what's worse: jumping out of here right away and leaving his dad with a million questions and potentially the drive to find out what happened, or staying and doing damage control. I close my eyes, thinking about talking to Admiral Wildason, about telling him part of what's been going on. My First Sense doesn't seem to mind, which, honestly, surprises me. The timeline is such a picky, finicky little thing I would've expected it to throw a tantrum.

On the other hand… I open my eyes and look at the admiral, *really* look at him. He's old. Somewhat frail, even though his eyes still have this sharp, alert glimmer to them. Maybe, and I feel bad thinking this, but maybe my First Sense doesn't protest because Admiral Wildason's future impact on the timeline will be minimal, to put it politely.

On that depressing thought, I make up my mind. "Okay. Okay. While we have no time, we also have all the time we need." I pat the pocket the disk waits in for me, and Kieran gets the hint. "But please be careful with the timeline, okay?" A slight smile lifts the corners of my lips. Maybe I should learn to live more in the moment, especially as a time traveler. Since I got accidentally thrown back to the *Pioneer* and met Kieran, I haven't paused. Yes, I slept. Yes, I ate. Yes, there were periods of inactivity, but overall there was always *something*. Get home. Save Kieran. Apprehend Mashaule. Put an end to the Temporal War. I haven't truly stopped and enjoyed a moment in a while.

And neither has Kieran.

I turn him back around by the elbow. "What about sitting down?" Looking past the admiral, there's a little sitting area under a gazebo framed with green bushes and colorful flowers.

"Please, let's," Kieran's dad says. "I need to sit. And I also need a drink." He pats Kieran's shoulder and holds on to it as he steers him down the way.

The older man takes the lead, holding on to his son, and I follow, my gait slightly uneven. Might be the grassy surface, might be my bioengineered left leg, who knows. Oh, never mind. It's probably from being thrown around through time and space.

Sigh.

The admiral's gazebo sits smack in the middle of this large garden. Looking around, I'd say it's not quite the size of a football field, but close. The grassy area is framed by flower beds, which again are framed by trees, and more trees behind those. At the end, partially hidden behind trees from here, I can make out a modern-style farmhouse in all-white with large windows and a pointy roof.

"Where are we anyway?" I ask Kieran once I catch up with him.

"Our summer home. Northern California. No neighbors for miles on either side here—or at least it used to be like that."

That definitely explains both the beauty of nature around us and the feeling of solitude.

Admiral Wildason releases Kieran's shoulder, leads the three steps up into the all-wooden gazebo, and takes a seat in one of the large wicker chairs with thick cushions and armrests. "Please." He motions at the two-seater wicker sofa across from him.

Kieran looks around as we sit down. "This is new."

"New to you, yes. I built it about ten years ago. Needed something to do after I retired." He leans to his left and lays his palm onto the control pad integrated into the small wooden table placed next to his chair. "One scotch. And…?"

"Water," I say, and Kieran nods.

"And two waters," he finishes. One second later, all three drinks materialize next to the pad. "Help yourselves."

Kieran reaches over and grabs our waters, handing me one as Niall opens a drawer in the coffee table. He grabs something and throws it over to Kieran. "Still like this?"

Furrowing his brows, Kieran catches the object. "What's— No way!" His eyes pop open as wide as the smile spreading across his face. "My favorite chocolate! You still have some!"

"In every room in the house. And, well, here. I had just received a big box of that stuff to send to the *Pioneer* for you when… well, when you *died,* or whatever we call it now. First, I couldn't even look at it, it was too painful. I—" The admiral swallows hard, takes a sip of his scotch, then smacks his lips. "Okay. Now I believe my eyes. Clearly, I haven't died and crossed into the afterlife. Nothing burns and grounds you like a scotch. But anyway, at one point I remembered how you always seemed to light up with a bite of these, and I figured I'd give it a try. And as you can see, I've come to like them quite a bit." Patting his belly, he shrugs.

Kieran blows out a soft laugh that fizzes out after a second. He inhales deep and holds his breath. "I'm sorry, Dad. Not that you took over my love of chocolate, but that you had to go through losing me." *After losing Mom*, swings in his words, even though he doesn't say it.

His dad swirls the amber liquid in his glass, not taking his eyes off Kieran. "Whatever happened to you, I doubt it was something you signed up for voluntarily. And here you are, alive and breathing." He sets the glass down onto the table. "I'm ready whenever you are."

Kieran nods, laying the chocolate bar onto the table so carefully as if it were the most delicate object in existence. "Nonie?"

I nod and scoot forward. This is my part. Telling the story and letting my First Sense guide me. "I wanted to start by asking you to be open minded, but considering whom you're seeing next to me, I think we got the open mindedness covered." I lay one hand on Kieran's leg.

"That we have." His dad nods.

"It gets even crazier though. I'll start with my perspective: I was born in 2277—"

"You don't look three years old to me, if I may say so."

"That's because I'm not. I'm eighteen. I went to the academy and graduated in '95—"

The admiral's eyes widen. "Are you telling me…" His mouth opens and closes, before he blows out a puff of air through pursed lips. "I thought time travel was impossible."

"Believe me, so did I."

"Me, too," Kieran adds. "Until Nonie popped up on the *Pioneer* in '55."

Admiral Wildason shakes his head. "'55? But you died, or whatever we're calling it now, in '57."

"That's correct." I hold out a hand. "To summarize it, my first interaction with Kieran and the *Pioneer* was accidental. I barely made it back home to my time. Turns out I have a knack for traveling through time, so I was recruited work for a part of USEF that deals with temporal safety. As I was working on a mission for them, I added one and one and realized Kieran wasn't dead, but had been trapped in a different reality, a realm outside our known universe, and one with different laws of physics and time. He was trapped in there until I got him out, which is why he hasn't aged. Time works differently there."

The admiral takes a sip of his scotch and keeps the glass in his hands. "And now you brought him back to this time?"

I cringe. "No, sir."

"Call me Niall, please. You're my son's girlfriend and rescuer, if I understand it correctly. No need for any formality between us."

O-kay. My cheeks heat. I'm still not good with dropping rank. But I'll do my best. "Okay, Niall." I try out his name, and it works. Helps that he is in a leisure outfit and not a full-blown uniform. So much for retirement, by the way. "I brought Kieran to my time, where I'm from. We landed here on accident. Again."

His dad narrows his eyes. "On accident. Did I understand correctly that you were trapped in a different reality for all these years?"

"Until '95, yes."

Taking another big sip from his scotch, Admiral Wildason moves the drink around in his mouth before swallowing. "I imagine that to be difficult."

Kieran huffs. "It was. To a degree I could communicate with… *them*, but it wasn't like we're talking now. In the end it helped—will help—us to establish a dialogue and for our people to understand each other, so even though I was trapped, I did something good, but I wouldn't necessarily recommend the experience."

Kudos to him for not mentioning the Essken-slash-Quaneez by name. Kieran might be new to time-traveling, but he definitely isn't new to limiting information. And he isn't new to tailoring said information either, in this case for his dad's benefit. We both know the last thirty-five years of living a nightmare were anything else but as easy as he just made it seem.

I give him a small smile in support. "Still better than being killed by a madman." At least he survived. He'll be okay, eventually.

The admiral freezes with his drink halfway to his mouth. "What did you just say?"

My cheeks heat up. "Uh, better than being killed by a madman?"

"Why would you say that?" Admiral Wildason tilts his head, eyes narrowed and gaze sharp, as if I'd given him a buzzword he'd been waiting for.

Whoops. Well done, FBTI-officer Thorburn. Kieran one, Nonie zero. "I'm sorry, Niall, I just said that without thinking. We're trying to not ruin the timeline. There are things we cannot tell you, just as you cannot act on anything you learn from us. Do you understand that?" The last thing we need is adding more problems to the ones we already have.

Niall waves his hand in an impatient manner. "Of course, that's a given. I took temporal mechanics at the academy. But tell me, why would you say *better than being killed by a madman?*"

Ugh. He won't let go. I sigh and focus on my First Sense. It feels… huh, encouraging, in a manner of speaking. I tilt my head and keep a close eye on Kieran's father. "Because my job description was hunting down a madman who was traveling through time, tasked to kill Kieran."

A muscle works in the admiral's jaw. He sits completely still, unblinking. Not even sure if he's breathing—

He slams his palm onto the PAD on his left. "Initiate protocol Wildason Alpha Three."

"*Acknowledged,*" the PAD replies, and *pop*, a little forcefield springs to life around the gazebo, shimmering and distorting the view the slightest.

"A vision shield?" Kieran raises an eyebrow and leans forward, forearms resting on his legs. "Now you have me curious, Dad."

"One can never be too careful, as I've learned over my eighty-six years." Sitting the drink back down, he leans forward, looking so much like his son in the same position, I'm in awe of genetics. Looking at his dad, I get an idea what Kieran will look like as an old man. He's going to age well, I predict.

"Why would you need to be careful right now, Dad?" Worry creeps into Kieran's voice. I remember him telling me about his dad's tendency for paranoia. It was his idea to install the secret drawer in the desk on the *Pioneer*, old-fashioned, but effective. I have the strangest urge to ask him if he knew Kieran kept chocolate in it, and not, as probably intended, USEF-secrets.

Niall's expression hardens. "Because I have a quite explosive theory I've been working on ever since your mom died."

Oh. Kieran and I exchange a look. That sounds like the paranoia I heard about.

Kieran pinches his nose and sighs. "Dad—"

"No. Don't start. I know what you're going to say, and I don't want to hear it."

"But—"

"No, *Captain.*"

Kieran rolls his eyes, then lifts both hands in an I-give-up gesture. "You don't need to pull rank on me, Dad. Go ahead, I'm listening."

His dad harrumphs. "And keeping an open mind, as you asked me to do."

Kieran takes a deep breath, but before he can respond with something he might regret later, I squeeze his thigh. Hard. "Yes, we will."

"Thank you." The admiral leans back and takes the PAD out of its charge pod on the table. He glides one finger over the screen, and the vision shield darkens the light shining in.

"Aren't you exaggerating a bit?" Kieran raises one brow.

"I want to show you something. And I don't want to announce it to the world."

More like to a bunch of squirrels and gophers or so, but okay.

Niall flicks his gaze to me. "Have you ever heard about the *Journey* incident?"

"Of course I have. The *Journey*'s drive malfunctioned and she exploded. After that, we limited jumps to avoid the strain on the drive we assume caused the issue." I keep my voice even. It's been forever for both men, but Niall's wife, Kieran's mom, was on that ship. Kieran once told me he was supposed to be on it as well, but luckily his dad had taken him to a conference instead.

"Correct. You know, for the longest time, I thought it was an accident. I considered myself lucky, to a degree, to only have lost my wife, and not you as well." The admiral puts *only* in air quotes. "Especially after you survived Addi shooting you. But when you died— or rather, presumably died—in that nebula, something changed for me. Call it a hunch, but I tried to look for a connection."

Kieran narrows his brows. "Dad, none of that is connected. The *Journey* was an accident. I wasn't even on it—"

"But you were supposed to be, you know that. Your name was still on the crew manifest."

"Yes, but I *wasn't* on it. And I went into that nebula out of my own free will. I really did. There's no conspiracy, Dad. There just isn't. Not this time."

The admiral scrolls through something on his PAD, then flicks his hand and throws the image into the air. "There's no conspiracy? Then look at this for me, will you? This is the duty roster for the *Journey*'s engineering when she was in space dock and getting her overhaul right before she left on her last mission." He circles a finger around the top area, where it says *drive functionality*. "Do you see those five names here? Burton, Pomm, Jimenez, Siddik and Wang? Those are the only people who worked on the *Journey*'s drive." He pulls up another document and displays it in the middle between us, so that it hovers over the wicker table in the center of the seating arrangement.

"Okay," Kieran says. "Only those people worked on it. That's not unusual though. The jump drive isn't easy to work on. It takes many certifications and qualifications to be even allowed near it. I wouldn't expect as many people working on the drive itself during an overhaul as, let's say, on the communications grid. Or the weapons."

Lifting a finger, Niall taps something else on the pad. "I agree. But look at this—this is cut together from their service records."

Kieran narrows his eyes. "Why do you have access to their service records?"

"Because I have friends in high places," Niall replies, keeping his face perfectly blank.

Knowing Kieran, he has about a hundred comments to that, but kudos to him, he keeps them all bottled up.

"Anyway." Niall scoots forward, pointing at each name as he comments on that person. "Burton. Left USEF six months later. Pomm, eight months. Jimenez, nine. Siddik, same. Wang stayed another two weeks, then she was gone, too."

"Huh," I say. "Agree, that's odd. If you're a highly-specialized jump-drive engineer, there aren't really many other opportunities outside USEF." Only two private shipyards manufacture all jump-capable private and commercial ships, and that's it. They share one space dock close to Pluto for repairs, but that one has a bad reputation. I wouldn't think people were eager to leave a well-paid USEF-position for either of those options.

Niall snaps his fingers. "Thank you for agreeing. Turnover in engineering is very low in USEF, so that struck me as odd. But what I found even more concerning is this."

The image between us changes to five smaller lists, each with one name highlighted.

"Every single one of these five people joined Humanity First right after they were off the USEF's radar." He claps his hands together once. "What do you say to that?"

I whistle through my teeth. Humanity First—I don't know if there has ever been a more annoying political group. The only positive thing to say about their movement is that it killed the last of racism amongst ourselves—but the bad news is they extended that same racism to other cultures. Even in my time, so many politicians and people with what I thought should be common sense are also members of Humanity First, it's frightening. Case in point, a good amount of USEF captains moving to attack the Essken before Kieran convinced them to hold their fire.

Kieran massages his chin, looking over the data sheets. "Not that I memorized all their release dates from USEF, but they all seem to have joined Humanity First about six months after they left."

Niall nods. "They all joined on the day six months later. Why, you ask? Because that's when USEF stops its counter-intelligence surveillance on former employees. And it gets even better, because look here. This is from their annual worldwide party convention that year, after all of the former USEF engineers had joined." He replaces the lists with a new document. "They filled all executive positions in the party that day. And look who scored."

It takes both of us a second to scan over the document, but there they are. All five names pop up behind a job description. Treasury—Pomm. Internal affairs—Burton. Wang even made secretary. They all were voted into higher positions within their organization.

Kieran's dad leans back. "I for one would think it unusual for five newbies to be trusted with those highly sought-after positions, wouldn't you agree?"

My jaw hardens. "You're thinking since they were appointed so shortly after they joined, they must have been associated with Humanity First before."

"Bingo. USEF doesn't let you enlist if you're a member of Humanity First or any other radical organization. I'm not saying that we're free of sympathizers, but no active USEF officer can also be an active member with Humanity First."

Kieran shakes his head. "So, what you're really trying to say when connecting all those dots, is that these people, and therefore Humanity

First, might have tampered with the drive and gotten it to explode? But why?"

"Bingo again." Niall points his index finger at his son. "Here's where my conspiracy theory comes in. Is it a coincidence you should've been on that ship? That you were assassinated three years later? Then—"

"Addi wasn't a member of Humanity First. That's ridiculous."

"Granted, that's where my theory becomes a bit more wobbly, but—"

"Dad…" Kieran lets his head hang.

"Nu-uh, keep an open mind, because it's getting even stranger."

"I really doubt that," Kieran murmurs, ignoring the glaring glance from his dad.

The admiral projects a new image into the air.

Kieran groans. "A finance statement? Of Humanity First? Dad, that's confidential information—"

"And again, I have friends in high places. Please look at these high sums donated to Humanity First. They all came in the day after Pomm was put in charge of treasury." He circles several donations, all in the millions, all from different accounts.

"Now see why I'm saying it's strange." He swipes again, and the image changes. The account numbers of the donors get highlighted. Then, names appear next to them.

"These people donated the money. But they're normal people. They don't have that kind of money. All of them got it from somebody else."

Arrows appear next to each transaction, all leading to a new name at their ends.

"But those people are also just normal people without a fortune to donate, meaning…"

More arrows appear, pointing at new names.

"So, we play this game another one, two, three, four times…" With each count, new arrows and names appear. "… and then we have one universal donor who spread their wealth to those people, who then passed it on."

Kieran laughs out harsh. "Money laundering. Wow. I didn't expect that, but I guess I should have with a party like Humanity First."

His dad cuts him a glance. "You should have suspected that, but you probably would never have expected who donated the money in the first place."

"Do I even want to know?" Kieran asks.

"Probably not, but I'm telling you anyway." One more swipe, and all arrows point to a final name and a picture of a black-haired woman next to it:

*Tala Torona.*

"A— A Magellan?" I blink, as if it could change what I'm seeing, but no, of course it doesn't.

Niall nods. "I'm as confused as you are. We know Magellans, while keeping to themselves, are a very open society. They're actively working to improve their relationship with us. We helped relocate them from Alpha Rubrum to Mag-2. Our peoples are friends. Or so I thought."

"Maybe not everybody agrees," Kieran says. "They're entitled to their opinion."

"That they are. But why go through the trouble of hiding their donation?"

And why would they support a group that actively fights anything Magellan? "Maybe they don't want to—"

"Or maybe something else is going on. The *Journey* explodes after five engineers have certified a well-functioning drive, all five of them leave USEF within the next ten months, not too soon and not too many at a time to draw attention to it, but they leave. They all join Humanity First as soon as USEF surveillance drops out. They all get voted into high positions, suggesting previous involvement and engagement, maybe even some kind of reward being dished out, and once they are, they receive high sums of money through questionable channels from a Magellan, like a payment. Tell me that doesn't sound off to you." The admiral crosses his arms in front of his chest.

"Well," I say, looking at Kieran and then back at his dad, "I think we do find that suspicious, but I fail to see a connection to Kieran."

Rubbing the bridge of his nose, Kieran leans back. "Nonie is right, Dad. When you put it like that… I agree, your reasoning is solid. But it sounds so far off, a Magellan supporting murder on a grand scale…"

"So, it did—and still does—to me. Here's the sad thing. I saw your reaction." He nods at me. "This was news to you, wasn't it? And that means that even in your time, nobody has held the people responsible for this disaster accountable." His shoulders droop forward and the glimmer in his eyes dim. "Of course, that could mean I'm on a complete witch hunt, but excuse me if hearing that somebody was out to kill my son— who was supposed to be on the *Journey*, who survived an assassination attempt by somebody we trusted—makes me a tad nervous. What if what you're talking about is also connected to the *Journey*? To everything? What if I'm missing the big picture? What if—"

Twigs crack, followed by a loud curse and a voice screaming: "Hey! Hands in the air! Hands up! Up!"

All three of us jerk from the unexpected yell coming from the right. We jump up to standing—

Oh, crap. "Sheridan," I hiss. How in the name of the universe did he find us? We're the needle in a haystack!

Sheridan keeps his rifle up as he prowls forward, carefully setting one foot in front of the other, aiming at us through a small screen hovering over the weapon's sights. "That's a cute vision shield you got there, but a tad behind the times, from where I'm coming from. Let's make this short and sweet. You're needed in the future. Time for your court martial."

"Oh, now it's a court martial?" Kieran calls out, sarcasm in his voice. "We got an upgrade."

Sheridan shrugs without moving the weapon off-target. "It should be, in my opinion."

No, it should not! "We have evidence somebody is tampering with the timeline! Somebody from our future!" Am I happy I picked up the disc earlier. Would just be my luck leaving it amidst the roses.

Niall flicks his gaze over to me, full of shock. Well, now he knows. Sorry.

Keeping his focus on us, Sheridan's steps only falter the slightest before he steps out of the bushes onto the path leading to the gazebo. "Evidence for tampering with the timeline. Really. *Great.* I'm sure the judge and the Taro will be very much open to hearing it, especially coming from the two of you." Sarcasm drips from his voice.

I take one step forward, dropping my hands. "You haven't even seen—"

"Hands up and stop right where you are!" He swings the rifle to aim directly at me.

It works. I freeze and inch my hands back up, sour rage rising like bile.

Sheridan sighs. "Look. I get that you're good people at baseline. I do. But I also have seen the evidence against you, and it's clear and unambiguous. And don't even think about it, there's no escaping me, and I don't even mean to be arrogant here. Our technology is superior, our knowledge is superior. You can't hide your Setayashi-trace. Even if you run, I'll find you, wherever you hide."

Our Setayashi-trace! That's how he found us. I curse under my breath.

"Finding doesn't equal taking us back," Kieran says.

Sheridan sighs once more, almost apologetically. "Unfortunately for you, it does."

"Fortunately for us, it doesn't."

Kieran's words and tone should've given Sheridan a hint, but I guess counting your chickens before they're hatched is a common mistake if you're the one with the weapon and the others aren't. To me, it's obvious he has an ace up his sleeve, something to get us out of this situation, like—

Kieran snatches his dad's rifle off the table and fires in the general direction of Sheridan while bringing it up to his shoulder.

I suck in a shocked breath. He fired first? That's so not Kieran! He wouldn't—

Sheridan yelps and jumps behind the same bush he ruined already, not that the plant would help him much had Kieran actually aimed at the agent.

Niall curses under his breath, but, as if they had rehearsed it, and not wasting the moment of opportunity and distraction, he slams his hand onto the PAD. "Emergency Beta-Two!"

With a little pinging sound, a forcefield pops up around us, distorting Sheridan's frustrated outcry. "Seriously? I was trying to not shoot at you, and that's what I get? So that's the game we're playing!" He jumps out from behind the bush and fires at the gazebo. As soon as the charge hits the forcefield, bright blue tendrils of energy sizzle over the barrier, like fingers searching for an opening, a weakness to exploit. Tiny little explosions pop up along the forcefield, something I've never seen happen before. Whatever these weapons are, their ammo is quite something.

Sheridan fires again, his shots landing precisely in the same area, all with the same result, only those explosions grow in number every time a charge hits.

"We don't have long," Niall calls out, panting, blood drained from his face. "The power is down by half already. What do we—?"

"He wants nothing with you, he only wants us." That's what I hope. Sheridan can't be stupid enough to remove Niall from the timeline. This, his current behavior, is already idiotic and damaging enough, especially for a self-proclaimed protector of the timeline, but that being said, we started it when Kieran fired first.

Sheridan keeps his focus and aim on the same spot as he fires in rapid succession at the forcefield. Nausea rises, courtesy of my First Sense. In a distant part of my conscience, I realize that's progress, because a few months ago my PTSD would've been triggered hard by all the shots. Now? Please. I've been through stuff lately. All Sheridan is doing is making me mad. Shooting at us *and* a native of this time? Not cool, First Executioner, not cool!

The admiral's expression hardens. "He wants you? Not on my watch. Give me that." He takes his rifle back from Kieran. "Get behind me. Both of you."

With Sheridan's last shot, the forcefield flickers. Crap. It's not going to hold much longer, and we all know it. Sheridan's inching forward with each shot, probably readying himself to grab us and jump us back to his time once the path is cleared.

We only have one way out, ironically a similar one Sheridan would've used, with minor differences in the details. I thrust my hand into my pocket and bring out the disk. "Kieran! Hold on to me. Niall—he won't do anything to you, please don't antagonize him!"

"Don't antagonize him? He's antagonizing *me*!"

Kieran smacks his dad over the head, lovingly and a tad desperate. "Dad!"

I press the button on the disk, feeling the radiation open my senses to the Maelstrom.

"No!" Sheridan curses and increases his assault to continued fire.

"Dad, get cover!"

Niall lifts the rifle to his shoulder. "I'll cover my a—"

I feel my body hum and tingle.

With a tiny *ping,* the forcefield snuffs out.

"Showtime," Niall says, and pulls the trigger.

Sheridan curses louder, Niall snickers, and the world turns blurry, as I pull Kieran and myself into the Maelstrom.

# Chapter Ten –
# Left Field

**The Maelstrom**

*This time I'm making it quick. I need a place to hide us, to think, to regroup. Where can we go, when can we go, when I'm sure Sheridan is going to follow us? How can we hide if he's using our Setayashi-trace to find us? I hold on to Kieran with all my might.*

*Time swirls, different strands billowing up and out, others retreating—Oh heck, yes, I got it!*

*I focus on the exact moment, the location, the feeling of the place I want to land, and—*

Kieran and I land standing upright, the shock of being slammed into solid ground reverberating through my body and compressing my spine. With an *oomph*-sound we stumble forward—and right into a wall of people standing slightly lower than us. Somebody behind us hisses. "Seriously? Dematting into an audience this late? What the hell is wrong with you?"

At the same time, the two people we pushed forward as we landed turn, anger on their faces. "Cut it out, it's not as if we could see more than you!" The one guy twists his shoulder away from where I grasped him to not fall, while the other one looks at Kieran like he'd seen a ghost, then shakes his head and directs his attention back to the front.

"*… the universe is a big place. Believe me, I've spent quite a while exploring it. It's big, and foreign, and sometimes a very scary place with deceiving beauty. It has taught me many things, one of them—*"

The moment it clicks for Kieran is the moment he sucks in a sharp breath through his teeth. "The Golden Star of Combat! My acceptance speech," he whispers at me under his breath. I nod and lay one finger across my lips, then grab him by the hand. We need to hide amongst these people, but also need to find a spot to talk, and preferably one where people don't look at Kieran like the guy we bumped into just did. Luckily, we're moderately high up in the arena—

A bright flash and quick outcry coming from the top of the venue catch my attention. I cringe. Yeah. Let's go to the aisle on the *other* side, because a slightly younger, very frustrated Nonie is going to come down the middle aisle in a minute or so.

I lead Kieran past the people seated or standing in our row. Most are annoyed at us for the intrusion and distraction. More than one or two throw us angry glances I wish they didn't. A woman in her early twenties, although she's keeping her gaze fixed to the stage, squeals under her breath.

"He's so cute! So heroic!" She clutches both hands to her chest. "*So cute!*"

Kieran, in lieu of other disguises, jams his chin all the way down to his chest and slumps his shoulders forward, the tension radiating off him doubling.

Nope, Kieran has never been a fan of his fan club. At least nobody's throwing bras. Yet, maybe.

Once we pass that woman, he tugs on my hand. "Do you think he's okay?" he whispers under his breath, loud enough for me to hear.

"Dad?"

I nod and keep pulling him with me. Sheridan doesn't want Niall, as I said. He also wants his future intact—something he should've kept in mind when he started firing at the gazebo, just saying. But yes, I think Niall is fine.

I hope.

My heart is thumping so loudly, I expect people to complain about that, too, but my main concern is of different origin. Every few steps, I throw a look back. Is Sheridan here yet? Would he even follow to the exact point, time and location? How? He hasn't yet popped up, maybe that's a good sign. Maybe his jumps are limited, just like with my SED. Maybe finding us is more complicated than he let on—heck, that's why I landed us here!

"We're trying to listen here!" A middle-aged man stands up to let us pass, glaring at us. "Get going, ma—" He stops himself when his gaze falls on Kieran, who turns his head. Only too late. The man narrows his eyes. "Are you—"

"There you are!" A woman pushes through the row toward us. "Come on!" She wears a long black sweater-dress, its hood pulled over her face hiding her features. A little bit of long black hair peeks out from underneath, maybe with the tad of a shimmer…? "Sorry," she says to the man as she's handing Kieran a baseball cap. "My cousin has issues." She sounds like she's smiling, even though I can't see her face.

With only a moment of hesitation, Kieran takes the cap and slides it onto his head. He pulls it deep into his face, but still keeps his hunched posture.

Grabbing us, the woman pulls out of the row and into the aisle.

Uhh—

"Keep walking, keep walking," she says, and turns into a small alcove to our right people use for picnics. It's made from the same material as this whole arena, a marble-like stone with a remarkable pink glitter and shine, depending on how the light hits it. This alcove is empty, probably since there's no stage view from here because of the little chest-high wall on all four sides. The table and two benches in the middle of it make this the perfect secluded picnic spot, but bad for following what's happening on stage.

The woman slides behind the table on one side and gestures at the other one. "Sit."

Kieran and I exchange a glance.

Humor laces her voice when she speaks again. "Your First Sense should tell you it's okay. Mine does." And with that she lowers her hood.

Long, shiny black hair frames a face so similar to my own we could be sisters. Her nose has the same upturn as mine, her cheeks the same high jawbones. Her lips are fuller, but I guess I gotta have gotten something from my dad.

"Mom," I whisper, then realize what I just did and slap a hand across my mouth. "Shit!" Way to go, Lieutenant! I'm not even born yet in this time and here I go and *mom* her!

A small laugh escapes her. "Don't worry about it. I know." She winks at me. "Come on, sit down, before your... your father wonders where I am." She blushes at the word *father*.

Right.

I swallow dry as I slide into the bench across from her. "I... I didn't know you were here." And by *you* I really mean both of them. I don't think Dad ever talked about attending Kieran's ceremony, not that I assume he talked about everything he did before I was born, but this sounds like an event worth mentioning.

My mom's smile grows. "I don't very often get the chance to see my space-faring brother, so we made it a trip."

Zio! "Right," I say. I'm kind of stuck mentally. Seeing my mom in the hut and actually interacting with her are two very different things.

Kieran keeps looking from her to me, and back, then shakes his head. "Excuse me." He takes me by the elbow and pulls me off the bench and to the side.

"What are we doing here?" he whispers. "I get it I shouldn't have brought us to my dad, but now you brought us to your mom—"

"I did not *bring us to my mom*," I hiss. Nu-uh, that was so not on purpose! "I chose this location, because I thought if Sheridan is looking for abnormal Setayashi-traces in the time stream, we could hide here."

Understanding flashes in Kieran's eyes. "Because you're here already. With the *Pioneer* for the ceremony. Which he should know about."

"Yeah. I'm somewhere there, frustrated." I nod my chin toward the audience and frown. "I didn't know my mom was going to be here. Had I known, I would've chosen some other time. It's not like there aren't any choices." It had felt right to jump to here and now, since I figured we could hide amongst the masses. Sheridan showed himself to Niall, but he can't possibly be stupid enough to contaminate a whole audience.

Again: I hope. Lots of hoping going on these days.

A little sting of worry shoots through me when I think of Niall, but I push it aside, then look at Kieran. "We need to discuss our next step. I'm not so confident anymore that we'll find open minds and ears when we present the evidence to the court. Not after what Sheridan said." *Clear and unambiguous evidence* against us. Sounds to me like innocent until proven guilty is not high on his list of priorities.

Kieran presses his lips into a tight line. "Agreed. But what would help us? Any proof of the Temporal War, of course, so more information that somebody is messing with time. But what kind of proof would that be and where can we find it?"

I shrug. "Good question. We need to look at the data on this disk and see what we can get from it. But yeah, you're right, we'll have to find a way to prove to the court the timeline is being tampered—"

My mom clears her throat. "I get it you're trying to keep time-sensitive info to yourselves, but you know that I'm a temporal specialist, right?" My mom raises a hand and waves it. "I'm just going to assume you have questions, or else I wouldn't know why my First Sense alerted me to your presence."

Mom was a temporal specialist? What else don't I know about her? Not that Dad could've known I'd need a temporal specialist in my life later, but he could've mentioned it!

As soon as I think it I take it back. He knew from the moment he saw Star Hopper after my kidnapping I would travel through time.

Maybe he was trying to not influence me in any way. Maybe he was doing the right thing, or at least trying to.

"I'm waiting," my mom says, tapping her fingers on the table.

Kieran and I exchange a glance. "You're the boss," he says, pointing at my stomach, like my First Sense sat there, and who knows, maybe it does. It doesn't act up, that's for sure. I'll never understand that thing—especially not after Mom said hers alerted her to us. She didn't come to see me last time I was here, when I was chasing Mashaule. This time, she picked us right out of the crowd.

Not a skill I could call my own.

Sighing, I nod at Kieran, then slide onto the bench behind the table again, Kieran following suit. "How did your First Sense know about us?"

She lifts and drops one shoulder. "My First Sense differs from many others'. It's why I'm in temporal mechanics. It's why I know who you are, which makes me slightly uncomfortable, I mean, Tom and I have been together for not even two years, so…" She cringes.

"I get that feeling," I murmur, thinking back to Kaytee, who's barely older than me, but decades younger, and my great-granddaughter. "How old are you anyway?"

"Twenty."

Kieran laughs softly. "Well, that makes me the senior in this group."

"And me slightly concerned, because if my First Sense is not mistaken, you're going to be my son-in-law. Which is really confusing, since *you* are giving a speech down there right now and *you* haven't even been born. Or even talked about," she adds under her breath.

I cock my head. "You know all this from your First Sense?" That's *so* not what I'm getting from my First Sense. I feel a tad cheated here.

"Yes, but it's not like a newsflash where suddenly all this knowledge pops up in my head. It's more a slow development. Like, I've been feeling off all day, anticipatory jitters, I guess. I had a *hunch* when Tom and I got drinks, which is now why you're wearing his favorite cap that he thinks he lost when he put it down." She points at Kieran's black hat with a golden symbol on it, *Academy Debate Team* embroidered on it. "Then, finally, I felt the disruption in time, which is why I came looking for you. I wouldn't call it a compulsion, but more like an imperative urge to find you. Maybe… maybe like some animals just know how to build a burrow, or just know how to do certain things. All I have to do is listen to my instincts."

Kieran raises a brow. "It still sounds quite confusing to interpret."

Mom snorts once. "No kidding. But hey, it's not as confusing as when I saw you on Alpha Rubrum and had a similar information dump. That one really messed with my brain. Thanks for not ratting us out to Tom's Captain, by the way."

"You're welcome," Kieran says, with a tiny bow of his head. "Wasn't a tough choice to make, uhh—"

"Kelia. And you're obviously Kieran Wildason, and you, Thorburn junior…" She taps a finger against her lips, thinking. "If Tom has his will, you might be named after some human athlete, but if I have my will… You're either Heather or Nonie."

I cringe. "You made the better choice. I'm Nonie."

Kelia beams. "Good to know I got my will, not Tom."

Indeed. I don't feel like a Heather, or like being named after a soccer player.

Somewhere outside our little alcove something clatters to the ground and breaks, probably a glass of sorts and a sound quite common in a public area where drinks are served, yet it makes me twitch and throw a nervous glance over my shoulder. How long will it take Sheridan to figure out where we are?

Kelia tilts her head. "You're running from somebody."

Either her First Sense really beats mine by a mile, or I'm just that obvious. I sigh. "Unfortunately. I'm not sure what I can tell you—"

"I know that some Magellans have a higher affinity for time, like myself. I can deduce, seeing you here, that you can travel through time. That's probably the combo with Tom's genes, I would guess. And since you're nervous somebody is following you, I'm also assuming that somewhen on the timeline something went wrong, and now you're trying to stay away from whoever is chasing you." She dusts off her palms, a pleased expression on her face.

"Well." Kieran scratches his head. "That's pretty much spot on."

I sit up straighter. "Okay, since you're a temporal specialist and your First Sense seems to be better than mine, tell me what we can do to convince somebody the timeline has been messed with. How do you prove somebody changed something." And keep them from doing it again, preferably. One step at a time though.

"Within your own timeline?" She shrugs. "You can't."

I groan. That's not what I wanted to hea— Wait. "Within *my own* timeline? There's only one—"

She looks at me, like, *really?*

I snap my mouth shut. Then open it. Then shut it again.

"Speechless?" Kelia grins. "You'd be right in line with ninety-nine percent of Magellans. My opinion isn't very popular." Her face falls. "Well. Judging by your surprise, it won't become popular either. Damn."

Kieran rests his forearms on the table and folds his hands. "Keep in mind I'm the one without temporal affinity here. I'm afraid I need a bit more of an explanation."

She sighs once and shakes off her frustration. "Look. You know there are infinite possibilities how anything can play out. I could've given you no hat. Or a different one. That's a minor change—"

"And the timeline would smooth out again, because it doesn't change the outcome."

Kelia—my *mom*—levels me with a glance I imagine I would've been the lucky recipient of quite a few times in my life had she been around when I grew up. "Not necessarily. Imagine I didn't bring a hat, and people recognized Kieran. Could've led to quite the chaos and the disruption of the speech, caught the attention of the media, et cetera, et cetera. Get my point?"

We both nod.

"Okay, anyway, there are multiple realities existing next to each other, every one slightly different to the next, if there's a reason for a split-off. It's quite fascinating thinking it through, isn't it?"

But wait... "And you're saying those other realities don't cease to exist?"

"Why would they?"

"Why would they not?"

"Because reality doesn't function like that. Mind you, I'm still in my studies, but I'm working on it. My plan is to come up with the mathematical and physical proof of the existence of a multiverse. I can guarantee you it exists."

I chew on my lower lip. A multiverse… timelines changing and not ending, but continuing on. It should sound absurd, but… I saw it with my own eyes: Other Nonie and the other, older, Kieran. She thought she was the main timeline, and I thought the same. What if we were both right, and nobody was in an off-branch designated to cease to exist?

It would be one heck of a game changer with ginormous implications.

Drawing in a leg, I turn to Kieran. "I think… I think she's right." All of a sudden, I feel small and lost. The world was big when space opened up to us. It felt even bigger when I learned there was a past I could travel to—and now? Knowing there are infinite multiverses, all with their own past and future? Feeling insignificant doesn't quite cut it. Inconsequential, maybe, but even that doesn't capture the utter feeling of unimportance threatening to overwhelm me. The world is big. Much bigger than I thought.

Surprise pulls Kieran's eyebrows up his forehead. "She's right? Isn't that against all theories—"

"Yes, but I've seen it." How I imagined time to work might've been a bit naive. There's no straight flow. There are bends and turns and paths started but not finished, yet others break free and continue on, forming a new timeline, and therefore a new world. A world I have seen.

"You have?" both say in unison, equally perplexed.

"I have. Once I jumped when I couldn't quite control what I was doing, and I got thrown off course." Courtesy of hearing Kieran's screams when I touched the Realm's strand. "I met myself. I met you, Kieran. Only… Only I was still my age, and you were old." That moment when I recognized his voice and then realized he was old, that he hadn't died… mind blown. Completely. How I had wished it was my timeline, how I'd longed for it—because I still believed Kieran to have died in that nebula.

Holy Universe—*that nebula!* I slam both palms onto the table. "Kieran, you didn't go into that nebula in that universe! And clearly you— " Whoops. My First Sense flares up. Caution, Thorburn! "Sorry." I grimace at Kelia and turn to whisper into Kieran's ear. "And clearly you weren't assaulted by Mashaule either. Another me was there, and she was different. She wasn't good at fighting—"

He pulls away to whisper a response into my ear, but I grab him and hold him right there. "I know what you want to say, that's not a big difference, but it is! I became good at fighting because of my kidnapping! If that other me isn't a fighter, maybe she never got kidnapped! And since the kidnappers were from the future and had one of those disks…" I pat my pocket with one hand, and release Kieran waiting for him to do the math. Maybe Other Nonie's timeline doesn't have a Temporal War, it would make sense!

He cocks his head to the side, letting my theory sink in. His chest heaves up and down quicker than normal. "It's a good thought."

"Thank you." I happen to agree, and it feels good to finally have something to work with. Like we finally had a leg up and weren't mere play balls of the future and the Temporal War.

We both direct our attention back to Kelia. "I guess I know where to start. Thank you, seriously. I can guarantee you, I wouldn't have thought in that direction."

"Few people do, you know? Happy I could help though. And if you don't need me anymore, I'd probably take off before Tom comes looking for me and this gets even more awkward." She slides out from under the bench. "It was really good meeting you, Nonie, and to see you again, Captain."

Kieran smiles at her. "Kieran. I want to ask you to say hi to Tom, but I guess that wouldn't be a good idea."

"Probably not." She swipes a strand of hair behind her ear, the gesture so similar to mine, it squeezes my heart. Before she can leave, I jump up.

"Wait."

Kelia gives me a questioning look and I feel my cheeks heat. I'm usually not this needy, but in this case… I wrap my arms around her and squeeze. "Thank you. That really helped a lot."

For a moment, she's stiff in my arms, then relaxes and returns the hug. I get it must be weird for her, hugging a daughter she didn't know she was going to have. I mean, same for me with Kaytee. I bet Kelia knows this means more to me than to her, but I'm still glad I said what I did and not what I thought. *I'm so happy I met you.*

Eventually we let go of each other. Kelia's lips spread into a full smile as she waves. "I'll see you in a couple of years!"

It costs me the strength of moving a mountain to keep my smile up and return her wave. She fake-salutes to Kieran, and then she's left the alcove.

My smile fades.

No, she won't see me in a few decades.

She'll die in childbirth.

We'll never meet again.

# Chapter Eleven -

# Nonie Squared

*Gemini-Colony, Exploration Plaza, July 21ˢᵗ, 2256, 1522hrs*

I stare after my mom, eyes burning with unshed tears. Fate is mean. Time is mean. Both have been messing with my family for a while now, and so much that giving me the ability to travel through time is adding insult to injury. Yes, without this nifty skill, I would've never met her, but thanks to it, it hurts even more *not* having her.

Now I know what I lost.

Kieran steps up behind me and lays an arm around my shoulders. "I would offer you some of my chocolate to cheer you up, but unsurprisingly, I didn't grab it when Sheridan found us. Believe me, I'll add that to his tab."

I laugh out short, although it ends in a sniffle. "You sound so grumpy about that."

"Well, I didn't appreciate him shooting at us—at Dad—or making me leave my chocolate." He leans in, but I take a step back, tilting my head to the side.

"You shot at him first," I say. "You didn't even try to talk it out, or to stall. *You shot first.*" I cross my arms in front of my chest. That's so gung-ho and out of character for Kieran I wouldn't even considered it as an option.

The muscles in his jaw harden. "He was aiming a weapon at you and Dad. There are times that call for peaceful negotiations, but this wasn't one of them." He rubs both palms over my upper arms, slipping a concerned smile over his face. "But that's not what I wanted to talk about. I think I know what's going through your head. Don't focus on the what-ifs, Nonie. Take this as a gift." He kisses my temple, and I let him, filing this discussion for a later point in time.

Leaning into him I wrap my arms around his waist and exhale deeply. "You're right. It is a gift. And maybe I'm ungrateful focusing on what I lost rather on what I just found, but..." I lift and drop my shoulders.

"It's tough, I know. But take it from somebody who just found out they'll never see their dad again, yet miraculously got one last chance to connect with him less than half an hour ago. You have to see that as a blessing, not a curse. You can't let it pull you down."

I look up at him, eyes narrowed. "Surprisingly level considering I had my whole life to come to terms with not having a mom, while you found out about losing almost everybody in your life only a mere day ago."

A wistful expression settles on his face. "Agreed. And believe me, it's what I'm telling myself. Maybe, if I do it often enough, I'm going to believe it." A bit of hardness bleeds back into his words.

For a moment we stand in silence, letting the words of Kieran's acceptance speech wash over us.

"*...don't believe this is us. Making war. Shooting before talking. You can trust the* Pioneer *will be there for you to defend you. We won't stand down and ignore a threat to you, our family. But at the same time, we don't want to be a weapon of mass destruction mindlessly used. We—*"

Kieran pulls me in tighter and swallows hard. "I was a different man then. So young, and I don't mean in terms of age, but in terms of experience. So sure we could stop the war, if only we put our mind to it and resources behind it. So optimistic and believing in the best in humanity. And yet, the worst of the destruction it caused was still to come."

It is yet to scar and haunt him, he means, and I get it. All of it, and maybe even a bit why he reacted like he did at his dad's gazebo. "The Essken survived, you know that. We didn't kill them."

"I know that, and it takes some of the guilt off my shoulders. Only some though, because I still saw their suffering, the pain they went through every time we destroyed their ships. No, they didn't die. But what we did to them classifies as torture under the Geneva Conventions." Closing his eyes he inhales slowly, controlled, before he opens them again. "I can't help but think we should've ended this war a long time ago. I should've convinced humanity war wasn't the solution. We could've saved so many, prevented so much misery on both sides. I should've done more. I should've worked harder to get USEF to let me pursue my leads how to communicate—"

"Kieran, stop." I turn toward him and lay both my hands on his shoulders. "No. You can't bear the weight of the war on your shoulders. It's not on you. You do *not* carry the responsibility for how the war progressed. You did all you could to minimize casualties and find a better solution wherever it could be found. You—"

"Didn't do enough, period." His jaw hardens and he stares straight over my head. "But, in a twist of irony you surely appreciate, it's too late to change it. Or, maybe not, if I understood your mom correctly." He closes his eyes and takes a slow, deliberate breath in, opening them with the exhale, shifting his gaze back to me. "So, what's our plan to stop that Temporal War?"

A messy, yucky lump forms in my chest. Yes, Kieran is doing a remarkable job staying level-headed considering, well, everything, but once in a while, the façade cracks and the trauma underneath pokes out its ugly head. But, I can't fix any of it stuck in the past, on the run from Sheridan, and while trying to literally save our future.

Prioritizing sucks.

So, I do what anybody my age would do: I ignore the problem. Fixing a fast smile on my face, I pat his shoulders twice before letting go. "Our plan? We'll see what Other Nonie has to say. If we find the differences in her world, we find out who wants us out of the way, and we find the person pulling the strings of the Temporal War. Easy peasy, right?"

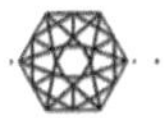

### *Hopefully: Other Nonie's Timeline*

Even before we slam into the carpeted floor, elation shoots through me: I did it!

In the split-second before gravity takes a hold of us and forces us into a stumbling unsteady crouch, I recognize the office. A familiar red sofa sits close to the wall across from the desk-and-chair combo in front of the large floor-to-ceiling windows. The same person behind the desk.

A grunt breaks from Kieran's throat as we land *behind the couch,* like I intended. Satisfaction floods me. Progress! I don't think I was ever this precise.

"You're back!"

Hearing *her* voice, Kieran wants to get up, but I pull him down again. "Me, first," I whisper, and he nods, making himself small behind the couch.

I stand up and raise a hand. "Hi! Yup, I'm back."

Other Nonie grins and gets out of her chair. "I was wondering if I'd ever see you again. Actually, I was hoping you'd come back."

Ah, cool. I did bring us back *after* our last meeting. Job surprisingly well done, Thorburn. Sometimes I amaze myself.

I shrug, like, no biggie. "You know, figured we should stay in touch. And, well, turns out I have a couple of questions for you."

"You know, we must be related, because I also have a lot of questions for you." She glances at her wrist PAD. "But you're not alone,

I see."

Of course, she'd check her PAD. Which makes me realize. "No alarm today?" Last time there was an alert when I landed, and I assume that's what ultimately brought this timeline's FBTI onto me.

She rolls her eyes. "Disabled that feature and equipped my PAD with it. Quite inconvenient how that went last time. Figured this gave me more control and them less. Good combo." She wiggles her eyebrows. "So, you brought…?"

Yeah. "I brought…" The man you're in love with? The man I'm in love with? I breathe a heavy sigh. "Come on up."

Kieran stands up from behind the couch, the cap my mom gave him a tad askew, and I swear Other Nonie's face loses all color in a heartbeat. Her mouth opens and closes, her eyes are wide as saucers, and I don't think she's breathing.

I suppress a cringe. Slightly embarrassing to see myself that obviously affected by Kieran. I mean, I am, but I hope I keep it under control a bit better.

I gesture at Kieran, then her. "I think you know who the other one is, but still: Nonie, meet Kieran. Kieran, Nonie."

"Hi," Kieran says, looking at her with curiosity. "Always good to meet another Nonie." He smiles and Other Nonie turns from white as a sheet to red as a beet.

"H-hi." She clears her throat and drops her gaze. "This is unexpected."

"Well, we had some unexpected complications we'd need some help with." I motion for Kieran to follow, and we step out from behind the couch. "I figured I'd ask someone I trust." Lame joke, but it breaks the tension.

Other Nonie chuckles. "You've come to the right place then." She gives me jazz hands, then points at the couch we just appeared behind. "What can I help you with?"

Kieran and I sit down, while Other Nonie grabs the chair on the other side of the desk and brings it over for herself. It is, by the way, quite odd to see yourself as an observer. Never noticed we Nonies don't move as gracefully as I imagined us to. Sigh.

Anyway. I take a moment to collect myself. "Well, we have an issue I'm not quite sure how to break to you. Remember when we found out that we must be from different timelines instead of being each others' future or past, because there were too many differences between us? And in our worlds?" I pat Kieran's leg twice, and she gets it.

"Believe me, I remember. But I also remember specifically what you told me after you saw my Admiral Wildason." She lifts a brow and gives a pointed look at Kieran.

I lower my head in a slow nod. "Yes. Obviously, things have changed since then. At that point I still believed Kieran had died, but shortly after that, I found out that he was in the Essken Realm. Long story short, I got him out—"

"But that's not the problem," Kieran says, cutting to the chase. "We're accused—wrongly, I might add—in a Temporal War we have nothing to do with. Or, maybe we do." He nudges his shoulder into mine, a move the Other Nonie doesn't miss, not the way she watches us. Neither did she miss how close we're sitting together. Or how I patted Kieran's knee. She takes it all in without a comment or change in her expression, but I know her. I know *myself.* The wheels are turning.

"A Temporal War?" She glances from Kieran to me. "That's new."

But it's starting to feel real old, I must say. Sighing, I take over. "I wish. People want to kill us—people from our future. They've tried to do so several times throughout our lives, so if we want to stop the war, we need to find out why we were supposed to get killed, which will bring us one step closer to the responsible party and their goal. Does that make sense?"

Other Nonie scrunches up her mouth. "Carry on."

"That's why we're here. I remembered you said you weren't good at fighting. I remembered your Kieran, who was older. Ergo, there are differences between us, and it stands to reason they might be part of why people want us dead. We find out why you don't have headhunters after you, we hopefully find ours. Very convenient to have access to an alternate reality."

Her brows fly up. "What did you call us?"

"Uhh, an alternate reality?"

"Why?"

The way she looks at me, brows narrowed and lips pursed, I curse on the inside. Should I not have said anything? My First Sense isn't protesting, but does that mean I should go sprouting my theory everywhere? Heck, nobody in my time—or in the future we got abducted to—is entertaining alternate realities as a possibility at all!

She gives me a look I never thought I could pull off, all serious and intense. "Why, Nonie? Why do you now call us an alternate reality and not a split-off branch?"

And I know that tone as well. She won't let it go. I exhale harshly. "Because I don't believe anymore there's only one timeline, or that deviations get smoothed back in or cease to exist. I believe they split off and continue on their own." I hold her gaze. Didn't mean to throw that revelation at her out of nowhere, but apparently it needed to be said.

"So, you really don't believe anymore that our branch will disappear? Or yours?"

"No." I shake my head. "We spoke to… a temporal scientist who is convinced multiple realities exist. I think you're in yours, and we are in ours. It feels… right."

Other Nonie sucks her lip in, then breaks out into a wide grin. "You just passed your test. Congratulations."

Wait, what? "Congratulations?"

"For figuring it out. I knew you were a smart one." She wiggles her eyebrows at me, looking so at ease with my literally world-changing revelation, there's only one explanation.

"You knew." She knew there were different timelines, all existing together, none of them fading out.

"I did. We have known for a while."

I furrow my brows, feeling all kinds of irritated. If I had known split-offs didn't fade out or stop existing… I would've never let Kieran enter the nebula. I would've held him back and then dealt with the fallout of that action, no matter what that meant for *us*. I would've had a *choice.*

A bit of disbelief creeps into my next sentence, combined with hurt. "You lied to me. You said you'd never ended up in a timeline that wasn't yours."

She looks at me from under her lashes. "Sorry. Yes, I lied. I—"

"You said I quoted the handbook!" I cross my arms in front of my chest. She cheated me!

Other Nonie rolls her eyes. "Get over it, other me. I was fishing for information, since you didn't give me much. It's protocol, assessing what the other person knows, always has been since I confirmed the theory about stable alternate timelines. But in my defense, when you popped up in my office and I realized you were not a future-me but from a different timeline it was quite the shocker, even though we did know about the possibility." She shakes her head. "Mind blown. Theoretically, I knew there was a possibility somebody could come and visit. But then, we haven't found—or rather, hadn't found—another Nonie who could jump between timelines. And I didn't tell you, because we believe in independent development of every timeline. That's not an excuse, but again, protocol. If you find out, you find out, but we stay out of your business."

Staying out of my business, right. "You gave me your SED!" That definitely helped my business!

Other Nonie grimaces. "Don't point out my inconsistencies, okay? Just because we have a protocol… doesn't mean I always stick to it. I felt sorry for you."

I blow a raspberry, then chuckle. She tested me, and I failed because for all I knew there was only one timeline. Do I like being played? No. Can I understand it? Yes, so whatever, I need to let it go. "Looks like we're both rule benders, huh? Okay, points all taken, but sorry, I don't have such noble guidelines. I'm here, asking for help."

"And that makes all the difference. It's an active request on your part, so let's get you the help you need." She taps the Hablamate on her left upper chest. "Thorburn to Outreach. You're needed in my office." Tapping it once more, she closes the channel before the response.

Hey! Not cool!

I pop off the couch. "Excuse me? Calling in the cavalry?" I glare at her. "Last time your FBTI wanted to lock me away. I don't think this time it's going to be any better." It was a risk coming here, I knew that, but I had hoped the benefits would outweigh those risks.

"Easy," Other Nonie says. "I'm pretty optimistic you'll be fine with the cavalry. It'll be a bit awkward, but that's it."

"Why would it be—?"

The rest of the sentence gets stuck in my throat when the air shimmers in front of me and the outlines of three people solidify until they've rematted completely. Out of the corner of my eye I recognize person number two and three, but it's the first one, the one who appears right in front of me, who occupies a hundred percent of my processing power.

Kieran.

Last time I was here, I didn't have the chance to see him from close up, and even if I had, I probably would've declined. It would've been too painful to see the signs of aging on his face when they were denied to my Kieran.

But now there's no looking away, no lowering my eyes. Other Kieran's gaze snaps to mine the moment he turns solid, and it feels like… like home. Like I feel with my Kieran. Small wrinkles crinkle at both of his eyes as they narrow, and the lines around his mouth are more pronounced when he lifts one corner of his lips for a small smile, but he feels like Kieran. I don't know this person, but I feel like I do. My body insists we know each other.

"Lieutenant," Other Kieran says to me when I stay silent, an intense seriousness in his eyes. "What's going on?"

Maybe I shouldn't have made fun of Other Nonie before, because this time it's me who can't get a sound out. Only an embarrassing squeak leaves my throat—before I do what I should have done the second he materialized: I point a finger at behind Other Kieran, at Other Nonie, at the same time as somebody else mutters an expletive.

Other Kieran whirls around, takes in Other Nonie—

"Uhh, Kieran…?" Other Chase says.

"Yeah?" comes the reply from both of them, one getting off the couch, and the other turning to face the source of the second response.

"Interesting." Other Zio looks from me to Kieran to Other Nonie and Other Kieran. "Due to the combination of obvious age discrepancy and duplication I assume alternate reality rather than a temporal transfer from our own timeline?"

My eyes pop wide. "*Everybody* knows-knows about other timelines?" *Zio* knows it? I sat down with *my* Zio and asked him about it—all I got to hear was something along the lines of science supporting the main timeline-theory.

Other Nonie grins. "Told you the truth and nothing but the truth. They're helpers."

Other Kieran's face splits into a warm smile. "You look good so young," he says to Kieran.

"You don't look too bad older either," mine responds. Then they each take two fast steps and bro-hug it out.

O-kay. Less awkward than I would've expected had somebody ever asked me how a meeting of this kind would go.

Zio addresses me. "Do you know who we are? Is there a version of us in your reality?"

I nod. "Yes. Admiral Zio Upinga and Admiral Chase Conolly, called Trip. You're Kieran's best friends and my mentors at the Academy."

Chase chuckles. "Well, good to know some things stay the same."

I narrow my eyes. "Not all do though. Zio mentioned the age discrepancy—and now I'm curious too. You two are older than your Kieran. By a lot." Looking at them, Chase and Zio look like mine in my time, while Other Kieran… isn't that old. Older, but not old. It bugged me last time already, but I had other issues to take care of.

Other Kieran lets go of his counterpart. "I had an unfortunate incident in the Essken Realm. Nonie rescued me out of it in eighty-one, which is the reason why I look twenty-four years younger than Zio and Chase. I didn't age in the Realm." He scans over Kieran. "I assume that didn't happen to you, since you look what—early twenties? Captain of the *Pioneer*?"

My Kieran swallows hard. "Yes. Yes and no. I also was trapped in the Essken Realm, but I didn't get out until ninety-five, when Nonie found me." He says it free of accusation, yet I feel like the worst girlfriend ever. Other Nonie got the job done faster.

She whistles through her teeth. "Holy Sun and Stars, you got him out in your native time—in your now? Genius! Really, genius. You totally avoided the age-gap, and—" Her gaze drifts to Other Kieran, before she snaps her mouth shut, closes her eyes for one second, and shakes her head. "Never mind. I wanted to say it was a good idea. And sorry, young Kieran, I have an idea how it was in the Realm, I know it wasn't pleasant. But, also knowing how the Realm works, I'm not sure if it made a big difference for you how long you stayed in, but definitely a big one when you came out…" She glances pointedly at our entwined hands. Her and her Kieran exchange a long glance, so sad, so full of opportunities lost, I absolutely know what she means, and I can't help but wonder… Are they bonded? If we have a common past and Nonie got sent to the *Pioneer*, they should be. And if they are… I can't even imagine how hard that must be. How frustrating. How defeating, if you can't have what your body and soul crave.

Chase claps his hands. "Okay. Sad stories aside, welcome to our reality. What brought you onto us?"

Other Nonie points at me, and I raise my hand. "I guess that would be me through an unfortunate mis-jump."

Other Kieran fake-punches Other Nonie into the upper arm. "Remember those?"

She harrumphs and rolls her eyes, fighting a smile. "No idea what you're talking about. And everybody, sit. This might take a while." She points at the couch for Kieran and me, while she takes the same seat as before and the guys pull chairs from the conference table closer to the door, Other Kieran placing his next to Other Nonie. Once everybody is seated, she brings them up to speed within twenty seconds.

"An interesting conundrum." Zio crosses his legs and leans into the chair. "You assume that our universes differ because of interventions from the future to both of your lives."

"Correct. At least we think it's part of the puzzle." Neither of us suffer from grandeur thinking our universe revolved around us, but well, certainly we're still part of its mechanics. "If somebody upstream is trying to specifically take us out—"

"Futural. Call it futural." Other Nonie points to the ceiling, then down to the floor. "Upstream and downstream is confusing. Some would think of the future as upstream, because we're living *up* to a certain age, and time is a ladder we climb *up*, so it makes sense—but then a stream flows downhill, meaning, the future should be downstream by definition. Right?"

I blink slowly. "Right."

"So, we call it futural if it's in the future and praeterital if it's in the past. Handbook, chapter 2, temporal terminology. Avoids confusion."

"Right," I say again. She's right and it makes complete sense, but: Handbook. Sigh. "Either way, now with the correct terminology, I was saying that if somebody *futural* is trying to specifically take us out, there must be a reason why. And that *why* should lead us to the person benefitting from the changes, I.e., our bad guy, who's *still* trying to neutralize us." Altering our behavior and turning us into mind-controlled zombies would count as such, I feel.

Zio nods. "That would make sense. Lieutenant, knowing you, I assume you have started an evaluation?"

"Puh-lease. First thing I did after the unexpected visit two weeks ago." She taps her wrist PAD—a pink one, by the way—and raises her hand. "PADdy, display interactive file Nonie Multiverse One." A split second later, her PADdy has projected an image into the air between us, to my left a picture of baby Nonie, and about two meters to the right a picture of her in her red uniform. "This is my native timeline. Born, grew up, Academy, and here I am. Tah-dah." She points at herself. "*You* on the other hand… PADdy, insert readings from previous scan two weeks ago."

"*Acknowledged,*" PADdy says in a voice so suave I immediately want for my PADdy as well, *and* the ability to scan without others noticing. I'm *so* going to request all of that. When I have my PAD back, that is. Also, I'd like an upgrade to pink, please.

*"Information added. Scan indicated the same origin with a divergence point around age nine."*

A picture of me pops up partially overlaying the image of baby Nonie. A line shoots out from our picture, a numbered dot every couple of inches marking the years, I assume: one, two, three… Once PADdy hits nine, Other Nonie's path continues up at a forty-five degree angle to her picture with what I assume is today's date underneath it, while mine dips down at a forty-five degree angle before ending at a picture of me right now, wide eyes and not the most intelligent expression on my face and all.

*"Several deviation- and critical decision points were detected. Match at eighty percent."*

"Thank you, PADdy." Other Nonie nods. "There's your confirmation: See those lines? Your temporal signature differs from mine, as we figured. According to PADdy's scan, it looks like there was a divergence point—"

"Divergence point? Where the timelines split?" I lean forward and stare at that divergence point as if it could tell me the answer.

"Yes. The two most important temporal mechanical terms to know are divergence points and focal points. Focal points are events in time that keep timelines together. Like a knot tied out of many strings, connecting them, tying them down in one location. Our birth, for example. When we were born, our universes-slash-timelines were still one. Or, an event that would always happen the same way. A divergence point on the other hand is a split-off, when one timeline drifts off the common path for whatever reason. FBTI-handbook, also chapter two, temporal terminology. I paraphrased though."

"Heck, I need that book." I groan. I *so* need that book.

"To continue my evaluation," Other Nonie says, pointing back at the display. "There was a divergence point at age nine, meaning, something happened to one of us, not the other, and it split our paths.

There were apparently a couple of other events after that had us drift further apart—"

I slap my thigh. My theory, basically proven, right there! "It can only be the kidnapping." When I see the others' confused glances, I explain some more. "I was kidnapped at age nine. Eventually, I found out the kidnappers were from the future or at least working for somebody in the future, since they had future tech. That abduction was quite traumatizing and it changed and shaped my life after. It explains why you're not good at fighting, while I am."

Other Nonie blows a raspberry. "No need to point that out, thank you very much."

"What about us?" Kieran says with a nod of his chin at his older counterpart. "Let's see if the theory holds for us as well."

"Sure thing. PADdy, scan and insert." Other Nonie aims her PAD at Kieran.

*"Information added. Scan indicates the same origin for both specimens with divergences at ages seven, ten, and twenty-three with additional several potentially neglectable smaller impacts."*

A similar timeline to ours pops up for Kieran, from baby picture— Other Kieran's I presume, not that it made much of a difference—to their pictures as they're sitting here. Of course, either Kieran's picture looks frame-worthy, not dorky like mine, but that's probably not what I should focus on.

My gaze follows the lines and the angles it cuts at seven, ten, and twenty-three. I stand up and point at age seven. "The *Journey*-incident. In our world, the *USEF Journey* got destroyed when Kieran was seven years old. His mom was on board."

Other Kieran's eyes widen. "Mom? That didn't happen for me. Mom lived a happy life until she died of old age in '87. I'm sorry that happened to you. Really sorry," he says to Kieran, empathy shining in his eyes. "I can't imagine not having her growing up, I…" He lowers his head and slowly shakes it. "I can't even go there."

For a moment silence hovers. Then, Kieran acknowledges his older self's words with a nod. "Thank you. Her death had quite the impact on me, as you can obviously imagine. But, this is neither the time nor the place to talk about Mom, even though I'd love to hear more from you." His glance at Other Kieran holds a mix of curiosity and sorrow.

I shove my hands into my pockets. And since we're on the topic of the *Journey*… "To spice it up, we've recently found out that Kieran's dad thinks the *Journey*'s destruction wasn't an accident but sabotage." Which of course, might be a puzzle piece in our game as well.

Other Kieran tilts his head, brows narrowed. "Sabotage? Why would somebody sabotage a USEF vessel? With which goal?"

Good question. Kieran's gaze meets mine, and I nod.

"Dad thinks they wanted to kill me," he says, leaning forward and resting his arms on his thighs. "But I wasn't on board as planned, only still on the crew manifest for that flight," Kieran says. "I was supposed to accompany Mom, but Dad took me to one of his conferences last minute. Nobody bothered to cross me off the manifest. Dad said Mom had reported to her CO that I wasn't coming, and that's it. USEF actually showed up to inform Dad of the death of his wife *and* son because of that error. Quite the bag of conflicting emotions for him."

I acknowledge his statement with a nod and point at the graph. "That explains the deviation between you two at age seven. Moving on to age ten, the next diversion of your common path. Kieran was shot and barely survived."

"Holy everything," Chase murmurs. "Who shoots a child? Accident?"

Kieran opens his mouth to answer, but I cut him off. After all, I was there, and… I have some information he doesn't know about yet, but ultimately needs to be filled in anyway. Here we go again. In a perfect world, we'd have time for debriefings, but not in ours. In ours we go with the flow and adapt on a whim. "No. Planned murder, if I'm not mistaken. Here's the thing: his nanny shot him, but he survived. And it gets complicated, because I'm the medic who saved him."

Kieran's gaze shoots to me. "That was *you?*" Surprise rings in his tone. "You never said— Never mind, of course you didn't say anything."

"Well, I found out about it only recently, so let's put it this way: I still have to get back and save you, or else you're in trouble. My FBTI knows you weren't supposed to die, so they sent—will send—me to protect you. Twice, actually," I add under my breath. Saving myself saving Kieran. Cue the headaches, right?

Other Nonie chews on her cuticles. "Why did anybody want you dead, Kieran? You were ten."

Kieran shrugs. "They said my nanny had a nervous breakdown—"

"I don't believe that's it." I cross my arms in front of my chest. Here comes the second part of *things you should know about the day you were shot*. "For one, my time's FBTI knew somebody wanted you dead in the first place, hence, they sent me. For another, when I was there, while I can't say I was paying that much attention after she shot you," thank you, disruption of the Bond, "I can tell you she cried something about how she was sorry and how *they made her*."

Kieran sits up stiff as a log. "They *made her*? Who?"

"Well, your guess is as good as mine. I would assume the same people who sent Mashaule after you and who kidnapped me?"

Other Nonie rubs her temple. "You could counter-check with the Zeroverse. I mean, since you can actively and willfully jump to different realities. Then compare, just like with ours. See what the default would've been."

"Check with the what?" I ask.

Other Nonie blushes. "Sorry. The Zeroverse is the universe, or timeline, that's the primary for multiverses related to ours. The default one, so to speak—what you referred to as the main or only timeline. The one we originate from, your timeline, and ours as well. I have no idea where the divergence is, but it's somewhere."

"Wait—so you're not the, uhh, Zeroverse?" How many are there?

"We're not. As far as I know me—us—traveling back in time to the *Pioneer* is what deviates us from the Zeroverse."

Holy Sun and Stars…! It shouldn't come as a surprise we're not the original strand with all the alterations in ours, but nothing to make you feel more insignificant than realizing you're not even close to it.

"Okay, so if I wanted to check the Zeroverse, how would I know where to jump to?" Needless to say, the possibilities are endless when it comes to time and location.

Other Nonie stops rubbing her temple and switches to tapping it with one finger. "Once you identify the strand, which shouldn't be hard, since it's quite obvious, I don't think you'd need to worry about that. You'd end up somewhere close to the other you, like you did here. Rule of Familiarity: you're drawn to other versions of yourself close to your native time first, then to other versions adjacent to your native time, then to familiar people or situations independent of your native time. Past over future."

Oh. "There's a rule for that?"

"Yes, like I just said." She narrows her eyes. "If you don't know that either… Your FBTI needs to crank it up."

"I whole-heartedly agree," I murmur. Besides the handbook, hers has better tech. Heck, last time she set a marker for me to get me back to Mashaule on the fairgrounds. I'm not sure my FBTI even has a Setayashi-device, and hers can set freakin' markers.

Chase rubs his forehead. "Pause here, Nonie. I'm used to feeling a step behind whenever you talk multiverse or time-travel, but this is getting complicated and you're ignoring something your counterpart just said: Mashaule? Admiral Mashaule?"

I think he meant the other Nonie, but this is my question to answer. "Correct. Our Mashaule had been in contact with somebody from the future who instructed him to kill Kieran before he entered the Realm. There were several attempts on Kieran's life, which I all defended." Barely, sometimes, but beggars can't be choosers. "The odd thing is that Mashaule did jump back and forth in time to kill Kieran, but he never tried after you came out of the Realm—maybe because he didn't know you'd come out." Because when he left on his crazy mission, Kieran was still presumed dead. I cringe and deflate when I realize my flaw in reasoning. "No, wait. The enemy from the future should know that Kieran came out in ninety-five, shouldn't they? So, they could've instructed Mashaule—" I suck in my lower lip and chew on it. "Or maybe they had a different plan for that in place, hence our abduction to 2299!" That could be it!

"Geez, you guys can't catch a break," Chase says.

No kidding. And I agree.

Zio stands up and paces back and forth. "Our Kieran left the Realm sooner than you did." He looks at Kieran sitting next to me. "Maybe, since Mashaule was trying to kill you minutes before entering the nebula, your Temporal War could wish to change Kieran entering the nebula. Question is, why. What did you do in there, or what happened while you were in there and what happened when you came out?"

Kieran lifts both hands and turns the palms to the ceiling. "No idea, I literally just came out, and then we got taken into the future."

Zio continues his pacing. "When our Kieran returned from the Realm, he convinced USEF the Essken weren't a threat. We stopped using Tau-radiation and we stopped hailing them. Took us a while to establish communication, but Kieran was there every step of the way. In fact, the peace treaty, the Essken joining USEF, and eventually the foundation of the UWO are all due to Kieran's efforts."

Other Kieran blushes. "It wasn't just me."

"UWO?" I ask.

"The United Worlds Organization, a collective of all different species we have discovered, with one common elected president and administration. A true step toward a multi-cultural, peaceful society. But without Kieran, neither peace with the Essken nor the foundation of the UWO would have happened," Zio says, then cocks his head and pauses. "Interesting statement."

The epiphany strikes the rest of us at the same time. Chase leans forward, blowing out air through pursed lips. Both Kierans recoil in shock, and Other Nonie and me look at each with wide eyes.

"No. No, that can't be. Somebody is trying to prevent peace with the Essken?" I whisper. "But... The war would've continued with many, many more casualties. Mashaule—and mind you, I don't know what is true of his claims—said killing Kieran would *save* billions of people. And what's so funny about that is that the FBTI in 2299 claims the same thing about both of us, taking us out would *save* billions of people."

And, like Kieran, I'm trying really hard to not let that accusation get to me.

"Somebody in the future is trying to eliminate both of you so that what—Nonie can't get Kieran out of the Realm, and Kieran can't make peace with the Essken? Is that what we're thinking?" Other Nonie's gaze jumps from one of us to the next. "Because, that's a biggie."

"It sounds like it must be wrong." Chase holds Zio by his arm, stopping the other man's pacing. "You're driving me crazy, Zee. And by the way, there must be a different reason. This one is nuts. Who would *want* a war to drag on?"

"But it does make sense. All attempts would have either killed Kieran before he could have gone into the Realm and get to know the Essken, or would have gotten rid of Nonie, so she couldn't have gotten him out of the Realm. Oh, holy Sun and Stars!" Other Nonie smacks her forehead. "You said you barely got freed from the Realm—and now they're after both of you. Of course! You haven't made peace yet! To whoever is behind this, their fight isn't lost quite yet! It makes sense!"

We stare at her, equally horrified.

"It is a valid theory," Zio says.

I swallow down the rising nausea. "Unfortunately, it is. It also makes your dad look less paranoid and rather clairvoyant, Kieran." Against all odds the connection the admiral saw could be real. "For all we know whoever made Addi shoot you, whoever set my kidnapping in motion, whoever got us abducted a century into the future, it could be the same person with one goal in mind."

Chase groans. "Your timeline is messed up. Usually I'm complaining about ours, but I take it back. Ours is just fine the way it is. Finding a name, the mastermind behind your temporal manipulation, is going to be impossible."

Kieran squeezes my knee twice, and I nod once in return. Great minds think alike, I guess.

"It's not impossible," I say. "In fact, we can tell you who is behind the *Journey* incident."

"How?" Other Kieran tilts his head.

"Dad," Kieran replies. "His paranoia turned out to be useful." The two men exchange a glance and the older version rolls his eyes.

"Never thought I'd hear that about him."

Kieran chuckles. "Me, neither."

"So, which name did he come up with?"

"Well," Kieran says. "To be fair, it came out of left wing, but he showed us the evidence. The clues ultimately lead to a Magellan named Tala Torona."

"That name is unfamiliar to me," Zio says. "Not that I presume to know every Magellan by name, despite our low numbers."

Other Nonie shrugs. "Let's find out. PADdy, display information about Tala Torona."

*"Acknowledged."*

A second later, a new image appears where Kieran's and my timeline were displayed before. It shows a middle-aged Magellan woman with the typical dark, shimmering hair cut to a stylish bob.

*Tala Torona*, it reads. *Specialist, temporal mechanics.*

"Temporal mechanics, that sounds about right," Kieran says. "Assuming our Tala Torona is similar to yours."

"Agreed." Nonie taps her PADdy. "Widen search parameters and display."

*"Acknowledged."* PADdy brings up a string of data.

"All research articles. All related to temporal mechanics. Which makes sense, if she was a temporal mechanics specialist." Chase scrunches up his lips. "But that alone doesn't make an assassin. Give us her latest whereabouts and contacts. More juicy stuff."

Nonie enters the commands into her PAD.

*Last known location: Mag-Two, 2287.*

Other Nonie frowns. "Eighty-seven? PADdy, display vital data for Tala Tarona."

*Tala Tarona, 2210-2287.*

"Well, that looks like a dead end." Chase huffs. "Pun intended."

"Classy joke, Trip." Other Kieran gives his friend a pointed stare.

"Hey, it was a good pun, don't diss it!"

Out of nowhere, a wave of nausea hits me, so overwhelming I double over. *Crap.* I know this feeling, and I really don't care for it, not now, not ever again.

Dizziness sweeps over me, twisting reality like someone drugged me, stretching the edges of my vision and compressing the center, worse than what I experienced in the Realm, way worse. Everything feels wrong, down could be up and up could be down, I can't really tell, just like I can't really tell what I'm seeing. For a moment I think I see Kieran as a child, Zio as a teen, or maybe I'm just hallucinating. The images are all translucent, like ghosts, and gone in the blink of an eye.

Kieran grunts, and I don't need to look to know the K'Zees are there. I feel their siren call, their pull on every cell of my being, like I did during every single one of these episodes, only it's getting worse. Lifting my gaze, I look around: coils, K'Zees, whatever, surround us. Some tug on Zio, some on Nonie, none on Chase. Zio looks pale, like Other Nonie. Other Kieran seems slightly uncomfortable, swatting at his shoulders, like a bug bothered him, whenever a K'Zee bumps against him, but they don't attack him, they don't shoot into him like curly arrows, like they do for my Kieran.

With every coil hitting him, Kieran jerks as if whipped. Somewhere in the recess of my mind I wonder how something so beautiful can be so deceiving and painful. Like in the Realm, they're beyond mesmerizing as they zip through the room, from one person to the next, glittering and shining so bright, I don't just see their beauty, I feel it. Everything inside my body aligns with the K'Zees, yearning for them, hungering for them.

And the only way for me to squash that hunger, to fulfill that need, is through Kieran. Not giving in, not touching him, feels against my nature, and that's not going to happen. I'm not denying myself the fix my body so desperately craves. I'm not resisting. I can't.

I reach for Kieran's hand, the tips of my fingers vibrating more and more the closer they come to him, and as soon as my hand touches his, the coils' energy shoots up my arm and into my core. Relief pounds through me, washed away by a hurricane of lightning bolts. I gasp and stiffen as the energy whirls around my core, igniting my First Sense. A rush of endorphins hits me as my body switches to autopilot and the energy shoots into my left hand, and… and lights it up like a candle.

Holy Universe, that's new!

I stare at my hand, glowing with the energy—

And *zip*, the episode is gone, leaving me doubled over, holding on to my stomach with one hand, and with the other to Kieran. No more distorted images, no more coils. No more pain.

"Well, that looks like a dead end." Chase flinches and waves a hand. "Never mind, not the best phrasing. This won't help us, I wanted to say."

"I agree. Whatever Tala Torona's reasons to sabotage the *Journey*, she didn't live long enough to be the future aggressor—" Other Kieran pauses. "Are you guys okay?"

Straightening up vertebra by vertebra, I slowly let go of my stomach and of Kieran's hand. That was intense, even by our standards. Other Nonie and Other Zio also still look pale. My counterpart works on a hard swallow.

"That was… odd," she says. "Did you feel that? As if there was an earthquake, but nothing moved?"

"Appropriate description." Zio takes a deep breath in and releases it slowly. "Quite disturbing."

"You… you felt that?" I stare at my counterpart. None of the others did on the *Achievement*, not even Koll. He said he sees the K'Zees only when in the Realm.

Other Zio and Other Nonie nod, neither of them looking too happy about it.

"Well, at least we're not alone," Kieran rasps, squeezing my hand once as he straightens up, one vertebra at a time.

Despite the lingering throbbing in my center, a small smile pulls on my lips. Agreed. Never have I been happier to have others share in the misery. "Have you experienced this thing before?"

"I haven't." Other Nonie shakes her head. "And I'm fine if I never do again. That was weird."

"Neither have I, but something tells me you have." Good to know Zio knows me well, no matter which Zio and no matter which me, apparently.

I lower my head in a slow nod. Don't want that nausea to flare up again. "It's been happening to us for a while now. Started after we were taken into the future, weird episodes with hallucinations and odd perceptions for me, plus energy bolts coming out of nowhere, which tend to attack Kieran." Which makes it so stupid for my body to crave them.

"It feels like being shot with darts of electricity," Kieran says in a flat tone.

Other Kieran rubs his shoulder absentmindedly, and I point at him. "They swarmed around you, too, but only poked you, so to speak. You felt it, right?" I rub my shoulder, like he did, and his eyes widen.

"That? Yes, I did. It felt odd, but not painful."

"Take it and run with it," Kieran comments dryly, taking off his hat and wiping the sweat off his forehead.

I turn toward my counterpart. "Nonie, what did you feel?"

She cringes. "Just… not good."

I lower my brows. "That's it?"

"Pretty much, yeah."

"No… pull? No weird buzzing? Your First Sense doing… *something?*"

"Uhh, no? I mean, my First Sense flared up, but I've had worse."

Dang it. Why is it only me? She *is* me, in the name of the universe!

My counterpart grimaces. "What did you feel? And do I want to know?"

I sigh. "You definitely don't want to go through it. It's a sharp, burning pain, until my First Sense kicks in. I feel it protects me." It did so during the episode in the Realm, and if I think about it, also the ones before, I just didn't pay attention to it. Sorry if I was mildly distracted by being taken apart one cell at a time.

Kieran looks from one to the other. "Overall, you guys are the first to experience it with us. Nobody else has been affected so far."

"I wasn't affected either. I'm just listening to this like I came late to the party," Other Chase says, crossing his arms in front of his chest and one leg over the other.

"Don't take it personal," Kieran says. "You're not missing out, let me tell you."

Both men grin at each other like they had known each other for years, and one could say they have. In a manner of speaking.

Other Nonie lifts a hand. "Uhh, I don't want to sound like I'm losing it, but did anybody else notice that Chase repeated himself? Was that on purpose? Because it for sure felt weird." She places one hand on her stomach, and I know what she means: her First Sense, just like mine.

"I did not repeat anything," Other Chase says, shaking his head.

But he did!

"Your joke about the dead end." I point at him, then Other Nonie. "You're right. He said it twice. It's not a complete match, but close enough that it counts. Something similar happened once before to us, time slowed down. Zee, what about you? Did you feel it the same as Nonie?"

Zio shakes his head. "No. I felt a profound disorientation but saw neither energy coils nor any repetition of events. But I think it is safe to say we are experiencing some temporal paradox, and we all know your sensitivity is much higher than mine." He points at Other Nonie and myself.

"What kind of paradox?" Kieran asks. "And why did I feel it *and* see those coils? I have no sensitivity to time whatsoever. Chase?"

"Told you, I'm your control group. Nothing at all."

I point at Kieran's counterpart. "But you did feel them, even though you didn't know what was going on." I mimic him swatting at the coils again.

"Oh, great," Chase says. "We have weird energy coils attacking Kierans."

"And only Kierans," I confirm. "Because none of the—excuse me— regular humans felt anything, neither now nor during the other events."

Zio shrugs. "I am unsure of the significance, but to me it felt like time was… broken."

My eyes widen. *Like time was broken.* Of course! I smack my forehead. "I saw images of a younger Kieran, a younger Zio, and other stuff I couldn't identify, like ghost images from the past! And come to think about it, I saw something similar once before, on the *Pioneer*!" I turn to Kieran, nodding like a crazy person. It got buried under everything else that happened, but I did see those ghostly outlines of people in the hallway when time slowed down, those echoes of all of us. Such a weird feeling. "As if the past was bleeding through."

Zio lifts one brow. "Like the fabric of time had thinned, or a temporal cleft occurred? Theoretically that is possible, but the consequences—"

"Uhh, guys? *Guys!*" Chase gets up attention focused on something behind Other Nonie. "This one I *am* seeing, tell me I'm not the only one!" He points at Other Nonie, who pops up from her chair, twisting at the waist in the direction Chase indicated. So does Other Kieran and the rest of us.

Next to Nonie's desk, where Chase pointed to, the air wafts and shimmers, billows and bulges like something was trapped in it, forcing its way out with sheer violence.

"What the—"

Chase doesn't get to finish his sentence. As if torn apart, reality splits open, ripping at the seams, as first a leg appears before two hands push the tear wider and a person squeezes through. *He* stumbles out, the rift closing the very moment his body has left it.

I suck in a gasp. "Sherid—"

Sheridan's gaze falls onto Other Nonie right in front of him. A satisfied grin pulls on the corners of his lips. "Thought you could hide? Not from me, but nice try! And sorry, but you changed the game on this!" He pulls a weapon from a holster on his hip, aims at her—

Crap. I jump forward and wave my arms, pulse pounding in my chest. "Hey, Sheridan! Might want to confirm your target?"

He whips his gaze to me, his mouth dropping open when he sees, well, *me.* "What the—? That—" Confusion settles on his features, deepening when he sees both Kierans, replaced one second later by a steely resolve. "Whatever trick this is, you're coming with me." He steadies his aim at Other Nonie—

*Pew!*

A high-pitched sound shoots through the room. Sheridan twitches and doubles over, moving in slow motion, while Other Kieran keeps his weapon aimed at him, jaw set tight and eyes shooting fire.

O-kay. I see his point, but Kierans seem to be quite trigger happy these days.

"Nobody is being taken anywhere here," he growls as he darts over to Other Nonie, weapon raised, a look of controlled panic and sheer determination on his face.

Yeah. No question about it, by the way. They're bonded.

Sheridan grunts, but doesn't fall over, doesn't lose consciousness, and instead brings the weapon back up.

Other Kieran shoots again, but something in Sheridan's clothing lights up when the charge hits. Sparks sizzle over his body, but the second shot doesn't seem to affect him.

Another shot fired by Other Kieran—with the same result.

Sheridan huffs out a laugh through gritted teeth. "Stunners. Ah, good old times. Sorry, that trick only works once, and even then not quite. Thank you, Essken shields." He curls his finger around the trigger—

Chase throws a chair, hitting Sheridan square in the upper body, driving him back. "Everybody, out!" he yells. "Now!"

Other Kieran grabs Other Nonie's hand and yanks her away from Sheridan, keeping himself between the agent and her. My Kieran jumps forward and grabs a hold of my arm as I press the button on the disk. "Sorry, guys, and thank you!" I yell, as my body begins to tingle when the radiation does its job. The world turns blurry as the Maelstrom begins to take over—

Sheridan cries out in frustration, loud. "Oh, come *on!*"

I look over my shoulder to see him swing the weapon around and at me, the motion barely discernible as reality fades out, but clear enough

to make my heart stutter.
    I focus harder—

# Chapter Twelve - 

# Different Baseline

**The Maelstrom**

*P*ain *hits me square in the back unlike anything I've ever felt. Nerve endings fry and sizzle, as every cell screams out in agony.*

*The panicky yells of Other Nonie and Other Kieran, of Other Zio and Other Chase get cut off as the Maelstrom swallows us up and throws us around, head over heels, as uncontrolled as on my first jump. I can't make sense of it, can't focus, can't—*

*Kieran grunts from the forces of the Maelstrom using us as a play ball. "Nonie!" He tugs on me, desperately and hard to pull me in, pressing me to his chest with one hand, the other frantically patting my body down. "Shit! Nonie! Nonie! Talk to me! Say something! Are you—"*

*Can't reply. Can't move. There's only pain in my existence, paralyzing me, similar to when the Essken shot me at First Contact, but somehow different and worse.*

*Through the chaos in my mind I feel Kieran stretch out a hand for something, then hear him groan in frustration. He keeps me pressed to his chest, but squeezes me harder. Relief. His body helps, as if some of the pain drained away from the contact. Because of him.*

*Kieran struggles, moves like a swimmer drowning, then, with another sound of frustration, circles both arms around me. "Nonie! Nonie! Are you with me? Hey, Nonie! Can you get us out of here? I don't know what to do. I can't get us into any of these times, they just pass through me. We need to take care of you. Nonie!" The worry in his voice together with the contact breaks through the mind-numbing pain.*

*Must act. Must do something.*

*Forcing my heavy eyelids open, a bout of overwhelming nausea washes over me. Can't function much.*

*"That's it, Nonie, that's it." Kieran kisses my temple with urgent desperation. "I know it hurts, but you can do it."*

*I can?*

*We're flailing chaotically.*

*There's one strand—*

*The biggest. The brightest. Calling to me.*

*Reflexes set in. With an effort close to moving a mountain I will us there, lift a hand—*

*And gravity takes over.*

## Somewhere, Somewhen

The rainbow colors of the Maelstrom pop out of existence, replaced by cool, bright white neon light. The split second I need to register we've entered normal space isn't enough to prep myself for the impact. Kieran and I slam into hard, white, unforgiving floors. The crash drives whatever air I still had left from my lungs. My head bounces off the floor, adding a whole new level of dizziness. Kieran tightens his arm around me as he takes most of the impact, grunting with the forces of nature bringing us to a complete stop, face down, a mess of tangled body parts.

For one eternal second, complete silence hovers.

Then, somebody takes a step, their shoes making little sucking noises on the floor. "What the actual—"

*"Intruder Alert. Intruder Alert. Intruder Alert Deck fifteen. Intruder Alert—"*

"Tell me something I don't know," the same person remarks. "What'cha guys waiting for? Go!"

I hear the urgency in their voices and I know I should be moving, I just can't. I really can't. Whatever Sheridan shot me with feels like it engulfed me in concrete—concrete spiked with barbed wire on the inside. My vision is blurry, my brain stuck on the slowest processing speed ever.

"Are you okay? Non—" Kieran tries to pull his arm out from under me, but he doesn't get to it: We're being grabbed and pulled apart, so roughly, my head bounces off the floor again. Ow.

"Stay down! *Down!* Hands above your head! Hands above your head! Move! *Move!*"

"No, we—"

They don't let Kieran finish his sentence. My blurry vision cranks it up just in time to see three people in red and black uniforms tackle Kieran, two going for his arms, the third for his back, pinning him on the ground, starfish-style. He struggles—

"Do that and you're going to regret it." The one guy with his knee on Kieran's back presses a weapon into his neck.

I don't feel how I'm being pinned to the ground by another three people, I'm too numb and too much in pain at the same time. But that image, Kieran on the ground, his chest heaving with heavy breaths, his hands balled to fists under the hold of those two men and with a weapon pressed into his neck, it makes my heart lurch into my throat, bringing a wave of panic with it.

Where are we? When are we? In which freakin' timeline, and what does that mean for us?

I try to move my hands, but can't against the hold. The cold floors feel heavenly against my cheek, but make me shiver. Or maybe it's that barbed wire-spiked concrete. Every breath hurts. It really feels similar to what being shot by the Essken felt like when I met Kieran, only less paralyzing, and more painful, but still quite similar.

*"Scan completed,"* a PAD announces above us, and somebody whistles.

"Sir, this is something you should see."

"I agree with you without even knowing the details."

I hear steps behind me, a moment of silence only broken by Kieran's frustrated, heavy breathing, and then a curse.

Somebody kicks my thigh. "Seriously, Cadet?"

Cadet?

"Get them up. *Now.* Search them."

The pressure on my arms and back releases as, just like Kieran, I'm being yanked up by two males in their late twenties. Neither of them look at us in any way I'd call friendly. I blink to get the haziness to retreat. Where they grab me, fiery pain shoots in all directions, as if they pressed the barbed wire in deeper. Another person pats me down and double-checks my right pocket.

"Only this, sir." She pulls out my disk, and air flees my lungs. Not the disk. Please, not the—

The man in charge steps forward. "Cadet Thorburn. Can't say it's a pleasure to meet you, but your name does ring a bell."

I blink harder and strain my eyes to get the man in front of me in focus: medium height, sturdy built, skin a few tones darker than mine, dark hair and a goatee. Dressed in a uniform that could be USEF. Lieutenant's pips on his collar. His light blue eyes pop as he's glaring at me. He checks his PAD again, looks at Kieran, huffs, and directs his attention back to me.

"Entering a USEF vessel without permission, Cadet? Strike one. Breaking through our shields to demat on board? Strike two. Tagging along some idiot with a genetic masker? Strike three."

I jerk my head back, ignoring the spike in headache. "Genetic—"

The officer gives me a look that shuts me up. "Speaking out of turn. Strike four. And don't play dumb with me. *Kieran Wildason.* Really. That guy. Sure. Putting a genetic masker on a young dark-haired guy doesn't make him a Wildason look-alike. Too slender. Do your research next time, if you're making such an effort." He steps forward, hands behind his back, looking me up and down. "I'm not sure what you thought you were doing or why you thought it would be funny, but it isn't. Use of a genetic masker and unauthorized demat onto a USEF vessel are both federal offenses and will get you locked away for years. Kiss good bye to your career, Cadet. *Dumb. Move.*"

He over-emphasizes the last words, and the bit of panic in my throat expands to a full-blown tsunami-wave of panic. Federal offense, locked away? I whip my head over to Kieran, ignoring the barbed wire digging into each and every muscle.

The cap my mom gave him is miraculously still on his head, and maybe that's helping us. Maybe. His lips are pressed tight, brows pulled down, muscles in his jaw popping. His fists are curled tight, and he looks like he was ready to break out of the officers' hold, but he doesn't. He doesn't say anything either, because we can't.

My next breath hitches as the heightened emotion clears some of the pain's haziness, and finally I can think, at least to a degree. At this very moment, we can only go with the flow. We're outnumbered, in an unknown timeline, with unknown consequences to our action.

All we can do is bide our time and play this strategically. Maybe hope for dumb luck, while we're at it.

The officer in charge throws my disk up in the air and catches it. "Brig, both of them. Lock 'em away, and I don't mind if you lose the key."

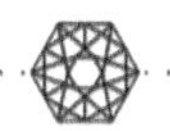

*Some USEF Ship, Somewhen, Some Universe*

Not even ten minutes later I've been shoved into a cell in the brig. I have no idea in which one Kieran is, can't see through the forcefield set on blur. Him they dragged along faster, I was the slow one. Couldn't move: barbed concrete. Eventually, we made it here, and even to those knuckleheads it was clear I wasn't faking it.

Inch by inch I lower myself onto the cot on one of the walls, then feel for my back: no wound, just a very, *very* sensitive area. Great, so that stuff hits any target and spreads through the body, causing universal damage. I let my head sink back against the wall, dragging in deep breaths accompanied by sharp, penetrating worry.

We got away from Sheridan, but at what cost? We're clearly not home, but in some other timeline. Even if I get access to my disk somehow and get us out, I'm really messing up this Nonie's life right now. So much for staying under the radar.

Crap.

And while I'm sorry for this Nonie here, my worry about Sheridan's next move is greater. We're sitting ducks behind the forcefield. And with that weapon of his… Could that be part of the tech the Essken have given humans? Not that it matters, as a general rule we should avoid getting shot again.

It matters more how long will it take him to find us. How does he even find us in different realities if they don't believe in them? I hate, hate, hate being at a disadvantage, and we haven't had a single stroke of good luck, unless you count not getting caught by Sheridan.

My heart hammers. I stab my fingernails into my palms. Focus, Thorburn. It's a mess, that much is clear, but there must be a way out of it that doesn't include waiting for Sheridan as our liberator from the brig.

I swallow hard, then draw my legs in and rest my forehead on them, despite the pain. I need the disk. I need Kieran. Or, maybe just the disk and jump out of here, and then come back for Kieran, maybe even the moment they close the forcefield in his cell. Doesn't matter when I pop in to get him, as long as I get him. If we're truly in this mess because somebody wants the war to drag on and prevent peace with the Essken,

Kieran needs to be protected at all costs. I—

A door-sized part of the forcefield turns clear, then sizzles out, catching my attention. A tall woman steps through, dressed in a white USEF uniform much closer in design to the medical uniforms I'm used to. Her long, black hair shimmers, and the way she walks…

"You're Magellan," I blurt out. Another Magellan in USEF besides Zio!

The woman laughs. The forcefield closes and blurs behind her as she sets a medic bag down on the cot next to me. "Always good to see one of your own tribe, isn't it?"

My own tribe? She knows I—this timeline's Nonie—is Magellan? "Y-yeah," I say, unfurling my legs and sitting up straighter. "Ow."

The woman's demeanor changes in an instant from jovial to concerned. "They told me you'd been injured."

"One could say so."

"They also told me you crashed onto the floor from about three meters."

Which explains why my head hurts so much. That, and whatever Sheridan shot me with. "Uh-huh."

She opens her bag and takes out a medical scanner, directing it over me. "How are you feeling? Did you hit your head?"

"I did. I—" An idea comes to mind. "I think I got a concussion. I'm confused."

"Well, crashing onto the floor from ceiling height could do it," she comments drily. "How bad is it?"

I rub my temples with both palms. "Quite. What's the date today?"

"March 8th, 2299."

Sun and Stars—I jumped into a different reality *and* four years into the future. I suppress a groan and any other reaction to the info besides a slow, knowing nod. "Okay. Uh, that's what I thought. And I'm on a USEF vessel, correct?"

"Correct." The doc drops the scanner into her bag and takes out a sub-dermal injector. "Which is quite difficult to pull off and has everybody on high alert. Pulling a stunt like this, breaching our security on the eve of the UWO anniversaries, wasn't a good idea."

"UWO anniversaries. Remind me?" That's the same acronym Other Nonie used—United Worlds Organization?

I grimace as she unloads the injector into my neck, but a split second later the barbed concrete melts away, only the slightest sting remaining. Exhaling slowly, I close my eyes for one second as my muscles relax. Better. Much, much, better.

"Cadet." The doc gives me a skeptical look as she moves her medical scanner over my body again. "The United Worlds Organization turns forty. You can't tell me you forgot that too."

They got UWO here, too, just like in Other Nonie's reality! Does that mean they're at peace with the Essken? It should? If there's anything to our theory at least.

Taking one look at her scanner's readouts the doc nods. "No concussion. You're in pretty good shape considering you're claiming memory loss."

I lower my gaze. Guess my acting really is subpar. "Okay, sorry. Everything's just…" I shrug.

"A mess?"

"Pretty much."

She sighs and shoves the injector back into the bag. "Can't say it isn't. You're definitely in trouble. Your friend too, even if he isn't USEF. I still have to look at him and disable his genetic masker. We need his true ID for the prosecution."

I flinch. Last thing we need is her finding out there is no masker, but that Kieran is real. Once they do, I can't assume they're going to greet us with open arms, no matter if they know about time travel and alternate realities or not.

Ergo, I need time. We need time.

And with a Magellan, there's only one chance. I look her straight in the eye. "How strong is your First Sense?"

Her brows lower in confusion. "It's quite well developed. Why?"

"Because I'd like you to listen to it. Give my friend a chance to settle his thoughts. I'm sure he will be more amenable to any kind of discussion if—"

"You must think I'm completely gullible." She snaps her bags closed. "That's not going to happen. I do my job as it is asked of me, and—"

The forcefield lights up in the middle and snuffs out as somebody enters with heavy steps, their body hidden behind the doctor.

"Doc, thank you. I'd like the room please. Meet me in sick bay."

I startle. That voice—

"But Admiral, I still have to take care of the other—"

"In sickbay, Doctor."

"Of course, sir." Her jaw tightens as she takes her bag and strides past... as she strides past an old Kieran, even older than the one I saw with Other Nonie. I was right when I thought Kieran would age well. He must be early or mid-sixties, but he still looks so much like Kieran, it makes my heart stumble. A few grey streaks show at his temples, but he still has a full head of hair with that same stubborn lock falling down his forehead. I know it so well, just as I know the way his eyes are narrowed, his jaw is clenched and his posture rigid. He looks just as mad as my Kieran was when he found out Nonie Magnetta wasn't the spacefaring, lost civilian she said she was.

"Cadet."

The way he says it, all calm and collected, is in complete contrast to the anger I feel bubbling under his skin.

"*Cadet*," he repeats, and it clicks for me.

I jump to my feet, wincing in the process, but I end up at attention, the barbed concrete much less bothersome than before the doctor's visit. "Sir."

"I'm in the middle of prep for the UWO anniversary. I'm busy, and I don't like to be disturbed. Yet, I get called up to the *brig*, of all places, urgently, and why? Because my mentee apparently decided to crash the party on a secured USEF vessel. The *Pioneer*—"

My brain gets hung up on two words, but processes only one. "Mentee?" Kieran is my Mentor? Like, *now*, since they all call me Cadet here, even though we're four years ahead of my native time?

He gives me a look as if I'd lost my marbles. "Yes, Cadet. Mentee. What are you playing at here? I asked you repeatedly to join me for the festivities. Celebrating the day we came together as a group of sentient beings to work as one seemed to me like a good reason for an off-world trip. You declined, for whatever unfathomable reason on your part, and *now* you're here? *Now* you break through a military grade code to crash us?" He spreads his arms wide. "I don't even know where to start! This is a career-ender!"

I know. I drop my gaze to the floor. Yes, this could completely kill this timeline's Nonie's career. It doesn't look good. I'm stuck between a rock and a hard place, and no matter what I do, I'm damaging this timeline, either by taking Nonie off her predestined course, or by contaminating them, telling them about alternate realities. On the other hand, they *could* know about alternate realities. Just because my timeline is barely figuring out about them doesn't mean they can't be ahead of us. Other Nonie was, so maybe this timeline is as well—there's at least a chance.

Keeping my gaze trained on the floor, I feel for my First Sense. At one point somebody needs to explain to me if it applies to my timeline only, or to whichever timeline I'm in, because it is annoyingly silent. I'll add it to the list of questions. Buzzwords *user manual*.

Lifting my gaze to the admiral, I make a decision. I need to find out where they're at when it comes to time travel and then make another, *informed* decision. "Sir—"

"No, Cadet! Do you even know what's going on behind the scenes at this very moment? You might think you got it bad in the brig, but believe me, it's going to get worse. As soon as USEF HQ gets our report, they will be on high alert because of your action! Where did you get the technology to demat through our shields like that? Who gave it to you, and who else has it? Do I need to tell you what a threat that is? That once HQ security gets their hands on you, you won't be seeing the light of day for a very, very long time again, no matter what your father and I have to say in your defense? Let me repeat, for emphasis. You are not leaving this cell or any cell for a very long time." He curses under his breath, roughly pushing the one stubborn strand of hair back up his head.

A tickle of panic rises in my chest, twisting my stomach into a figure eight on its way up. Admiral Kieran doesn't know it, but he might be right. Once they know we're not who they think we are, this Nonie should be fine, but Kieran and me? We're still a threat and entered the *Pioneer* through her shields. Oh, Holy Sun and Stars! I sway back and forth before I get my rising dizziness under control. No matter the timeline, you don't breach security like we just did and get away with it. People get nervous when safety is compromised, no matter which universe you're from. If they judge us to be a risk, we'll be locked away, no doubt about it.

A wheezy breath leaves me. Our only chance is an open mind in these people. "Admiral, I—"

He holds up a palm. "Not done yet. And to top it off you bring some young guy with a genetic masker of all things, an illegal masker, posing as me? What were you even thinking? Hell, what is wrong with you?"

The words hit me like a slap to the face. I jerk back, shaking my head. "Admiral—"

"No, Cadet. There's nothing, absolutely nothing, you can say to improve the situation, so I recommend—"

"Admi—"

"—not saying anything at all until—"

"Admiral!" I raise my voice, to no avail.

"—you have a lawyer present and—"

Patience goes *poof*, and powered by frustration, I yell. "Kieran! Holy Universe, listen to me!"

He freezes in mid-yell and I realize my mistake. *Mistakes*. Plural, unfortunately. One, I yelled. Cadets don't yell at admirals. Two, cadets also don't call their admirals by their first names. I snap my mouth shut, but the damage is done.

The admiral's eyes widen and his lips part. For once I'm not sure what he's thinking.

Silence hovers, thick and heavy.

The admiral swallows. "You called me Kieran." Contrary to the dressing down I expected, his voice is soft. Curious.

"I… did." I cross my hands behind my back. "I apologize."

He steps closer, head slightly titled to the left. "You never call me Kieran."

Aw, crap, crap, crap. Of course, I don't, I'm a cadet. Way to go, Thorburn. Way to go! "Again, I apologize, sir."

His gaze hardens. "Apology not accepted. What's going on here, Cadet? You've always been exemplary with your behavior. Separating business and private life like no other cadet I've ever worked with. Hell, you didn't even come when I invited you to Addi's birthday party. I offered to take you on this trip, because as I have said a hundred times, the anniversary of the foundation of the UWO is an event worth witnessing, especially when it's close to the Essken Realm, but you declined. You declined, and now you're here. Acting… odd." Gone is the rigid posture, the anger, replaced by an older version of the man I know. The man I trust.

Okay then, here goes nothing: "This is an out-of-the-blue-question, but do you think time travel is possible?"

The admiral's jaw drops open. "What? Time travel? What the absolute hell, Cadet?"

Oh. Well. That doesn't sound like a yes. That also doesn't sound like I jumped to the *Pioneer* when this admiral was its captain or else I'd expect a different answer. Heat creeps to my face. "That's a no then?" My voice ends in a little squeak.

Kieran keeps his gaze glued to me. "That's a no to a question that has absolutely nothing to do with the situation you're in. If you're wishing what you did didn't happen, so do I, but alas, life and time don't work that way." He chews on his lower lip and shakes his head. "Everything about this is highly unusual. This isn't you. What's going on here? Talk to me."

Problem is, now I can't. Or can I? I mean, what do I think is going to happen when they find out this timeline's Nonie is where she's supposed to be, so there's two of us? Or when they find out my Kieran is the real deal, not some guy with a genetic masker? They will realize there are different realities. And once USEF security knows, USEF knows. From there, the knowledge will spread and voilà, thank you for contaminating this whole timeline, Lieutenant Thorburn. Rock, meet hard place.

I really need a handbook. I need rules and guidance. I'm swimming in the dark.

His gaze bores into mine, intense. "Talk. To. Me."

I look down to the floor and lower my voice. "I apologize, sir. I don't know what got into me. I—"

"No. Don't pretend like I don't know you or like you just made a simple mistake in an assignment. There's more behind your actions. I can't help you if you don't talk to me honestly." A moment passes, and even without seeing his eyes, I feel his heavy gaze on me. He takes in a slow controlled breath, holds it for a second, then lets go of it. "Talk to me, *Nonie.*"

My gaze flies to his and what I'm seeing there, unguarded and open… it takes my breath away. So many emotions reflect in his eyes, so many… I'd expect to see none of them in an *admiral* looking at his mentee. I'd expect to see all of them in *Kieran* looking at me.

His gaze doesn't flutter. He doesn't close himself off. Instead, he stands there, open and vulnerable, allowing me to see the emotion crossing his face. A small, sad smile picks up the corners of his lips. "Look, I… I get we have a complicated relationship. You know that and I know that. Maybe I shouldn't have taken you as a mentee, but I've known you since you were little and your dad… he asked me, you know? And it felt right. You are one amazing young woman, Nonie. Full of promise. We can't lose you to solitary confinement over what happened here." He pauses and wets his lips. "*I* can't lose you to that." The apple in his throat bobs up and down.

For one eternal moment, we look into the other's eyes, and it's what I needed. Like a dam broke, my First Sense swells with the knowledge of what to do, bringing a surge relief with it. *Finally.*

I suck in my lower lip and release it again. "I trust in you to do the right thing with what I'm about to tell you. I can't stress enough how important this is."

Admiral Kieran nods. "Of course. I appreciate your trust in me."

Nodding my chin toward the blurry forcefield. "I assume it's soundproof?"

A shy smile pops up as he regards me from under his lashes. "Do you think I would have said half of what I just did if it weren't?"

I chuckle once. "No, probably not. And no audio or video in here, because—"

"—it violates prisoner privacy, correct."

This timeline is better than ours as it progresses. Sheridan's stupid bubbles showed everything to the guards outside. Not cool at all.

I nod. "Do you mind if we sit? I'm a tad woozy." The doc's injection helped a lot, but some of the barbed wire concrete is still there, only not as bad as before.

His brows fly up to his forehead. "No. Not at all, I'm sorry, I—"

"Never mind, no problem." I wave a hand. Emotions ran high, I get it. Letting myself fall onto the cot I pat the space next to me.

Admiral Kieran hesitates, but then sits down, somewhat stiff, hands on his thighs.

I chuckle softly. "You know, it's odd seeing you like this."

He cocks his head. "Sitting next to you in a brig? I sure hope it's odd." A glint of humor shines in his eyes, and I smile.

"Yes and no. But… I'm not used to you as an admiral." I wanted to say I wasn't used to him as an old man, but that's a tad too mean.

"You've only known me as an admiral. All your life."

I look up to meet and hold his gaze, willing him to listen and not freak out. "No, I haven't. Where I'm from, you're a captain. Where I'm from, you're younger. Where I'm from, things are different."

Admiral Kieran's chest rises sharply. "You're saying—" He twists at the waist to better look at me. "No, that can't be. You look like her. I mean maybe… maybe a tad younger, but…" Knocking the aberrant curl out of his face his gaze bores into mine. "Are you saying you're from a different universe?"

My smile widens. "That's what I'm saying. Your Nonie and me, we obviously have certain things in common, but at one point our paths split." Probably when I was kidnapped, if our theories hold. "In my timeline, I went to the Academy and graduated early. I'm a lieutenant with USEF."

Admiral Kieran's eyebrows pop up. "Is there any proof to what you're saying? No offense, but you could be going for insanity to lower your sentence. It's a smart thing to do."

"None taken. Proof. Well, if you scan me for Setayashi-radiation it should show positive."

"Setayashi-radiation? What is that even?"

"A by-product of time travel." I swipe a strand of my hair behind my ear. "Since you don't know that I assume there really is no time travel in your world?"

Admiral Kieran huffs. "Definitely not. Or at least, not that I know of."

Oh. So like I assumed, this Nonie never got thrown back to the *Pioneer*. Her and Kieran never met when he was young.

The admiral gives me a pointed look. "And traces of that radiation won't do the trick. You can tell me all you want, and I can't prove it."

Point taken. I look him in the eye. "You can check on the man who came with me. I think that would clarify a lot."

"The guy with the masker?"

"Or rather, the guy without a masker." I hold his gaze, waiting for him to do the math.

His jaw works. "Now you really have me curious."

I shrug. "Or you can hail me. Your Nonie. Check in on her." She'll be right where she's supposed to be.

Admiral Kieran gives me a skeptical glance, then swipes his palm over a small wrist PAD. "Call Cadet Thorburn." He angles himself away from me, but still I stand up to give him some space.

Not even two seconds later, an image of the other me pops up at eye level for the admiral.

"Admiral," she says. "Is everything all right? I wasn't expecting to hear from you for a while."

His response takes him a second too long to be truly convincing. "Yes. Yes, of course, Cadet, I was just… I was just calling to tell you once again you're missing out."

This Nonie smiles, and dang it, it's not a smile a cadet gives an admiral. It's the smile I give people I like. I would know, because she looks like me, duh, although a tad different somehow. It's not only that her hair is shorter and cut into a bob—not a bad choice, by the way— but that she's a noticeable four years older. Huh. I definitely look more mature. Suits me. Still doesn't change that this Cadet Nonie likes Admiral Wildason.

"I know I'm missing out, Admiral, but it's better I stayed home."

"I happen to disagree."

"I know, sir." The corners of her lips drop the slightest as her eyes dull, and it tells me all I need to know. I've spent enough time with myself to recognize when I'm shutting down for emotional protection.

For a moment, silence hovers. Then Admiral Kieran nods. "Anyway. Carry on. Sorry to have bothered you."

"You never bother me, Admiral."

They both smile at each other, then the admiral ends the call. He presses his lips together and shakes his head. "Dammit," he curses, then taps his Hablamate. "Wildason to Captain Chocho, private channel."

*"Chocho here."*

"Initiate full communication lock-down. Has USEF security already been informed on the intruders?"

*"Negative sir, Karakunnel is still working on his report. He wanted to add the doctor's scans as well—"*

"Disregard that. As of now, the arrival of the intruders will be kept top secret and on a need-to-know basis. Limited access to the brig. This is not going to be discussed amongst the crew. Please assemble the officers who know about this and have seen the intruders in the conference room."

*"Sir?"* Chocho sounds confused.

Admiral Kieran sighs. "I know what it sounds like, Captain, but you know me. I have a reason for my actions, and it's a good one. I'll let you know as soon as I can. Wildason— Oh actually, one more thing. Please demat the male intruder to this location. Thank you. Wildason out." He taps the Hablamate, then looks at me. "How ready do I need to be?"

"I'd say you're doing a pretty good job reacting to these curveballs. You'll be fine."

He huffs and stands up as well. "I sure hope—"

The high-pitched whine of a re-materialization interrupts him. Within two seconds the swirls and little sparks still, leaving my Kieran in the middle between his counterpart and me, his back to the admiral. As soon as he sees me, he darts forward and wraps me in his arms.

"Nonie!" Kieran buries his face into the crook of my neck. "Are you okay?"

I hug him back. "Now I am." Now that problem one is solved, us being separated. I tap his shoulder. "You might want to meet our visitor."

Kieran stiffens, then pops his head up and whirls around, keeping one hand clasped around my arm, as if he wanted to make sure I wasn't going anywhere.

Both men inhale sharply, but it's Admiral Kieran who turns pale and takes a stumbling step backwards. "You—"

My Kieran, at this point a pro at time travel and weird timeline jumps, lets go of me and raises a hand to the visor of his cap to greet his counterpart. "Hi. Yes, I'm you. Just a bit younger." He adds a smile to his words.

His older version rakes a hand through his hair in a very familiar motion, then drops it. "Well. I think your statement has just been confirmed. Time travel…" He shakes his head. "Or inter-dimensional travel. What do you even call it?"

"Good question," I mutter, then shrug. "We're pretty new at it. I'm the only person where I'm from able to do such a thing." Which, I'm realizing, is technically a lie. Sheridan is jumping realities, too. He has help though, I think, like Mashaule and au contraire to me. I'm a natural.

"If only you can switch realities, why are you both here?" The admiral points at Kieran.

"I kind of dragged him along. It's complicated. Fair to say we didn't expect to land here. Something went awry, and I took the wrong exit, so to speak. I wasn't trying to come here."

"That's good to know, yet somehow disturbing knowing what exists beyond the walls of our limited comprehension."

My Kieran shakes his head, the few locks that escaped the cap bouncing. "I don't think you'll have to worry about that. And your universe will get there when they get there."

"But the big question is, what will you do about it. About us?" I gesture at Kieran and myself.

Kieran slides his hand from my forearm to my hand and holds on to it.

The admiral's eyes widen, as the apple in his throat moves. "I... I think I gave you a good idea of what I'll be doing. Your existence will have to be top secret. If word gets out time travel is possible and that our Nonie potentially can do that as well, I don't know what may happen." He paces back and forth through the brig. "At least I need to be able to control the narrative to a degree and to give her a heads-up. With the knowledge that we can be breached the way you did, and Nonie at our hands, they might turn her into a tool of defense."

I frown. "Okay, that's basically what I am." Recruited by the FBTI and sent out to do damage control. "But I don't feel like a tool, just FYI. I'm happy and proud I can help the USEF."

A smile tugs on the corners of his mouth. "That's so very you," he says. "Either way, this will stay top secret until we feel like it can become common knowledge. Any of it." His gaze darts from his younger counterpart to myself, only snatching on our entwined hands for a moment. "Now, you said you landed here on accident. Let's be real. Once I report you, there's no way you're going to be allowed to leave, at least not for a while, and..." He lifts his sheepish gaze to us. "...I'm partial to both of you. So, before anything goes on the record, is there anything I can do to help you get back home?"

That's easy. "Actually, there is. When we were brought here, a small disk was taken from me. I need it to generate a spike of Setayashi radiation to help me jump back home."

"That's it?"

"That's it."

"And then you'll leave and…?"

"And never come back. Again, I didn't plan to get us here, and I don't think we should be doing timeline-hopping."

The admiral leans his head left to right. "It for sure would make people less nervous if they knew this was a one-time occurrence. And, knowing your counterpart, I trust you. To a degree—no offense. After all, you're like her, but not her. Probably a few years younger, too."

"No offense taken," I say.

He looks at his younger self. "But you… I haven't looked like you in decades. Why are you so young?"

"Believe me, looks are deceiving. I don't feel young."

I jerk my head over to Kieran. The way he said it, somewhat resigned, somewhat angry—

He sighs. "In our timeline, I was trapped in the Essken Realm for close to forty years. I didn't age, so when Nonie got me out, I looked the same as I did on the day I entered." Kieran spreads his arms wide, only the slightest shake in his voice hinting at the emotions connected to his statement.

The admiral jerks back. "Trapped in the Essken Realm? You survived that? When we first encountered them, we tried to send ambassadors, but they either died or lost their minds."

"The Bond," I say, gesturing from Kieran to me and back. "It protected him."

His mouth drops open. "The Bond. The *Magellan* Bond? Are you telling me that you and you…" He moves his index finger from one of us to the other, like I did. "That's… unexpected. On many levels."

I roll my eyes. "Was a surprise for me as well, believe me."

"Get in line." Kieran motions behind him. "Imagine my surprise when you left and I was torn apart from the inside."

I cringe. "I know. Sorry."

"It's all good." A gap of silence hovers. "That pain was nothing. You and me are about the only good thing that happened since the war started." He lowers his gaze, but I still catch part of the anguish he feels whenever the war is mentioned. Goosebumps run down my spine. The pain of a disrupted Bond was nothing? In comparison to what—what he went through in the Realm?

My heart skips a beat. Maybe I'm still underestimating what it was like during those decades trapped, what it truly meant.

The admiral whistles through his teeth. "If you were in the Realm, who made peace with the Essken?"

Kieran stiffens. "No one. At least not yet. We're working on it. Who made peace in your reality? Was that… you?" We exchange a glance, and judging by the look on his face, we're thinking the exact same thing.

The admiral nods, a light red tinging his cheeks. "It was me. We were lucky. For a few weeks, it seemed as if war was unavoidable, because the Essken were that destructive—the Magellans warned us about that and we almost went to war because of it. Eventually I figured out how to communicate with them. Once you truly understand each other, it's much harder to find a reason for fighting."

"You figured that out?" Respect and awe flares in Kieran's voice. "How?"

"Couple of things." The older man shrugs. "Assumed their senses differed from ours. Hailing resulted in attacks each and every time, and once, when I encountered them planet-side, I could've sworn they tracked by scent. We came up with a theory and workaround and established very basic communication within a few days, then eventually came up with a peace contract."

Just like my Kieran did. The exact same thought process, only uninterrupted by war and, well, me. Every muscle in my body locks up. I don't want to hear the details, but the luxury of prioritizing want over need isn't one we can afford. "W-were you ever a victim of the Essken's Mind Crucification?"

The older Kieran jerks his head back. "Me? No. I think I escaped narrowly once, when we got a distress call from them. I dematted down and was greeted—and I'm putting that in quotation marks—by armed Essken. Thing is, I had Zio—you both know Zio?" We nod, and he continues. "I had Zio treat me with an injectable anti-odorant before I went, just on a whim, and it worked. Apparently, I didn't smell aggressive to them. Twenty seconds after I materialized, they lowered their weapons. And, well, the rest is history."

Yeah. Their history. Their history uninterrupted by my traveling to the past. Who distracted Kieran with her presence? Me. Who distracted him from his idea of tracking by scent? Me. Once he came out of the Mind Crucification, USEF didn't give him another chance. They enforced the hails at every encounter, the ones Kieran always suspected triggered the Essken.

All that war. All those years of war because of my distractions. Because of me.

If Kieran is thinking he should've stopped the war sooner, what am I supposed to think? Because he would have, if it hadn't been for me. I was the variable, the Diversion Point. I was the reason he didn't figure it out and the war continued.

My throat feels tight all of a sudden. Struggling to pull in air, I wonder how much responsibility one person can shoulder. How much weight can they carry before they break? How much guilt has to build up before one's soul is crushed under it?

And how much is one allowed to crumble under all of it when what remains of our world is on the line?

I push down the bile rising up my throat and file Old Kieran's information to be processed—and cried over—later. Like Kieran, I need to be functional now. We can't afford to not be at least close to our best, but both of us will have to unpack some baggage when we have the time.

Old Kieran scratches his neck. "Those were our first steps into founding the UWO. The Essken have made us stronger and a better people."

His words and awe transform the younger Kieran's face. I haven't seen him smile that radiantly in a while, a long while. Not since around the time when I jumped to save him from Mashaule during his acceptance speech for the Golden Star of Combat. *I was a different man then*, he said, a couple of hours ago when we met my mom there, and his happiness for his older self's success highlights that difference. Kieran hasn't smiled worry-free in a long time.

He feels for my hand and pushes his shaking fingers in-between mine, twisting the ring on my finger. "Somehow I like this timeline," he whispers into my ear. "Even though it confirms our theory."

I agree with both. We have peace, not a war dragging on for decades, Kieran survives, and the UWO is founded, like Other Kieran did. Seems like a good outcome to me—but maybe not everybody shares that point of view. Namely, whoever wants to make sure there isn't any peace. We're on to something, I can feel it.

Smiling up at him, I squeeze his fingers. "Yeah, this timeline has its benefits." I would like to add though that listening to my First Sense is still a work in progress, but I knew, I *knew* in the depth of my heart that had Kieran not been pulled into the Realm, the war would've been shorter. I said it before—I felt it, my whole life.

He squeezes my hand like I did to his. "But there's a very big difference to our universe." He lifts our entwined hands and places a kiss onto my knuckles.

I pale.

Correct. Without the Essken Realm, Kieran and I wouldn't be where we are now.

And it makes me ridiculously happy that him and I exist at the same time, but it makes me also feel incredibly guilty. We found each other, while billions of beings died during a war that wasn't stopped because of my presence in the past. Because I interfered.

Kieran lowers my hand. "Are you okay?"

I fix a quick smile onto my face. "Yeah. Yes. Sure. I'm fine." And I will be, once I've accepted I had no choice. I was thrown into the past and acted according to what I knew at the time, incorrect temporal rules and blossoming First Sense included. I was a cog in a wheel spun by somebody else, namely the true responsible party.

That doesn't mean I don't feel guilt over what I did, what I caused. I do, and I probably will for as long as I live.

Kieran narrows his eyes, the movement emphasizing the darkish circles under them, and also a clear sign he doesn't believe me. The older Kieran comes to my rescue, his gaze fixed on our entwined hands.

"I can't believe you're bonded. I should be more perplexed by the fact that time-traveling and different universes exist, but apparently that's not what affects me the most." He laughs out harsh and pinches his nose. "It is quite eye-opening to see other possible realities."

Thankful for the interruption, I nod. "I can imagine what you're talking about." I saw him interact with my counterpart. No matter the universe, there seems to be a connection between Kieran and me. It led to heartbreak for Other Nonie and Other Kieran, and it led nowhere with this Admiral Wildason and his Cadet Nonie, but that doesn't mean there isn't a connection. Maybe we're a focal point. Maybe we always happen, to varying degrees.

The admiral looks up from our hands. "I assume our timelines split when we made peace and you didn't? We then founded UWO and you… didn't? It would make sense a split happened there, wouldn't it? Is that how it works? Only that we, our universe, assumed split offs would decay while only one main timeline persisted."

I nod, and choose to ignore the part about the split-off. Self-protection. I can't break down bawling now. "To be honest, that's exactly what we thought until recently." It's also what everybody else at home still believes. Guess they're in for a surprise. I wonder what became out of my mom's ideas. Her life was cut short, but she must've made progress in the years until her death. Where is her research? How far did she get, and what happened to it?

The admiral paces through the small cell. "Alright, so you need the disk to leave and once you do, you'll likely not come back, which is helpful, yet not. Could you stay for a while?" He stops to look at us. "It would help support the story."

"It would, but I don't think it's a good idea." I give him my best apologetic frown. "We ended up here because somebody is chasing us. Long story, but we need to get out of here before he finds us. Not only because we don't want to be captured by that person—"

"Again," Kieran mumbles under his breath.

"—but also because I don't want any harm to come to you." Wouldn't that be fantastic? I accidentally jump us here and get Admiral Kieran killed. A shudder runs down my spine. Not going to happen.

"That's appreciated, but I can hold my own. I do see your reasoning though. It unfortunately leaves me with not much for my officers and USEF to go by besides my word."

"Not quite." Kieran points at the sensor strip inside the ceiling. "You should be able to get a Setayashi spike that should match the one from our appearance. Your Nonie—"

"Is at the academy," I add. "There's the alibi, including your call to her location. You'll have enough to get them thinking."

Admiral Kieran chuckles. "Understatement of my career. But okay, I understand." He reaches into his pocket, pulls out the disk, and wiggles it.

My eyes widen. "You had it this whole time?"

Shrugging, he tosses it over to me. "We didn't know what it was. I wanted to question you about it. For obvious reasons, I figured you'd be more amenable to talking to me than to the Chief of Security." He winks.

I catch the disk and grunt with the sudden movement, when the left-over barbed wire digs in deeper.

Kieran snaps his head over to me. "You're still hurting?"

"I'm not quite back to a hundred percent." I shrug, like, no biggie. "But this makes me feel much better." I wiggle the disk like Old Kieran did, a shuttle load of pressure falling off my shoulders. "Thank you, Admiral. For everything, and that includes having an open mind."

"Right back at you. Thank you for opening my mind. I foresee some very interesting conversations ahead of me."

"That for sure." Especially with one very specific person. I wonder how that will go. Pity they can't send me a message to update me.

"Excuse us for a second." I turn to Kieran and lower my voice to a whisper. "We need to come up with a game plan overall. We're running and acting as a response to Sheridan's actions, and I don't like it. I get it he has the better tech and his origin time is… *futural* from ours, which gives him all kinds of advantages, but that shouldn't mean we've lost the battle already."

"Agreed," Kieran whispers back. "What do you suggest?"

"Even though we didn't exactly plan the jumps we took, we have way more information now. What do you think about jumping back to our now? We need backup. Chase and Zio should be able to help us figure out who is behind the Temporal War."

Kieran's jaw tightens. "Agreed. We need that backup and protection."

I nod. "Then it's a plan. Ready?"

"Ready."

I press the button on the disk, my body warming up a split second after, as soon as the radiation takes a hold of my cells.

"It was very nice to meet you, Admiral," I say to the older man.

Warmth radiates from his eyes. "The pleasure was all mine to meet both of you."

The tingling in my body grows stronger and stronger, until the Maelstrom takes over and the image of Admiral Kieran Wildason fades out.

# Chapter Thirteen - Different Path

*The Maelstrom on the Way back Home*

The moment reality fades away and the Maelstrom takes over, I look out for the swirl of time and events feeling the most familiar to me. To my utter relief—because let's face it, I'm not a pro at inter-reality jumps—I feel and see it right away. There's no mistaking it. Maybe I could even find it blindfolded the way my body hums and pulls me in its direction.

"Do you see it?" Kieran asks. "Because obviously I don't, but that being said, everything looks... more colorful. Brighter, somehow."

I look up at him. "Yes, I see it." I point in the general direction of what feels like home. "You're getting used to the Maelstrom. If you continue like this, I'm going to be out of a job soon." I elbow him in the side and he grins.

"No, thank you. I'll stick to starships to jump from one place to another. It's more—"

Dizziness rolls over me in a series of shockwaves, every new one worse than the previous. I groan as everything begins to spin, as reality cramps up around me. Holy Sun and Stars—what's going on? I've never experienced this during a jump, I—

*Everything around me billows, rears, bubbles—*

*"Nonie!" Kieran calls out my name, pulling on my arm. "What's going— Crap!" He grunts and doubles over—surrounded by bright, luminescent coils.*

*I gasp as a sharp bolt of pain shoots through my midsection. Doubling over, I cry out. Another K'Zee-attack—in the Maelstrom! The break we had was too good to be true. And it's worse than before, like somebody had cranked up the volume. Dozens and dozens of K'Zees attack Kieran from all sides, all of them thicker, longer, and brighter than ever before, merciless in their assault. Kieran stiffens, then bows back, his face contorting into a grimace of pain.*

*That's all the warning I get before more of the coils shoot through him and our connected hands into me, not only doubling the pain, but tripling it. Quadrupling. As though I'd touched a live wire, my muscles lock up from the sheer energy slamming into my body. To top it off, another wave of nausea and dizziness swamps me.*

*This is new. And bad. Really bad. The intensity is on a whole different level, and without any of the bliss or the endorphins that accompanied the K'Zees, only that cutting pain. My breath comes out in short little wheezes. Couldn't let go of Kieran's hand, even if I wanted, my muscles are frozen in place, held in position by a reflex I can't control. Can't see clearly, either, everything blurs—no that's not me, it's the Maelstrom blurring, distorting. Kieran is as clear as day; me, too, like the strand belonging to the Realm, but everything else… not, as if it's stretched too thin.*

*Ignoring the searing pain, I try to grasp what's happening, why this is different. A part of me knows it's important I pay attention, but it's close to impossible.*

*Time swirls around me like the strands were thrown into a blender— ours, others related to it, others that don't even look remotely familiar. Nothing is orderly and calm anymore, events blow up and contract, faces, cities, things, all accompanied by a cacophony of noise. What the absolute—?*

*A bright white flash blinds me. I cry out, squeeze my eyes shut and throw my hand up to my face—*

*Holy. Everything.*

*Gone is the noise of myriads of events happening at the same time, all replaced by deafening silence. While my insides are a complete chaos of coils and pain, everything out here is the exact opposite, absolute peace and silence. For a moment, I consider having lost my hearing, but Kieran's suppressed grunts contradict that theory.*

*I let the hand protecting my eyes sink down, fighting the dizziness and the tearing sensations on my inside. The outskirts of my vision black out, but no doubt about it, this is real. Not me seeing things. Real. Pulling myself together with sheer force of will, I focus on ignoring the burning in my core and yank on Kieran's hand. "Kieran, look!"*

*My croaked words echo through the vast emptiness around us. Where a mere second ago billowing clouds of time and events surrounded us, an utter black chasm cuts through everything, and I mean* everything. *Like somebody had taken a knife and sliced through timelines, cutting them in half. Some are only cut open, others completely severed. The thin band of the Realm glitters in the distance, unaffected, like our intact strand a reassuring presence against the sensation of complete destruction. Uber-bright flashes light up the edges of this gorge, the image made even spookier by countless energy coils rippling along its borders, many of them veering off their path to find their way to Kieran, like moths to a flame.*

*My knees buckle as another wave of fiery K'Zees shoots from him through me, their force threatening to overwhelm me. I grit my teeth. Can't let it distract me, this is huge, and I don't mean that I can't make out a beginning or an end to this… this cleft, but the fact this is happening at all.*

*Nothing should be able to put a cleft through freaking all timelines, nothing!*

*My breath comes out in short, cut-off bursts. No doubt, it's a cleft for sure, like Other Zio said—a temporal cleft. Were the other shifts clefts, too? This one feels way worse than the others—because we're in the Maelstrom, maybe? And what is the cleft, where does it come from? How do I make it go away?*

*Kieran contorts under the onslaught of another wave of coils. Knowing they're coming does nothing to help with the agony when they reach me. This time, my vision truly blackens at the periphery as my body is ripped apart one cell at a time, fried, disassembled, and fried again. But finally— finally!—the relief sets in. Something happens inside my body and instinct* takes over. I feel my First Sense flare up like a cramp in the depth of my core, protecting me, turning those razor-sharp edges into the softest cotton, soothing my aching cells and wounded soul. It pushes the energy out of my body, away from my core, away from where it hurts. Out of the corner of my eye, and with the last bit of conscious thought left, I see my hand light up and glow, like a beacon of light illuminating the darkness. It warms to the point of burning—and just before I think I can't take it anymore, my body rids itself of the coils' energy as it bursts out of my fingertips like it was trying to rip them off.

I yelp out and yank my hand back, fingers cramped up and throbbing—

Without any warning whatsoever, the cleft flashes, and the two sides of the Maelstrom reunite in a clash of colors and time swirls, the impact's shockwave crashing into us, throwing us head over heels through time and space.

I scream out, and so does Kieran. The joy of hearing him yell and realizing the pain, the coils, are gone, is very, very short-lived as the powers of whatever-that-just-was use us as a play ball. Inertia forces my head back, Kieran's hold loosens on me, and with a panicked scream I throw myself around to grab onto his arm with my other hand, damned if I let go of it. Can't lose him, but also can't hold on much longer.

Times and events of multiple timelines—I think—rush past us and through us, time and dimensions pulling on us as if they wanted to tear us apart and turn our insides out. Can't get a footing, can't even control my flailing limbs.

We need to get out of the Maelstrom.

Like, now, before we get separated, injured, or killed.

I grunt and focus, trying to ignore the panicky pressure inside my chest cutting off air, cutting off oxygen.

Another temporal wave of sorts crashes into us, the impact like stepping in front of a starship about to jump, throwing us back in a spin and tumble with absolutely no chance to control our trajectory, or anything.

That's when I realize we're not going to make it home.

Our priorities have just changed.

I don't see our timeline, and I don't think I have the time to search.

I make an executive decision, focus, feel for something *familiar*, anything, *and—*

Kieran and I slam into concrete, the force of the impact bringing him to his knees and me to all fours.

"Crap," he gasps, bracing himself with his hands on the hard ground, sucking in long, deep breaths. "That was…" He shakes his head, puffing out air.

"New," I wheeze. "I—"

"Wait." Kieran's tone is serious. "Are we home? Our timeline, our time? It looks like we could be. Houses, street… some suburban area."

I try to shake my head, then change my mind when intense nausea flares up, like my First Sense was injured. Opening my eyes works, at least long enough to get a glimpse of concrete and part of a white picket fence to my right. "I don't think so, it didn't feel like it." To be sure, I would have to get up, or at the very least lift my head or keep my eyes open longer, and sorry, neither nor is going to happen right now. I don't think I can move yet.

Kieran pushes himself up into a low squat position, much slower than I usually see him move, even after a fall. "Can you jump us again?" The question is asked in his captain's voice, the one I'm used to hearing on the bridge, and while I'd love to give him a positive answer, jumping us would mean I'd have to move.

Sucking in one long breath before I slowly exhale, I nod. "Not right now, but soon. Yes. Believe me, it's my priority. I just need a minute, but also, I think the Maelstrom needs a minute." Or two, or three. Can it even recover from being sliced through? What if it can't? What would that mean for us, for—

"What was that thing?" Kieran whispers, swallowing loudly. "Was that what Other Zio meant when he said a cleft?"

"I… I don't know what that was." Besides scary beyond belief. "Did you… did you see it *cut through* timelines? Not ours, not the Realm,"— yet, maybe—"but through so many." What does that mean for the affected timelines? Do they continue on? Disintegrate? What happens if the past is cut off from the future?

"No. No, I didn't." He swallows audibly. "I was living in the moment, meaning, trying to keep it together."

I huff out a broken-off laugh, but cut it short. Ow. "Geez, that wasn't fun." Sorry I sound whiny, but it's not without reason. Every single one of my superficial breaths wheezes in and out. I feel like I aged sixty years overnight. I feel empty, drained, my First Sense aching, which makes for a weird stomach-churning throbbing sensation. To top it off, I'm a bit offended by my body. This whole yearning for those coils, only to be roasted from the inside by them is a bit of a betrayal.

"That jump had more of a punch to it than usual." Grunting, Kieran works himself up to standing and dusts off his palms on his thighs, then looks around, a worried expression on his face. "Nobody around. It still looks like home."

I lift my head, but nausea rises, and I slam my eyelids shut. Nope. Nope. I'm not going to throw up. Raising and waving one hand, I hold my head still. "Wonderful. Maybe I didn't bring us too far off from home. Not that I could control much of where we went."

Kieran blows out a puff of air. "I'm amazed you got us out at all, and safely so. The forces at play... unimaginable. The K'Zees also attacked with a newfound intensity, like they were trying to take me apart."

"Agreed." I try to sit up from my position on all fours, but abort the movement when nausea roils inside my stomach. Never mind. All fours are fine.

"And we still don't know what's causing any of it, the coils, or that cleft." He kicks at a pebble on the ground. "My reflex is to blame Sheridan, because I find it quite coincidental that he's chasing us and something else is trying to take us out, but I doubt his powers are that developed."

I shake my head once, then flinch. Not a good idea. This is the worst transition I've ever had, after the worst jump ever. Fitting. "There's no way he would be able to pull off something of that magnitude. It was literally like time was torn apart. No way he can do that."

"Feels good to hear that. The question then becomes, besides how can we stop it, what is that cleft, why is it there, and why is it affecting us more than others?"

I breathe in slowly through my nose and out through my mouth. Quite annoying it takes me so long to recover. Kieran is up and standing, while I… am not. "I'm the only person we know of with a mixed human-Magellan genome, so maybe it's something about that. Zio was somewhat affected, so maybe Magellan genes are sensitizing, but only in the combination with human genes does it lead to what I'm experiencing?" My First Sense does protect me though, which I really, really appreciate.

"Where does that leave me? My genome is as boring as they come."

I shrug, the movement not half as nauseating as expected, if I keep my eyes closed, at least. Reassured by that, I sit back on my legs, samurai-style, my bruised knees unappreciative of the change in position, although my biosynthetic left knee doesn't hurt as much. Appreciate the Magellan's quality of work.

That being said, if I had a better grasp of our landings, I'd be in better shape. I'm getting so much better at the jumps, current obstacles and complications excluded, but the landings I still mess up, besides the one behind Other Nonie's couch I was so proud of. In my defense though, nothing about this last jump was normal. "No idea where that leaves you. Other Kieran wasn't as affected as you, so maybe it's our Bond?" It would make sense. After all, it helped Kieran in the Realm and to recognize more details in the Maelstrom, so why not assume it also sensitized him in a similar way?

Kieran takes me by the upper arm and helps me up. "Take it easy. I'm still a bit off balance." He pauses. "And you know, normally I would put more resources into finding out about this cleft. It doesn't seem like it's something good."

"Agreed. But?" I keep my eyes closed, since my brain is insisting gravity doesn't exist. How can things sway when I don't even have my eyes open?

"But right now, there is no normal for us, and we don't have any resources, being on the run. As much as it annoys me, we have to figure out problem one before we can even think about tackling problem two."

Agreed. "Problem one is getting us back home. I don't want to make it easy for Sheridan, and I don't want us to be sitting ducks, but for that, I need the Maelstrom to be normal again." Or we won't stand a chance. "So, I guess problem two then is taking care of Sheridan, and problem three, the events and coils."

Kieran's voice hardens. "And when you say taking care of Sheridan, I would like to add that I will *take care* of him whenever I get my hands on him. I hope for his sake his protective field works against my punches as well. He shot you in the back."

And while I don't appreciate that either, Kieran's response is another sign he isn't as even keeled as he used to be. "Threatening violence on my behalf? That's—" I snap my mouth shut and swallow my next comment. Not the time and place, or even the universe, to open up that can or worms. Instead, I fix an amused smile on my face. "…archaic, yet romantic."

My comment breaks the tension as Kieran chuckles. "I know. I'm just not the biggest fan of Sheridan's methods, no surprise there."

"So I've noticed." I smack my lips. Although I doubt Sheridan is one of ours, not that I cared what he thought. "But anyway, I agree with you. I don't like Sheridan's methods either."

Kieran exhales a little too forcefully to pretend he wasn't holding his breath, then harrumphs. "It's majorly concerning he found us in a different timeline, especially after the judge told us there was only one— and yet he jumps to different realities? Preaching one thing and practicing another. Can't say I like it."

"Same here. Thinking back though, he did look surprised when he saw my double. And you." Like he hadn't expected that.

Kieran dusts off my pants for me with one hand, keeping the other firmly wrapped around my upper biceps to keep me from swaying too much. "You're thinking he was surprised by an alternate reality? Not so sure. I think it's reasonable in general to be surprised by the exact conditions he's appearing in. I mean, do you always know exactly what you're jumping into? And by that, I mean circumstances, not only the time and place, but the exact location. Who is there, what is there, and all that jazz? And speaking of… any better idea where and when we are?" Turning once around his axis Kieran takes in the view. "It looks somewhat familiar."

"I have no idea." I sway a little more as I lift my head to look around, only to slam my eyelids closed again. Ugh, stupid dizziness.

Kieran stabilizes me by my arm with a force as if he worries I'll fall flat on my face.

To be honest, I don't think it's an unreasonable concern.

"Easy there." He squeezes my arm. "I think standing on your own is imperative before jumping."

I exhale a shaky breath and open my eyes. My gaze falls onto the single-family homes with pretty front yards and white picket fences—

Recognition hits, no matter in which universe.

My eyes widen. How did I get us *here*, of all places? "I know where—"

"Oh, how inconvenient." Somebody clicks their tongue. "And that would be twenty-four hours of lock-away and a mark on your record. You know the rules. ID out, come on, come on, I don't have all day."

Kieran whirls around, his hand still on my arm—and freezes. "Shit," he mutters under his breath, then moves to shield me, but not fast enough for me to not agree with Kieran's assessment of the situation. I recognize a patrolling officer when I see one, and this one isn't happy. At all.

The man, about thirty or so, is dressed in a black uniform not unlike the FBTI's and scowls at us, a PAD in his hand. *Shit*, indeed. This isn't what I would call staying under the radar.

My muscles are hard and rigid. I'm dizzy from standing up, and I have no energy to jump us anywhere right now when I need to be able to run. To fight. To get us out of here—

The man sighs, then makes a circling motion with his hand. "Get it going. Ignoring General Mashaule's Law is bad enough, but refusing cooperation? Or do you think curfew doesn't apply to you?" He narrows his eyes at us, tapping his PAD with one of his fingers. "I'm waiting. You—"

"Shouldn't be out here, which is what I said about a million times, Nonie." Hearing my name said by *that* voice, I jerk, then twist at the waist toward the one person I really didn't want to meet.

Dad.

I mean, not mine, but some other Nonie's.

Dressed in a USEF uniform with different markings and color codes, Dad stands behind us, hands crossed behind his back, in a wide stance, glaring at the other man, whose demeanor changes completely.

"Ambassador Thorburn." He bows and lowers his PAD. "I didn't expect to find you here. It's after—"

"And I didn't expect my daughter out here after she promised she was going to be *up in her room* and *studying*." Doesn't matter which timeline, I know that disappointed and annoyed expression. He glares at me, and, born out of years of kind of being this man's daughter, there's only one response. I go with the flow.

"Just getting some air, Dad."

"Right." Dad puts his hands on his hips. "And you are?" He looks up and down Kieran, ignoring the other officer.

Before I can make up my mind what kind of lie to come up with, Kieran tips the visor of his cap with one hand, then holds out his other hand. "Colin Cortez, nice to meet you, sir." He's definitely a natural at this.

Dad harrumphs, but shakes Kieran's hand. "You the tutor to help Nonie with her admission test for the academy?"

My mouth drops open. "My *admission* test?" Admission? I started the academy as the youngest student ever, I—

I snap my mouth shut when Dad gives me *that* look. "Yes, your *admission* test. We talked about the very important fact that carrying my name means you have to perform better than everybody else."

Well, at least some things haven't changed. The other officer shifts from one foot to another. Nothing worse than being caught in the middle of a higher-ranking officer's family quarrel. Okay, I can make it more awkward. I sigh and drop my head. "Yes, Dad, but you didn't have to rub it in like that. Colin just arrived and is probably already thinking I'm an imbecile after the way you said that."

"Would never," Kieran says, rocking back on his heels, hands behind his back. He looks utterly at home in the situation since Dad showed, au contraire to me, even though this is my dad. Somewhat.

The officer clears his throat. "Sir, if it's alright with you, I'll go back patrolling. I feel you have the situation under control." He salutes sharply.

"Thank you, Larson. Let's hope you're right. Apparently, you never know with the young folks." He rolls his eyes then points his thumb over his shoulder. "Off you go. Consider yourself warned for today."

I snap my mouth close. Guess we're going inside. "Okay, okay," I mumble. I open the gate and walk through, every other step spiking pain through my body from my soles to my head. Forcing it down with one big breath I ignore it. "We're gonna go and get started."

"Yes, we are." Kieran follows me through the gate right past Dad.

Just before we reach the entrance door, he calls out, "Colin?"

"Yes, sir?" Kieran turns around.

Dad tips his forehead with one finger. "Academy Debate Team. Had some of my best times at the Academy there."

Academy—Oh. *My dad's* hat Mom gave Kieran.

Grinning like he was in on the joke, Kieran tips his cap. "Arguably *the* best."

Dad chuckles.

"Good one." He pauses, tilting his head. "You remind me of someone."

Kieran shrugs and replies without missing a beat. "That's possible, sir. My granny says I look like this Texan soap opera star I forgot the name of. That could be it."

Dad wrinkles his forehead. "Nah, I don't think so. More like…" He scratches his head under the hat, then smiles and holds that finger up. "Ah, you look like a young Kieran Wildason. That's it!"

Keeping my reactions under control deserves an award for acting it cool. *A young Kieran Wildason.* Bonus points to Dad, but can't he be less observant?

Kieran's eyebrows shoot up. "Really? Wow, okay. That's a compliment I can live with. Thank you, sir." He grins at me. "Hear that? I might charge you extra now."

I roll my eyes. "Thanks, Dad," I call over my shoulder and face the door, thankful when I hear it unlock after recognizing my face. Am I glad this Nonie here didn't get a nose job or something.

Dad's only reply is a satisfied quiet laugh I cut off as soon as I enter the house that isn't mine and close the door behind us.

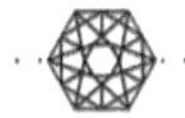

### Thorburn-Residence, Somewhen, Some Timeline

Silence.

Kieran drops the grin at the same time as air whistles between my teeth from my sharp exhale. That was close.

"I don't think I'll ever get used to different versions of us or people we know," Kieran whispers.

"No kidding," I whisper back. "One overbearing dad is enough, but two?"

He nods and brushes a strand of hair out of his eyes. "This timeline seems to have curfews. USEF enforced curfews. Military government? And... *General Mashaule's Law?*"

I nod and give an exaggerated shudder. "Military government, and I don't want to know the details if Mashaule gets to make laws. Plus, curfew, and twenty-four hours of lock-away for breaking it? Yikes." The grass is definitely not always greener on the other side. It feels weird being here in general, but especially in this house. This is my home, yet isn't. For one, the wall color is off. The carpets look different. And it smells like cat food.

Kieran peeks through the curtain of the window next to the door and jerks back. "Crap. Your dad's coming!"

I whirl around and look through the electronic peephole. Dad's four steps away from the door.

Crap, indeed.

Adrenaline chases the left-over dizziness away as I grab Kieran by the hand and yank him toward the stairs. If I understood Dad correctly, I'm apparently in my room, which I hope is also upstairs, like mine. "Not enough time to jump!" I hiss-whisper. I initiate the jump now, Dad's going to enter right when things get interesting, and there goes not contaminating this timeline. Even worse, what if he initiated house lockdown when we were ready to jump, and the shields popped up? No idea what would happen, but it probably wouldn't be good.

We dart upstairs and make it about six steps up before the door opens.

I drop Kieran's hand, and like we rehearsed it we stop. Kieran laughs once and continues a sentence he never started.

"—offering me any baked goods, you're saying I'm safe accepting?" He points at one of the many, many pictures hung along the wall, this one, like all of them a family picture of… of *all* of us. I swallow dry. In this timeline, in this universe, my mother is in all pictures. Not only did she not die, but she's in *all pictures*. A Magellan. Openly posing for pictures with her human-slash-half-human family, and, judging by the one Kieran's pointing at which shows her with this timeline's pre-schooler aged Nonie baking cookies in a mess of flour and tools, living with us.

I take a half second too long to truly be smooth with my response, but my brain needed a moment to come to terms with that fact. "I have years of practice, as you can see. Baking."

Closing the door behind him, Dad clicks his tongue. "I'd still be careful, Colin." He looks up to us and, well, just stays where he's at. Gah! Nowhere else to go but up.

I harrumph and lead the way. "Stop selling me out, Dad."

Dad lifts both hands. "Sorry, couldn't resist."

I roll my eyes at him and continue up the stairs, doing my best not to look at the pictures we're passing, but how could I not? They offer fascinating and tantalizing glimpses into a life that could have been. Mind blown. Of course, I expected a different timeline to be different. It's the name of the game, after all, but I didn't expect it to be such a biggie. My heart skips a beat.

Like any person could or would, Kieran tugs on my sleeve and points at a picture a bit higher up. "Oh gee, that one's cute," he says with a warm smile and loud enough for my dad to hear. Then, he drops his voice to a whisper. "It's you, even if it isn't."

An acute sense of longing, of having missed out on so many things, crashes over me when I look at the image Kieran indicated. Dad carries Mom on his shoulders, and perched on top of hers, preschooler Nonie is throwing her arms up with obvious glee in her expression.

I swallow. Yeah, I missed out. I knew that. Now I realize it even more.

"Which one?" Dad yells from downstairs, from… the kitchen, I would say? At least in my home it would be the kitchen.

"You carrying the weight of the world, Mom and me," I yell back.

"Ah, good one," his voice comes back muffled, then louder as he steps into the hallway again. "And now go and study, Daughter!"

Kieran and I exchange a glance and I lift both palms. What am I supposed to do? He's right there. Still can't really jump in front of him, can we? I point a finger up, then at my pocket, and Kieran nods. Once we're upstairs in the hallway, I can jump us.

Which means that for now I do the only thing I can do and lead the way up the stairs.

Downstairs, Dad opens a can of something, probably a sparkling water, if he is anything like my dad. In passing I glance at the remaining pictures, wishing I could stop, if only for a moment, to take them in some more. To savor them. But, as always, there is no time to rest and enjoy the moment.

As always.

I clench my jaw so hard, my molars hurt. Can you get burnout from a few weeks of time-traveling? Maybe, if the pressure is high enough?

And does it matter?

No, it doesn't. There's no way but forward for us, even though it might include going backwards and zigzagging sometimes.

As we reach the top of the stairs, Dad puts the drink down onto the side table in the hallway and comes up the stairs as well, in his normal, unhurried pace.

I suppress a grunt. Seriously? I mean, yay, it doesn't look like he's suspecting us to be intruders from a different reality, but could fate cut us some slack please and let us have those few seconds we need to jump without contaminating his timeline?

My mind races. Dad realizes something is off, I'm sure he's going to put the house on lock down. No idea if that'll work for my SED as well, but no demat would come through, in or out. No communication either, besides Dad's emergency code. My dad initiated lockdown once, about six months after my kidnapping, when he thought we had intruders. Turned out to be the neighbor's cat trapped in the living room, doing a typical cat-tight-rope dance around all of Dad's memorabilia lined up in the bookshelf and dropping them one after the other.

Two words of Dad's and the house's internal safety protocol will turn on, and then… we might be trapped for real, since only Dad can lift the protection.

I really don't want that to happen, so no, we can't stop and jump.

The only alternative is the other me, who I presume is doing what she's supposed to, and in her room, studying. The house would initiate lock-down on her orders as well, but I doubt she-slash-I would do that. Or, let's say it this way: I'd rather take my chances with myself.

Arriving in front of the door I'm pretty positive is mine I don't stop, I don't hesitate.

I walk right in.

Here goes nothing.

I open the door and enter with three fast steps, giving Kieran enough space to follow and close the door behind him right away. Buzzword privacy.

My counterpart sits on the cushioned wide windowsill, a book in her hand. "Dad, I told you—" Her jaw drops and her eyes pop comically wide when her gaze falls on me.

"Hi," I say with a little wave of my hand, then put my finger across my lips. What do you tell yourself to not freak out? "Sorry to intrude, I promise, we mean no harm. I'm—"

Her mouth closes and opens again. She blinks. Hard. "You... You're me." She tilts her head and lowers her book. "But you're not from my past. You look too young to be from my future and your hair is weird. Look at that. The only logical conclusion is that you're from a different timeline. I'd never wear my hair like that." She swipes one of the dozen or so blue strands scattered throughout her hair behind her ear.

Oh.

Okay. That... that went better than I expected. No freaking out, just a logical conclusion based on... hairstyles. Sure. Why not. Still, respect.

I nod and give her a thumbs-up, ignoring the barb about my *weird hair*. "Yes, you're correct, we're from a different timeline. So... different timelines are common knowledge here?" I point a finger down at the ground.

Blue Nonie slides off the windowsill. Her room might be in the same location as mine is at home, but it's got a different vibe. For one, the walls are painted in a soft pink. For mine I chose a warm yellow. I like what she did to the windowsill, widening it and turning it into a cushioned, comfy place to read. Mine is normal, for a lack of a better word, holding a trophy I won for fastest SAR during the academy. Even the bed, tucked into the right corner of the room, has covers I wouldn't have chosen myself. Frills aren't my thing.

She cocks her head as she comes closer. "I grew up with temporal theories. Our mom is a temporal specialist. Or, wait, maybe yours isn't."

Well, she is, but... "My mom died when she gave birth to me."

Blue Nonie stares at me. "Mom... died?" She says it with such sorrow I wonder how close they are in this reality. What I might have missed in mine.

I nod. "I grew up with Dad." Saying it after having spoken to Other Nonie and about Kieran's mom dying makes me realize how similar our fate is. Another sad fact of life, or rather, death, to bond over.

Her eyes widen. "With Dad. That must've been intense."

"You have no idea. Or actually, you might."

We grin at each other like two sisters.

Behind me, Kieran clears his throat. "Excuse us," he says to Blue Nonie and turns me aside. "What about not influencing other timelines?" he whispers in my ear. "This isn't it."

"What am I supposed to do?" I whisper back. "I had to say something after storming into her room. Plus, you know, I'm making this up as I go." I smack my lips and shake my head, the words coming out next feeling more than right. "Just because Other Nonie had a rule about not influencing others doesn't mean our timeline is going to come up with that. I agree we don't want to mess with anything in our past, but an alternate reality?" I shrug. "I'd treat it more like a first contact scenario. See where it leads us." We don't have the luxury of Other Nonie's ethical regulations. Not while on the run and trying to figure out our fate.

Several long moments pass before he nods once. "Okay. I feel that's fair. At least until smarter people than us can come up with something else."

"Please. Can't wait for the handbook." I huff, then turn back to Blue Nonie. "By the way, this is Kieran." *My boyfriend,* I want to say, yet don't. Just because I'm telling her some things about my timeline, doesn't mean she needs to know everything. Picking and choosing? For sure. I'd call it minimizing the contamin—

"Kieran?" Her gaze darts across his face as if she was trying to figure him out. "Why do you look familiar? Did we go to school together? Why do I feel I know you?"

"Well…" Kieran scratches his neck. "I told your father people think I'm that soap opera—"

She shuts him up with a wave of her hand. "No. You look like…

nah, that's kind of impossible, but yeah, you look like Captain Wildason. You know, from like fifty years ago or so? You totally—" She snaps her mouth shut and pales when she sees our faces. "Are you him? You're *him*?"

Kieran lifts and drops a shoulder. "Bull's eye."

As if a bomb dropped Nonie jumps back a step. "Holy everything! You're *the* Kieran Wildason? You're alive in your reality?"

Dread forms in my stomach. "He… he isn't in yours?" Maybe I just haven't gotten him out of the Realm yet, but I should've already been thrown back to the *Pioneer*—

Oh, heck. Color drains from my face as nausea rises. She hasn't been at the academy yet, Blue Nonie is studying for her *entrance* exam, at my current age. That means she hasn't traveled back to the *Pioneer*. And that means that—

"Captain Wildason died as one of the first victims during the beginning of the Quaneez Wars. Quaneez Mind Crucification." Blue Nonie looks at Kieran, grimacing. "Sorry."

"N-no problem." Kieran gives her a small smile, but it doesn't reach his eyes.

The Mind Crucification… Of course. I close my eyes. For whatever reason, this Kieran must've not figured out how to communicate with the Essken, like Kieran we met in the brig. And without me being flung into the past… Even though we didn't know it at the time, we were bonded already. According to Koll and Lorr, it's what helped Kieran survive the Mind Crucification and the Realm. No other human came out as intact as he has—and we have the Bond to thank for that. But in this Nonie's reality, she never went back. She never bonded with Kieran, and therefore she wasn't there to keep him alive during the Mind Crucification.

And he died.

I swallow hard.

Time is complicated.

Time sucks sometimes.

Blue Nonie points to the couch on the left side of the room, across from the bed. "Sit, please. You don't look so well. Anything to drink? I'm sorry, this is a bit awkward."

Kieran lets himself fall into the couch, still a touch pale. I move to stand next to him, not feeling much better, to be honest. "No, thank you. We—"

"Or, if you don't want anything to drink, I got some cookies, or chocolate?" Blue Nonie offers a bowl filled with several types of cookies and small chocolate bars to Kieran and me.

Kieran's eyes light up. "Yes, please. And thank you. That's a lifesaver." He takes one wrapped bar and reads the print on the back. "Looks good."

"It's my favorite." Blue Nonie grins and holds the bowl out to me, but I wave a hand.

"No thank you. We've really got to get going, actually. I'm sorry we barged in here, but we landed here on accident, and I was kind of running from Dad."

"He saw you?" She sits down on the soft, fluffy carpet in front of the couch, crossing her legs.

"He got us away from that officer patrolling."

She draws her legs in and wraps her arms around them. "You were caught after curfew? Happy Dad was there, I really don't need that on my record. I do want to join Mom at the MTI, you know?"

"MTI?"

"Ministry of Temporal Integrity?"

I choke on my next breath and cough. "Ministry of what?"

"Temporal Integrity. You don't have that?"

I glance at Kieran, waiting for protest before I divulge more information. "I don't know how much I can tell you—"

"Please." Blue Nonie waves a hand. "Don't tell me some crap about preserving our timeline. As we all know, there are infinite numbers of timelines. In this one you popped up here and told me what I asked and vice versa, in another one you didn't. In yet another one, you gave me some, but not all information. You get the point. Stop thinking of timelines as fixed entities. They evolve."

This time my jaw drops. "Are you for real?"

She brushes the same stubborn blue strand back behind her ear once more. "Very much so. I'm also the daughter of the Minister for Temporal Integrity, so I know my temporal theories."

"Mom is a Minister?" I squeak. "For the Ministry of Temporal Investiga—"

"Integrity. And I guess that answers my question. You don't have that."

Well, she's right. "No. No, we don't. We have a Federal Bureau of Temporal Investigation, but it's top secret within the USEF."

"Huh. Interesting. Ours is definitely not top secret. Would've been better for Mom if it were." She scowls.

Curiosity won't let me ignore her comment. "Why?"

"Because she was surprised at work a few months ago—by a thief from a different timeline. He shot her and stole some tech—"

I yelp. "He shot her? Is she okay?" My heart hammers for the woman I don't even know, but feel I do.

Blue Nonie nods, anger shining in her eyes. "Yes, she recovered, but that despicable Magellan got away. The Praetor was not happy about either. Mom is his right hand."

Blowing out a puff of air, I will my speeding heart to slow down. "Glad she's okay."

"Believe me, me too. And I'm glad things calmed down, because we were *this* close to developing a timeline task force within the MTI."

"But you didn't," Kieran clarifies, sounding a tad worried.

"No. We decided to take care of our own universe and instead added staff to the Ministry for Space Exploration."

I whistle through my teeth. "We don't have that one either." I wish we did. It sounds like we should have it.

"Geez. What do you guys even have? Ministry for Colonization?"

"Nu-uh."

"Ministry for Astro Warfare?"

"Astro Warfare?" Kieran leans forward. His fingers still on the chocolate's wrapping paper, leaving the top of the bar partially open. "Is that what I think it is?"

"Well, if you're thinking it's the ministry that makes sure we don't get dragged into another war, then yes. They—"

"Do you have a UWO?" I shoot the question out so fast, Kieran swings his head toward me in surprise.

"A what?" She narrows her brows.

"United Worlds Organization?"

"Why would we need that?" I wouldn't say disgust swings in her voice, but definitely not an open mind.

"Uhh, not important, just asking." Sounded like a no to me.

"Look, we don't need some kind of roof organization. Like I said, we got the Ministry of Astro Warfare. They work hand in hand with the Ministry for Space Exploration, and thanks to them, we've been able to dominate all new species within weeks of their discovery. Losses were minimal." She flexes her biceps on both sides, like a body builder. "We lost four percent of all humanity during the Quaneez Wars. We learned."

Four percent! That number gives me chills, but it's another word that makes me very much uncomfortable. "Dominate? You mean admit to the USEF? As members?"

"Sure, if you want to phrase it like that." She lets go of her legs and stretches them out.

Something dawns on me, so ugly and horrible I'm afraid of the answer. "What happened to the Essken?"

"Essken?"

Kieran clears his throat. "The… Quaneez."

Blue Nonie huffs out a laugh. "Oh, them. Gone."

"Gone? What do you mean, gone?" She can't mean gone-gone, maybe they retreated, maybe—

"We eventually destroyed their Realm. Used Tau-bombs. Never heard from them again." She blows on her cuticles, unaware of the horror close to overwhelming me. They found the only way to truly kill the Essken and destroyed the Realm. Like, the whole Realm? Or one Loch'Rm? Does that affect *our* Essken Realm in our universe? Does it not? I have no idea how that works, and it doesn't really matter to the Essken in this reality. Billions, as Koll said. They're gone. All killed. Beings who would've lived forever, snuffed out. Gone.

Of course. That's why she still calls them Quaneez. Not Essken, because they never got to the point where Kieran found out how to talk to them. Instead, they were all killed when the Realm was blasted with Tau-bombs.

An uneasy feeling spreads in my stomach. Scary as it is, it might be our answer to what differs here. The more timelines we jump to, the more it becomes obvious Kieran, the Essken, and the foundation of the UWO—or the lack thereof—are a divergence point. It's too clear a connection to overlook. No Kieran—no Essken, no UWO. I—

"You seem surprised. How did your USEF win the Quaneez Wars?" Blue Nonie looks up from her cuticles.

"We didn't." Kieran works one hand through his hair, then drops it onto his thigh, next to the opened, but untouched, chocolate bar. "The fight is still ongoing in our now, which is 2295."

"Whoa!" Blue Nonie blows out a puff of air. "Is that why you're here? To figure out how to win? Like I said, Tau-bombs should do the trick—"

I hold up a hand. "No, that's not why we're here. In our timeline, somebody is trying to alter our history, and we're trying to figure out why." And how to stop them. Yes, the war stopped early in this Nonie's timeline, but at what cost? Genocide. I won't even consider that as an option.

Blue Nonie huffs again. "Here, I'd have Mom on it. The Praetor wouldn't have any issues diverting resources to something like that, especially if it threatened our lives."

"Praetor." Kieran lifts an eyebrow at her. There is that title again.

"Praetor Izola? The guy in charge of all USEF? All species? Everything? Ah, never mind, he came into power when the Magellans figured out how to kill the Quaneez. You guys never did, so probably no Praetor. Boy, your timeline is way different from ours."

"Yeah, I'm beginning to think that too," I mumble under my

breath. Magellans consenting to and committing genocide. I didn't expect that. At all. Maybe I should have, given that Kieran's dad tied Humanity First to a Magellan financing them.

I frown. I need PADdy to keep track of all the things we're learning. Time traveling, especially when jumping through timelines, gets confusing. And I still need more. Theories need to be proven. "Do you mind if I run a few things against you and see what else is different here?"

"Sure, go for it." Blue Nonie lets go of her legs and leans forward, all attentive.

"Okay. I feel like I know some of the answers already, but still. One, did you get kidnapped as a nine-year old?"

She jerks back. "Heck, no! Calm and uneventful childhood."

As we figured that might have been one point of divergence. "Good for you." I nod. "Two, did you ever get thrown back in time or travel back in time?"

She bursts out laughing. "No, of course not." She brushes her hair back and taps something metallic behind her ear. "We know it's theoretically possible, but make sure it doesn't happen to people with the enabling genome. We like our timeline unaltered. Theory has it that repeated willful alterations can wear out the fabric of time, so the Praetor decided to make sure we stay safe. Hence, this." She taps the metallic device again.

I exchange a glance with Kieran. Didn't Kaytee have something similar behind her ear? "That thing stops you from traveling through time?" I nod my chin at the device behind her ear.

"That it does. Not many people have—or need—one. I'm special like that. As you know." She grins. "No, actually, you're more special. You're actively jumping between realities, that's quite something. We know they exist, but we didn't think it was possible to cross until that thief popped up, but who knows if he even made it back home. Mom theorizes that trans-universal jumps lead to disruptions in the nucleotide bases of our DNA and ultimately, death. I'm surprised you're in one piece." She gives me the one-over. "I mean, you look pale and not exactly fresh, but neither of you looks like you're dying."

"Uhh, okay." I swallow hard. Note to self: maybe limit jumping through universes until we know we'll make it out alive? Kieran and I exchange a worried glance, and while I see where she's coming from when she says he doesn't look exactly fresh, I refuse to worry about that now.

Kieran cocks an eyebrow and nods, on the same page as me, then directs his attention to Blue Nonie. "Is there a *USEF Journey* in your world, and is it still intact?"

"Yes, and yes. In fact, the *Journey* was instrumental in the Quaneez Wars. I think her first officer… Her first officer was gunning for some payback, if you know what I mean."

Oh heck, we do. In this world, Kieran died at the hands of the Essken. I really, really like our timeline better.

"Holy Universe," Kieran groans. "Mom?" He lowers his head into his hands, shoulders heaving with deep, purposefully slow breaths.

A shiver runs down my body—a chill, like the air was charged all of a sudden, like before a thunderstorm or—

Reality wafts and billows between Blue Nonie and us, it tears—

"Shit," Kieran whispers, jumping up. "Nonie, it's—"

"Sheridan! I know!" How did he find us here? I'm fumbling for my disk in my pocket, but Sheridan's too fast. This time he bursts out of that invisible bubble like it spat him out. He flies forward, arms and legs flailing—and crashes right into me.

The impact throws us back, half onto the couch, half off of it, me buried under Sheridan's weight. I grunt as the collision drives the air out of my lungs. The couch moves back with a screeching sound, tearing down some boxes stored next to it, their content spilling out onto the floor in a clattering mess. Before Sheridan can get a grip on me, I've dug my forearm's blade across his face, turning his head away from me. Where the head goes, the body follows. My palm glides over his sweaty face—

With the force of a fist to the stomach, fear slams into me, the distinct sensation of unease, of confusion, of—

Sheridan roars as I push him up, the sensations gone as fast as they appeared. Getting my feet in-between us, I kick him back at the same time Kieran grabs Sheridan by the shirt and yanks him off me.

I blink hard, chasing away that odd sensation. No time for it. Other Nonie yelps and scrambles out of the way as Kieran shoves the agent into the desk. I want to yell at him to be careful, but Kieran is a captain of the USEF and driven by about the same obsession as me to never be helpless again. To never be victimized again. And… maybe by a wee bit of pent-up aggression.

He rams his fist into Sheridan's face with a satisfying smacking sound. I guess that would be a no to Kieran's earlier question about that forcefield and protecting Sheridan from punches.

Sheridan stumbles back, but Kieran is on him. Following his first punch with two more, the other man's head whips left to right. An animalistic, roar-like sound bursts from Kieran's throat with each impact. He grabs Sheridan by the shirt and shoves him into the wall next to the desk, then pulls him forward and drives him back with such force, Sheridan's head bangs against the wall and bounces back, eyes rolling up.

I expect Kieran to let go of Sheridan, but he doesn't. Instead, he winds up for the mother of all punches, face pulled into an aggressive grimace as his eyes are shooting daggers at the executioner.

"Kieran!" Holy Universe, he's going to take the guy's head off! I pop up to standing, heart beating at double the healthy pace, shoving my hand into my pocket for the disk. "Kieran!" I yell.

Kieran freezes in mid-motion, fist cocked and ready to punch. For one long moment I don't think he's going to stop, that he's caught in this rage until I physically drag him back from Sheridan, but then his higher brain function seems to kick in.

Glaring at Sheridan, he lowers his balled fist—and throws a forward elbow at Sheridan's temple.

Well. So much for the higher brain functions.

The other man's head snaps back, and Kieran uses that momentary distraction to push him over the desk. He snatches up the weapon Sheridan pulled on us before and throws it onto the carpet, out of reach.

Blue Nonie squeaks and finally scrambles up, wobbly like a newborn foal, clearly in over her head, judging by her freaked out expression. Guess I found another difference between our worlds.

With one quick step I'm at the weapon—

"Horace, engage!" The agent pushes the words out in a gurgling, throaty outcry, blood dripping from the corner of his mouth—and the stupid, annoying weapon jumps into the air and hovers at eye level, two red lights glowing maliciously.

*"Temporal deviation registered. Three non-FBTI targets acquired."* A third light pops up and with it a thin, laser-like beam of light to each Kieran, Blue Nonie, and myself.

My heart stops. Not good. *So* not good. And offensive: I *am* FBTI!

Sheridan straightens up with a groan. He wipes the back of his hand across his mouth and nose, and it comes back bloody. "Nice try, Wildason. Nice try—" His gaze falls on Blue Nonie, then darts over to me. For the shortest moment, his pupils widen and his composure slips, before he carries on as if this was a regular day at the office, only with a bloodied face. "Adding assault of an officer to your crimes. And for what? Nothing. You're still coming with me. And sorry, you, too." He nods his chin at Blue Nonie.

"Me?" She squeaks in a high pitch I didn't know I was capable of producing.

"Yes, you. I don't know what game is being played here, but I intend to find—"

*Bang!*

The door bursts open and rams into the wall behind it with a crack so forceful, several of the knickknacks in Blue Nonie's shelf topple over and hit the ground.

"Not so fast!" Dad stands in the doorway, the personification of paternal wrath and protectiveness, wide-shouldered, in his fighting stance, a gun at the ready and aimed at Sheridan.

Before either of us can process the sight of my dad as an avenging angel he fires once, twice—

The first shot hits the hovering weapon smack center. Without a sound, the lights turn off and it clatters to the ground. The second shot finds its target in Sheridan. He grunts with the impact of the first round, but for the next, just like before, *something* happens and the charge gets absorbed.

He roars. "What is it with people shooting at me? Horace—"

Dad bursts forward, faster than I've ever seen him, lightning personified—no, *anger* personified. He lifts his weapon up high, and brings it down onto Sheridan's head with the force of Thor's hammer.

The agent twitches once, then crumples to the ground when his legs give in. His eyes roll back and his mouth goes slack.

And Dad still towers above him like he was deciding whether to squish that bug in front of his shoe or not.

I sneak a look at Kieran to catch his attention, then slightly jerk my head. *Come over here.* I'd like us to get out and away from here.

"Dad!" Blue Nonie hyperventilates, eyes wide. "Dad!"

"Nonie!" Dad—Blue Nonie's dad—steps away from Sheridan and wraps his daughter in his arms, still keeping his weapon aimed at the unconscious agent. "You okay?"

Blue Nonie nods. "Just scared."

Kieran uses the distraction to inch closer to me. The moment he wraps his fingers around mine I dig my other hand into my pocket—

"That's a no to whatever is in that pocket, my dear." Dad swivels and aims the gun at me. At us. We both freeze.

"Uhh," I say. Not the most intelligent response, but it's my dad glaring at me and aiming a gun at me. That kind of messes with your head.

"Dad!" Blue Nonie yelps. "They're the good guys! She's me from a different timeline!"

Dad rolls his eyes. "Honey, I knew they were from a different timeline the moment I saw them."

My jaw drops. "You did?" I thought I deserved an award for my acting performance, or at least Kieran did—turns out it's my dad who should receive such an honor.

"I did. For one, I might be a guy, but I know my daughter's hair.

For another, I know her, and you weren't it. No offense," he tags on when I grimace. "Lastly, I served with Captain Wildason, and you *are* him." He gives Kieran a challenging look.

"Touché," Kieran says.

Dad grins. "I haven't been married to the Minister of Temporal Integrity for nothing. I trust Nonie—all Nonies, I want to say—but I'm still this one's dad, and staying alert is in my job description." He lowers the weapon. "Didn't expect another person though when I heard chaos break loose in here."

I point at Sheridan. "It's a long story, but he's one of the reasons we're here."

"He's giving you trouble?"

"You could say so." Even though I bet he'd say the same about us.

Dad nods. "I assume you have a way of leaving here?"

Finally I pull the disk out of my pocket and wiggle it. "We do."

"Then I suggest you do so while I delay this gentleman a bit more. But," he says, holding up one finger, "I won't keep him here. We don't want any other timeline's troubles."

"We understand that. And thank you… Dad."

Dad smiles at me, and he's so much like my dad, it's mind blowing. "Any time, second daughter."

I look over my shoulder at Kieran, who nods. "Ready." He takes my hand. "It was nice meeting both of you."

A wistful expression crosses Dad's face when he looks at Kieran. "And it was really good to see you again. I'm happy your timeline seems to be different from ours, no matter the downsides." He jerks his chin at the unconscious Sheridan.

"I'm with you on that one," Kieran says, throwing a longing glance at the chocolate bar that's now smushed into Blue Nonie's carpet before taking my hand. "Let's go."

"May your First Sense always guide you back," Dad says, laying one palm over his heart.

"And may your First Sense always guide you safely." I lift my hand for one last goodbye to myself and my, uhh, second dad, then, press the button.

# Chapter Fourteen – Home Turf

**Hopefully: Back Home, Right Place, Right Time**

*T*his time the Maelstrom is back to normal. Thank whomever for small favors. Muscle memory takes over. Once I'm in the Maelstrom with Kieran holding onto my hand, I relax. For once, I got this.

*Scanning the orderly chaos of wafting colors and strands, I feel ours like a homing beacon.*

*"You okay?" Kieran asks, tugging on my hand.*

*"I'm fine. Just want to be fast and shake off Sheridan."* Before you try to take his head off again, *not that I minded too terribly.*

*"I'm supporting that idea one hundred percent," Kieran says with a bit of a bite to his words, looking around the swirls of colors and events. "This direction, I think?" He points to the exact area I was going for.*

*I raise an appreciative eyebrow at him. "Not bad for a beginner."* Said the other beginner.

*Kieran chuckles, and man, that sound, proof he's back to normal, recharges my empty batteries. "I think I have you and the Bond to thank for that, so don't be too impressed."*

*"Well, Mashaule screamed his lungs out when I jumped with him, so there's that." How did he even make it to the correct point in time? Maybe a pre-set destination? Hopefully, the disk will help us figure that out—to figure everything out.*

*Our strand comes closer, and maybe Other Nonie is correct with that Rule of Familiarity, because I see myself: preschool, school, academy— There!*

*I will us out of the Maelstrom—*

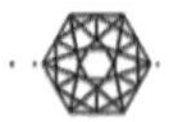

Like two professional time-travelers, we land on our feet with only the slightest stumble. The air smells like home, conditioned and cool, with the faintest hint of medical cleanliness.

*"Code Magenta. Code Magenta. All non-essential personnel please return to your quarters or assigned stations. Code Magenta. Code—"*

I let go of Kieran's hand and spin around my axis once. A medical bay. A deserted medical bay. None of the diagnostic beds lining the walls are occupied.

"Where are we?" Kieran asks. "And when?" He definitely got the hang of the important questions faster than I did. His brows narrow. "Are… are we on the *Hope*?"

"Well, I was planning to bring us to Chase and Zio, and close to after we were abducted by Sheridan. This is our timeline. But I could be off with the timing, or I—"

The doors leading out into the hallway hiss apart, making room for—

"Zio!" Relief rushes through me, bringing a wide grin to my face. More, faster steps come closer from the hallway, and two seconds later, Chase jogs into the sick bay, falling in step with his friend, looking like he'd seen a ghost.

"Guys!" Chase pulls me into a hug while Zio bro-hugs Kieran.

When we separate, both men exchange a glance. "We were worried sick about you. You've been gone for two weeks!"

Two weeks? I draw in a sharp breath and choke on it. Coughing, I clear my throat. "Two weeks? So much for me getting the hang of precise jumps."

"Two weeks without a trace of where you went. One second we could track you in Kieran's quarters, the next you were gone. A tiny spike of Setayashi radiation was all there was, but not at the usual levels. What the absolute heck happened?"

Kieran lays a hand on Trip's shoulder. "That's a long story, but for now we need some precautions before we can bring you up to speed and ask for your help."

Those words catapult both of Chase's eyebrows up his forehead, then down into a V. "I'm all ears."

"First, we need Zio to check if Nonie is okay. She got shot with something a few hours ago, and while she received some care, we need to make sure it won't leave any long-lasting damage."

"I'm fine—"

Kieran's glance shuts me up. "I've had you crash on my bridge with a knife in your chest. Excuse me if I'm a wee bit traumatized from that and would really like to make sure you're okay."

I snap my mouth shut. Point taken. In my defense, yes, I get he's worried, but he doesn't exactly look like he's had a long, relaxing nap either with those dark shadows under his eyes. Plus, it wasn't me who lost it a few minutes earlier.

"You were *shot*?" Chase exclaims, while Zio takes out his medical scanner.

"Elevated neurotransmitters. Reduced dopamine. Some damage to neural plates." He looks up from the device. "What kind of weapon did this, dear niece?"

"Something about a hundred years ahead of us, dear uncle." I frown. "It's a long story, like Kieran said, but before we get to that Kieran is right, we need to get those precautions into place. Remember when I came back last time with Mashaule? I need the same level ten containment field with subatomic stabilization around wherever Kieran and I are. If it makes it easier for us to remain—"

A mischievous grin splits Chase's face. "Done."

I cock my head. "What do you mean, done?"

"I mean that you guys left without a trace, and we assumed it was probably not willingly. Your dad was livid, Nonie. So, we decided to play it safe. The *Hope* is now equipped with universal containment field emitters throughout the whole ship. As soon as we detect any trace of Setayashi-radiation and Code Magenta goes live, the containment field keeps everybody in or out, depending on the point of view. Figured it would be helpful either way. Zio's idea. My implementation."

I whistle. "You guys never cease to amaze me." That moment when you realize your team—your friends—have your back. Ah. Nice.

"Should've known you guys were ahead of us." A satisfied, proud look crosses Kieran's face.

"It didn't feel like we were ahead, more like we were chasing wildly without a clue where to look. Quite frustrating. And we were getting quite nervous, too."

"And why would that be?"

Funny how they haven't worked together in decades, but Kieran picks up on Chase's discomfort right away, switching from a relaxed to a straightened stance.

Zio raises an eyebrow. "Because everybody has been asking for you, Kieran. You vanished right after your speech to the fleet, but understandably people wanted more of you, needed to see you and hear from you. So far, we've been keeping them at bay saying you needed medical care and time to recover."

I throw a pointed glance at Kieran. "You're right with that one."

Kieran pops up the hat and scratches his head before shoving his curls back under it. "Only two weeks in a medical spa are hard to come by these days. I'll cope. Okay, now here I am, where are the fires I need to put out?"

"Funny you're talking about fires." Chase crosses his arms in front of his chest. "That would be Humanity First. You, my friend, have an invitation for tomorrow to meet with nobody other than *the* Travis Roodt."

Travis Roodt. A groan breaks from my throat. "Why isn't he in jail?" He should be, after the stunt he pulled with Humanity First. If it hadn't been for Kieran's address to the renegade parts of the fleet, we'd be in the middle of a flared-up war right now with even more names to add to our statistics.

Derision drips from Chase's voice as he sneers. "Because he didn't make any of the captains turn against USEF orders. It was their decision following his thinking."

Kieran narrows his brows, looking from me to Chase and back. "Who's that Roodt person?"

"The very annoying, very narrow-minded leader of Humanity First. He's the one who's been trying to influence the election for USEF President toward Mashaule—"

"Say no more, I got it." A muscle ticks in Kieran's jaw. "And I know the type. So, tell me, am I really meeting with him or are we ignoring him?"

"We can't ignore him, even though that man is close to terrorist status, in my book," Chase says. "At this point, he wants to meet with you, we comply in the interest of peace, because, as always in our lives, the situation doesn't lack complications. Kieran, you remember we're having a cease fire with the Essken, right?"

"Yes, I do, as clearly as I remember having to talk down half the USEF fleet to not engage the Essken."

"And we've dealt with the officers who sympathized with Humanity First," Chase says. "But now, for the last close to two weeks, the Essken have repeated a pattern. The same ship appears at the same nebula you entered their realm in. It waits for exactly twelve hours, then reenters the nebula and vanishes. It comes back two days later, same pattern. Weapons powered down, just waiting. We assume it is an invitation to talk, which we can't do without the two of you. Unfortunately, even this non-threatening maneuver is making several groups on Earth quite nervous, namely Humanity First."

Another groan breaks from my throat as I let my head drop back. "Of course. And that's why we can't have nice things."

Chase presses his lips into a narrow line. "I completely agree. I guess a cease fire over all doesn't have enough killing for them, or maybe they feel their support by the general public slip. Either way, they're pushing for an attack before they lose even more momentum—which, right now, they still have. It gets worse though. Somebody has been whispering in their ear lately, somebody from one of our science vessels. They analyzed the data from you entering the Realm, Nonie. They found out that Tau radiation destroys the Realm."

Kieran and I suck in a sharp gasp at the same time. "We know how to kill the Essken." I close my eyes for one eternal second.

Chase nods. "We do. *They* do. And it's a major problem, as you can imagine. Humanity First has been rallying intensely over the last weeks. They've amounted enough political counter-pressure for us to only have one more appearance cycle of the Essken to successfully communicate before the governments of Eurasia, the Americas, Afrika, and Oceania will veto the USEF's current plan."

Dread forms in my stomach. "They can do that?"

"They can. If united, Earth government has the right to veto. Also, imagine what would happen if USEF, and by that I mean your father as its president, ignored the request, especially if spoken in unison." Zio puts request in air quotes.

"The public outcry about USEF's current path regarding the Essken is already loud," Chase says. "Kieran's speech may have aligned USEF behind him, to a degree at least, but to the people out there, the voices they've known their whole lives matter more. So, yes, Humanity First has done a good job, from their point of view. They've gotten people angry. Now they see a chance for payback and to destroy the Essken once and for all. USEF may be independent from Earth governments, but if we go against a public opinion this riled up…" He shakes his head. "Civil unrest is a word not strong enough. It's going to be civil war. Mutiny, wherever you look. If we don't make peace with the Essken, USEF will have no other choice but to drop Tau-bombs on the Realm.

And I don't need to tell you that while we will suffer casualties, it will wipe out the Realm and the Essken. We will be committing genocide."

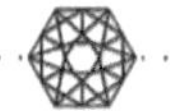

### *USEF HOPE, 14:35hrs, Conference Room, September 28th, 2295*

Twenty minutes later, both Kieran and I are freshly showered and dressed in clean USEF standard uniforms. After Chase's revelation, I would've loved to take longer under the shower just to wash off the sensation of doom, but time, as always and ironically, is still of the essence, especially now. That being said, I'll never ever underestimate the value of a hot shower and clean clothing again. I'll have to do the math for how many hours we had neither, but needless to say, jumping through a few alternate realities doesn't make for a fresh feel overall.

The water and snacks on the table in the *Hope*'s conference room also feel way more luxurious than they should. Rewind to a few weeks ago, and neither nor would've gotten me excited, but today those few nibbles and fresh, cool water get five out of five stars from me. Small amenities are underrated when you take them for granted. When did we eat last? Also, no idea. Sleep would be nice too, but for now, another strong coffee will do the trick. Priorities.

Only our small crew of Zio, Chase, Kieran, and myself is assembled in the conference room. Dad is at a meeting on Earth regarding the Essken and scheduled to demat back on board tomorrow. He'll have to catch up. There's no way we can wait for him.

Kieran, by the way, appreciates the snacks at least as much as me. Popping a piece of dark chocolate in his mouth, he closes his eyes. "Finally." A peaceful expression slides over his face—one I've seen way too little of recently.

Zio raises an eyebrow and opens his mouth, but Chase cuts him off. "Don't say it, Zee."

"I—"

"He's been through a lot. He deserves some chocolate."

Zio snaps his mouth closed as Kieran peeks through one half-opened eyelid. "Did you just get Zio to give in?" He opens both eyes fully. "Does that mean I only have to get abducted to the future, be chased through time, and thrown into the brig for me to be allowed chocolate?"

Chase snorts. "So it would seem. Or maybe the fact that you said split-off timelines are *stable* messed with his head."

Kieran and I spent the last forty-five minutes giving a painstakingly detailed report of what happened since Sheridan abducted us, while Chase and Zio did their best to not interrupt, even though I, too, could see Zio readying himself when I first mentioned Other Nonie's timeline was stable. Just sayin', I called it first, about forty years ago, back on the *Pioneer* when I was evaluating all my options during my chase of Mashaule, but I called it. Not that I blame young Commander Zio for shutting down my theory about stable alternate timelines, not at all. We were a long time from where we are right now, with much less to go by.

Zio harrumphs. "My head is fine, thank you very much. Let's just ignore my temporal lapse in my medical duty in regards to Kieran's chocolate consumption and carry on."

"I feel like I should ride this out longer and enjoy it, but as so often, you're right." Chase takes a big sip of Lubbeck's, eyeing Zio for a response that never comes.

He sets his glass down again and gives me a weird look from under his lashes.

"What?" I ask.

"No offense, and you and Zio are the experts, but are we still sure it's okay for you to tell us all this? About the future? Other universes?"

I set my water back down. "Let me put it this way. While it's a bit odd, I'm not getting pushback from my First Sense, and even if I did, I would still tell you guys part of what's going on. Sorry, somebody is bending the rules of time to their liking, why should I stick to them?" Changing my tune from protecting the timeline at all costs to, well, *not*, makes me feel a bit like a rebel. *Rawr.*

"Plus, while there might be an infinite number of universes and this conversation possibly going differently, I bet you it's not. Knowing myself and where we are right now, I would always decide this way. This isn't a Divergence Point. This is a Focal Point, to use those expressions." I'm sure of it. Whichever way our future will go, and whichever strands will branch off, this meeting isn't it.

Chase rubs his nose, then drops his hand. "Okay, all I need. Then we're not holding back. Cool. Somebody tell me then how we ended up where we are, in our timeline, which is not the Zeroverse, correct?"

I shake my head. "Nope. That was the one strand that had a different pull, for a lack of a better description. In that one, Nonie never traveled back, and Kieran made peace before the war even broke out." The one where we landed in the brig. Nonie never traveled back, but Kieran figured out quickly how to communicate with the Essken, because she—I—wasn't there to mess things up.

Chase pouts. "Okay, I can live without being in the Zeroverse even though my ego is taking that personally, somehow. But how did we end up here, in our timeline, then? It's so vastly different." He raises both hands at Zio in a tell-me gesture.

"Don't look at me." Zio shakes his head. "Apparently, I'm late to the party when it comes to accepting different stable timelines as a reality. Even my late sister seems to have known years ago. All I can presume is that every major change, as we assumed, leads to a split-off."

"A divergence point," I remind him. At least Other Nonie had terminology. A handbook!

"A divergence point. Only that, against my previous assumptions, it forms a stable, ongoing and continuing new timeline. Then, another change happens, and another split-off follows. We, as we sit here right now, might be in the fourth or fifth branch."

Chase groans and lets his head hang. "Geez. Fourth or fifth?"

"Or more. Imagine the baseline, Kieran ending the war before it begins. Nonie does not travel back in time at all. Now go through this somewhat chronologically. Kieran, you're ten years old and shot by your nanny. There's the first alteration—divergence point, I apologize—and a new timeline begins. But also, this change ripples through the timeline and gets picked up by Taro Magona, I presume, and she sends Nonie back in time to save you, Kieran, to restore the original flow of time to the timeline she is in."

I nod. "That's what happened with Other Nonie. But she also had traveled back before, to the *Pioneer*, like I did."

"I believe you're skipping ahead, Nonie. And I believe we're missing a couple of Divergence Points."

Chase groans again, louder this time, and rests his face in his palms, elbows on the table. "Fantastic. Why is all and any of time travel so complicated? What are we missing?"

Focusing on a spot somewhere behind Chase's head as if it held all the answers, Zio takes a second before he responds. "Imagine Nonie saved Kieran from being shot as a boy. Whoever wanted to achieve a change, did not meet their goal. Hence, they had to try again, and maybe the next step included trying to remove Nonie from the equation. No Nonie, nobody to rescue Kieran."

"My kidnapping." I raise a hand.

"Exactly. Only that the same thing happened, and future-you was— or rather, will be—sent back by Taro Magona's FBTI to save yourself and preserve the flow of the timeline, so that you'd still be able to eventually travel back and meet Kieran, and save him from being shot and killed, and the Quaneez Mind Torture." He uses air quotes with this. "Ultimately that plan to reshape the timeline also backfired. And so, another attempt was started, which could have been trying to kill Kieran on board the *Journey*."

It all fits, layer after layer, it all makes sense, but— "Wait a second." I pale from where my next thought leads me. "If the past changes, we're now assuming a split-off happens and the new timeline reflects that change futural—in the future—from the event. Meaning, I go back and prevent my mom from dying during childbirth, me here in this timeline would still have grown up mother-less. Only the Nonie in the other timeline, the new split-off, would have grown up with her mom. My point is, it would be nice of me to keep her alive, but it wouldn't help *me.*" I jot my index finger into my chest.

Chase keeps his face blank. "I did mention I'm getting a headache? Futural? Is that what we're calling things now?"

Kieran lowers his chin in a quick acknowledging nod. "Futural if it's in the future, praeterital if it's in the past. We had help with terminology."

Blowing out a breath of air, Chase closes his eyes. "Finally, something that makes sense in all this chaos."

"Yes, *Nonie,* correct." Zio ignores his friend's comment with a pointed glance. "You yourself would not benefit from the change. This theory is a very big shift from our single timeline theory, where every change would have resulted in an immediate effect downstr— futural from it." He sighs. "While I understand it, I cannot say I like it."

I smack my lips. They feel dry, like my throat. I swallow hard. "Neither do I. Somebody *changes the past* and *realizes* it didn't work the way they intended and then *tries again*? If somebody is able to realize their plan didn't work, they must be able to access that new timeline where the change took place and see what changes stuck. That somebody must be able to not only jump through time, but also through timelines." I stare at the guys, wide-eyed.

As if I didn't just drop the biggest revelation ever onto them— because until what feels like five minutes ago, we didn't even know other timelines were stable—Zio only lowers his head in a slow nod. "Also correct."

Kieran sits up straighter. "So, we're looking for a time-traveler across universes. Needle in a haystack, anybody?"

"I'm not looking far. My first suspect is that Sheridan guy." Chase pulls his brows into a displeased expression. "I got a couple of issues with that man—and the people from our future in general, so let's talk about that, please, because it needs to be said. I know you. It needs to be said." He gives Kieran a worried glance. "For the record first and foremost, I don't believe any of their accusations. Don't know about you guys, but I for one find it extremely unlikely that one single person—or two, for that matter—could have the potential of killing billions, especially if they're not bad people, which, no surprise there, you're not. Yes, I know, once the dominos fall, things happen, but still. It didn't sit well with me, for many reasons, when Mashaule spouted that nonsense of needing to kill Kieran to save the world. I don't like this new accusation any better. It's getting old. And it makes me wonder if those accusations come from the same source. I mean, what are the odds they're not?"

Zio lifts one eyebrow. "One billion—"

"Rhetorical question, Zee." Chase gives him *the* look. "My point is that there must be more to it than meets the eye, like you said. Are you really responsible for a disaster of this magnitude, or is that a ruse? Part of the Temporal War? And if so, why?"

I tap my index finger on the wooden table. "Exactly what we've been thinking. And my First Sense says we're innocent." It didn't agree when Mashaule tried to kill Kieran, and it didn't like what the judge had to say any better.

"Okay, then let me give your First Sense the benefit of the doubt and say it's right. Neither of you is responsible for anything that kills off close to all humanity."

Kieran flinches. "I wish you would stop saying that."

"Sorry. But for what it's worth, even if it wasn't for Nonie's First Sense, I'd be on your side." Chase squeezes his friend's shoulder once. "Anyway, hear me out—and mind you, I'm not calling myself an expert in the topic of time traveling and timeline jumping—I'm wondering now how much this Sheridan guy and the judge are involved in the Temporal War. If we're operating under the assumption you two are innocent, then why do they toot the same horn as Mashey did? Are they the cause of it or just another cog in the Temporal War?"

"I have no idea." Either is a possibility. The Temporal War could originate from the time we were abducted to, or from further futural. We can't disregard what Chase just pointed out though: we could have found our Unknown Bad Guy or Guys. "And remember what I told you. Comparing the other timelines to ours, there's a pattern. Kieran is alive, eventually we seem to make peace with the Essken, depending on when he enters the picture."

"Quite reassuring, by the way." Chase pats Kieran's shoulder.

"I try," Kieran says. "In every universe, apparently."

"As I would expect of you," Chase says.

"But," I carry on, "to point out the other side of the medal, if Kieran isn't there, the Essken Realm is destroyed and the war is over sooner."

"With a couple of downsides, besides the Essken and me being dead," Kieran says. "No UWO, but a military government that didn't seem like fun."

"In their defense," I say, "and I mean that somewhat jokingly, they were developed very well though. Ministry for Space Exploration, Colonization, Astro Warfare… They had the tech—" I suck in a harsh, sharp breath as acid flares in my stomach, pushing bile up my throat. My stomach cramps as my whole body spasms. "Holy Sun and—" I gasp, pressing both palms against my abdomen.

"Nonie?" Kieran leans forward, a worried expression on his face.

Waving one hand, I straighten up. "I'm fine." Holy Sun and Stars! That was one of the biggest gut feelings my First Sense has ever produced—but for a reason! I tug on Kieran's sleeve, eyes wide, heart skipping an excited beat. We might be onto something!

"Kieran! Blue Nonie said something about a Magellan stealing tech from them, remember?" I turn toward him, drawing one leg under my other thigh. "That could be the person we're looking for! Right? Could a Magellan have the knowledge and skills to pull that off, Zio? To jump to a different timeline? I'm only half-Magellan, and I can do it, there must be others with greater affinity to time than me." I can't be the only one. "And you told me some Magellans have greater sensitivity to time, and that your people were hunted once because of it."

"That used to be true. There were Magellans with the ability to travel through time, at least that's what the old legends say."

"You also said your people had operatives who corrected what needed correcting, right?" He dropped that bomb on all three of us when I first came clean I was a time traveler.

"Seventeen interventions; seventeen corrections." Zio lowers his chin in an affirmative nod. "But, as you know, you are the first with the ability in several centuries. There are no recordings of any time traveling since the time of our sun entering its final stage. It's possible the required genetic setup disappeared as our population shrunk. All we have now is a First Sense, our ability to sense changes in the future and past, and even that can present vastly different. For most it is nothing but a sensation, for some with a stronger First Sense, it can come with an image, like a distant memory or blurry dream."

I tap my temple. "I only had that once. A premonition, like before Mashaule jumped back in time." When I had just returned from the *Pioneer* for the first time and was recruited into the FBTI. It feels like yesterday, yet eons ago. So much has happened since, I'm a different person than back then, ridiculous as it sounds. "All three of us felt something was changing. Me, you, Taro Magona."

"Of course. As the acting Taro, she has the highest sensitivity to time, the most refined skills, and the best honed First Sense."

Giving his friend a look from under his lashes, Chase grins. "Aww, Zee, are you blushing?"

"I'm not," Zio replies, rolling his eyes.

"'Course you aren't." Chase chuckles. "Ah, Taro Magona…" he whispers under his breath.

"My point was," Zio says a tad louder than necessary, "that while some of our people were able to time travel, it seems we have lost that specific ability." He glances at me. "Although I would most likely re-examine that assessment, knowing what I do now, but my point is I don't have enough data to say if currently a Magellan is able to travel through time any better than a human or not."

I tilt my head left, then right. "Judging by what Blue Nonie said, I would go with a yes. And I actually have two more reasons to suggest we focus on said tech-stealing Magellan, and not only because of the sensitivity to time."

"Do tell." Chase opens his palms to the ceiling.

"One, Blue Nonie." I tap a finger onto my mastoid bone behind my ear. "She had a device behind her ear that's supposed to keep her from time traveling, like other people with the enabling genome. So, in that timeline, and in the future, they know some people of Magellan descent can travel through time. Sheridan I'm sure has some Magellan genes as well, annoying as it is."

"Your theory makes sense," Zio says. "What is your second reason?"

"Your dad." I nod at Kieran, then look at Chase and Zio. "I feel Niall Wildason's theory is a good place to start from." I have a bad feeling about it, in, well, a good way. Meaning, I feel it'll lead to something. It's too much to be a mere coincidence.

Chewing on his lower lip, Kieran nods. "The Magellan Dad found out about, Tala Torona, the one who funded Humanity First—

"A group with the goal of keeping humanity to itself and not forming alliances with others, like us Magellans," Zio adds. "And who is very much in favor of attacking the Essken, even at this very moment."

Silence falls, the shocked, horrified kind. We're all doing the math and arriving at the same solution.

I swallow hard. "That could be it. Torona could be it." She's our best lead, and it makes sense, in a very disturbing kind of way. "Humanity First has always been a pain in the behind, but Torona worked with them, we know that. Zio is right, for the last decades, all Humanity First did was sow hate and discord against non-human life. And even though they tried to keep humans and Magellans apart, I would argue that there's no better hiding spot for a Magellan trying to influence public opinion to get rid of the Essken than within an organization so anti-Magellan nobody would suspect them to be hiding in plain sight to achieve their goals." I slam my palm onto the table when the next gears click into place. "And guys, as a matter of fact, you told me that we only have one more chance to successfully communicate with the Essken, or else Earth will withdraw support to USEF and urge us to destroy them with tau-radiation—and who is behind that? Again, Humanity First, potentially influenced by a Magellan, namely Torona, potentially to get to the same goal as in the other timelines, killing the Essken and preventing the UWO from being founded."

Kieran whistles. "As I said in a different world, literally—Geez." He shakes his head. "Words I never thought I'd speak in earnest. And yet, here we are. Anyway, as I said in a different world, I think Dad had a good, solid base for his paranoia. Let's look into it, we need to know all we can about her."

"Yes, let's. We have nothing to lose." I shake out my arms. Here goes nothing. "*Hope,* please display data for Tala Torona." My heart skips a beat and hammers at an unhealthy pace. Please let it lead somewhere.

Without missing a beat, *Hope* answers. "*Tala Torona, specialist, temporal mechanics, born 2210, deceased 2287.*"

"Hate to break it to you, but she's dead though," Chase points out. "I don't think she's responsible for anything after 2287." Leave it to Trip to make the same jokes across timelines. Here's to consistency.

Holding up my pointer finger I raise one brow. "Are you sure about that?"

"Well, yes. Magellans live a lot longer than humans, but not after they're pronounced dead."

Suppressing an eye roll, I shake my head. "That's not what I meant. I think we're limiting ourselves by not keeping the flow of time in mind. *Hope,* display family tree for Tala Tarona, descending."

Within a second two lines jot out from her name: Toa Lupora and Klino Tupela.

"Two children. Neither name ringing a bell." Chase drums his fingers.

A knot forms in the pit of my stomach. Maybe I'm on a witch hunt, but man, I feel like it's the right way, kind of, when my First Sense kicks in. "*Hope,* display next generation."

One name pops up under Toa Lupora: Dalon Izola.

*Izola.*

Dizziness makes me suck in a sharp breath as my heart speeds up. I blink, but the name stays the same. I look at Kieran, the weight of the world—or rather, several worlds—falling off my shoulders, because if I'm not mistaken, we just had a breakthrough. "Tala Torona is the grandmother of Dalon Izola. Izola as in—"

"Praetor Izola," he finishes my sentence. "And worse, we've heard that name somewhere else."

"We have?" Chase asks.

Nodding, I point at myself. Excitement buzzes through me, energizing every cell. Finally, we're making some headway! And finally, we might know when the Temporal War originates. Not two-hundred or more years in the future, but about a hundred, because… "In *our* future, Izola is going to be the Taro! He makes it to power in at least two timelines, in our future as the Taro and in Blue Nonie's as the Praetor."

We look at each other, wide eyed. My heart races, like I just ran a marathon. This is huge. Gigantic. We have a lead that's not just a hunch but comes with evidence and logical reasoning.

"We're thinking that is the long-term plan? Grandma Torona changing the past so her grandchild Izola can rule as a Praetor or something similar?" Chase turns in his seat to get a better look at Kieran.

Kieran doesn't hesitate. "I do. My dad's reasoning was solid. Something is off with that Tala Torona. One, she's a temporal specialist. Two, she connects directly with a descendant who comes into power in at least two universes, I'd say that's enough of a motive until proven otherwise."

"Targeted genocide through temporal manipulation." Chase breathes out fast and thrusts a hand through his hair. "That's evil on a whole new scale. The Essken are being slaughtered to elevate one person to power? What's wrong with people?"

I huff drily. No idea. Had somebody told me a mere few weeks ago we'd suspect a Magellan of genocide and tampering with the timeline, I would've thought they were certifiable. Alas, you live, you learn.

"We have to think carefully about our next step." Chase drums his fingers in typical impatient Chase fashion. "Your reasoning is solid, but it isn't evidence. With the responsibility of a whole people's fate on our shoulders and the future being one step ahead of us, I for one would need to know for a fact that we're not barking up the wrong tree."

"And our options right here and now are limited," Zio says. "We cannot take the only living Magellans connected to this into custody for a deed they might not have done yet. After all, supporting Humanity First isn't a crime."

"It should be," Chase mumbles.

"But it isn't. Dalon Izola is a child at the moment, and his mother Toa Lupora, an adult, but if we cannot prove she is currently involved in fighting or initiating the Temporal War, we have nothing to hold against her. This is a war, but we are not ignoring the rights of a person, or we're no better than the ones initiating said war."

"Relax, Zee, I've got a plan." Chase leans back.

"I don't know whether I'm reassured by that."

"You should be." Chase pats his friend's shoulder. "Here's the deal: either Taro Izola and Sheridan follow a course laid by Izola's grandmother—or maybe it was vice-versa, she is following their instructions."

Zio taps a finger against his chin. "An intriguing idea. You are proposing Izola went back in time and recruited his grandmother's help to set certain events in motion."

"Now you're following me." Chase gives Zio a thumbs up.

"Not only am I following you, but I am overtaking you. Your thinking follows linear temporal theory. Izola travels back to his grandmother, she changes the past, and those changes affect the future Izola is born in, in this case one presumably without Essken, UWO, and with a chance for him to become Praetor. Am I summarizing your train of thought correctly?"

"Yes, but I don't see what's wrong—"

It hits me like a sledgehammer to the face. "A Diversion Point," I whisper, then continue louder. "The past is changed, a split-off happens. The Izola asking his grandma for help wouldn't benefit from the change, which would come to pass in the newly split-off timeline."

"Correct. And he wouldn't know whether he failed or succeeded, which would have me wonder why several attempts have been made to change the past unless he is not only able to travel through time, but through different timelines."

I get Zio's implication. "That brings us right back to what we talked about earlier: A Magellan, potentially jumping not only through time, but timelines. You're saying that person not only knows about the multiverse, but is able to transfer themselves into the new timeline and continue from there." Is that even possible?

"Exactly. The technology required for that is—"

"—probably something Blue Nonie's timeline could've had. It could have been stolen from there. But—" I shake my head, thoughts racing. "She also said my mom had come up with a theory that transuniversal jumps lead to some kind of DNA-disruptions. Not sure if that's true, but if it is, how would they stay alive?"

"Even though I would trust my sister's research in any timeline," Zio says, "I cannot answer that."

"But I know somebody who can." Chase puts on a smug grin. "Y'all didn't let me finish my plan. And yes, Zee, it remains the same despite you making it complicated. Again."

Before the other man can come up with a retort, Chase looks at me, one eyebrow cocked. "You said Sheridan works for Taro Izola, correct?"

"Yeah, he does—oh." A shiver runs down my spine. This is definitely something we can work with. I crack my knuckles. "We know where Sheridan chased us to. We can go jump back to get him—"

"If you think I'm going to let either of you jump anywhere, or even go to the bathroom without me knowing, you must've lost some marbles over the last jumps." Chase crosses both arms in front of his chest, giving me a glance I've been the, uhh, *lucky* recipient of quite a few times during my academy training. "We have other options available, so I'll be damned if I let you guys out of my sight."

"Do tell," Zio says, keeping his expression blank.

Chase cracks his knuckles. "Well, we have choices, like I said. Several, but one of them is slightly more convenient than the others: Nonie's idea was the right one."

I look up at him. "Thank you? I guess?"

A half-smile tugs on his lips. "A plus for logical reasoning, B minus for execution. This guy Sheridan is chasing you. Let's catch him and see what he can give us. We want information, we want to see if and how much Izola is involved—or his grandmother—and I'm sure Sheridan has some of the intel we need. So yes, I propose we invite this gentleman in for further questioning. Align our forces, so to speak."

"How do you propose to do that then, exactly?" Zio asks.

"Ye of little faith in my cunning abilities," Chase replies, a smug look on his face, and that look, it gives it away. To me, at least.

"He'll come to us!" I jump up and begin to pace back and forth, excitement shooting through me. Chase's idea is pure gold! "And as their only executioner, the only one jumping through time, he must be high-ranking and know more than he lets on—and he's letting on quite a bit already. You're absolutely right, he's our best source. And the best part? We don't have to put an effort in to get him. He will come to us."

Kieran mimics Chase's knuckle-cracking. "Agreed. He's chasing us down. He found us everywhere so far, including the other timelines, so he'll find us here. Who knows, maybe he's here already, but can't pop in like he did before because of your containment field."

I fold my hands behind my back while pacing. It could work. We might for once have the upper hand. "And we'll use a containment field to trap him. But to do that…" I whirl toward Chase. "Tomorrow is the day Kieran is supposed to meet with Travis Roodt? And in two days the Essken are going to wait for us?"

A grin spreads across his face. "Yes."

"And nobody knows what to do and you're all waiting for Kieran and me."

The grin widens. "Not very flattering, but well summarized."

I look at Kieran, then my two mentors. "Tomorrow then. We catch Sheridan tomorrow." Everybody is waiting for us, so history will have us marked as present and ripe for the picking. Sheridan will try first when Kieran meets Travis Roodt. He won't wait until we see the Essken, not if avoiding peace if their goal. Sheridan is impatient like that.

I tap my chin, thinking. "When he abducted us, Sheridan chose a point in time right after Kieran's speech to the fleet, suggesting whatever we will do happens after. He'll find us in this time, just like he found us before, so I don't think we'll have to try to get his attention. This level

10 containment field we have active should protect us from him popping in, but with his tech, I wouldn't bet on it for too long, he'll find a workaround eventually. He's a hundred years ahead of us when it comes to technology. Once he knows why he can't demat in, I'm sure he's going to figure out a way around it. Which means, we got to have our trap in place."

Pride shines in Chase's eyes. "Happy to see we trained you to use your brain. That was my idea as well. Much easier for anybody in the future to find you where history documented your location compared to any given regular day. He'll be there. Plus, it might be petty, but I like that Roodt wants to use us, but instead we're using him."

I have to agree with Chase in all points, and not only because of logical reasoning. Call it my First Sense, I don't know, but somehow, I have a feeling that's when he's going to strike, no matter if he's already here or only arriving then. My only problem with it is predictability. "I'm asking this because I'm really not sure of the answer. Whatever we do, won't he know, because history should've documented what we did?" Changes we make now travel into the future, as far as we know. "In a single timeline, I'd say yes, but trying to think about it in a multi-timeline manner makes me wonder—"

"I don't think there is a difference." Zio shakes his head. "All we will have to do from this very moment on is keep our plan beyond secret. Off the books, as much as possible. Not talk about it with others, who could document it and pass it on. If we keep the information from traveling into the future, Sheridan won't have access to it. It will be forgotten by history, so to speak. Mind you, I'm no temporal specialist, let alone one for a multiple-timeline theory."

"You never have one of those when you need them," Chase quips. "Sure would come in handy."

"Agreed. But, we have a plan. And in the meantime," Zio says, holding up my disk, "I will see what I can get from this. Any additional data can only be helpful. Until then, I suggest you two rest. We have a catch to make tomorrow, but Kieran also has to make peace with the Essken people the day after."

Steely resolve shines from Kieran's eyes. "I can't wait." The muscles in his temple tighten. "And if we're lucky, we'll not only end the Quaneez War in the next two days, but also the Temporal War. Let's get it done, people."

# Chapter Fifteen -

# Not a Break

"You know, when Zio said we were supposed to de-stress, I'm pretty sure he meant for us to sleep." I slide onto the barstool in front of the tiny kitchen island in the *Hope*'s Guest quarters. This time, nobody tried to give us separate quarters, though I'm sure they'll all plead ignorance when Dad's back on board.

"I'm taking the liberty of interpreting the doc's orders." Kieran picks up a carrot, throws it in the air, catches it, and points it at me. "Cooking relaxes me. Plus, we get a fresh meal out of it. Tell me that's not relaxing."

I grin, resting my chin on my palm, elbow on the table. "It is. Especially for me. I'm just sitting here, watching you." In my PJs, because it's late in my book. It's comfy, I don't mind it, and since Kieran is in his as well, I don't feel underdressed. Plus, we didn't really pack a suitcase for the whole time-traveling thing, so we've got to live with and sleep in what USEF gives us, and that would be one set of standard issue

PJs and one set of standard issue uniforms per person.

"I don't mind. I like it when you watch me." The slightest blush of pink colors his cheeks before he turns his back to me and continues chopping the carrots. "It's something that should be normal for two people, but with the limited time we've had—and the limited potential future, let's be honest—it hasn't been something I assumed would happen a lot. So yeah, I'm enjoying this moment. It's homey. Normal."

Normal. "True. We really haven't had anything normal so far." Not how me met. Not how we kept on meeting. Not how we spent the last couple of days.

"Well, maybe it's what's normal for us."

I sigh. "Maybe. But my life wasn't like this before my first jump to the *Pioneer,* so I'm really, really hoping it won't be once this is over."

Kieran lays the carrot on the chopping board and wipes his hands on a kitchen towel. "The sad thing is that when you say when *this* is over, we have to clarify. Are we talking about the Essken War? The Temporal War? Us being chased by a timeline-changing Magellan? I mean, we have choices."

I huff. "No kidding. But at least we've got a plan in place. That's progress. We're not helpless anymore, we're not reacting to their actions, but making them react to ours, because we finally know the Essken War is connected with the Temporal War—and you made peace in other alternate realities, so you can do it here as well. Let's be honest, you would have forty years ago if it wasn't for me."

Something in my voice makes Kieran freeze in mid-motion. Knife hovering over the carrot, he pauses. "You know it's not your fault, right?"

A hot rush of emotions digs into my core like a skewer fresh from the fire. My cheeks flush. "I—"

"Did you jump to the past with the plan to prevent me finding out the Essken tracked by scent?"

I shake my head so fast, my vision turns blurry. "N-no, I—"

"Or did you come up with your alibi with the intention to cover up any of it?"

"No, I didn't even know they used scent. None of us knew."

Kieran turns around, knife still in hand. "Then I don't see how any of it is your fault. I see the fault in the person who caused you to be in the past, and who therefore changed many a thing, it seems. Yes, your report about having been on the planet changed my approach, but let's be honest, USEF had many chances to let me do my thing. I might've figured it out eventually. I bet if you check other timelines, I did. Just, in ours, the course was set differently. And even though I don't think it was your fault, I get why you're having a hard time with that, because, well…"

"Because you also think it's yours," I whisper.

Kieran nods, slowly, while chewing on his lower lip. "Of course, I do. Other Kierans did better than I did." He laughs out once, dry. "Heck, they made peace and founded the UWO. What did I do? Spend a couple of years in the Realm, and now I'm feeling sorry for myself? That's not me. That shouldn't be me, at least, and yet…" He lowers the knife and lays it onto the countertop, then folds his hands over his chest and drops his gaze to the floor.

I shake my head. "Don't minimize what happened to you. Don't pretend like it was nothing and that you should shake it off. Your counterparts were incredibly lucky they didn't experience what you did. And give yourself some credit—you kept USEF from attacking the Essken basically the minute you came out of the Realm. You're not the reason we're in this mess."

Lifting his gaze, he looks at me. "Neither are you."

For the longest time, we stare into each other's eyes as silence hovers. His throat works on a hard swallow, and there's this swooshing sound in my ears making it hard to focus. The moment Kieran pushes off the countertop, I slide off my chair.

We meet in the middle, between the kitchen area and the bed. Gently, as if I were a delicate flower, Kieran takes me in his arms, resting his chin on top of my head when I cuddle into his chest. His heart beats fast, too fast for somebody who looks this calm.

"We're a mess, huh?" I whisper, and get a little chuckle as a reward.

"I feel like I'm the bigger mess, though."

"It's not a competition, you know that, right?"

He chuckles again and tightens his hold on me. "I know. And if it was, for once, it would be one I wouldn't want to win. It's just…" He sighs. "You have everything under control, Nonie. Heck, you can jump us through time and through timelines. I'm along for a ride where I'm no help at all."

"I have everything under control?" I lift my head off his chest. "I have nothing under control. Half of the time I'm lucky things work out the way I planned them, and the other half I'm navigating us into even bigger messes!" I dropped us onto the bridge of a USEF ship, landing us in the brig. Because of me, we popped up with Blue Nonie, first getting into trouble with the officer enforcing curfew, then with Sheridan. I'm navigating everything blindly, as much as I'm trying to do the right thing.

Kieran stares down at me, frowning. "Well, I happen to see that from a completely different point of view. Don't sell yourself short, Nonie. I don't know where I'd be without you, and I don't mean that in a literal sense, because I know. I'd be in the Realm. Figuratively, I don't know where I'd be without you. How I'd be dealing with everything, because clearly I'm not exceeding at it right now either. But without you, I wouldn't know up from down." He reaches up and cups my neck, sweeping his thumb across my skin. "Trip and Zio are here, but they're old. We're still friends, but… it's different than it was. Obviously."

I shake my head the slightest bit, then nuzzle my cheek into his palm. "But they're still your friends. They never stopped. In either timeline we visited. They're another constant in your life."

"I know that, and I'm loving them even more for it, even though it's not the same—it can't be the same as before. But you and me… we *are* the same." He pauses for a moment. "You said Zio and Trip were a constant. Did you notice what else was? Who else?"

Heat skates up my back when I get what he's going for. I nod. "You and me."

"Yeah. We're a constant, and that's so ironic given the nature of our relationship. But in some form or another, there's always a connection between us, no matter the timeline. I'd be lying if I said that didn't mean the world to me."

He drags his fingers up and down my back and I want to respond, I swear, I want to say something totally cool and wise, or at least something helpful, but any response I might've had becomes unimportant the moment he lifts me up like I weighed nothing and carries me to the bed. As he's sitting down, he pulls me onto his lap, so that I'm straddling him. Wrapping his arms around my upper body, he presses me against him and nuzzles his face against my chest, then turns his head to press a kiss against my throat.

"Remember my letter? The one from the drawer?" His voice sounds rougher, deeper.

"Of course, I do." How could I not? A myriad of conflicting emotions skates through me. That letter…

He clears his throat. "Do you… do you remember what I wrote under it?"

*For me, you were it.*

"Yes," I whisper.

"I wasn't in a good place when I wrote the letter. Not sure I'm in a better place now in general, but I know from the bottom of my heart that those words were and are true. For me, you are it. I'm in awe of you and what you can do, now more than even when I wrote the letter. Without you, I'd be lost."

He pulls me closer, so tight, I feel a hint of desperation in his embrace, but that sensation is gone as soon as he kisses the side of my neck again. No idea why the soft contact of his lips against my skin shortens out my brain, but it re-prioritizes everything.

He trails soft kisses up my throat and to the line of my jaw, stopping at the corner of my mouth. "Did I ever say thank you for figuring out I was in the Realm? For getting me out?"

"Yes—"

"But did I really?" Grasping my neck, he pulls me down into a kiss.

The moment our lips connect, my body clicks into full Kieran-mode.

Kieran kisses me full of confidence, slow and deep. It brings fire to my heart and soul, and boy, do I want to stay immersed in that feeling. Gliding his hands down my back, he wraps them around my waist, then slips one under my standard issue USEF PJ shirt. I gasp as goosebumps run down my spine, and feel Kieran smile against my lips.

"I like it when you make that sound," he whispers, dragging his nails up over my back, then circles the little sunburst scar we share from that shot going through my shoulder and into him as I was protecting him from the Essken, back when I didn't even know who he was.

I squeeze my legs tight, locking his hips in between them, and dig my fingers into his shoulders. I need to hold on to something, because it feels like I'm falling, out of control, spinning. Or, it may be the room, who knows, and who cares. Nothing matters besides Kieran's kiss and the way he moves his hands over my back and ever so slowly to my sides, and then… to the front.

His thumb brushes the underside of my breast and I wonder how nobody has found out Kieran must possess magical powers. He must. His touch ignites my skin in a way only magic could.

Kieran tilts his hips up, connecting us in all the interesting places, and all of a sudden, I'm out of patience. I drop my hands to the middle of his chest and yank his shirt up and over his head, throwing it to the side. It lands on the couch, next to where he threw his hat when we arrived. My heart skips a happy little beat ahead, as if it had waited for me to finally take action.

A mischievous gleam lights up in Kieran's eyes. "Too slow?"

"Heck yeah." Our life's been too hectic and too full of surprises to take things slow. I shove him backward by the shoulders. Gently, of course.

Kieran being Kieran, he would have ample time and strength to resist me, but I don't think he wants to. He lets himself sink back onto the bed, hands finding my hips as I still straddle him. "Always so impatient."

For a moment I allow myself to appreciate the view of a shirtless

Kieran. Tight abs. The little scar we both share. The wave of goosebumps erupting as he gasps when I lower my weight down onto him.

I should take it slow. Enjoy it more. But as it is, I'm fresh out of patience. Guess I always am, when it comes to us finding time to enjoy each other. Hence, fabric is unnecessary and in the way.

"You know what? Let me help you out." Reaching for my own shirt, I rip it off and throw it somewhere behind us.

Kieran's eyes widen, the simultaneous gulp and stiffening of his body empowering me, making me bold. The last time I touched Kieran, *really* touched him, was literally decades ago, and even though that night has burned itself into my memory, the memory isn't as good as the real thing. As this.

Kieran is like an addiction, and I just got my first hit after a period of abstinence, so yes, I'm bold. I peel his hands off my waist and place them on my breasts. He sucks in a sharp breath, then lets out a small sigh as he cups them. That sigh... it does amazing things to my body. It releases an abundance of hormones and tingles all over my skin. It adds to my Kieran addiction, big time.

Kieran sucks his lower lip between his lips. His eyes take on a hooded, lazy quality as he slowly moves his thumbs in small circles over my skin, until they've reached my nipples. The moment he touches me there, my body responds on autopilot. I push my hips down and into his, tilting my pelvis until I feel resistance. Kieran's entire body jerks, as if he'd been shocked—

And in a heartbeat he has reversed our positions. I squeak as my back meets the mattress, not from the impact, but the sudden change in position.

Kieran grins and raises one eyebrow. "Too slow, agreed." He lowers his head, grazing his lips over my cheek, down to my collarbone and back up. I glide my hands over the skin of his naked back, feeling him erupt in shivers wherever I touch him. He holds himself low as he kisses me, keeping our bodies flush and aligned *very* well. So well, I wrap my legs around his hips and buck against him.

This time we both draw in a sharp breath.

Kieran supports his weight on his forearms next to my upper body. He looks at me, reverence in his eyes. "It sounds cheesy, but... I feel your touch so much deeper than on my skin." His whispered words brush over my lips. "Maybe that's the Bond, I don't know, but I was wrong earlier. I don't need cooking to get my stress levels down. I only need you. Always only you. No matter the time we're in, no matter the situation. Always. Only. You. Seeing all the other versions of us... I'm happy we're here. Now. Together." The last word he emphasizes by rolling his hips against mine.

A rush of sensation hits me all at once, triggered by his words and powered by his touch. "Oh heck," I gasp. "Me, too. Very happy, currently."

Kieran chuckles, the sound light and full of warmth. "Glad to hear it. *Hope*, cut the lights."

The lights snuff out, leaving us surrounded by nothing but darkness and our love for each other.

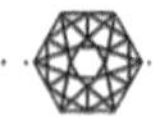

### *USEF HOPE, Guest Quarters, 23:55hrs, September 28th, 2295*

It's the middle of the night when I'm awoken by the abrupt onset of overwhelming nausea. I jerk awake, the small movement making the near-total dark room spin.

Oh no.

Not again. I know that sensation, and I can't say I'm looking forward to the next seconds or minutes. At least I know what to expect and brace for. Shooting one hand out, I wrap it around Kieran's forearm, because one, he needs to be prepared, and two, might as well shorten his misery and connect myself to him.

He startles awake from sleep. "What—"

Before he can get a coherent sentence out, reality billows, blows up, then contracts, only to expand again.

"Crap," I wheeze, eyes wide. Crap. This feels strong, like in the Maelstrom.

With an eardrum splitting *BOOM,* an explosion of never ending blinding white rips reality apart. We both scream out, the sound drowned by a thunderous noise—then replaced by all-encompassing, complete silence and the same type of tear we saw when in the Maelstrom, only now… we're in the middle of it, floating in dark, cold nothingness.

As though somebody had taken a zipper and yanked it open, our reality is visible in the distance to our left and right, its outlines ragged and torn. Behind and around it other timelines waft and float, the Realm's thinner band as well, straight and unaffected by the rift.

"Holy crap," Kieran whispers. "Another cleft. It's gigantic." His hand tightens around mine. "Where are the K'Zees?"

Before I can reply, my body hums and buzzes in anticipation mere moments before I feel the first twitch of electricity in the arm holding on to Kieran.

"Ah, there they are." He grunts, tightening his grip on my hand.

Yes, there they are. I suck in a breath, but it gets stuck halfway down to my lungs. "Holy Universe," I wheeze, as my body cramps up. If I thought the coils were more aggressive the last time, they're even worse now. Peeling off the edges of the tear, they hone in on Kieran with admirable precision. An *oomph* sound breaks from Kieran's throat as he bows back, buried under the swarm of bright, thick lightning bolts. They're coming from the edges of this cleft, rising up in swarms, all heading for us, not just dozens or hundreds, but thousands.

*Hundreds* of thousands, and we're floating in the middle, completely and utterly alone, and at the mercy of those K'Zees.

Panic hits hard at the same time as my center is set on fire by the coils. I pant and grunt as they swirl around inside of me, giving my body what it craves, yet stabbing me with countless little knives. Kieran's grip on me is so crushing, I'm not sure my bones will stay intact. Sweat dots my brows. Focus, Nonie. Focus. How did we end up here? How do we get out? Because we *need* to get out, if the growing unease in the pit of my stomach is any indication. I've got enough experience at this point to know when my First Sense isn't happy.

Sucking in one sharp breath after another, I ignore the burning inside my guts and all around my hand, forcing one foot in front of the other, like I normally would do in the Maelstrom, dragging Kieran with me, the equivalent of a human-sized balloon on a string.

After a few steps, I slow, then stop. Usually I'd have crossed some distance, but I don't think we made any headway toward the enticing edges of reality, not that I can tell, at least. My heart skips about five beats ahead as pain and nausea rise to previously unknown heights and the outlines of my vision turn dark. Holy—!

With a violent jolt, my First Sense reels, the sensation so strong, it feels my body is attacking itself with such an intensity, angry and violent, urgent and demanding, and too overwhelming to adapt to it. Not good. Not—

A chill snakes around my insides, so potent, a shiver runs down my back at the same time as a big, rolling motion below me catches my attention. Out of reflex I draw my legs in and look down.

Oh—

"Holy Universe!" I jerk upright, squeezing my eyes shut and clamping one hand over my mouth or else I might throw up from the overwhelming sense of doom shattering something in me, something the coils must have loosened. My First Sense cramps as energy keeps on shooting through me, in from Kieran, lighting up my hand, and out the other side, a constant stream of contradicting pleasure and ripping agony, but paling in comparison to what I just saw.

To what I just *felt*.

Heart pounding and every muscle cramping, I force my eyes back open to the same horrifying scene as before: Far, far down, at a distance impossible to estimate, the temporal tendrils of the Maelstrom flow and waft, and no, that's not the part that triggers my First Sense or brings the sense of doom choking me. It's the darkness beneath it. A never-ending dark cloud grows and expands, jumping from one colorful time wave to the next. Where it touches them, the colors leave, the light leaves, and only the darkest of all blacks remains, so deep, the only word to describe it is *dead*.

Dread wraps around my heart, slowing down its frantic beat. *That's where the sense of doom is coming from, as if a million souls cried out in agony and pain.*

Timelines move faster than I've ever seen them move, trying to escape the darkness. Some of them crash into the unperturbed realm's strand, bounce off, and find another way for escape as the black clouds pick up speed, drift higher, like powered by the will to ingest everything in their path. They move up, up, *up*—

With a jolt I realize they're going to get us. They're fast, and I've been too shocked to move, too caught in fear—

"Kieran! Move!" I scramble, trying to move up, away, but it's hard to force my locked-up muscles into motion, hard to tell whether I'm making headway at all, hard to drag a half-frozen Kieran with me.

The dark clouds rush at us, passing the Realm while swallowing more and more time tendrils, like a monster on a binge. Coldness wraps around my soul, squeezing it, draining it of everything good and warm, of what makes me, me. Paralysis grips my extremities and stills them. The coils grow frantic, upping their assault on Kieran, and therefore, on me, but even if I wanted to, I couldn't let go of him, my body wouldn't allow it. I'm the opposite pole to his magnetism, no matter the coils are tearing me apart. I'm nothing but a useless conduit as my First Sense gets rid of them, forcing them out my body, expelling them through my heated and lit up opposite hand.

If my world wasn't made only out of pure horror at the moment, I could at least appreciate the beauty of the soft stream of colorful swirls shooting into the nothingness we float in.

The black cloud races toward us, bouncing off the Realm's strand and continuing its scurry up toward us, growing by the second. It's so close, I can't see its end, but yet I cannot estimate how close it is. Miles? Mere meters? The sense of *death*, of irrevocable ending, is so suffocating my next breath *feels* like it might possibly be my last. Sorrow swamps me. If only I could've protected Kieran better. We—

*SNAP!*

I scream as the margins of our universe reunite in a deafening, bone-shattering thunderous *clash*, as if drawn together by magnets. Reality, gone a split second ago, is back, like we hadn't been floating in the Maelstrom, about to be extinguished and snuffed out like a candle by some unimaginable darkness. All that is gone, replaced by good, old, normal reality as we know it.

The *Hope.*

We're back in bed, on board the *Hope.* Some smaller coils sizzle around the edges of my awareness before they vanish and everything is back to how it *should* be, pain free.

A chopped-off wheeze breaks from Kieran's throat, and within a split second, he has pulled me against him, gliding his shaking hands down my back before he balls up my shirt's fabric in his hands and holds me like he never wanted to let go again. Throwing my arms around his neck, I squeeze tight. I don't care if I choke him, I need to feel him, need to feel that we're alive, that we're here. I gulp in a fresh breath of air and Kieran's scent. My lungs rejoice, my heart skips a couple of beats, only to hammer away at an unhealthy speed. A strained wheeze leaves my throat as Kieran's chest moves fast against mine, his pulse hammering at the same heart-attack rate as mine. Each of our breaths is labored and harsh. His body shakes, and so does mine.

I cling to him like he clings to me, like we just came back from a cliff we could've fallen over.

We *would've* fallen over it reality hadn't snapped back into place.

Ever so slowly my pulse calms down. Kieran swallows, then shifts his shaking hand higher, into my hair. "That was bad," he whispers, voice hoarse. "Really bad." He pulls back, cups my cheeks with both of my hands and rests his forehead against mine.

I blow out a puff of air through pursed lips. "I… The cleft… Did you… did you see?"

Kieran tenses and holds his breath. "Only coils, all around me, there were so many. What… what did you see?"

*Darkness so deep and evil, so complete and cold.* I swallow hard. "I saw—"

*"Upinga to Wildason."*

Kieran raises one eyebrow, still but otherwise holds completely still, not letting go of me. "Wildason here." His warm breath tickles over my cheeks, a calming reminder that we're back on the *Hope*, alive and in one piece.

*"Kieran… is Nonie okay?"* Zio's voice sounds rough.

"Yes and no," Kieran replies after a short second. "I assume your First Sense acted up?"

Zio takes a moment before he answers. *"Indeed. It was… rather disturbing."*

A small, half-crazy laugh bursts from my throat. "Understatement, Zio. Understatement."

Kieran sighs once and brushes his thumbs across my cheeks. "Come on over, Zio. This looks like something we need to talk about. Bring Chase, for good measure."

*"I will see you in five. Upinga out."*

As soon as the channel is closed, Kieran gives me a peck on the nose and pulls back. "Good?"

I nod. "Yes. We definitely need to talk to them. We need to brainstorm. Especially with what I saw." I reach for both his hands and peel them off my face, squeezing them once.

"Whatever it is, we'll figure it out. We always do." He tries for a smile, but it feels fake. His face is too pale, the circles under his eyes too dark and deep. Have they been getting worse? I frown. Probably.

Kieran presses a hand to his stomach. "This one was the most intense yet." He huffs, then sighs. "As if we didn't have enough problems with the future gunning after us."

I snort. "True." I kick the covers off and swing my legs out of bed, the motion stirring up some nausea and residual dizziness. "Do you think—"

The doorbell chimes, and Kieran jumps out of bed, his PJ pants almost indecently low on his hips. "Whoa." He sways, but gets a hand out to stabilize himself on the corner of the bed before he can lose balance, then throws a worried glance over to me. "That's new."

The doorbell chimes again. Kieran sighs and reaches for the shirt I threw over the nightstand earlier. "Enter."

The door opens to a quite disheveled looking Chase and a somewhat fresher looking Zio, both in USEF leisure outfits.

"You guys were fast." Kieran motions for them to come in as he slides the shirt over his torso.

"Emergency demat to this location," Zio answers. "I didn't want to lose time."

Kieran gives them a skeptical look as they enter. "And yet, you rang the bell. Couple of decades pass and you learned manners? Can't remember when you rang the doorbell at my place the last time."

Chase snorts. "True. But then, you were alone in your quarters. We're knocking as a courtesy to Nonie, not you."

"'Preciate it." I give a mock salute in their direction, hoping I'm not blushing too much. Feels like my face is on fire, courtesy of the memory of last night. *This* night. And hey, I'm happy we put on some clothes after, even though I had to go looking for my PJs. The pants I found close to the kitchen island. Yes, Kieran really wanted those off and gone, fast.

I suck my lower lip between my teeth, holding back the smile wanting to break free. Somehow, it doesn't feel right smiling and feeling happy after what we just witnessed.

Kieran rolls his eyes. "Of course, you're not knocking as a courtesy to me. Thanks, I feel so cherished."

"You always are." And even though Chase slaps Kieran over the back of the head in a playful manner, seriousness saturates his tone. He grabs a chair and pulls it over, while Zio does the same. Since we're out of other options in this small room, Kieran and I take a seat on the bed, him with his feet on the ground, me, criss-cross applesauce. It feels weird to be on the bed together with Kieran, while Chase and Zio sit across from us. It has something parental to it, a little bit like being caught in the act—I'm sure they know we didn't only sleep tonight. And that's...

just awkward.

I drop my gaze and let my hair fall into my face. I need a moment to recover from that traumatizing thought. At least Dad isn't here, thank whomever for small favors.

Kieran, on the other hand, gets right to business. "Thanks for coming over, guys. We didn't get to talk about this issue yesterday, but frankly we can't *not* talk about it anymore. It affects both of us, and to a lesser degree, others." He gives Zio a pointed look. "And it's increasing in intensity. Now might be a better time than later."

"Agreed," Zio says, much paler than usual.

Chase's gaze darts from one of us to the other and back. "Obviously, I'm not part of the club. I get that something urgent happened, but what did I miss this time? Because y'all look like crap, no offense."

The first time since I've known those three guys together, Kieran ignores a barb from his friend. He gives me a questioning look, and once I nod, replies to Chase. "Short version: We've been experiencing some weird phenomena, like some kind of distortion in reality or temporal disruption. Zio's counterpart thought it was a chasm in time."

Zio stills. "A very astute description. I agree. Whatever this was, it did not feel right. It felt like—"

"Like the end of time," I whisper hoarsely. Like this was it, we were all going to die.

"Zio?" Kieran asks and looks past me, at his friend.

The apple in the other man's throat moves up and down, hard. "It... was a sensation and experience I do not wish to repeat. Nonie's description is apt. It felt like approaching death."

"If this has been happening before, I assume it wasn't as bad before or we would've heard about it?" Chase narrows his eyes. "You mentioned something, Zee, but it wasn't like this."

"No, it wasn't. But this phenomenon seems to increase in frequency and intensity, I agree with Kieran."

"And it happens throughout universes," Kieran says. "Nonies and Zios seem to react to it, suggesting the Magellan's sensitivity to time plays a role."

"Your counterpart also felt the coils, just not as much as you did," I remind him.

"Coils?" Chase raises an eyebrow, and I sigh.

"Yes. Koll, the Essken from a century in the future, called them K'Zees. Either way, I don't have any better name for them, but whenever these events happen, little coiled lightning bolts of energy attack Kieran. They're painful to him, and once they hit him, I'm drawn to him. I cannot *not* touch him, it's like…" I lift and drop my shoulders. "Like imperative magnetism, which sucks, because it's also painful to me. Only positive side effect is that they seem to go away when I touch him. They leave his body through mine. Lightning conductor, right here." I wave my hands.

Kieran frowns at me. "I still wish you wouldn't touch me when that stuff happens," he whispers, eyebrows pulled down into a V. Before I can reply, the frown turns into a soft, close to imperceivable smile. "But I do appreciate it. It makes all the difference to me."

For one short moment we look at each other. We're in this together, obviously, and *that's* what makes all the difference.

Chase blinks. "Geez… Did you experience it like that, Zee?"

"I did not. The previous episodes have been more an acting up of my First Sense, but nothing compared to this latest one."

"I don't think anybody else had the same experience we did," I say. "And yes, agreed. They've been getting more aggressive." And that's not everything. I shoot a questioning glance at Kieran. "And this time, we're still having side effects. You can't tell me you're not feeling it." I make a spinning motion with my finger next to my temple. "Dizziness."

Kieran grimaces. "Well, yes. I do. That didn't happen before."

Well. I beg to differ, because the nausea and dizziness lasted quite a bit for me the last time, too, and I do remember how slow he got up after we crashed in front of Blue Nonie's house. But I'm not about to point that out. Instead, I lift and drop both shoulders. "See? The attacks are worsening."

Zio cocks his head. "You are having symptoms from it?"

"Like Nonie said, some dizziness, Zee. Not a big deal." Kieran waves his friend's concerns off.

"I would still be remiss in my duty if I didn't check you." He reaches into his pocket and takes out a medical scanner, waving it first over Kieran, then over me.

"Zio. We had a talk about not taking your medical scanner to bed with you. It might be a few years in the past, but I remember it quite clearly." Kieran raises an eyebrow at his friend, but when Zio doesn't respond and keeps on scanning, his expression changes to worried. "Zee? Come on man, you're making me nervous."

With a look of intense focus on his face Zio scans himself.

Looks at the read-outs.

Lays the scanner aside.

Folds his hands in his lap.

Closes his eyes and takes a long breath in.

"Zee, seriously. You're freaking me out. Would you please talk to us? I just had a very unpleasant encounter with those coils, I'm not really in the mood—"

"You're dying. Both of you." He regards us with a somber seriousness, one that leaves no doubt that he means what he says.

All the tiny hairs on my body rise in response. "W-what?"

Zio takes another long breath before responding. "I didn't like your scans yesterday, but I couldn't specify what was wrong with them. Call it a hunch. Now looking at the scans I just took it is obvious."

"I don't like the way you say that," Kieran whispers. He scoots closer and takes my hand, pressing his thumb against the rainbow ring as if it could give him hold. "At all."

"And I do not like saying it either, but… your cells are destabilizing. They are falling apart at a rapid rate. Comparing the two scans, it's clear what you experienced is speeding this process up, and going by the current rate…" A muscle in his jaw pops.

"Just say it," I force out through clenched teeth, tightening my fingers around Kieran's.

Zio looks me straight in the eye. "Going at the current rate, neither of you will survive another attack like the one you just went through."

# Chapter Sixteen -

# One Moment in Time

We all sit in shocked silence.

Kieran and me, fingers entwined.

Chase, mouth agape.

Zio, holding on to the scanner, the slightest tremor to his hands.

"Our cells… are falling apart?" Kieran clears his throat. "And… you have no reason for that other than—"

"Other than what you experienced, correct. One scan alone wasn't able to detect the cause of your un-wellness, but the direct comparison is unambiguous. Those events are causing your cellular decay, without a doubt."

*Without a doubt.* There goes Blue Nonie's theory trans-universal jumps could cause damage to our cells—or maybe they are, but it's not like it mattered at this point.

Goosebumps run down my skin, but I feel empty. I should be more shocked, more outraged. My heart should be beating faster to protest

Zio's prediction, but instead it keeps up its usual rhythm, seemingly unaffected.

"Not to offend your medical skills, but are you sure you can read that from two scans?" Chase glides a hand over his head, face ashen.

"No offense taken, and yes. The data is unambiguous, as much as I wish there was an error in it."

"But there must be something we can do to protect them," Chase says, jumping off his chair. "What are these events, how can we predict them, and how can we make sure those coils don't affect them? Or affect them less? How can we reverse the damage?"

"I don't have a response to either of your questions."

"There must be something somewhere we're overlooking. What about other Magellans, or the other versions of us, the other Zio? Anything that's useful?" Chase gets up and walks to the replicator. "Lubbeck's, extra-large."

As if in a trance, I shake my head. So unreal. I hear what Zio is saying, I understand it on an intellectual level, but not in the depth of my soul. "N-no, they didn't report anything else. Overall, it seems Kieran and I are the most sensitive to it." So sensitive, we're falling apart.

"And I have not heard from anybody else anything close to what you are reporting," Zio says. "I checked with the Taro. She felt something similar to what I did, but not at the same level. Maybe the effect depends on the location of the person experiencing it—"

"Or the level of sensitivity they have. Or a combination of both, proximity and sensitivity." I lean forward and press my palm against my forehead. "And maybe you should scan yourself, because—and I know you're going to protest—yours might be higher than the Taros'. Your sister, also known as my mom, found us in a whole audience full of people and knew so much, all from her First Sense. Stands to reason it could run in the family." Plus, I need to have gotten my First Sense from her as well, and if half her genes can make me jump timelines, Zio, as her brother, could also have an elevated First Sense, and who knows if that's an asset or a risk at this point.

"I did." Zio raises the scanner, then places it onto the table, neatly aligned with its edges. "My scan is normal. Sensing the events does not seem to cause the same harm as does your exposure to those coils, or so I assume."

"That's good to know. At least something positive." Kieran lowers his head once in a curt nod, a lock of hair falling into his face. He's so young. So very young. Not that I wasn't, but having seen two older Kierans recently, it drives home how unfair life is. How unfair fate plays. Kieran just came back from the Realm, only to be abducted and to now find out he might die soon. To find out *we* might die soon.

He gloves our entwined fingers with his other hand, smoothing his thumb over my skin. "Why us then? What's different? Maybe knowing the differences can help us find a way to get out of this mess."

When we were in the Realm with Koll and I joked we were special, I really didn't mean it that way. I'm fine with normal. Really. Normal is all I want.

I shrug. "The biggest difference between us and all other versions of us is we experienced the episodes more intensely than them. So maybe we were sensitized by frequent time jumps? That's how it worked for me in the Maelstrom and with my jump precision—for you, too, you're able to see more and more in the Maelstrom, and the Realm—so why shouldn't it be the same with these coil attacks? They could be getting used to us, given that we're jumping back and forth these days. Maybe even our Bond plays a role, too." That's the working theory for the Realm, and until I have a better one, I'll use it for this as well.

Zio clenches his hands and releases them. "I don't have enough data to answer those questions."

"But you will get that data, right?" Chase swallows hard, his hold on the gigantic glass of Lubbeck's so tight, his knuckles turn white.

"That is a question you didn't need to ask, Trip."

"All right, yes, I know. Apologies. I don't do well with these kinds of things. It gives me the creeps thinking you might not be—" He pauses and cocks his head. "Wait. You guys were in the future. You met your great-grand daughter, and as far as I know, you haven't made any babies yet. That—"

A groan breaks from my throat. "Chase. Can you please not talk about making babies?" While I'm in my PJs? On my bed? That I slept in with Kieran? Could it be any more awkward?

Chase waves me off. "Get over it, whatever—but my point is, if you're supposed to have children, doesn't that mean you'll survive?" Hope colors his voice as he looks from one to the other.

And I hate to take it from him. From us. "In short, no. We're not going to survive just because we've seen our impact on the future. This right now might be a Diversion Point. This is something bigger than our timeline, or any timeline, and just like the Temporal War strives to achieve, these time spasms and coils can change the timeline's course or cause a split, especially after what I saw with the last event." I suck in a big breath, which does nothing to calm the roiling sea of nerves inside my stomach. "Which brings me to my point, which is that we're missing the point."

"You'll have to elaborate on the one," Chase says drily, taking a big sip of Lubbeck's.

I reach over, steal the glass from his hands, and take a large gulp. I feel we've reached that level of both friendship and desperation.

Worry creases appear on Chase's forehead. "The point we're missing is that bad?"

"Well. Yes." I hand the glass back to him. "Don't get me wrong, I don't want us to die. I want us to grow old and live a somewhat normal life, and those coils eating us up from the inside doesn't help with that at all." I swallow hard. "But that being said, we're not what we need to be concerned about. The events are changing. In retrospect, everything is so much clearer, but… we didn't have much time to think, to *really* think." The muscles in my jaw tick. Maybe I could've seen a pattern sooner, if we didn't have to fulfill five job descriptions at once. "The first attack by those coils wasn't so bad in the grand scheme of things. After that, I started seeing different versions of people, like different timelines bleeding through. Once time slowed to a crawl. We theorized these events had something to do with temporal abnormalities, so far so good, but then, tonight, I saw for the second time a literal *chasm* tearing through space time. A void, for a lack of a better term, an abyss of nothingness. And here's the truly scary part: It *deleted* timelines. It snuffed them out. They were gone, just gone, where it touched the Maelstrom. It was about to reach us, before the rift collapsed and reality went back to normal. But for those few seconds, I was sure whatever that thing was, whenever it would touch me or us, we'd be gone, just like the timelines it turned into nothingness."

Blood drains from Kieran's face. "That's why it felt so… final." He rakes a hand through his hair, letting go of a slow, controlled breath. "I see why you're saying we're missing the point. Those events are bad news for us, but worse news in general. Let me ask you the important questions here, since you're painting the bigger picture than our potential untimely demise. Is this thing destroying time in general? Is that what it's doing? How much of a threat is it to us, and—you know I'm going to ask this—could it be part of the Temporal War, like, the ultimate weapon? I know I keep harping on that, but we initially thought the FBTI had something to do with those attacks on us—what if we were right?"

The ultimate weapon… what a scary thought. It would be an ultimate weapon for sure. That dark cloud, it didn't mess around. It *deleted*, leaving nothing in its wake. A shudder runs down my back. It *ended* what got in its way.

I shake my head. "I can't imagine anybody being able to manufacture a weapon of this magnitude. It can't be artificially made." How would one even design a time strand-eating weapon that rips reality apart?

Kieran drops his hand, shoulders slumping forward with his exhale. "I feared you would say that, and I think you're right. Against all odds I was hoping—and I'm using this word lightly here—it could've been man-made. If it's a natural phenomenon, our chances of stopping it are even slimmer. I can keep whoever is deploying a weapon from doing so, but I can't get a natural phenomenon to stop, especially if I don't understand it."

I drop my voice to a whisper. "No. No, I don't think we can stop it." We were lucky this time, that's it. The Realm was lucky, too.

All of a sudden, I feel cold. Drawing my legs in, I wrap my arms around them. "It felt like the biggest force of nature I've ever experienced." Forcing down a hard swallow, I look at the three men. "And Kieran is right. I don't think we can stop it. I can't imagine anything that could withstand—" I crunch up my nose. Actually... "Come to think about it, the Realm wasn't affected. Or maybe not as affected? It's hard to tell, I—" I wave a hand and sigh. "Never mind. I don't know what I'm talking about. We were lucky this time, that's it, and the Realm was lucky, too."

"Luck isn't really trust inspiring," Chase says, lips pinched together.

Shaking my head, I drop my gaze. "No, definitely not. And what makes it even worse is that with our plan we might be successful—no, we *will* be successful—in stopping the Temporal War, but we have no way of stopping the chasms through reality." The futility of our situation is absolutely infuriating.

We're doing what we can to save the Essken and to stop the Temporal War. We're trying to save lives, as many as possible.

But in the end, Kieran and I are one K'Zee-attack away from cellular death, and our timeline still could be gobbled up by a hungry dark cloud of doom.

In the end, we still *all* might die.

And there's absolutely nothing we can do about it.

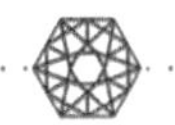

*USEF HOPE, Guest Quarters, 00:30hrs, September 29th, 2295*

"We'll see you tomorrow then." Kieran lays one hand on Chase's shoulder as he guides his two best friends to the door. "Try to get some sleep."

Chase huffs. "Right. Fat chance."

"I know." Clapping Chase's shoulder twice, Kieran raises his hand at Zio, already out in the hallway, focused on his medical PAD. "See you tomorrow, Zee."

When Zio doesn't respond, Chase sighs and rolls his eyes. "Well, some things never change, you'll be happy to hear. Let me make sure he doesn't run into a wall while he… while he does whatever he's doing." He takes the Magellan by the elbow, but looks back at Kieran. "You *will* be here tomorrow. Nothing else is going to happen. You both will. Be. Fine."

It takes Kieran a second to reply, and when he does, his voice sounds rough. "We will. Bye, Chase."

"Bye, Kieran."

For another ten or fifteen seconds, Kieran stays at the door, looking after his friends, before he steps back and it closes behind him. His hands are buried deep in the pockets of his PJ pants, his head lowered, gaze trained to the ground, chest heaving up with a long inhale. The same misbehaving unruly lock as always falls into his face. He chews on his lower lip, and when he looks up, his gaze finds mine. "That was unexpected. Everything."

I exhale roughly. "Another understatement, but yes." I pat the spot next to me on the bed, and Kieran shuffles over, shoulders slumped forward, head bowed. He lowers himself onto the mattress, sitting down, his legs crossed, facing me.

He looks miserable, like the last twist of fate broke something irreparable inside of him.

"How are you holding up?" I cup his cheek with one palm. He nuzzles his face into my touch, the softest smile on his lips, even though it doesn't reach his eyes.

"The question should be, how *you*'re holding up. You're young, this is your time period. You shouldn't be dying."

"Neither should you."

He drops his gaze to the bed. "I'm a dead man walking, Nonie. Don't forget, I was considered dead for decades, and it surely felt like that while I was trapped in the Realm. I had it coming, one could say. My life was only on loan since the moment I entered the Realm. I never expected it to last." He tries for an unaffected calm tone, but squeezes his eyes shut a little too hard to be truly convincing.

And I understand.

A shudder runs down my spine. This is the weight he carried since I got him out of the Realm, the true weight on his shoulders, on his soul, the reason for his off behavior, his atypical aggression, his casual way of dealing with threats of death. Not that Chase and Zio are older, his dad gone, not any of the million other problems and obstacles thrown in his—our—way.

*This* is the chain around his soul.

*I'm a dead man walking, Nonie.* How can you live when you consider yourself dead? My heart goes out to him.

*My life was only on loan since the moment I entered the Realm. I never expected it to last.*

I keep my voice soft. Caring. "I know."

He opens his eyes, brows narrowed. "You… do?"

Brushing my thumb back and forth over his cheek, I try to soften my words to ease their sting. "Since I got you out of the Realm, you've been off, Kieran. Not always, but I noticed." How he wouldn't stop beating Sheridan, when the old Kieran would've only used violence as necessary. Or how he disregarded all common sense and tried to attack the FBTI-agents on the *Pioneer* when we were clearly outnumbered and outgunned, as though he didn't care what happened to him—because he considered himself dead already.

My heart breaks once again, with a crack as deep as the time chasm right through its middle.

I can't say Kieran's revelation is coming as a big surprise. When I saw him last in his time, on the *Pioneer*, just before entering the Realm, he clearly was depressed. The war, the loss of life, it weighed on him. Did I expect him to miraculously feel better after coming out of the Realm? Did I really expect him to feel better when he realized he missed decades, outlived friends and family, and was caught in the middle of a temporal war in addition to the ongoing Essken War?

Had I thought about it more, the answer would've been *no*.

But I didn't, because we were busy with too many things, too many threats, too many more important concerns. And because sometimes, he seemed fine. Like last night. Yes, we've had moments where some frustration broke through, but then... then we had us.

But that doesn't mean Kieran is fine.

Holding his face in my hands, I try to put as much emphasis on every single word as I can. "You aren't a dead man walking, Kieran. You're a survivor who's been given another chance." As short-lived as it may be in our case. "I don't want you to see yourself as dead already," I whisper, eyes tearing up. "You're here, with me, and right now we're still alive. I need you to be alive, Kieran. For as long or as little as we have, I need you to be alive."

He sucks in a sharp breath, face pinched tight, as he shakes his head. His answer is spoken so low, I can barely hear it. "I don't know if I can do that, I—" He snaps his mouth shut and swallows once. Rubs his hand across his forehead, then opens his mouth again, only to shut it. "I—" Holding his breath and then releasing it with a big sigh, he deflates, like he was giving in. "I've tried. There are times where I think I'm succeeding, and others where it's clear I'm not."

He forces his fingers to splay onto the blanket we're sitting on. Like the dam was broken and blown into pieces, the words spill out of him. "Sometimes, I'm hopeless, but mainly I'm so incredibly angry about *everything*, angry at fate to get me stuck in the Realm, angry at the Essken for not realizing time is linear for me and for what was happening to me. I'm just plain *angry* all the freakin' time! And I know I shouldn't resent the Essken; it wasn't their fault, they tried to help me, and believe me, it makes me even more angry that I know that. It denies me a perpetrator, a guilty party, to focus my anger on, because all I want is to scream at somebody responsible, and yes, beat them up. I want to get the aggression out of my system, maybe then I'll feel better. Knowing the Essken aren't at fault is great, but it leaves me with a whole motherlode of frustration and anger I have no way of getting rid of." He balls the fabric of the blanket into his fists so hard, the veins on the back of his hands pop out.

Inhaling once, he fights for composure, shaking his head, a dark lock of hair falling into his face. "And if it was only that anger, yeah, I might get over it as time goes on, but the way I feel… I have these high ideals for myself. I'm a captain with USEF, the youngest at my time. I have values I uphold in myself and others, and now? Now I can't find it in me to honor those values. If there was a person responsible for what happened to me and I met them I couldn't guarantee their safety, Nonie. I don't think I could control myself. And that, the fact that I'm considering harming, and potentially killing, another person as retribution, that scares me. That's not the person I want to be, but it is apparently the person I've become."

Tears shine in his eyes, but he doesn't look away as he whispers the next words, nodding. "And then I feel ungrateful, because you're right, I *am* alive, I did make it out of the Realm. I have Chase and Zio. *I have you.* Living without you in my time would've been torture, in general, but also with the Bond being disrupted. I know I'm lucky to be alive and to be with you. I want that. I just wish I could feel the way I'm supposed to, and not so freakin' angry and lost all the time." He squeezes his eyes shut, and a single tear rolls down his cheek.

I swipe it away with my thumb, then drop my hands onto his thighs. My heart is pounding so violently from his admission, I pray it won't distract him, it won't break the spell. He needs to get this weight off his chest. In normal life, he would've been to a USEF-assigned counselor already, because we know about the impact of trauma on one's mental health. Kieran had more thrown at him than any other officer I can think of, yet we haven't had the time to take care of anything else but physical injuries. Him trying to open up right now is huge.

He draws in a shuddering breath. "I always knew the risks of the job. But I was so cocky, I thought whatever fate threw at me, I could handle it. Work my way out of it. Until the Realm happened, and then the Temporal War. Now I'm nothing but a chess piece, and that's the last thing I want to be. I don't want to play somebody else's game. You know how much it is in my blood to be in control, and…" He rubs a palm over his eyes, expression tortured and torn. "… and I'm scared of what I'm willing to pay to regain some of that control. I would give… *everything*." He inhales deeply and blows out the air softly.

"Everything," I repeat softly, trying to make sense of the word, trying to grasp the magnitude of what he means with that.

He stills. "Exactly. *Everything*. I would give my life if it meant I'd die a free man and on my own terms." Lifting his gaze to mine, sadness shines in his eyes, and maybe some fear courtesy of his admission. "And I shouldn't be thinking that. I shouldn't be thinking about death, but life. Not about endings, but about beginnings, but… Since I flew into that nebula, the choice of what to do with my life was taken from me in that very moment. My life, as I had envisioned it, was gone. Did I know that was a possibility as a USEF officer? Heck, yes. But that doesn't mean one isn't always hoping for the best. And maybe I would deal with all of *this*"—he makes a circling motion with his hand—"in a better way if I didn't feel so used. No control. The lack of understanding what's going on. It chips away at me. Turns out, sometimes you're just a play-ball. Sometimes you're just helpless. And that realization… I think it broke something in me. I lost my footing in my life. I feel like I'm drifting, and I don't know how to get my feet back on the ground." His voice cracks with the next choppy inhale.

"And now that we might die with the next shift and there's— again—nothing we can do about it… I realize I've been wasting those few days I had. I was given a chance to live, and I wasted it. *I wasted it*." He squeezes his eyes shut. "I'm so sorry, Nonie. So very sorry."

My heart, a soft, melted, buttery mush after his words, finds its backbone again. "There is nothing to be sorry for, Kieran. Nothing. Everything you just said is normal, you hear me? Normal." What a weight to carry. His anger, aggression, desperation. *I would give my life if it meant I'd die a free man and on my own terms.* I understand it, all of it, but it makes me so unbelievably sad for him. Or rather, angry there's nothing I can really do, no quick fix. We're stuck in this war, with these shifts and coil attacks, and, like he said, we're only chess pieces being moved around.

Yeah.

I get where his anger comes from.

I get why clinging to your ideals and values might be difficult when you're used like a means to an end.

And I get why that all eats at him.

I look at the man I've felt an inexplicable connection to ever since I saw a picture of him. The man who's so much more than history made him out to be, who has still so much more to offer to the world.

The man I love with all my heart, Bond or not.

And I want him to know that I understand. That I'm here for him, and that despite the darkness, there's always a spark of light. I see it, and I hope I can make him realize it's there.

I draw my leg in and scoot closer to him. "You know, I'm with you on the anger part. I'd love to uppercut somebody for having you go through what you did in the Realm, but you know what? I'm also so very happy you did end up in the Realm, because you're *here* and you're *alive*. I grew up learning you died when you entered the nebula. Every single moment I spent with you in my past, I knew that. You said you're a dead man walking now, but that's not true. Back then it was. You were a dead man walking, and knowing that was beyond heartbreaking.

I swallow hard. "I don't know what's going to happen with those shifts. If we're truly doomed, as Zio says. Since apparently the timeline isn't as special as we thought, I also don't know what's going to happen in our future—yes, we could survive, or maybe we won't. I don't know. But I'll tell you one thing. I know that you and I will make the best of the time we have. We won't give in to anger or despair, because we're better than that. Because we got us. And I'm not willing to spend what potentially could be our last hours not honoring the people we were before fate threw us in for a loop, nor do I want to waste a single second with you."

Before I lean my forehead against his, I look into the eyes of the man I've followed through time, and whom I'd follow wherever and whenever he went. "I love you, Kieran. I'm so incredibly sorry all this happened to you, but so incredibly happy you are here. I. Love. You." My voice breaks with the last word, as emotion clogs my throat. I only said those words once, before he went into the nebula and I thought I'd lose him for good. They're big, they're scary, but they need to be said, and they need to be said often. I couldn't live with myself if… *something* happened to either of us and I hadn't told him how much he meant to me.

Kieran lets go of a stuttered breath, cupping my cheeks like I'm holding his. His touch feels like *more*, like it tethered our souls together so that mine could keep his afloat. "I love you too, Nonie. So very much, it hurts. So very much."

For a moment, silence hovers, only interrupted by our harsh breathing and the fast beat of our hearts. I focus on the feel of his forehead against mine, the caress of his breath down my cheek, the sensation of his hands on my cheek. I want to burn it all into memory and keep this moment safe and sacred, because right now, right here, with Kieran and me in our little bubble, we are okay. We will be okay.

That will change the moment we step out of this room and back into the hurried pace of life, trying to win the Temporal War and hoping there won't be another shift, but for now, we got us.

We need us.

Kieran peels my hand off his cheek, brings it to his mouth, and kisses the ring he gave me in what feels like a different life. Entwining his fingers with mine, he sneaks our hands between our chests. "I understand what you're saying," he whispers. "I want to be alive, Nonie. I really do. I want to be alive with you and enjoy every second we have left, but I don't know if I can flip the switch like that." He makes a snapping sound with his fingers.

"I don't expect you to," I say, shaking my head. I wouldn't even know if that was possible.

"But I want you to know that I'm trying. I want to be in the moment, and with you. I'm trying."

He kisses the ring and then each of my knuckles. "Nonie?"

"Yeah?"

"Can I… can I just hold you for a while?"

My heart stutters at the vulnerable quality in his voice. I nod. "I'd like that. As long as you want."

Kieran smiles—not the thousand-watt go-getter smile, but one of relief and content. A small one, reaching his eyes and giving them some well-needed spark again.

"I might never let go." He brushes his lips against mine, then lays down, head on the pillow, pulling me with him so that my head comes to rest against his chest. He brushes my hair out of my face with one hand, while sneaking the other under my neck and into my back, then grunts and rolls on his side, hooking over my legs with his top one, connecting our fronts. "There we go." He kisses my forehead, then rests his chin on top of my head, taking a deep, controlled breath in and exhaling it over several seconds.

Cuddling into him, I press my ear against his chest, the calming dub-dub sound of his heart fixing up holes in my soul I didn't know needed patching. And even though our timeline is in danger, reality might be falling apart, and we might be dead soon, in this moment, none of that matters.

All that matters is living, enjoying the moment, enjoying each other, and taking from time what she's trying to deny us: the hope for a future together.

# Chapter Seventeen -
# Snap Goes the Trap

The next morning, both Kieran and I have way darker shadows under our eyes than either of us would like to admit.

"You look like you rested about as well as I did," Chase comments when he enters the demat room, a lidded mug in his hands.

"Good morning to you, too. Can't say we slept much." Kieran sighs, and then puts on a small mischievous smile, so much like *before* it makes my heart hurt and rejoice at the same time. "And no, I know the way your mind works. Don't say it, you're old now, I don't want to hear it."

Chase chuckles but doesn't take the bait as he normally would. Guess we're all still recovering from and dealing with last night's revelations. Turns out sleep isn't really an option when the world could end courtesy of the Temporal War, or a time-eating mega-chasm out to end all timelines, and for sure to end us. Whoever said choice was good must've never faced a triple-threat whopper like this.

I steal a glance over at Kieran. Despite the crappy situation, I feel he looks better today. He just joked with Chase, that's a good sign. And while neither of us slept, I still feel more recharged than I've felt after a whole night of sleep. This night did both of our souls well.

Chase raises his lidded cup, an impish half-smile spreading over his face. "Here's something to cheer you up, because universe knows we all need that today." He clears his throat and stands up righter, raising his mug. *"A glass of Lubbeck's to start your day makes all your troubles melt away."* He looks from Kieran to me and back when we cringe, his face falling. "No? Marketing came up with—"

Kieran waves both hands, a pained humored expression on his face. "No. Hard no. But thank you for making me smile. And then cringe. That being said, whoever came up with this, have them work harder." He shakes his head, grimacing.

"Nonie—"

"Sorry, Chase. I'm with Kieran on this one." But I love him even more for not making it awkward, like we were already marked for death. And here's to being optimistic about our future and planning ahead: Whenever we have peace and quiet, I want to hear all about Admiral Conolly's involvement and history with Lubbeck's. I feel like I should get an honorable mention or something, after all, it was me who got him hooked onto the flavor. I'll add it to the ever-growing list of things to do once there's time. If *we* have time.

Double-sigh.

Chase frowns, but takes another sip of his drink, probably to sweeten the rejection. He swallows and smacks his lips. "Okay then. Got a couple of updates for you two. One, your dad's held up on Earth, Nonie. I gave him a report last night—only the outlines, no details, for obvious reasons, espionage being one of them. Oh, and that certain conversations shouldn't be held over the comm. I did emphasize the need for a timely return though, because… you know." He looks down into his mug and swirls the liquid.

Yeah, I know, cellular decay, etc.

"I think he picked up on the urgency and he'll join us as soon as he can."

I lower my chin in a nod. "Sounds good." It hurts knowing Dad is in the dark about my impending demise, but he needs his head in the game as much as I do, and I don't need him fussing over me every minute he's here. I'd love to see him, now more than ever, but remembering how he went all uber-protective Dad on me when I came back with Mashaule before I went into the Realm to meet the Quaneez and free Kieran, I don't need to have a repeat-performance of that. I'm distracted as it is, and keeping Dad's worry off my shoulders in addition to my own might break me, hard as it is keeping information of this magnitude from him.

"Two, everything's set on Kataki, and when I say everything, I mean *everything*. Roodt requested absolute privacy in your meeting room. No recording. No surveillance. Only you, and nobody else, Kieran. Obviously, that was a hard no, not that I'd tell him that. So, I had my work cut out for me last night. We took precautions and secured the heck out of the meeting area. Nobody gets harmed on my watch." He presses his lips into a thin line, the only indication he isn't only referring to down on Kataki.

I whistle through my teeth. "You did that already since our impromptu end-of-the-world midnight meeting?" No wonder he needs a Lubbeck's pick me upper.

"Yes and no. I wish I could've done it myself, but everybody besides Kieran is blocked from dematting down there. So, I got you the best man for the job if I can't do it, and sent—"

A beeping noise coming from the demat console interrupts him. "And perfect timing." Setting his cup down under the sign that says *No Liquids in the Demat Room,* Chase moves around the console and cracks his fingers. As he handles the controls, a high-pitched whine fills the air. "I believe no introductions are necessary," he says, motioning to the person materializing on the platform.

As soon as the demat process is complete, the older, white-haired admiral steps off the platform. "Officers," Admiral Bas Grazer greets us, bowing his head in our direction.

"Bas," Trip replies, taking his Lubbeck's again. "Glad you could join us."

"Wouldn't miss this party for the world." He gives me a curt nod that I return. Given that we have a bit of a complicated history and a ton of issues between us, this equals a heartfelt reunion. Intellectually I know why he behaved so abrasively and dismissive toward me, but my soul still hurts form the futile effort it poured into being seen by Grazer.

How hurt was I when Grazer wanted to downgrade me to a B for one of my drills? And how happy was I when Mashaule praised me for that same drill and recommended me for D-2 and the mission that was supposed to kill me, a planet full of Essken, and destroy Dad's chance for the presidency?

I suppress a shudder.

Yeah.

Grazer downgrading me had nothing to do with him disliking me and everything with me single-handedly undoing years of effort of keeping me safe and under the radar. *Now* I know why Grazer wasn't happy.

Hindsight is truly 20/20, because that's *so* not what his behavior toward me felt like. Mashaule played him too, just like he played all of us for decades. Grazer lost as much to that traitor as we all did. The Magellan woman he fell in love with, command of the *Pioneer*, and who knows what else. Probably some of his independent decision making, being under the thumb of a madman.

Huh.

When I put it like this… I think I can get over my hurt ego when it comes to Grazer. Sometimes, my maturity surprises even myself—or maybe perspective changes when the rest of your life seems shorter all of a sudden.

Grazer takes two more large steps and halts right in front of Kieran. "Captain Wildason." He holds out his hand, a look of wonder in his eyes, as he slowly shakes his head. "I saw your transmission to the fleet. I understand what happened. Yet, seeing you here, looking the same as you did when we served together… It's hard to wrap my mind around it."

Kieran takes the other man's hand. "Believe me, *Admiral* Grazer, it's quite the adjustment from my point of view as well." He says it like the old Captain Wildason, the one who captivated large audiences with his presence, not like the man who was so at odds with his fate last night.

Grazer chuckles. "I believe that without even knowing all the details. I also apologize for the same mess still being an issue since you left. Sometimes, forty years pass in a blink and mean nothing." He sighs, letting go of Kieran's hand. "How does it feel having to put out fires left and right the moment you're back?"

Kieran's gaze darts over to me for one split second, before he focuses back on the admiral. "It keeps me busy and from thinking too much about those forty years. Other than that, I can't say I'm happy about the progress—or lack thereof—when it comes to the Essken. The Quaneez."

"Amen to that, Captain. But it is my sincere hope we will be closer to peace after your meeting with Mr. Roodt today. I take it you have been briefed?" Grazer's gaze drifts over to Chase.

"Somewhat. We had another… emergency last night, so time has been limited."

Nicely phrased, Trip. Nicely phrased.

Chase takes the last sip of his drink, a slightly desperate look on his face when he realizes the cup is empty. "Kieran, Bas is the head of D-Two. He can get stuff done where I can't, a.k.a., down on Kataki One with a demat-block in place. Am I right, Bas?"

Grazer wiggles his eyebrows. "Indeed you are. And it's my pleasure to do whatever in my power to catch you a time traveler for questioning and to keep you safe, Captain. I still haven't forgotten Alpha Rubrum."

Kieran inclines his head. "I stand to what I said back then. Peaceful coexistence is the future of USEF."

Grazer smiles and claps Kieran onto the shoulder. "You had the talent to be a pain in my behind, but I'm happy you're back."

"Thank you, sir."

Putting his empty cup down under the same sign as before, Chase turns back toward us. "Everything is set on the ground, Bas?"

"Everything is set. I can't tell you how much fun I had sneaking in under their noses and installing those emitters. As soon as even a hint of Setayashi radiation is detected, the forcefield will be in place. That man you're looking for won't know what hit him."

"Speaking of." I step forward, hands folded behind my back. "A word of caution. His clothing functions as armor. You might get one shot in, but the second will be absorbed. A rotating frequency might give you better chances of quickly neutralizing him." Fool me once… I rub my fingers over my back where Sheridan hit me. Being a hundred years behind his tech means we have to be on target with everything we do, and if that shield is truly related to Essken-technology, as he said… Well, we had to look for a way through their shields before, we can do it again.

Grazer lowers his chin in a nod. "Understood, Lieutenant." A small smile tugs on his lips, and it comes with an apologetic glance at me. "I still regret fate was not in our favor. D-Two would've benefitted having you join the team."

Heat washes over my face. Getting a compliment is one thing, but getting it from Grazer, the man I tried to impress—officially unsuccessfully so—all my academy life? Whole different animal. "Thank you, Admiral. I regret that, too, but taking recent events into consideration, I do think the FBTI suits me more." For as long as I'll live, cue the dramatic music, sigh.

His smile widens, and boy, is it unsettling to see that look on him, even though it feels genuine. "Point taken, Lieutenant, point taken."

Chase claps his hands. "If everybody is ready—"

The doors swoosh open, admitting Zio. Like the rest of us, he looks like sleep hadn't been an option last night. His uniform is as wrinkled as the dark circles under his eyes, and given that Zio never accepts anything less than perfection in himself, his look is worrisome. He nods at everybody. "Good morning, Bas. Good to see you again."

"Likewise, Zio." Grazer lowers his chin at Zio. Interesting to hear him address the Magellan in a more civil manner. His nonchalant and slightly racist way to talk about my mentor always made me uncomfortable around him, but maybe… maybe that was part of his cover to stay under the radar with Mashaule. Like, pretending to be a reformed man after his unfortunate misjudgment of dating a Magellan woman.

"Trip, I need to have a moment with Kieran and Nonie." Zio gestures to the far corner of the Demat room.

"Of course. We have another few minutes."

"Thank you." Zio strides ahead, and we follow. Once we're in the corner and out of earshot for everybody except sound-sensitive Magellans, he opens the pouch he brought and takes out two round, flat, coin-sized devices. "This might help you stabilize your cells. It is all I can develop on short notice, but I want you to at least wear these while I continue my research. I cannot promise it's going to work, but at least we're not completely helpless. Niece?" He motions for me to lower the neckline of my shirt, then sticks the device under my right collarbone. "I was out of mental energy to come up with a better name than the device's description. It's a cellular stabilizer. If you can avoid encountering one of those events, please do. Otherwise…" He sticks the second device onto Kieran's skin. "Otherwise, I hope this works."

Kieran adjusts his shirt, gratitude shining from his eyes. "Thank you, Zee. Really, *thank you.* Hopefully we don't need it, agreed, but if we do, I have full confidence in your skills. This will work."

"Your word to fate's ear, Kieran."

A smile pulls on Kieran's lips. "Fate owes me one, I've come to realize. I'm calling in her debt. Speaking of, could I have a moment with Nonie, please?"

Zio nods, closes his pouch, and joins Chase and Grazer. Taking me by the shoulders, Kieran turns me, so that my back is against the wall and him in front of me.

"I've said it before, but this time you have to listen. If another event hits us, I don't want you to touch me," he says, voice serious. "I want you to let me be and do your best to get out of whatever situation that is and get back home."

I stare at him, open mouthed. "You're joking." I can't just leave him floating in whatever time chasm without a way to get home.

"Not in the least. We assume the coils are causing our cells to decay, and they're only attacking me. There's no reason for you to touch me and expose yourself to them. There's no reason for you to die, Nonie."

I blink hard, trying to get a myriad of emotions sorted out. I love that Kieran is so protective of me, I really do, but he forgets I make my own decisions. I meet his gaze. "If I don't touch you, you will die." He probably would've died the very first time the coils attacked him, for all we know.

"But then you don't."

"What makes you think I won't?"

"So, what, now you want to speed it up?" He throws up his hands.

"No, but I also can't just stay by and let you suffer and die, stupid!" I stomp my foot, and while it's a total kindergartner move to do, it drives my point home. There you go.

Kieran's gaze softens. "I understand that. But imagine how it would make me feel if I knew I was pulling you down with me."

"Imagine how it would make me feel seeing you die in agony without having helped you, when I could've." I cross my arms in front of my chest. "Besides, I don't even know if I *can* control it. Once those K'Zees are inside of you, it's like a compulsion. Like you're a siren calling to me. It overrides something inside my brain." I slap my forehead twice. "Even if—if—I agreed with you, I don't know if I could uphold that deal once it happens." Because the pull to touch him is *that* strong. I could hold my breath longer than I could hold back from touching Kieran once the coils are inside of him.

For one long moment, we look at each other. Then Kieran pulls me in for an embrace. His chest heaves up and down together with a long sigh. "I guess we'll see what happens. And I'm still hoping Zio's thing works."

Wrapping my arms around him, I nod. "Yeah. It will." I don't let any doubt enter my mind. I can't afford that. Plus, Zio is possibly the best medical officer USEF has ever had. If I had to place my trust in somebody, it should be him.

Creating some distance, Kieran looks at me. "Great-grandchildren would be nice."

I chuckle. "Going out on a normal date would be nice."

He grins. "That, too." He kisses my nose. "One problem at a time, eh?"

"One problem at a time."

Chase waves over to us. "Ready? Travis Roodt should be waiting for you. And if we're lucky, Sheridan as well." And with him our hope to shed light into the mystery of the Temporal War.

Kieran nods and cracks his neck. "Ready when you are. Let's go and catch ourselves a time traveler."

Yup. One problem at a time.

## USEF HOPE, Stable Orbit over Kataki One, Demat Room, 08:18hrs, September 29th, 2295

The next minutes drag like hours.

Coming up with a plan is great, not being the one executing it is torture. Not that I don't trust Kieran, or Grazer, for that matter, but I don't trust either Travis Roodt or fate. Both have proven to have a mean streak. Add Sheridan to the mix, and no wonder I feel nauseous. At least it's normal nausea, not my First Sense's foreboding of potential doom.

Chewing on my nails, I pace in front of the demat platform. "How long?"

"About thirty seconds later than when you asked the last time," Chase says, then sighs. "Four minutes and fifty-two seconds. Kieran is safe down there, Nonie. Grazer knows what he's doing, and Kieran is one of our most capable officers. The last forty years haven't taken that from him."

They only took some of his spark, I know. But, to be fair, I stand by what I thought earlier: our late-night talk appears to have helped.

Kieran seemed more relaxed, even though something's still holding him back. But at least some of the weight has been lifted, I think. Or maybe, shared with me. "I know. I know. *Intellectually* I know all of that. Emotionally, I'm behind the curve. I—"

The demat console beeps, and both Chase and I suck in a sharp breath. He dances his fingers over the data input surface. "Three people, incoming."

Three people: Grazer, Kieran, Sheridan. Please let it be those three.

The whine of the demat process cuts through the tense silence, and three seconds later exactly the three people I wanted to see materialize, one of them quite annoyed, by the looks of him.

But, instead of growling at me, or making threats, or being an unkind annoying person in general, Sheridan stays silent. His bound hands are balled to fists, knuckles turning white. Maybe he's mad we caught him, maybe he's mad Kieran beat him up the last time, and I would understand that. Apparently, a future time-traveler doesn't necessarily have the means to heal himself faster. The area under his left eye is blue and swollen, his temple on the same side red and puffy, from where Kieran's elbow hit him. A cut runs through the right side of his lower lip, and somehow his jaw looks swollen there too.

Still, his gaze is alert as it bounces around the room, taking in his surroundings, the muscles in his jaw so tight, I'm worried he might crack a molar.

But he doesn't say a word. Doesn't fight.

And boy, if that doesn't make me nervous.

I take the prison hood we brought and step forward, holding it out toward Grazer. "As planned?"

"As planned," Grazer replies, keeping a good grip on Sheridan as he takes the prison hood.

Kieran gives me a curt nod, lips tight. Uh-oh. I know that expression. He didn't like what Roodt had to say. But I guess that will have to wait.

Chase claps his hands. "Okay, let's escort our guest to the conference room. We have lots to talk about, and I don't think the brig is the most conductive environment for that." *At this point,* swings at the end of his sentence, unsaid. Admiral Chase Conolly, good cop. I guess that makes me the bad cop, but I'm pretty sure that's who I am in Sheridan's book anyway.

Leading the way, Chase sets a fast pace through the *Hope*'s hallways. The crew is ordered to stay in their quarters or at their assigned stations, since tempting fate has rarely led to a positive outcome. Grazer follows, with Sheridan in a tight grip. He has a thick, metallic bracelet around his ankle, with a blinking light. That must be some kind of demat blocker, courtesy of Grazer and D-Two.

Kieran and I fall in step behind everybody. He reaches for my hand and slides his fingers in-between, squeezing my hand once before he lets go.

"How did it go?" I whisper.

"As expected," Kieran whispers back. "I don't think there's any reasoning with that man."

I huff. Didn't bet on that. But as long as Kieran is back in one piece and we got Sheridan out of this meeting, my boxes are ticked.

"He demands USEF to sign a contract agreeing to stop making contact with new species. Oh, and to *never build a federation of mixed alien races.*" He lifts his other hand for air quotes and shoots me a telling look. "Which sounds suspiciously similar to the UWO. A little birdie might've dropped hints, who knows. And if we don't comply, he and Humanity First will push for using Tau-bombs on the Realm, and he feels they can influence the majority they need."

I flinch. So, this is what it feels like when history is about to repeat itself—only the path was modeled in a different universe. "You're telling me the only good thing from that meeting was that we got Sheridan and got our theory about Humanity First's involvement confirmed." Humanity First. Boy, do I have a bone to pick with them. If they're this time period's accomplice in the Temporal War, I wouldn't be surprised if they were involved in my kidnapping, or in Kieran's nanny shooting him. For so long Dad thought I was abducted because of who he was, a high-ranking admiral with a strong pro-inclusion stance, but no. It was for some mad person's idea of reshaping a timeline to suit their needs, aided by misguided and blinded others.

Kieran harrumphs. "Pretty much that, but I didn't have any hopes for anything else anyway." He shrugs one shoulder as we enter the conference room, where Zio is waiting in his usual seat.

My former mentor eyes Sheridan with a curious expression on his face as Grazer frees him of his prison hood and cuffs, then pushes down on his shoulders as a somewhat obvious hint to take a seat. Once he does, Grazer takes the chair next to him, across from Zio and Chase. Kieran and me sit at the other head of the table closer to the door, opposed to where Dad sat the last time.

Chase clears his throat. "Not sure if introductions are needed, but my name is Admiral Chase Conolly. Admiral Zio Upinga"—he points at Zio—"and I'm sure you know Captain Wildason and Lieutenant Thorburn. Admiral Bas Grazer is the gentleman who was so nice to bring you to us."

Sheridan keeps his gaze trained at the table in front of him and nods once. "Pleasure."

Like me, Chase crunches his brows, because it almost sounded like he meant it. It surely wasn't dripping with sarcasm, like when he normally talked to Kieran or me. What the heck is he playing at? A drop of cold sweat runs down my neck, tickling between my shoulder blades.

"And while I believe I do know whom I'm having the pleasure of talking to, I'd appreciate a short introduction of your person." Chase gives Sheridan the same look hundreds to thousands of cadets have gotten from him over the course of his career: Talk.

Sheridan nods his head in slow motion. "Of course," he says, voice level and quiet, and so very un-Sheridan like, I squirm in my seat. "My name is Cormac Sheridan. I'm the First Executioner for the FBTI in 2399. Born 2366."

When he falls silent after, Chase nods. "Thank you, Mr. Sheridan. I take it you're aware we apprehended you because of our dissimilar interests when it comes to the timeline and Officers Wildason and Thorburn."

The apple in Sheridan's throat moves up and down. "I'm not so sure about that," he whispers, staring at that one spot on the table as if it held the answer to life's questions.

"Not so sure about what?" Chase leans forward, lifting one hand behind his ear.

Sheridan swallows again. Chews on his lower lip. Takes one large breath in, which he holds. Slowly he lifts his gaze to meet mine. "I'm not so sure our interests are dissimilar."

Uhh…? I cock my head to the side before I reply, thoughts racing. What is he playing at? What am I missing? "You—and I'm talking plural here—did accuse us of changing something in your past that would annihilate the future as you knew it." And a couple of billion people, apparently, but I leave that out for Kieran's sake.

"That we did."

"And now—"

"Now, I'm not so sure what we tried to do is right. Or that we even had the correct information."

His words, spoken so calm, so flat and without intonation, bring a shiver to roll down my spine. This is what a beaten man sounds like. I wouldn't peg Sheridan as a good actor, but what do I know? Him finally seeing the light is too convenient. We capture him, he's suddenly on our side? Right.

I cross my arms in front of my chest and glare at him. "What do you mean? Why would you suddenly change your mind?"

Sheridan holds my stare. "Because I followed you. I followed you to places that I was taught—I was *assured*—were impossible to exist. And yet, they did." A muscle in his temple pops. "With my very own eyes I saw other timelines, the same as ours, yet different. I saw stable timelines that didn't perish, and that means…" He shakes his head, eyes dull. "How can we justify what we set out to do? How can we justify interfering with the past under the pretense of keeping our present the way it is?"

"I don't think you can. Looking at what I understand of multiple timeline theory, if you changed your past, there wouldn't be a change to your present, your now. All you would have accomplished is to create a new timeline impacted by your change," Zio says.

Sheridan nods, then shakes his head. "I'm having a hard time coming to terms with that fact. All I wanted, all I was trained to do, was to protect the timeline—"

"And it turns out it needs way less protecting than we thought," I finish his sentence. Quite the bummer, I know.

"Exactly," Sheridan whispers, and, Holy Sun and Stars, gives me a faint smile. Old Sheridan I would've checked for brain damage, but this new Sheridan… Maybe there is a human under the façade of arrogant superiority.

"May I ask you when exactly you became aware that multiple timelines exist?" Zio asks.

The executioner takes a moment to think. "That's difficult to describe. It was the jump I followed the captain and lieutenant after they slipped away from me at Admiral Wildason's backyard. There was another version of each of you," he nods at Chase and Zio, "and of course another version of each of you." He nods at Kieran and me, then huffs. "I had no idea that was possible. The jump and transition had felt different, but I didn't know why. So, when I saw your counterparts, especially yours, Captain Wildason… I literally couldn't believe it."

He did look like he'd seen a ghost, I remember.

Kieran must've thought the same thing. "I believe you, Mr. Sheridan. You seemed quite surprised when you saw all of us."

"That's an understatement, but yes."

Kieran acknowledges his words with a small uptick of his lips. "You said the jump felt different, and I assume, from what I know from Nonie, that it had to do with jumping to a different timeline, but to start with the basics, I would like to know how you traced us down. How did you find us when we jumped and hid in time, or when we jumped to different timelines? Just with a Setayashi scanner?"

Sheridan nods at Grazer. "Yes and no. With the tool Admiral Grazer took from me. It's what I use to jump. My temporal aptitude is higher than most, but nowhere near the lieutenant's. I can't orient myself when jumping, so I need my device to guide me to my destination. Besides opening a portal, it's able to scan for Setayashi-traces, lock onto a person's DNA and temporal code and track through time—and obviously through different timelines as well, as I know now. If there are many hits, it just takes the device longer to come up with a destination."

DNA and temporal code! The DNA-part is obvious, and I'm assuming the temporal code, whatever that is, would make sure he finds the correct version of a person. Me and my DNA are all over the timeline, from my birth to when he abducted us, plus a few extra pop-ups in my past, on the *Pioneer* etc. Just searching for my DNA might bring him to any of those points in time, but adding a temporal code to the search parameters helps to secure the person at the age needed. Smart. And, of course, annoying for us.

Grazer takes a thin wristband out of his pocket and lays it on the table. "A DNA and temporal code tracker. Is that common technology in your time? Who manufactures it? FBTI?"

Sheridan nods. "Yes. Well, and no, again. It's unique. We only have one of it. The Taro worked on it for years before I could start using it."

The Taro. We wanted to find out from Sheridan how much he and the Taro know about everything, from alternate timelines to the Temporal War. Guess we just got a good step closer to our answer.

Kieran leans forward. "Does the Taro know about stable alternate timelines?"

Sheridan looks at him like he'd lost his mind. "No! Of course not, or he would never have ordered any intervention. It's going to come as a shock to him once he finds out. He—"

"Could I ask you for a favor?" Zio leans forward, his PAD in one hand.

"Sure. Yes, of course." A skeptical look crosses Sheridan's face, but he shrugs it off. "I feel like I'm limited in that regard, but of course."

"Could you identify this device for me? Have you seen it before?" He produces the disk I took from Mashaule and retrieved from the drawer in Kieran's desk on the table.

Sheridan eyes it with scrunched brows. "Never seen it. What is it?"

"Interesting you never saw it. This device originates from your present. My scans indicate it was constructed in 2398."

"I'm sure many a thing is produced in '98 I don't know about."

"But how many devices do you know that emit Setayashi radiation and can communicate through time?" I point at the disk. "Because this can." And much more. Buzzwords three-dimensional hologram through time.

Confusion colors Sheridan's words. "Communicate through time? Impossible. The technology needed for that hasn't been invented yet, even at my time. Once I jump, I'm on my own. There's no way to communicate through time."

"Then how would you explain this?" Zio pinches something on his PAD and throws it into the middle of the table. The holographic matrix picks up on it and displays it for all of us to see. Smack above the middle of the table hovers a three-dimensional graph, several lines zigzagging through it. "I was able to access most of the disk's data. It contains a quite fascinating collection of events."

"What exactly is that?" Chase tilts his head left and right, then spins the image with the twist of his raised hand. "One axis says time, the other space, and the third—"

"Is not labeled, but I believe that to refer to the location within a temporal multiverse, for a lack of a better term, with this here being the devices origin." Zio points to a red dot at 2398 and in an area shaded green.

My jaw drops. "Are you saying this thing knows where it is, when it is, and whether it's in its original timeline or not?"

"Exactly. You see how a line goes from its origin at 2398 straight back in time, staying in the green?"

We all nod, even Sheridan.

"It travels back to January second, 2254, and from my short time to analyze its functions, it appears every use is recorded." He double-taps his PAD's screen, and the dot on the second of January, 2254, lights up, together with Mashaule's voice coming through the speakers.

*"Eclipse, reinforce shields, get me visual! Who the hell is firing on my ship?"*

*"That's none of your concern."*

Sheridan jerks when he hears the second voice, eyes widening.

*"None of my concern? There's a freakin' ship firing on mine—"*

*"They won't fire on you anymore. They'll target the colony."*

*"The colony? I've got my crew down there, the Magellans! Eclipse, ready weapons—"*

*"Don't."*

*"Excuse me? They're attacking—"*

*"They are. And for the greater good, some of the people on the ground must die. It is unfortunate, but necessary."*

*"W-what did you do? That was you, wasn't it?"*

*"I did what was necessary to get their attention."*

*"That's why you asked me to do the modifications from here and not the bridge! You didn't want me to hear the alert for the approaching ship! How dare you play me—"*

*"I dare because it's necessary. This attack is one of many more to come, and it's part of the plan to improve the future."*

*"Who are those people? I've never seen a configuration even remotely close… They're firing onto the colony! The Magellans have done nothing to those people!"*

*"That assessment lies in the eye of the beholder. Don't forget, you invaded their territory."*

*"Whose territory? There's nobody around for lightyears!"*

*"Ah, yes… The twenty-third century…!"*

*"And either way, I've got to help them! Eclipse, bring us between—"*

*"Belay that."*

*"I have to do something!"*

*"You have to adhere to our plan. I'll take care of the Eclipse's logs. Nobody will know you chose to not help. I'm sure you can find somebody to take the fall and distract from this situation."*

"I think we have heard enough." Zio turns off the recording.

Him, Chase, and Kieran are all equally pale. I might've witnessed this very event, but they've lived through it, only on the other side, down on the planet. They were attacked by the Essken, they were on the ground, helpless, until Kieran took matters into his own hands.

"Well," Chase quips, "At least Mashey *tried* to help us. That's more than I assumed, honestly."

Zio keeps his focus on Sheridan. "Did you recognize the voice?"

The other man closes his eyes and inhales a deep, controlled breath. "It sounds similar to Taro Izola—"

"Can you confirm it's him?" Chase asks, leaning forward.

The executioner scrunches his face into a pained grimace. "No, I can't. Yes, it's similar, but that doesn't make sense. I don't think it's him. He'd never interfere. The integrity of the timeline is *everything* to him. There is no way the Taro would've said any of what I just heard, I would bet my life on that."

We all exchange glances, but Zio replies. "I wouldn't recommend betting your life on that fact, Mr. Sheridan. It might not end well for you."

Frustration spreads through me, making me antsy. A *maybe* doesn't help us, we need a confirmation if we want to hinge our whole defense strategy on it. I tap my chin with one finger, then point it at Sheridan. "I was there when the disk recorded that event. I saw a three-D hologram from behind, tall, wide shoulders, short cropped hair… He was wearing some kind of uniform, but I couldn't see any insignia."

Sheridan lifts and drops both hands. "Yes, sure, that could be him, but it could be a hundred thousand other Magellans—or humans—as well. Unless you have proof—"

I cut him a glance and pop an eyebrow up. "Actually, I do have proof. On my wrist PAD, which, inconveniently, you took from me."

He lifts his hands again, palms facing me. "I'm sorry, it's protocol, obviously. The judge has it. And if—*if*—you're right and he interfered—without my knowledge—it must have been to protect the timeline. Something must've been about to go wrong. I cannot imagine the Taro interfering otherwise, I really cannot."

And until a few days ago, I would've agreed with him. Magellans have been hunted to be used to predict—and alter—the flow of time. They kept their First Sense hidden for centuries for fear of abuse by other species. Our Taro is the embodiment of integrity and ethics, imagining her going against the timeline feels wrong.

But that doesn't mean every Magellan and every Taro is the same and shares the same values. And while I wish everybody would act to the high standards we hold them to, unfortunately, reality—ours at least—is much, much different. "Then how would you explain this disk? Such a powerful tool, originating from your time, and yet you never knew about it. It would need somebody high up the food chain to plant it where it was needed, wouldn't it?"

Sheridan presses his lips together. "Or somebody else, a criminal mastermind. I'm telling you, you're chasing the wrong guy. And I would also ask you to weigh your next steps carefully, because so far, I am on your side and I'm willing to put in a word with the Taro and the judge for you, but you have to stop focusing on the Taro. It's a dead end."

Yikes. That it is, for sure. Before I can respond, Zio has taken over, one eyebrow raised.

"Maybe it is time to show you the other evidence we have, collected in our past, by one of our admirals. Have you ever heard about a Temporal War being fought in our time, and possibly beyond?"

Sheridan slams his brows down. "A temporal *war*? No. Nothing is documented in the FBTI's records, I'd know about it. What—?"

"Considering you are the First Executioner and pretty close to the Taro, from what I understand, if there was a temporal war, shouldn't you know about it?" Kieran asks. "Shouldn't it be in your records if we know about it?"

"Yes! Absolutely! There is no way I wouldn't know. I know what the Taro knows."

"Right." Kieran drags the word out. "The Taro, again. History is written by the winner. Or by the one in power." He gives Sheridan a pointed look, waiting for the hint to sink in when Zio holds up a hand.

"Mr. Sheridan, you have Magellan genes, correct?"

"Yes, my grandfather—"

"Then please, listen to your First Sense. Your intuition. And listen to what I have to show you next. We have more data I'm interested in hearing your opinion about."

Sheridan takes a deep breath. "All right."

"Thank you." Lifting the disk and placing it farther in the middle of the table, Zio carries on. "The event on the *Eclipse* seems to have been the first time the disk was used. If you would please direct your attention to the graph and the trajectory for the next recorded use."

Zio taps his PAD, and the line shoots from 2254 to 2295.

"Looks like that was only a few months ago," Chase says, looking at the graph critically.

"Correct. You and I both saw the disk in use when Mashaule jumped out of USEF jail right in front of our eyes and Nonie followed. But please note the location of the event." Zio spins the image so that we can see the position of the next access point better.

Kieran blows out a puff of air. "It has shifted." Grabbing the edges of the projection, he enlarges it as if he'd grown up with the technology and not only recently been thrown into this time. "You said this axis refers to the position in the multiverse, or something like that. The data dot didn't stay in its original timeline. It shifted."

"It shifted." Zio nods. "But what's even more interesting is that the green shading continues to surround it, suggesting whatever the disk was involved in, there was a split-off, and the disk continued on in the new, altered timeline, still recognizing the timeline had split off."

*A time-traveler across universes*, taking his tools with him. Something about that makes my First Sense act up. I wonder—

"That… makes sense, from a temporal mechanics standpoint, as little as I like it." Sheridan swallows loudly. "Seeing this data, this device, is quite shocking, I must say."

Chase gets up and walks to the replicator. "Lubbeck's, anybody? Because I for one need a little something to go with these discussions. My brain can handle only so much temporal science."

"Lubbeck's?" Sheridan's face lights up. "Yes, please. Thank you! It's my guilty pleasure."

A slow, wide grin spreads across Chase's face. "I've decided I like you, Mr. Sheridan. You have good taste."

Zio opens his mouth, then shuts it, rolling his eyes. *Well, at least now we know Chase definitely won't go hungry for the foreseeable future. Lubbeck's will apparently still be around in a hundred years.*

Taking two full glasses and setting one in front of a quite delighted Sheridan, Chase takes a seat again. "Could we put the data into simple English, please? I get the disk was sent back, Mashaule used it at Alpha Rubrum, when he was kept from interfering during the Quaneez attack. Because of that interference, a new timeline split off, and that's the one the disk now was in. Correct?"

"Correct," I say, tapping my fingers on the table, Chase-style. "And if I'm not mistaken… Zio, display the next dots please. I could bet we'll see the fair at Ortega One, the raspberry farm, and the shuttle where Mashaule wanted to kill Kieran before he entered the nebula." *Because that's when he used the disk, so the data should be there.*

As expected, the dots pop up in a zigzag fashion throughout the graph, labeled with exactly the time and locations I predicted. Sheridan chokes on a sip of Lubbeck's. "That means we are several junctions away from the original timeline!"

"We are." *I mean, we-slash-I knew that. Been there, seen that.* "As little information as we have, the Zeroverse doesn't—didn't—know about time traveling. I never went back to the *Pioneer*. Kieran made peace with the Essken before the war could break out, and they continued on happily ever after." *More or less, at least. Both, that timeline's Nonie and Kieran, have been missing out, from my point of view.* "Just in case anybody was interested."

Silence hovers for a few seconds.

Eventually, Kieran sighs. "The next question I have, is how did the disk get to its destination? I doubt you'd open up a portal, throw it in and hope for luck to take it where it needs to go, or are you telling me it could travel through time on its own?"

Zio aligns the disk with the grain of the wood of the tabletop. "No, it cannot. And you raise an interesting point. Somebody will have to have brought the disk to Mashaule for him to use it."

"Wasn't me." Sheridan lifts both palms. "I swear. Today's the first time I'm seeing this thing."

But somebody will have to have brought it to Mash— Oh, holy Sun and Stars! Heat swamps me together with an epiphany. "I have no idea who brought it to young Mashaule at Alpha Rubrum, but..." I smack my lips. Could I be right? Because he had the disk when he was in USEF jail, from where he started his mad hunt for Kieran. I'm sure they searched him before locking him away, but he still had it. And I think I know who gave it to him: "The ensign," I blurt out. "When we ran to Mashaule's cell, there was an older ensign we almost crashed into. He greeted you two and—" I facepalm myself. Man, sometimes I'm slow, but in my defense, we were busy and in borderline panic mode. "And he greeted me, calling me Lieutenant! At that point nobody knew I wasn't a cadet anymore. *He* did, so that makes it a good chance—"

"He's the one who came from the future and brought the disk to Mashaule," Kieran finishes the sentence for me. "That's our best lead. Nice, Nonie!" He bumps his shoulder into mine, a proud grin on his face. Mine turns beet red probably, but oh well.

"Looking through USEF database and video recordings for the specific date and time..." Zio scans through his PAD. "Here we go. Visual of the ensign." Pinching the image and throwing it forward it gets displayed next to the temporal graph.

Sheridan chokes on his sip of Lubbeck's. "That's... that's..." He coughs hard, eyes wide, wheezing, as he sits up straighter and points at the picture of the man hovering in the middle, face paler than a wall. "You were right. No doubt about it. This is Taro Izola."

# Chapter Eighteen -

# Old Secrets

*USEF HOPE, Stable Orbit over Kataki One, Demat Room, 09:11hrs, September 29th, 2295*

"All right!" Chase slaps the table with his palm, an expression of wild satisfaction on his face. "It's official. Now we know who's calling the shots for the Temporal War!"

I exhale slowly, letting relief take over. That we do. And while we suspected it might be the Taro, knowing that we were right is somewhat scary. What the Taro did… Not sure what I would call his crimes. Attempted genocide? For sure. But what do you call the repeated manipulation of time to benefit himself? Egotemporal manipulation? How sad we have to invent a name for his despicable selfish acts.

Sheridan's face has lost all color. The apple in his throat moves up and down with an audible swallowing sound. "He… he trained me. Picked me personally for my skills. Every other human-Magellan offspring with even a potential genetic disposition for time travel has a temporal blocker in place." He taps the bone behind his ear. "I didn't get one. Because he believed in my skills. Because he believed in *me*." He swallows once more, and Kieran and I exchange a glance. A temporal blocker—now we have a name for that thing Kaytee had implanted behind her ear. I suppress a shudder. Not the kind of future I want, taking away people's freedom. Not that I want everybody jumping through time, but let's be honest, only a few probably could. The temporal blocker feels... like shackles.

Shaking his head slowly, Sheridan lifts a shaking hand to the bone behind his ear. "But did he truly believe in me? Or did he pick me because I was the easiest to manipulate? What have I done for him? What crimes? And would I even know? Or are there countless other versions of me, in different universes, who have done his bidding, each guilty in their own way?" He lifts his gaze to Zio, eyes wide. In this very moment, I feel sorry for Sheridan.

"Admiral Upinga?" Sheridan repeats, when Zio doesn't answer.

"Excuse me?" Zio snaps his attention from the door behind us back to the discussion. "I'm sorry, I thought I felt— Never mind. To answer your question, it becomes complicated with multi-timeline theory. I—"

The com chimes. *"Demat room to conference room."*

"Go ahead." Chase taps his Hablamate.

*"Ensign Blume here. We dematted two visitors from the* Pioneer *over. They're on their way to you."*

Chase scrunches his brows together. "And you're only now telling me that? Who authorized the demat?"

*"Sir, there wasn't an option to refuse it, and I was ordered to forget this encounter. Which I'm doing right now."*

Chase huffs. "I get you, Ensign. Thank you. Conolly out." He taps the Hablamate again, then looks at us. "Guess our Taro is paying us a surprise visit."

Zio sits up straighter, the faintest smile on his lips. "Indeed. A pleasant surprise."

Kieran tilts his head and gives his friend a glance, the kind where I know he'd tease him if we were alone. Alas, thanks to the presence of Grazer and Sheridan, Zio gets away un-teased.

A mere two seconds after Zio has finished his sentence, the conference doors slide apart.

"Taro Magona." Zio bows his head, a certain warmth in his voice. He's the first to stand up, followed by Chase.

"Taro," Chase echoes. "An unexpected treat to have you join us. We could really use your help—"

The Taro holds up a hand and Chase snaps his mouth shut. She enters the room, and only now do I see that somebody is behind her. A tall person, wearing a wide cape-like gown with a big hood pulled into their face, obscuring it completely. The way they walk, a bit hunched over, I can't even tell if they're male or female. Curiosity rises, together with a weird tingling sensation. I press a hand onto my stomach, just like Zio does, our gestures not unnoticed by the foreigner.

Once the doors close behind the Taro, she inclines her head. "I apologize. Precautions are unfortunately necessary. This room is secured?"

"Double and triple." Chase pulls his shoulders back. "You know all of our security clearances. We can have Mr. Sheridan escorted to his quarters—"

"That won't be necessary. His input will be valuable during our discussion."

Surprise flickers over Sheridan's face as he sits up straighter.

"Very well." Chase sits down again, like Zio. "Please, have a seat." He gestures to the two chairs at the head of the table, opposed from Kieran and me, where Dad usually sits.

"Thank you." The Taro makes her way over to the assigned seats, while the foreigner stays behind, closer to Kieran and me.

Instead of sitting down, the Taro rests both hands on the back of a chair and looks at me. "None of the information shared in this room can leave it. You all know what's at stake, and I know you can all be trusted." I feel like she emphasizes *all* in an odd way, as she glances at Sheridan, before her eyes land back on me. "I regret to say that our precautions proved to have rightfully been taken, but I personally am glad we can put an end to this charade. I have come here today with my

Temporal Advisor, a specialist in multiverse theory. I believe no introductions are necessary." She nods at the person she brought with her, who reaches up and drops her hood back.

*Long, black shiny hair.*

*A nose with the same upturn as mine, cheeks with the same high jawbones.*

A whoozing sound swooshes in my ears. For the first time since we cured the Reptilian Flu, I miss having a face mask to hide how my jaw drops. I suck in air, but the air must be broken, it doesn't seem to hold any oxygen at all.

The Temporal Advisor smiles at me, and that smile… I know it. It's mine, and I've seen it down on Gemini, in that alcove.

"Mom," I breathe. "Mom."

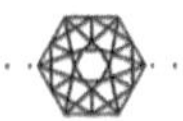

### USEF HOPE, Stable Orbit over Kataki One, Demat Room, 09:16hrs, September 29th, 2295

Zio stands up, his chair toppling back. "Kelia." His voice shakes, disbelief coloring every syllable.

"Kelia," Grazer echoes softer, his mouth gaping open. "That's—"

"Professor Okata," Sheridan says, admiration in his tone. "What a pleasure."

My mom—*my mom!*—smiles at him. At everybody. "The pleasure is all mine. It's been too long since I saw any of you."

I open my mouth, then shut it. Open it. Blink. Blink again. Sit up and lean forward. Rub a palm across my eyes. None of it changes that this is my mom, the same person I met on Gemini, only with a few more wrinkles. Otherwise, the same twinkle is in her eye, the same somewhat mischievous expression on her face.

"Mom," I say, my voice equally shaky as Zio's. Kieran lays a hand on my thigh under the table and squeezes, but it doesn't register to me.

My mom is here. My *mom*, who, as I was told, died in childbirth.

Her gaze softens as it falls on me. "Nonie. It's good to see you again. It hasn't been long for you, has it?"

I shake my head. "N-no." Blinking again, I address the elephant in the room. "You're alive." Not that I'm complaining, but... I don't know what to think. What to do. Part of me wants to jump up and hug the ever-loving daylights out of her, but I'm frozen to my seat. Not that Zio was doing any better.

"Indeed you are," he says, the three words carrying a myriad of emotions, but mainly three: love, surprise... and hurt.

My mom sighs when she looks at her brother. "Zio. I'm so sorry my disappearance was necessary. I apologize to all of you, but you'll understand the reason for me hiding. But, first things first." She steps forward and pulls me up and into the biggest hug I've ever been the recipient of. I wrap my arms around her and squeeze just as tight as she does, resting my head against her shoulder. We stand like this for a good thirty seconds, holding on to the other person as if we were trying to make up for lost time. I know I am.

There was always this little voice inside my head, the one that couldn't believe she was dead. Maybe that was my First Sense trying to get me to listen, only I didn't.

After a while, my mom glides a hand over my back and chuckles. "You know, obviously you knew more than me when we met on Gemini, but since then I have mentally kicked myself in the behind many a time for not enjoying holding you more." As we pull apart, her eyes shine with unshed tears.

"I wasn't even born then," I whisper. "I'm sure it was weird for you."

Mom brushes a strand of hair out of my face, and that tender, motherly gesture... boy, it makes it hard not to tear up. "Weird, yes, but I am and was so happy it happened." She squeezes my shoulder once, then lets go and winks at me. "Let's handle this here first, and then I cannot wait for some mother-daughter time, okay?"

"Okay." I suck in my lower lip and bite down hard, or else those happy tears might start spilling. Wouldn't be the worst in front of the people assembled here, but still.

Mom and the Taro and I take a seat. Man, do I wish Dad was here. He's in for the shock of his lifetime when he comes back. Surprise, Dad! Look, multiple timelines exist, and oh, your wife is also alive, by the way. Ah, and sorry, slight downer ahead, and your daughter's decaying on a cellular level, thought you should know.

I cringe. Poor Dad.

Poor Mom, when she finds out.

Poor me, if I die before we can spend some time together.

I push those thoughts away. As always, priorities.

Folding her hands in front of her, the Taro lets her gaze drift over every single one of us before she gestures at my mom and speaks. "The advisor approached me about nineteen years ago when she feared for her life. We—"

"Feared for her life?" Zio sits up ramrod straight. "Why did you not tell me, Keel?" Only the slightest bit of offense swings in his words.

My mom lowers her gaze to the table. "You were the first I wanted to tell, but…" She lays a hand over her stomach. Her First Sense.

Zio blows out a frustrated puff of air. "I understand." He relaxes the slightest bit, but still seems hyperalert since his sister dropped that latest bomb on him.

Lifting her gaze back up, Mom's jaw is set tight. "I was young, just beginning my temporal research, and pregnant with Nonie. The threats I received were more than believable, and after three of my colleagues were killed—mind you, all were working in *my* department on *my* research—it was clear I needed a different level of protection than to carry a weapon or install professional security alerts around the house. My First Sense showed me the way and I was left with no other choice than to fake my own death to throw them off mine and my family's scent."

My heart cramps up. Fate really hasn't been kind to our family. I feel bad for Mom, missing out on Dad and me, bad for Dad, clearly missing Mom so very much, and yes, bad for myself as well, knowing by proxy what I missed. Thanks for those family pictures on the wall,

Blue Nonie.

"Who is *they*?" Grazer asks, true anger tightening his features. This is the man I thought to be a racist, xenophobic bigot for most of my life. Seriously, in Grazer's case, I didn't even know half of it. I wonder if in a different universe, where Mashaule didn't threaten his career, where unions between humans and Magellans are legal, Grazer would always be how we see him now: a decent human being, maybe even a defender of the Magellan people.

"*They* are Humanity First, from what I know now," Mom says, bitterness in her voice.

I exchange a glance with Grazer and Chase. "Aligns with what we thought." Humanity First is everywhere, meddling in and with everything.

"When your mother approached me, she made it clear the threats were against her person and her research, of which she refused to tell me the details." Now Magona sounds a bit sour. "She asked me to trust in my First Sense, which I did, and helped her hide. I didn't have any direct interaction with her for all those years, until she contacted me a few days ago and told me it was, ironically, time."

She pauses and reaches for a bottle of water. "Imagine my surprise when she told me the exact topic of her research."

"Multi-timeline theory." Mom looks at me and winks. "Told you I'd be working on it, didn't I?"

A grin spreads over my face. "That you did." I vividly remember her disappointment when we met her on Gemini and she realized we from the future didn't know about her theories. That must've been way before her path became clear.

She chuckles. "The Taro was quite speechless when she saw my data."

"It's not every day your perception of the world and all you have worked for your entire life is challenged," Magona retorts drily. "But at least I understand now why hiding Kelia was important, and why not only she, but others, had to pay a price." She pointedly looks at me, then Zio. "I have said so before but will say it again. I regret your exile was necessary, Admiral, for… many reasons. I realize none of our actions, mandates, or restrictions were fair to you, but we couldn't risk having you on Mag-2. The bond between siblings is too strong. You would've noticed your sister was alive, no matter how well Kelia was hidden within the FBTI."

Sitting ramrod straight, Zio lowers his chin once, a muscle in his jaw ticking. "I understand."

But that doesn't mean he has to like it. It wasn't my place as his mentee to comment or ask, but even though Zio was and is one of the calmest, most even-keeled people I know, his people's actions hurt him. They for sure didn't help his stance within USEF, at least not with the xenophobes. A persona non grata amongst his own people? Exiled for his actions? Forbidden to bond? Clearly something must be wrong with him, right?

A wave of sorrow for Zio crashes over me. He didn't deserve any of this. But then, neither did any of us.

"And for you, Lieutenant Thorburn," the Taro carries on, directing her attention to me as if she heard my last thought. "I apologize for taking your mother from you. It was not an easy decision, but one born of necessity." She nods at my mom, who returns the gesture.

"And it was the decision I fought the most, but my First Sense was clear. You needed to be with Tom. Although, had I known what exactly was in your future, I might have not cared about changing the timeline, even if only a single one existed." She shakes her head. "But just because split-offs happen and multiple timelines exist, doesn't mean the integrity of every single one wasn't important. In fact, it's still paramount to keep them from destabilizing. Hence, once the events had passed, I knew your destiny was to save Kieran and bring the plants to cure the Reptilian Flu, but I would have given all I had to get the same results without putting you through all that you have been through had I known the details." Giving me such a look of maternal love and warmth it doesn't feel like we missed out on years of building a relationship. It feels like we'd been a team forever.

A lump forms in my throat, but I swallow it down. If I let the tiniest bit of emotion take root, I don't think I could stop the floodgates from opening. Deep breath. Deep. Breath.

"And now here we are, all of us fighting a temporal war neither the Taro nor me anticipated until the first intervention happened. We both felt it—a disturbance from the future. We thought it was a single intervention, but they kept on coming, event after event, alteration after alteration. To be fair, they helped me verify and prove my multi-timeline theory. I wouldn't be where I am now without the repeated attempts to change the past, even though the goal behind them still eludes me. I—"

"We can shed some light on that." I lift my hand. "Kieran and I have been to a couple of alternate timelines, and it helped us figure out a pattern. Plus, we had help." Within two minutes, I summarize our experience for Mom and the Taro. While my mom's eyes light up with pride the longer I talk, Sheridan looks more and more nauseated. I come to the end of my little speech, shrugging. "So, at this point, we assume Taro Izola has been manipulating time to get himself to power by eradicating the Essken. As you can see, comparing the events in different timelines highlights the differences. Kieran and I are there, peace eventually happens. Kieran is dead, the Essken people are killed, and the Taro comes into power."

Mom closes her eyes for one long second. "While I wish the circumstances were different, I'm pleased to hear my theories were correct. It's also somewhat of a relief to have confirmation of who was behind the killing of my colleagues and who was—and probably still is—a threat to my life." She glances at Sheridan, whose eyes widen as he pales.

"No, not to you. I cannot remember the Taro—Taro Izola, my Taro—ever talking about any danger coming from you—"

"But also, my theories aren't commonly known, correct?"

Sheridan's pallor takes on a slight blush as he looks at my mom from under his lashes. "While we never heard about your multiple timeline theory, you're quite famous for all your other temporal work, you know."

Mom takes the compliment in stride. "And while I'm happy to hear that, somebody made sure my work was buried deep. If I wanted to sow fear of timeline changes, it wouldn't serve me well if people knew the timeline would continue as is, unperturbed, and the changes only come into effect in a new, split-off universe."

Sheridan sucks in a harsh breath, then rakes a hand through his hair with shaking fingers. "That— You're actually right with that. That fear is the only reason why the Taro was allowed to establish our temporal task force." His wide, worried gaze meets mine. "Had we known other timelines exist, the judge would never have granted authority for time-travel and patrolling the timeline. We would never have tried to intervene at any point in time."

"There's your answer then." Mom lifts both hands and drops them onto the table, looking clockwise at each of us. "So, since we're on that topic, I would like to bring you all up to speed with some quick and dirty temporal theory, although I'm sure you figured most of it out by now."

"Please, go ahead. I'm bracing myself for the headache to crank it up," Chase says, sighing.

Mom grins, and it's like looking into a mirror. I might've had to do a double-take when I travelled back and saw young Chase and Zio for the first time, but seeing my mom like an older version of myself is even more… I don't know, freaky, in a good way.

"Somebody get the admiral a Lubbeck's. I hear it improves his attention span."

Zio raises a brow at my mom's one-liner, while Trip chuckles and wiggles his glass. "Appreciate the thought, but way ahead of you. Do I want to know why you know that about me?"

A playful gleam lights up in Mom's eyes. "You'll find out eventually. But anyway, temporal theory. Rule one, temporal inertia. While there might be an infinite number of timelines, for every single one of them the law of temporal inertia prefers a body to stay on its own path, on its own course. Simplified, veering off course is not what time prefers. Rule two, temporal similarity. Every timeline likes to stay as close to the main strand as possible. Birds of a feather, right? To understand those two rules, you have to stop thinking linear, as if tomorrow hasn't happened yet. Everything in every timeline"—she taps the table—"is predetermined. Timelines are fixed from beginning to end, not that there is one, but let's not get too technical. So, imagine the timeline as one infinite strand, like a story that's already written, no matter on which page you open the book. Yes, natural development happens. Split-offs happen. But overall, the timeline is a sluggish, lazy thing. It has a course in mind, and it would like to keep said course. That's why not every event leads to a split-off."

"So, you're saying getting a new branch to split off requires a major change, correct?" Drumming his fingers onto the table in the same annoying rhythm he's always preferred Chase smacks his lips, forehead scrunched into wrinkles. "So, why doesn't the Taro go all out? He tweaks here, he tweaks there, he only sends you, Mr. Sheridan, a single executioner? What is one person supposed to achieve? No offense."

"None taken." Sheridan straightens his shirt as he leans forward. "And for that, I know the answer. The Taro's problem is not manipulating the past, it's his now, the opposition he faces. His power isn't unlimited. In fact, Judge Alberti outranks him. She is the FBTI's president. She calls she shots. She's also the one who was against patrolling the timeline and against more than one executioner."

"That is actually good to hear. At least we have one person with common sense on our side." Chase takes the last sip from his Lubbeck's and sets the glass down on the table. "Okay, now that we understand what led to where we are right now and somewhat understand multi-timeline theory, what I still don't understand is why you're here, right now, Kelia. Not to play devil's advocate, but this isn't what I'd call staying under the radar. What changed? Why are you here?"

Steely resolve shines in my mother's gaze. "The Temporal War. This is where it comes to an end, one way or another." She lets her gaze drift over every single one of us as she lays her hand onto her stomach. "And we *must* ensure it ends. The continued alterations…" She grimaces and rubs her index fingers over her temples. "Like I said before, the continued alterations to the timeline aren't good, as you can imagine. I can't say what the consequences may be if we fail to stop them, but the fact that I can't, makes me very, very concerned. I've always been able to feel the progress of our timeline, like I could up to a few days ago. Now, I can't."

An icy shudder runs down my back. "What does that mean? Our timeline ceases to exist?" Because it would align with what we saw during the last event, timelines simply ceasing to exist. *Snuff*, they're gone.

My mom's wide-eyed gaze meets mine. "I don't know," she whispers. "It feels like time is about to end—"

Out of nowhere, a weird sensation washes over me, bringing the hairs on my body to rise. Dizziness swells, the sensation of shifting—

"Oh no," I whisper at the same time as Kieran curses under his breath. My heart drops. No, no, no. Not now. Throwing a frantic glance at Kieran, I reach for his hand, only to find him fishing for mine already. Our gazes connect, wild, panicked, afraid.

"It's happening." His voice wavers at the end.

"Shit," Chase spits out.

A chair topples over, followed by another one.

"For crying out loud, get out of the way—"

I can't get air in. I'm not ready. I don't want to die. Not yet. Not *now*, of all times.

Dizziness hits hard, nausea, too. The edges of reality shift, pull apart, and stretch until the mirror cabinet is back. I gasp, blinking, but those ghostly outlines stay, more than last time, way more. I think I see a version of Dad in one. An older Kieran. Chase, Zio. Mom, in some of them. I don't see me—

Kieran twitches, yanking on my hand.

I tip my gaze over—

Coils.

My heart sinks. There wasn't a doubt in my mind they'd be here, but I was still hoping we'd come out alive. I want to go back to normal reality and say goodbye. Hug my mom once more. Talk more to Kieran, cuddle into him, feel him more. I want to make more memories before

I have to go. I want to finish fighting the Temporal War, I want—

I want so many things.

Too many.

And I won't have time for any of them.

If I had the time or the brain space for it, I'd laugh about how nonchalant I accepted our sentence. *Yeah, we're falling apart. One more event and we'll die. Sure, I'll deal with it.*

How easy to say when it isn't happening, when you're not right in the very moment—right in your very last moment.

Talking about the end is easy. Facing it is harder.

A long, wheezy breath escapes Kieran. For the longest second, our gaze connects, his holding the same regret as mine.

Then, the coils dart down on Kieran, merciless, like assassins presented with their target, digging for a way to enter him. The device lights up green under his shirt, and so does mine, but the K'Zees don't give up. They dart at Kieran with a desperate intensity, shooting at him, bouncing off, and trying again.

And eventually, the first ones succeed.

Kieran twitches and tenses up as a handful of K'Zees shoot into his body. I feel the hum, the buzz, the anticipation of the high through our connected hands. Like my body didn't care about its betrayal, it opens up my First Sense and awaits the coils. They shoot through Kieran into me, through me, warm me up, tear me apart, light up my hand—

A sharp, burning sting shoots from my collarbone through my body. I cry out at the same time Kieran does—

And the next second, the pain is gone. Reality wafts and bends for another minuscule moment as my hand stops glowing and the hum in my body ceases, and then, *zip*, it's back in place.

No mirror cabinet.

No coils.

Only the *Hope*'s conference room with everybody, including Kieran and me.

*Kieran and me.* Alive. Breathing. Panting. Wheezing. But alive.

Mom has one hand pressed to her stomach. "That was—"

Zio squeezes my shoulder. When or how he got next to us, I have no idea. He looks down at his medical scanner, then at Kieran and me. "That was another episode." It's not a question, but a statement. I still nod.

"Uh-huh." I sound like I partied all night and didn't get any sleep. I wish.

The muscles in his temple pop as he looks at his read-outs—and then lets the scanner sink and exhales forcefully. "It worked. Barely."

"I can tell," Kieran croaks, still squeezing my hand like our connection anchored us together. "Wasn't exactly pleasant, but I'll take it. We're here."

My mother stands up. "What I just felt—you both felt that?" Urgency colors her voice.

I nod and swallow, trying out my parched throat to give her the quick version. "Yes. Kieran and I are sensitive to those events. To us, reality is changing, sometimes ripping apart, energy coils attack us, and the problem is—"

"The problem is they're dying, Kelia." Zio says, standing up. "The episodes, or rather, those energy bolts, disrupt their cellular matrix. I outfitted them with a stabilizer, which apparently worked, but I don't know how often or for how long."

Mom slaps a hand in front of her mouth, then scrambles for something in her pocket, a scanner similar to Zio's. "You're saying you're seeing reality rip apart?" She moves the scanner over us. "What else? The energy bolts?" She chews on her lower lip, just like I tend to do. "Nonie. Details. *Now.*"

I blink. "Y-yes. When you said time was about to end, that's what I feel, too. That's what we saw. Something's destroying timelines." I close my eyes, willing myself to focus. "The energy bolts. They aim for Kieran, they hurt him. They attract me though, my body wants them, for a lack of a better term. And—"

"Reality ripping apart, destroying timelines. Tell me about that." Mom's intense gaze darts from her scanner to me and back.

"Yes. Well, that's new. Overall, different things have happened.

With the latest few events, I saw variations of the people we're with, like echoes, or silhouettes, transparent. Reality ripping apart happened twice, once in the Maelstrom, once last night, where literally a tear through reality develops. And… and last night I saw a dark mass moving through that tear and… destroying timelines." A shudder runs down my back thinking back at the utter feeling of despair during those moments.

Mom sucks a sharp inhale through her teeth, her eyes wide, chest heaving up and down in a fast rhythm. "It's not a rift, as you call it. It's a temporal collapse," she whispers. "It may look like a tear, but it's a temporal collapse waiting to happen." She takes a second to rub a hand over her ashen face, and the seriousness in her next sentence brings a cold shiver to run down my spine. "And if the collapse isn't halted, it will consume everything."

Shocked gasps break from everybody around the table.

"Hold on," Grazer says, leaning forward and holding up a hand. "Define *everything*."

"Everything, Bas!" Mom throws her hands up. "Reality as we know it. I don't know what's causing the rift and therefore the impeding collapse, but if we don't stop it, it's not only our timeline, our universe that will cease to exist, it's *everything*. Every. Thing."

Silence hovers, the shocked kind.

Zio is the first to break it. Kudos to him for keeping his voice calm and level. "Is there a way to stop it?"

Laughing out once, dry, my mom drops her gaze and folds her arms across her chest. "I don't know. It might be easier stopping the origin, the reason for it to happen. If we don't, we'll have these rifts to deal with. And—"

"Could I… could I be causing it?" A muscle ticks in Kieran's jaw. "The things, those energy coils, come out of nowhere, but only affect me. They search me out. Am I causing this somehow, am I ripping time apart?" He keeps his back straight and chin up.

"No." Mom shakes her head once. "That's literally impossible. But…" She taps her finger to her lower lip, then points at me. "You are craving these energy coils, as you call them, they swarm you both, but only attack Kieran?"

I nod. "In the beginning, I tried to touch them, but it's like I repel them. Kieran doesn't, but he's the only one they attack."

"Then Kieran is an attractor, but the question becomes, why. Why are you like a magnet to them?"

"I don't see what's so different about me." Kieran waves his hand down his body. "I'm not doing anything special."

Mom counts off her fingers. "Well. I don't know. You're human, but so are many others in the room. Nonie has parts of human and Magellan genomes, but so does Mr. Sheridan, and—"

"I didn't feel a thing," he says. "Clearly my watered-down Magellan ancestry is not enough for me to be affected."

"So, what else is different?" Kieran asks. "Finding out what is might help us figure out what's causing it, or what's driving it. Any information is good information at this point."

I tap a finger against my chin, not even realizing my mom did the same thing a mere thirty seconds ago. "The only thing I can come with is that from all versions we saw of you, you were the longest in the Realm. Could that have affected you somehow?" The event we experienced in the Realm also felt—

I suck in a sharp breath as an epiphany strikes. "The Realm—it wasn't affected by the rift when I saw it in the Maelstrom! The timelines *around* it were snuffed out, but the Realm itself..." I stare at a spot on the wall, trying to remember the details, but details are hard to come by when you're fearing for your life and the destruction of everything you know. "... I don't think the Realm was affected!"

Kieran turns in his chair, the thrill of an idea lightening up his features. "What about the episode that happened when we were with Koll inside the Realm? He wasn't affected either, but he could see the coils. Was anything different about it for you? Did you see a rift or those images—"

I get what he's going for and sit up straighter, powered by the knowledge that we might be onto something. "Nothing! It definitely was different than all the other times. And the episode was much shorter—" I smack my forehead when the memory comes back. "When he held on to me it was as if he'd made my First Sense flare up, and then—"

"Your First Sense? Is your First Sense involved when these episodes happen?" Urgency colors Mom's voice.

"Yes." I nod. "It's a by-product, it's protecting me—"

She waves me off. "After it flares up, what happens?"

I shrug. "It's not like there's a distinct order of what happens when. I know it flares up, which makes me tolerate the coils a bit better. It feels like it's helping my body get rid of them, pushing them out." I wave a hand, spreading my fingers for demonstration.

Mom opens her mouth, then closes it, her eyes as wide and dark as when Zio used to space out, i.e., was using his First Sense. "Pushing them out..." she whispers.

I nod and drop that hand. "The coils make it glow, and last time I actually did see the energy leave my body that way. It makes a big difference." The relief felt heavenly in comparison to the burn of these coils.

A short, surprised laugh bursts from her throat. "Unbelievable. It's you. The rift, you're weaving—"

Without warning, a bright, blinding flash crashes through the room. All eight of us cry out in unison. I squeeze my eyelids shut and throw my hands up to protect my eyes, but the flash is gone as fast as it came, leaving me half-blind. That's not the beginning of an episode, what's—

"Execute," a male voice I don't recognize calls out as something cold and metallic is pressed against my neck—

And everything turns black.

# Chapter Nineteen -
# Unplanned

My vision comes back after what feels no more than a split-second, but I wish it hadn't. No, not true, it's not about the vision. It's about the situation we're in.

All eight of us—Chase and Zio, Grazer and Sheridan, Taro Magona and Mom, Kieran and me—have rematerialized in what looks like the same courtroom Kieran and I were in before, after Sheridan abducted us from the *Hope*. The large podium is there, only empty right now, the FBTI's seal displayed on the wall behind it, the room as devoid of chairs and tables as the first time we had the, uhh, pleasure.

Problem is, this time there are more people. Eight, to be precise, one standing behind each and every one of us, a weapon pressed against our temples.

"What the absolute—!" Sheridan is about to turn, but the man behind him, like the others dressed in the same uniform Sheridan wore before, grabs him by the shoulder and rams the muzzle of the gun into the executioner's temple.

"Not so fast." Malice swings in the man's words. "You've caused enough trouble."

Sheridan jerks. "I— Wha— I'm the Executioner! Let go of me, or—"

"Cormac." The sound of doors opening and closing accompanies those words, and the eight soldiers straighten up when they hear the voice from the right behind the judge's podium. The sound of slow, leisurely taken steps echoes through the large, empty room, until a man steps out to the side of the podium.

I suck in a fast breath. "Taro Izola."

The good thing: we don't need to worry about how to find the bad guy.

The bad thing: he found us, it appears.

Not how I imagined things to turn out.

A cold smile crosses his face. "Indeed. Nonie Thorburn. Kieran Wildason. And everybody else who has been making it really difficult for me to take care of time as I needed to."

I scoff. "Happy we could throw a wrench into your plans. Manipulating time for your own good? It takes quite the ego to put your needs above everybody else's." I glare at the man who ordered Kieran killed and who wants the Essken eradicated, merely to gain more power.

Izola lays a hand over his heart, his dark robe sliding up and revealing a bracelet made out of a beautiful, shimmering and iridescent material. "You misunderstand. It is you who are causing the problems. All I'm doing is helping my timeline progress the way it should be."

Sheridan, careful to not aggravate the man behind him again, lifts his chin. "I don't believe anymore that's what you're doing. This here"—he nods at the men holding us captive—"proves you've crossed a line."

Izola makes a *tsk-tsk* sound. "I was quite disappointed when you didn't return, Cormac. It took me weeks to come to terms with your betrayal. And it took me months before I had the judge convinced of the threat you're posing, enough men trained to track you down and bring you back, and the tech to break through this very annoying and very surprising demat-shield. Everything could've been so much easier had you only done what you were ordered—"

Kieran gives him a glance that should make the Taro glad a couple of guns keep him from getting too close. "Ordered to take us out of the equation so that you can make sure the Essken die and you become Praetor?"

Some of the officers look at each other, a confused look on their faces, as the Taro's cold smile freezes. Anger lights up in his eyes. It takes him a good two seconds to get himself under control before he responds. "Now, another lie. Is there nothing holy to the two of you, not even the sacred timeline itself? I'm glad we were able to apprehend you before you could commit more hideous crimes, especially with the company you've been keeping. Officers, bring the prisoners to the medical cells. They will have their memories altered and personality corrected for the safety of the timeline."

He waves a hand, the bracelet catching the light and reflecting it in a rainbow of colors, but before the man holding me can react, I have. And, to be brutally honest, it's the Taro's fault, or rather, it's thanks to him. He had me kidnapped when I was little, and that kidnapping made me swear to myself I'd never be helpless again. It's why I overcame my PTSD, to a degree at least, and practiced self-defense like a madwoman. I'd never be at a disadvantage again if I could help it.

Before the man behind me can react, I've shot my right hand up and wrapped my fingers around the muzzle of the gun. With one fast twist I turn it forward, the muzzle of the weapon pointing at the Taro, as I yank my head backwards and out of the line of fire. I'd like to not get my brain blasted out, thank you very much. Lightning fast, I bring my other hand up to cup the gun's butt, pull it tight into my shoulder, then push it forward with all my might as I buttcheck the guy behind me. With an *oomph,* he lets go of the weapon, and while usually I would enjoy beating the crap out of him, tactics require a different approach. Angling off to the side, I get behind him with two fast steps and reverse our situations, only I grab the fabric of his uniform with my left hand

and ram my forearm diagonally into his back to keep him from moving like I just did.

He grunts and steps forward, as if to turn and attack, but freezes in mid-motion when I tighten my grip on him and grind the weapon into his back. "Not so fast." I look the Taro in the eye from behind my hostage. "I get it, you still hold seven people, me only one, but all I want is to talk." To buy time. "None of us here are in favor of getting our memories removed and personalities corrected. We—"

"Hold it a second," a female voice comes from the door behind the podium as fast, hurried steps approach. "What is going on—" Judge Alberti gasps and stops dead in her tracks as her gaze falls upon all of us, the Essken following her barely evading running into her. To the judge's credit, she only needs a second before steel laces her voice. She puts both her hands on her hips and glares at Izola. "Taro Izola. Care to elaborate? I believe you were talking about a *surgical extraction* of the executioner, Captain Wildason, and Lieutenant Thorburn, and now here you are with—"

"Admiral Zio Upinga," Zio says, giving the smallest nod.

"Admiral Chase Connolly," Chase says next, followed by everybody else besides Sheridan. For him, no introductions are needed.

"Taro Magona."

"Admiral Sebastian Grazer."

"Temporal Advisor Kelia Okata."

When my mom says her name, the Essken—Tinn, I assume—tilts his head to the side, and the Judge's eyes widen. She chokes out a cough. "*You* are K. Okata?"

Mom smirks. "The one and only. Happy to see my reputation precedes me."

Admiration shines in Alberti's eyes. "I grew up reading your work. It's why I applied to the FBTI. I could quote the Temporal Principles by heart at age three: *First Principle: changes to the timeline reflect futural.*"

Her smile fading, Mom brushes a strand of hair behind her ear. "While that is wonderful to hear, it pains me to say that my work has been taken out of context. *First Principle: changes to* any *timeline reflect futural into a new stable split-off, leaving the original timeline intact."*

Kieran and I exchange a knowing glance. Mom is using the same wording Other Nonie taught us: futural. Makes me wonder if it was her coming up with that term, in either universe.

Mom glances at Izola, and that look she shoots at him makes me almost happy I had all my teen-quarrels with Dad. "That's what you should have learned, but I'm wondering if part of my work has been purposely held back."

For a second, silence hovers until the judge closes her mouth again. "Held back—a new stable split-off? Are you being serious? Is—"

Taro Izola bows. "Judge, I beg your pardon and apologize for bringing all those people, but the situation was less than optimal. We were able to apprehend them right as they were planning to attack us here, in our now. As you can see, we're dealing with delusions. Inability to grasp simple concepts." He shakes his head, the ultimate look of shock and horror on his face. "Their planned attack on us must've been the change in the timeline I've been feeling, the change that would undo our world as we know it. Our only hope is to proceed with our plan—"

"With *your* plan, you mean!" I move my hostage a bit, so I can see Alberti and she can see me, keeping my gun in a tight grip. What did Sheridan say? Taro needed the judge on his side. He doesn't have all-encompassing power just yet. And Izola himself admitted it took him a while to convince the judge of the next step, so what I'm taking from all of this is the judge is our friend. Potentially, at least. So, I go for it. "Your Honor, I'm sorry to tell you, but this man has deceived and played you. In fact, he's played all of us, including the timeline, like a fiddle."

Izola makes a gasping sound and presses a hand to his midsection, eyes wide, as if I just socked him into the stomach. "The timeline! Judge, please don't listen to them. The timeline!" He breathes out a wheezy puff of air. It's quite the performance, and the judge... she buys it.

"Crap," she curses under her breath. She yanks her arm up and points at somewhere behind the podium. Her shirt moves up, revealing something silver and shiny dangling from her belt. "Agents, take the prisoners—"

An epiphany hits me smack in the face. "I have proof!" I yell. "Proof I can't have tampered with! Izola is manipulating the timeline, please, Your Honor, you have to listen!" Maybe it's the word *proof*, maybe it's my tone of voice, the sincerity and plea in it, but Alberti drops her arm. None of the agents move, as if they too were wondering where this is going. Zio and Chase exchange a glance, Chase shrugging, like, *no idea what she's talking about.*

But for a change, I do know what I'm talking about. Happened rarely enough in the last few months. Hint-hint, temporal manual.

I lower my voice and speak calmly and clearly, as if raising the volume could change the judge's mind. "You have my wristPAD. You took it from me when Executioner Sheridan brought me here. It had been on me for months before I was brought to your time, and it shows proof of the Taro's involvement." I nod my chin at PADdy sticking out of her pocket. She's still keeping it close—isn't that a sign she doesn't trust the Taro? Or at least that she considers it important evidence?

"Ridiculous," Izola spatters. "Judge—"

Alberti lifts a hand, cutting him off. "I dislike being surprised. I dislike changes to a plan we both agreed on. I dislike both very, very much, and I will spare a moment to evaluate my options."

Izola deflates, looking like somebody kicked a puppy. "I'm sorry if I made you feel that way, Judge. Of course, check what the traitor is saying. I can promise you it won't be anything of substance." Gone is the hurt expression when the judge's attention isn't on him anymore, replaced by an arrogant smirk, oh-so-cocky and sure of himself.

Alberti rolls her eyes. "Very graceful of you, Taro. Thank you. Agents, hold."

A huge weight drops off my shoulders and my next breath comes in easier. "Judge, if you wouldn't mind activating the PAD, so I can voice control it?"

Alberti looks at me like I was dumb, eyebrows raised and with pointed glance, like, *really?*

I sigh and release my hostage, laying the gun onto the floor. "I'm pretty sure if I say something you don't like, you outnumber me."

Keeping her gaze glued to my every move, the judge removes PADdy from her belt. "Okay then." She wakes the device up and nods as Tinn steps out from behind her for a better view.

Adrenaline shoots through me. It's only our lives and I don't know, possibly the whole timeline depending on my data. No biggie. "PADdy," I call out, "please play recording from January second, fifty-four, visual and audio." My heart beats like crazy. I never checked the recording, who knows how clean or not it turned out. PADdy is top of the line, but Murphy's Law is mighty.

*"Displaying data,"* PADdy announces a second before projecting an unsteady image of the *Eclipse's* engine room, taken from my hidey-hole, into the air in front of the Taro. Only when everything is clearly recognizable and more weight falls off my shoulders do I realize how worried I was my recording wouldn't cut it.

But heck, it does.

No, it's not Oscar-worthy cinematography. It's shaky and all over the place from me moving my hand, but it captures what needed to be captured: Mashaule, at the console, the disk on it—and the blueish projection of a tall male dressed in a uniform looking suspiciously like Izola, now that I know the man.

As if they rehearsed it, Alberti, Izola, and Sheridan take a sharp breath in.

"Son of a gun," Chase mumbles under his breath, pride in his voice. Guess he's even happier now he gifted me PADdy.

The judge's eyes narrow as she cocks her head, looking from the projection of the Taro back to Izola himself, as if she couldn't believe it. And Izola…? Izola lost the arrogant expression the second he realized what the recording was: his downfall.

The audio starts, and I allow myself the tiniest smirk.

The Mashaule of times long gone gapes at the projected Taro. *"None of my concern? There's a freakin' ship firing on mine—"*

*"They won't fire on you anymore. They'll target the colony."*

Mashaule's choke and response are drowned in the murmur going through the room when the judge and the agents realize who is talking, that there's no doubt about the person's identity.

"—Eclipse, *ready weapons*—"

"*Don't.*" The projected Taro holds out a hand, a bracelet similar to the one he's wearing today on his wrist, and the judge gasps audibly. Maybe she just realized Izola is actively interfering in the past, doing exactly what he wasn't allowed to do.

Mashaule freezes mid-word. "*Excuse me? They're attacking—*"

"*They are. And for the greater good, some of the people on the ground must die. It is unfortunate, but necessary.*"

I can't say it gets easier hearing the detached and cold way Izola sentences the people on the ground to death—if it hadn't been for Kieran, that is.

Mashaule stutters, the look on his face one of pure disbelief. "*W-what did you do? That was you, wasn't it?*"

"*I did what was necessary to get their attention.*"

If the judge wasn't convinced of Izola's wrongdoing before, at this point she is. Her jaw sets as she presses her lips into a thin line.

Izola, probably feeling like he's losing ground, lifts both hands and shakes his head. "This is crazy talk! A manipulation designed to frame me—"

"This PAD has been personally guarded by me, Taro. I would choose my next words very carefully if I were you."

"*—didn't want me to hear the alert for the approaching ship! How dare you play me—*"

I know exactly which sentence comes next. I remember the horror I felt when hearing them spoken for the first time, and I can imagine how the judge must feel hearing them this time around.

"*I dare because it's necessary. This attack is one of many more to come, and it's part of the plan to improve the future.*"

One of the agents, the one behind Kieran, lets his weapon sink down, a look of complete disbelief on his face. Kieran stays still, but I can see the muscles tensing under his shirt. He's ready to spring into action, not that I had any doubt about that.

Judge Alberti looks at me. "I've heard enough."

I nod curtly. "PADdy, stop playback." Mashaule's borderline panicky voice gets cut off right after *Magellans have done nothing to those people*, a fitting emphasis on the Taro's coldhearted, calculated, and self-centered approach to change the past to his liking, no matter the cost. "I enabled recording for all spectral channels. You should find what you need to prove this wasn't tampered with," I say quietly.

Silence hovers, and it's loaded.

The agents holding the rest of us hostage are clearly torn. They exchange glances with each other, shrugging. The ones holding Chase and my mom step back and take their weapons down, holstering them. Alberti still glares at Izola, shaking her head.

"I am appalled at what you've done," she says, anger tightening her voice. "Disgusted. You are the Taro. You are tasked with protecting the timeline, protecting the people—*peoples*—and yet you tried to manipulate it to your own gain?" She hooks PADdy back to her belt with one hand, then motions at the agents with the other. "Agents, arrest the Taro. He will have to answer for the crimes he committed."

Her words make me release a breath of pure relief. The agents step away from all of us and aim their weapons at Izola instead. A small, easy smile tugs on the corners of my lips. We did it! Man, we had tons of luck on our side, but we did it. We stopped the Temporal War.

I'm about to step closer to Kieran, when the Taro slowly raises his hands. "Well, well. I have to admit, I didn't see this coming. It will be a lesson learned, so I thank you for that." He brings his hands closer together, and in this very moment, I know.

"The bracelet," I whisper, then scream it out. "The bracelet! Don't let him touch the bracelet, it's a Setayashi—"

Too late.

Izola snorts. "Right idea, late realization. Say goodbye, half-Magellan. This time I will get rid of you myself."

And, with a dirty laugh, he twists the bracelet.

## *Confederation Headquarters, Somewhen*

Horror shoots through my veins like ice as a burst of *something* spews from the bracelet. It's invisible, yet I feel it in my very core, not unlike Setayashi-radiation, but… like it was tainted, had gone bad. For the longest second of my life, my First Sense shoots a bolt of pain right through my center as reality is being ripped apart, only to throw me almost instantaneously into the Maelstrom and its myriads of colors, my body flip-flopping head over heels.

A scream bursts free as I'm desperately trying to control my flailing limbs. Events and timelines rush past me, too fast to make out. The noise is deafening and wrong somehow, disturbed, not the usual cacophony of history. Catching some resemblance of an upward position, I dig my heels in and throw my body forward, like I was pushing against a storm—and it works. My wild tumble slows down until I come to a standstill.

Sucking in deep breath after deep breath, I bend forward and rest my hands on my knees. Holy Universe—what in the heck was that? I never transitioned with such an uncontrolled violence and it never felt this… bad. I sneak one hand off my knee to cover my stomach. The pain is gone, which is fantastic, but it doesn't erase the sensation of general wrongness, which drives home my priorities, now that I have control over my body. I can't let the Taro manipulate time again—any of it.

I whirl around. Where is—

There, about twenty meters away, if one can measure in meters in the Maelstrom: Izola! Nobody else seems to have transitioned, maybe because nobody else has an affinity to time to equal ours, not even Sheridan. But just because I'm alone doesn't mean I can't fight. Whatever he's about to change, I doubt it's for the better.

Balling my fists, I sprint forward. Tendrils of time slither away, evading my mad dash. "Hey!" I yell. "Stop!"

Izola ignores me, a look of intense focus on his face as he scans the timeline. His moves are slow and sluggish, as if he was fighting through quicksand. Like a picture taken of a speeding starship, motion blur follows every dragging move he makes. He twists parts of his bracelet—

My First Sense seizes— And Holy Sun and Stars, all the swirls of time align!

I repeat, for emphasis: All chaotic swirls of time *align*, responding to and obeying his command!

It should be impossible, yet they obey like soldiers ordered to attention as they zoom around me and the Realm's unaffected strand: ours, countless others, some feeling familiar, others not all, all rigid instead of billowing, their colors pulsing at an incredible speed, like they were trying to break free from invisible restraints, lining up to form a magnificent wall of time around us.

Is a sight to behold, breathtaking and scary at the same time.

My mouth gapes open. The bracelet must not only be a Setayashi-device, but also somehow control the timelines. Izola's bracelet is *controlling the timelines*—how is that even possible?

A loud, high-pitched laugh bursts from the Taro. "Finally! It finally is perfect after all those wasted attempts!" He twists and pinches some part of the bracelet and my First Sense cramps so hard my muscles lock up in mid-run as nausea slams into me like a jumping starship.

Panic steals my next breath as inertia carries me forward into a fall I barely get my hands out for. No, no, no, please no, I know what this feels like, and I'm nowhere near Kieran! I crash down and bounce back up at an odd angle, extremities flailing as I'm trying to get control again. Gravity feels off somehow, or not right, at least. I—

Izola cackles. "Serves you right, you annoying thing. You're like weeds, I take you out, and yet you come back. But not this time. This time I'm in *full* control. Oh, what am I going to do? Choices, choices... Ah, I know. Now that I can jump with precision and without rejection there's no more need for any unreliable helpers, like the idiots who were supposed to kill you but couldn't pull it off."

The ones who—what?

He spits to the side in disgust, then gestures up and down my body as I finally get my limbs back under control. "They couldn't even break you enough to stay out of my way. Turns out, I need you dead to have the timeline develop as I want it. Even when you're damaged you're still a threat."

That's when it clicks. "My kidnapping! You—"

A cruel grin splits his face. "Don't worry about it. I'll go back and kill you myself this time, and since I'm in a generous mood, I might even do it before those halfwits shatter your leg." He squeezes some part of the bracelet and—

Lightning crashes through the Maelstrom, making the Taro jump, then jerk. A deafening thunder follows it right on its heels. The sound is so deep and powerful, I feel it in every bone in my body and down to a sub-cellular level. Did his bracelet cause tha—

Holy—!

A pull of a strength unlike any I ever experienced forces me a few steps forward, my body humming in well-known anticipation, even though I don't see any coils.

And really, I don't want to see any.

I work myself up to standing; my heart hammers as if it knew the moment the coils appear, its remaining beats might be numbered. I ball my hands into fists and take a few insecure steps. We will be fine. *Fine.* Zio's device has worked once, it will work now. It must. Too much hinges on it, too much.

Walking is hard at this point, like my body wanted to make sure I stay away from the man who could kill me, but my body got it wrong. Taking on the Taro *might* kill me, but not doing so will *surely* kill me. So, I ignore the burning accompanying my First Sense, the muscle cramp, and override my body's refusal to move with sheer willpower.

I'm almost there.

More and more lightning crashes through the Maelstrom as if it was out to get Izola, one barely missing him, hitting the timeline closest to him. He yelps and hops to the side, getting himself out of the way. I wish it had hit him straight in the chest, at least then—

Oh, crap.

The burst of lightning doesn't fizzle out, no. Dividing into hundreds of little tendrils of light, it cuts through the timeline it hit like a knife, shearing off little pieces and bigger chunks. They drift off, turn dark, grey, and then poof out of existence.

My throat constricts. Those pieces… they're gone. What does that mean for those people in the timeline? Horror freezes my blood, making the cramps courtesy of my First Sense feel like beginner's pain.

"What— No. That's not supposed to—" Izola shakes his head and takes a dragging step back, motion artifact making it look like he was in two locations at once. Still, he only narrowly avoids getting hit by another lightning rod shooting right at him.

And another.

Another.

Another.

Another, all of them attracting me, pulling me in like magnets.

Another lightning bolt hits, this time close to me, too close for comfort, but—

Recognition strikes. It's not lightning! How could I not have seen the difference when I felt it with the very first blast. Enormous coils! They're *coils*, K'Zees, only way, way bigger—ragged lightning bolts of different colors, zigzagging through the Maelstrom and digging into one or another timeline, chopping bits off, leaving huge areas to turn grey and into glittery dust.

Holy Universe, the K'Zees are destroying the timelines! No wonder Kieran and I are falling apart.

I scramble forward, faster, faster, heart hammering at hummingbird speed, yet not pumping enough blood. My body hums at a high frequency, demanding a fix no matter it will kill me.

More and more coils rain down on the Taro, dozens and dozens of bolts—so many, he can't evade them all. The ones that hit shoot right into his bracelet, bringing it to a scalding red glow. The Taro screams and jumps back, shaking his arm as if he wanted to fling off the bracelet. He thrashes about like a puppet on strings, manipulated by the

Maelstrom around him, pulling and pushing on areas of time that somehow seem connected to his body, causing images of reality to bleed through: The courtroom, some city location I don't know, a beach …

The Taro dodges another bolt-shaped coil with a yelp and frantic jump. The more he struggles and moves, the more strained the Maelstrom becomes—

And with a deafening *crack*, it tears apart at the seams.

Both of us scream out as the transition yanks on my body, stretching it and compressing it at the same time. My First Sense flares up—

And my feet hit solid ground.

I stumble and land in a crouching position, one hand on the cool hard floor for stability. Every breath is harsh, short, and doesn't bring enough oxygen. Lifting my gaze, I blink against the sudden brightness—

The courtroom, like we never left, only—

"Nonie! You guys were go—" Chase chokes on the last word as his eyes widen in shock and wonder. "What the absolute…?"

Yeah. The Taro and I might be back in the courtroom with the same people, but also, we're not. Or rather, we brought something with us.

Clearly, something broke in the grand scheme of things. Last time I checked, the Maelstrom wasn't supposed to be flowing around us like we were in the eye of the storm, surrounded by temporal swirls moving so fast and furious, I can't make out any details. The noise is deafening. Thunderous, hissing, swooshing. Winds lift my hair and whip it around my head. And still coils continue to shoot at the Taro's bracelet, which means if they're here, they're also aiming for—

"Nonie!"

Hearing Kieran call my name, I whirl around, imagining the worst—

But for once, we're lucky.

Coils crowd Kieran, coils of every size, from thin and short like earthworms to a meter's length and the width of my forearm. They swarm him from everywhere, tugging on his body without mercy, but only a few are successful in entering him, thanks to Zio's device, its green glow visible under Kieran's shirt. I feel their tantalizing call, but I'm missing the compulsive need to connect with him.

A weight the size of a boulder falls off my shoulders. It's still working. His cells are still stable, even though I'm sure the coils are hurting him.

Chest heaving up and down in a much too fast rhythm, his wide gaze meets mine, the same relief radiating off him I'm feeling.

We've been granted another reprieve.

Somebody screams—the judge?—and I whirl around.

The Maelstrom and reality only clashed a mere few seconds ago, but those few seconds have made all the difference to life as we know it. The laws of nature have changed around us, obviously. What once was the courtroom is now no more than a floor with gravity keeping us tethered to it. Gone are the walls, the ceiling, part of the podium. The Maelstrom is swirling and billowing in their place, events passing at a supernatural speed, from past to future, from one timeline to another. I can't even distinguish whether it's ours or a different one, everything is mixed up, like timelines were put into a blender. I have no idea if we are in the Maelstrom or if the Maelstrom is around us, but it doesn't matter. It's wrong, it shouldn't happen, and yet it is.

The judge screams again, staggering back from the coils breaking off the Maelstrom's rippling clouds, lapping at her like a hungry monster. Hands up, as if that would do her any good in defense, she stumbles as Tinn pulls her back, a look of sheer horror on her face—but the K'Zees follow.

Call it my First Sense, but I know that if they reach them, they'll be gone, irretrievably absorbed into time.

I dash forward, ready to help Tinn, yank them back and to do— I don't know, do *something*, but as soon as I get close to them, the K'Zees recoil back and retreat, hovering at a safe distance, calmer than before.

The judge pants, clinging to me like to a lifeline. "Sun and Stars, it was about to— It was about—" She gasps for air, but there's no time consoling her.

People scream or shriek.

The agents.

Sheridan.

Zio.

Chase.

Mom.

Hungry coil-tentacles protrude from the Maelstrom, reaching for them, flaring deeper and deeper into the little bit of normal space left to us.

Oh, crap.

My heart drops. Not sure what I can do, but I can try. When I sprint toward Chase and Zio, the tentacles retreat, just like they did with the judge. The K'Zees never liked me anyway, they only wanted Kieran. Maybe I'm a repellent, who knows, but I'm surely going to make use of it. The noise cranks it up to beyond deafening, to a painful ear-splitting howling of the Maelstrom.

Just before I can reach my two mentors, dizziness and the feeling of absolute death and destruction sweeps over me like a dark blanket, cold, suffocating, and so, so *final*.

Oh, heck.

My blood pressure drops to my feet. No. That can't be real.

Please, no.

Izola stands a mere four meters away from me, a shocked expression frozen on his face, the hand with the bracelet outstretched as if he is trying to distance himself from his own body part. A small, dark swirl trickles out of his bracelet, slicing through reality with surgical precision, followed by a cracking noise blasting through the air as it rips the room apart, straight through the judge's podium and beyond, through the maddening swirl of timelines. Holy everything, his bracelet is causing the chasm—

Somebody screams as time tendrils and coils protrude from the chasm, licking at reality, breaking off little chunks here and there, turning them into grey dust with the most horrendous high-pitched screeching sound.

It feels like death has just arrived.

I whip my head around toward Kieran, to make sure he's still safe, he's still okay, and my heart stops. Coils have all but surrounded him. He looks like a blur of colors, as if a toddler had taken a crayon, tried to color him in, and failed to stay within the lines. His eyes are wide, his teeth clenched, body shaking, but to my utter relief, the device is still glowing green under his shirt. We're still safe. *He* is still safe.

Judge Alberti yelps out in pain. "What is that?" She squirms under the coils' attack. "What's happening?"

"It's Izola's bracelet," I yell back. "It's causing a cleft in time!" I tap my wrist. And the coils are coming from the rift, attacking us. "Izola! Turn that thing off!" I lift one hand, as if it could protect me from the onslaught of temporal swirls whipping through the room.

"Off? I'm just getting started!" Face distorted into a desperate grimace, Izola twists the bracelet, but nothing happens. He grabs it with his other hand and squeezes. "Dammit, move! *Obey me!*"

Like a swarm of hungry bees, more and more coils slither through the gap, every new one bigger than the last, wrapping themselves around the people present. The judge, the agents, Zio, Magona, my mom, Sheridan, Grazer—they all start to frantically swat at things they can't see, their grunts of pain and confused shouts intensifying by the second, as the K'Zees tear and bite into their bodies.

Never have they affected anybody else but Kieran and me, but this time the rules don't apply, not when reality is breaking and the rift is about to delete us, like it deleted those other timelines I saw. More and more bits and pieces of our reality turn black, grey, and into dust, the screeching sound of the disintegration ringing in my ears.

I stare at Izola, frantically trying to get the bracelet to do *something*. Look back at Kieran, attacked by a myriad of coils, but stable, then at everybody else, squirming, swatting wide eyed. And I take in the coils eating away at reality, turning parts of timelines into dust, more and more, the longer they work: No doubt about it. We're about to die.

Grazer drags himself forward against the storm and onslaught of the Maelstrom. "We must destroy the bracelet! Do you hear me, everyone? It must be destroyed at all costs! No matter if Izola is still wearing it or not, I really don't care at this point!"

"No!" Mom yells, holding her scanner in one hand, while swatting left and right at hungry coils with the other. "You can't destroy the bracelet now; it's going to rip time apart! The only way to end this is to close the rift, at least enough that it won't cause a temporal collapse!"

I shake my head, hair flying everywhere. "Close the rift? How do we close a freakin' rift in time?" This thing is bigger than us, bigger than *everything*!

Mom looks at me with absolute horror and sorrow in her eyes—and then it clicks.

A weird calmness washes over me, as if I wasn't part of this reality anymore, but on a different plane.

Because I understand.

What did she say, before we were brought here? *"You're weaving—"*

Exactly. We're *weaving* the coils together. Kieran and I, together.

It makes sense, only I couldn't see it.

I'm not a repellent to the coils, quite the contrary. The coils were never out for Kieran. They always wanted me, what I can do to them. *For* them.

The first time I saw them they came for me, they wanted me, but they bounced right off. Kieran was their detour to me, so that— So that I could weave them together. That's what my First Sense does, it fixes these coils back together. That's why I start feeling better, why this euphoria happens, and when it does, the reunited K'Zees leave my body—and every time they do, the attacks stop and things go back to normal.

My mom is right, and it sounds so easy. Kieran and I can fix it. We can stop the rift.

*Kieran and I* can heal it.

But it's not easy.

Not at all.

Because in order to have the coils pass through us and my First Sense transform them to whatever it is the rift demands to be healed… For that, we will have to turn off Zio's device.

And that means…

It means we're not going to survive, not when we barely did so before, with way less coils out for us, and much smaller ones.

Kieran and I will die to fix the rift.

In the end, the Temporal War will have killed us, just differently than we thought we might go. Not by gunfire, not by being erased from the timeline, but because of a device ripping the very fabric of time apart, a device that never should've existed.

An ache opens up in my chest, as deep and all-consuming as the rift. We won't have a future. Nothing to build on.

But it will mean time as it is will continue to exist.

I draw in a harsh breath of air as I curl my fingers into fists. The decision isn't an easy one, but it's a logical one.

We've got a time chasm to stop, no matter it will kill us.

Because two lives lost are better than reality gone forever.

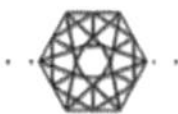

## Confederation Headquarters and the Maelstrom, 2399—or Any Time, Any Timeline

I whirl around and lock eyes with Kieran, swamped by the coils, teeth gritted as they tug on him. We don't need words. He knows. He understands.

His chest rises with a slow, deep inhale as he closes his eyes for a second. When he opens them, resolve shines in them. "Yes." He says it no louder than a pained whisper, but I hear it easily over the coils' noise in the room, over the jarring concert of the Maelstrom and the dying sounds of our timeline.

Our decision is made. We both know there's no other option.

I fall into a sprint, and maybe the urgency in it makes it click for Zio and Chase—or maybe they did the same math I did, or maybe they just read me really well. Either way, they know.

"Nonie, no! It's going to kill you both!" Chase tries to follow, only to be doubled over by overeager coils. He grunts, but I have no time to tend to him, no time to chase away the hungry K'Zees.

"You and Bas take care of the Taro, Chase! When we're ready, the bracelet needs to be destroyed! We need you, Trip, *please!*" That please, it carries a buttload of meaning. *Please* don't keep me from doing what I have to, no matter how hard. *Please* don't make it any more difficult for us. *Please* make sure the bracelet will be destroyed, and *please* make sure the Taro won't get away.

For a moment our gazes connect, and dang if his didn't hit me like an arrow to the heart. It's a goodbye, I realize. Before I can let myself fully understand what that means, before I tear up, I force myself to focus: fixing reality. Fixing existence.

With three fast steps, I'm next to Kieran, so swamped by coils, his features are blurry. The determination shining in his eyes is clear though. Crystal clear.

Like me, he understands.

*I would give my life if it meant I'd die a free man and on my own terms.*

At least he will have that. I will have that. In the end, we dictate how the game is played. We win.

Somewhat.

Kieran takes my outstretched hand, sorrow resonating in his words. "While we're taking back control, I wish it felt better."

Funny how the Maelstrom's howling drowns out everything but him. We're the eye of the hurricane. It's not quiet around us by any means, but it feels quiet, as odd as that sounds. Maybe reality is already broken where we stand, because I see everything about Kieran in sharper than 20/20. His dark, unruly hair blown into chaos by the Maelstrom's storm. The brown, warm eyes, framed by thick lashes. His wide shoulders and strong frame.

I swallow hard. Can't go down that road, or I'll lose it. I nod, ignoring the lump in my throat. "This is how it ends."

He sucks in a harsh, cut-off breath, his hand not holding on to mine curling into a fist, like I did. "I guess we were always meant for something more than normal duty. Together." He squeezes my hand, then brings it to his lips and kisses the ring he gave me in another lifetime. "I've said and written it before, and I stand by every single word. For me you were it, Nonie. For me, you were it." Brushing his thumb over the ring he lowers my hand, a slow smile curving up his lips.

I force down a hard swallow, doing my very best to ignore the zing of K'Zees shooting from Kieran to me. It's going to be a whole different ball game when the protection from Zio's device is gone. There's so much to say and so little time. I need him to know how much he means to me. How much of him is keeping my heart beating and my soul intact. I need him to know how I wish things had been different, luckier for us.

But in the end, I settle on two words that encompass all I feel for him. "Everything. Always," I whisper with a crack in my voice. "You're everything to me, and always will be."

Kieran closes his eyes, an expression of peace settling over his face, as if my words had given him new strength. My words... How funny I was so afraid to say I loved him, and in the end two other words held so much more power: *Everything. Always.*

He opens his eyes, gaze finding mine, a myriad of emotions flickering across his face, and mine, probably.

Regret.

Heartache.

Determination.

*Love.*

"I wish we'd had more time," he whispers.

I swallow hard. "I wish there was another way."

More than anything, I wish somebody else could fix this, not us. We've done enough, been played enough, been messed with enough. But there's nobody else. It's only us.

Kieran lifts his hand to the device under his shirt. "Together?" He squeezes my hand.

"Together," I say and squeeze it back, raising my other hand to the metallic disk under my collar bone.

"Kieran, no!" Chase yells, half doubled over, yet shlepping himself closer to the petrified Izola. "It will kill both of you! We'll find another way—"

But we won't.

Kieran allows us one more second of relative peace, before he nods, giving the signal.

Like him, I reach under my shirt and rip off the device and some skin with it, not that it mattered. I close my eyes, channel my First Sense—

And we both get hit by the full force of temporal energy on the loose.

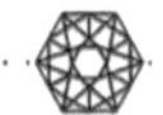

## Confederation Headquarters and the Maelstrom, 2399—or Any Time, Any Timeline

Pain rips through me like a shockwave. My body cramps and contorts, I couldn't stand straight if I wanted to. "Holy—" I grunt and gasp. I knew it was going to be bad, but this is bad-bad, with a capital B. There's no gradual increase, it's like being hit by a truck while tied to the front of another truck, both ramming into each other at maximum speed. The onslaught of coils is crushing.

Kieran spasms next to me, a strangulated choke bursting from his throat. I can only imagine how bad it must be for him—actually, I can't. He's always been affected more, and I'm already at what I consider my max.

Somebody screams—Grazer, the Taro, I don't know—but it makes me force my eyelids open against the urge to squeeze them shut and endure the torture.

No more than four or five seconds have passed, but the situation around us has worsened, if that was even possible. The rift originating from the Taro's bracelet has widened to at least five meters, cutting everybody off from the door behind the judge's podium, not that it led anywhere at this point.

Through the coils, the chaos, Tinn looks from one person to another, head tilted as if he was trying to figure something out, his stillness the complete opposite of the utter turmoil around us. The amount of coils breaking loose from the chasm's edges is unbelievable. They swarm out, looking for anything and anybody to attack, biting into people, biting into reality, tearing at it and taking it apart.

I have enough mental processing power left to know that's really, really bad.

The rift's winds are whipping around us, lifting my hair, tousling Kieran's, but I barely feel it. I focus all my senses to support the one I need the most right now, my First Sense. Every coil using Kieran as an entry point to me needs to be reconnected to its collective, or else the rift is going to tear us apart—is going to tear *everything* apart. I focus on letting my First Sense work its magic, on fixing those K'Zees together. It's a weird, coiling sensation in my core, the only good sensation I can pick up on, a bright light in the growing darkness drowning me.

Kieran holds on to my hand like a bench vise, his body rigid and face contorted.

"Nonie! Kieran!" Chase yells, face contorted into a mask of desperation. "Dammit, Zee, do something! Do something!" He fights for every step closer to the Taro, against the power of the Maelstrom, against the attack of the coils.

Like lightning bolts on steroids, they use Kieran to get to me. When I realized this was the only way to go, I knew it was going to hurt, but I didn't expect it to be at this level. I've been in pain before. I was kidnapped, stabbed, beaten. One could say I've had my fair share of... *things* happening to me, but this is beyond the physical level. It's pain shooting so deep it rips apart cell after cell. It feels like there isn't going to be any coming back from. Sadness swamps me, but I don't let it rise to the surface. Can't let that get to me.

I focus on drawing in the coils, on knitting them together, on fixing the fabric of time. Brighter, thicker coils shoot out from my hand and into the rift, knitting it back together little by little.

Only it's not enough.

Izola's bracelet keeps ripping time apart, and much faster than we can fix it.

Kieran stumbles forward, nearly falling. He's pale, eyes rolling back over and over again, and every time he shakes himself back to attention.

Somebody screams, an agent, I think, as something in a timeline somewhere to my left implodes into glittery nothingness.

Izola curses and steps back, cradling the arm with the bracelet. "Stay away from me or—"

"Or what?" Trip lunges for the Magellan, grabbing him by the biceps. "Doesn't look like you're in control, so sorry if your threats don't pack a punch!"

With a crazed outcry, Izola twists away from Chase. "I *am* in control, I—Ngh."

Trip lands a well-aimed right hook across Izola's temple, knocking him into a heap on the floor. If I wasn't fresh out of empathy for him, I'd feel sorry for the headache he's going to wake up with.

"In control. I can tell," Trip grumbles as a wave of dizziness swamps me. When everything has aligned properly again, I hear him curse.

"I can't get the damn thing off!" He digs into the bracelet harder, using some kind of power tool he must've pulled from his belt. "This is some type of resistant metal I've never seen before, I need something with more energy to destroy it!"

"Take my weapon!" one of the agents screams at Chase, holding out his gun.

Chase shakes his head, eyes pinched to slits against the onslaught of wind and debris from the crumbling timelines. "Too hot, it will melt whatever mechanism is in there! If we're unlucky, it's going to get stuck on this setting, and then we're doomed for sure!"

"We don't have much time left," my mom yells. "Everything is disintegrating, and it's starting to take out whole timelines! We have to turn off the bracelet and fix the rift!"

"Well, what do you suggest?" Chase throws his hands up. "It won't budge!"

Mom sucks in her lower lip, then whirls toward me. "Nonie! Can you give us more output?"

Give more—

I have to blink hard to bring meaning to the words, but once I do, I nod twice, fast. Can't lose too much focus, or I'll lose my grip on reality, but I think I know what she wants.

Mom fights her way against the whirlwind of time toward Izola. "Bring him over, Chase!"

Trip nods. "Bas! Bas! Help me carry him!"

Grazer fights to get to the two other men, then grabs a hold of Izola's other arm. Three of the agents come running as fast as they can while avoiding flying debris and coils, lifting the unconscious Taro by the legs.

If Mom is right, we may have a chance. I throw one last look at Kieran, willing him to understand it will get worse. He gives me a curt nod, before his eyes roll back again, and it's all I need.

Taking one last deep breath, I let go of the last bit of restraint I held up—the last bit of a barrier intended to give us a chance to stay alive. Instead, I focus on opening myself up, on drawing in as many coils from him as I can. I need power.

A loud, choked gasp breaks from Kieran as he stumbles forward, taking me with him—but we don't let go, we don't fall. I call to the coils like they call to me and they obey, assaulting Kieran, penetrating into him to get to me—but at a price. What the coils did to him on the outside, they're doing to me on the inside. The more they pass through me, the more of my life force they take with them.

"It's too much," Chase yells, his words being ripped from his lips the moment he forms them. "You have to let go, Nonie! It'll kill both of you! *Please!*" His last word is as pleading as mine was a few minutes ago as they drop Izola in front of me.

But I can't let go. He knows that. He just doesn't want to accept it. We let go, everything collapses. This way, we have a chance. *They* have a chance. We need to get that bracelet to stop tearing everything apart before we can start fixing the Maelstrom.

My body contorts on its own accord, twisting in a seizure. Kieran is limp behind me. I don't dare to look. The pressure inside my chest rises and rises to true bone-crushing levels as I feel something break inside me, something that I'm sure shouldn't be broken. Can't breathe. Can't—

Can't do… anything.

I choke on my next breath. Just… can't…

Chase was right, it's too much. It's killing us too fast for me to destroy the bracelet.

My eyes roll back into my skull, and when I have them under control again, everything's even more blurry—or wait, no, that's from the Maelstrom wreaking havoc. Everybody's movements seem sluggish, with the same motion artifact Izola had when he directed the timelines. Mom. Chase. The Judge. Tinn—

No, wait. I blink.

Tinn's movements look sharp, not blurry.

I blink again.

The air around Tinn is calm, no wind, no debris, not blurry, like when—

Somewhere in the depth of my mind a memory stirs, something important, something I know.

*Koll in the Realm—how the coils avoided him, and when he touched me— And the clefts we saw, the Realm—*

Another wave of energy crashes into me. I grunt as liquid heat spreads on my insides, like fire.

Not good.

"Move!" Somebody yells, then screams right after. "The ground is falling apart! Sh—"

*Focus. Focus.* I squeeze my eyes shut. I need to focus, I need to remember. It's important, I can feel it is. Clefts. Koll. The Realm—

The Realm!

The. Realm.

For one teeny-tiny moment, hope rises as I force my eyes to open wide. "Tinn," I whisper.

Mom, suddenly by my side, bends down. "What did you say?"

"Tinn," I croak. "I need… the Essken." He's my only chance to get through this. "The Realm—"

"Honey, what—" Confusion colors her voice.

"The Realm." Tinn's slightly artificial voice is calm amidst the storm. When he came to stand next to me, I don't know. I blink— And he's gone, popped out of our plane of existence before I can explain. Disappointment hits, hard, snuffing out the bit of hope, though looking at what's going on, I can't fault him for leaving, for getting himself to safety.

But at least one of us will survive this mess.

"Honey, I know it hurts, but you've got to try." Mom lays her hand on my shoulder, and that simple touch, so gentle amidst all this chaos, destruction, and violence, helps me remember what we're fighting for. She squeezes my shoulder. "You can do it. You and Kieran *both* can do it."

Chase lifts the Taro's arm up for me to reach. "I wish you didn't have to do this," I read off his lips, he's speaking too low to be heard over the noise of the wind.

Still, I give him the hint of a devil-may-care smile. It's all I can muster as I reach out with a shaky hand, wrapping my fingers around the bracelet, pushing the doubt away.

It will work.

It must.

We can hold on to life long enough.

Then, I focus on sending all the energy I can into that bracelet. The relief that comes with letting go, with releasing all that contained energy is momentous.

Mom and Chase yelp out and jump back as bolts and bolts of temporal energy shoot into the Taro's bracelet. I channel what I can get through Kieran into the bracelet, willing it to zip up like I helped the coils unite again. It warms under my palm, first glowing softly, then brighter and brighter, in a harsh orange.

Some inner warning system has me withdraw my hand before part of the bracelet turns to liquid, molten metal dripping onto the Taro's arm and onto the floor, and it falls off his body. Smoke wafts from the unconscious man's blistered and charred wrist, the stench nauseating.

"Yes!" An excited squeal comes from my mom. "You did it, honey, you did it!" She squeezes my shoulder once more, giving the remains of the bracelet a quick shove with her foot. "Keep it away from Izola, Trip. And keep Izola away from Nonie whenever he wakes up!"

"My pleasure." Trip and Grazer grab Izola by the feet and drag him away from us. I only peripherally notice his head bounces around on the floor, because my job isn't done; must get that rift to close.

Calling on my First Sense once more, I throw everything I have into fixing that rift. Now we stand a chance. Every little last bit of energy I can scrape together I use, even though it's not much anymore. My body feels like it's vibrating, or maybe that's the ground, I can't tell. A myriad of colors, all twisted into a thick, sparkling strand, shoot from my hand and straight into the center of the rift, first sputtering and spitting, then more steady.

"It's working," Grazer yells out, "they're fixing it!"

Through the haze and dizziness threatening to pull me under it dawns on me he's right: the energy shooting out from me is pulling the chasm's edges closer together, like a super magnet. Fewer and fewer coils break off from it, but they all find their way to Kieran, and therefore to me.

"You got this, Nonie." My mom's voice is a lifeboat in the chaos surrounding us, keeping my mind afloat and from going under, from going dark. "You got this!"

I blink hard to make sense of what I'm seeing. Without the bracelet countering my efforts, the rift has narrowed by at least two meters. Still a long way to go, but finally it's closing.

It's closing.

That's much better than I thought I could do, given I'm running close to empty. My vision blurs and clears, little black flecks floating everywhere. I blink again, but the movement only makes me dizzy. For a long, scary moment, everything turns black and quiet, so, so quiet. Problem is, when the noise hits me again full force, I can't say whether

I was out for a second or a day.

Can't breathe that well either, and neither can Kieran. His breath is harsh, with a stridor, like mine. I don't think I'm getting any oxygen in, it doesn't feel like it. Woozy. Definitely woozy. My frame wobbles, but I push my shoulders back. I got this.

I got—

My vision blacks out again, longer.

No, I don't think I got this.

The screams get louder, more urgent. More panicky.

"It's growing again!"

"Move! Move! *Move!*"

"Get away from the rift, go the f—!"

Pain knifes through me at a level I never experienced, yet I don't let go of Kieran. To the contrary, I grip him tighter, with all my might, as his fingers begin to relax in my hands. For a moment I wonder why he would let go, but then he sinks to one knee, face pale, ashen, eyes staring straight ahead.

Screams surround us.

"These things—ow! They're everywh—Ow! Holy Sun—"

"Move everybody back! It's advancing! *Move*, people!"

My heart cramps in a painful spasm completely unrelated to the coils as Kieran falls down onto his other knee, upper body still upright, but only barely so, swaying. His gaze is losing focus, breath coming out short—

He's dying.

I realize it the moment my knees give in and I sink onto them next to him. Can't stay standing. Too hard.

Looks like I'm dying, too.

And here I thought we might've stood a chance.

Breathing is an effort I'm not sure I can sustain. Everything turns blurry around me, no matter how often I blink, but blinking is also hard. The pain on my skin from all the coils is nearly as bad as the pain in my core. Part of me realizes that must be what it feels like when your cells are disintegrating, this ripping, melting sensation of falling apart, but I can't stop it. I can't keep it together. Not much is left that I understand. Not where I am. Who I am. What's happening. I only know one thing: I cannot let go of the hand I'm holding, if I did, people would die.

I want to breathe in, but my body doesn't obey my orders.

So dizzy.

So cold.

So weak.

My fingers loosen around the hand I'm holding. Their bones must be fused with lead. Heavy.

Must grip tighter, I know that, but the darkness is so tempting. So peaceful.

A voice calls to me, but it sounds so far away, and I can't really make sense of it. Screams get louder. More desperate, maybe surprised. On some level, I know that isn't good, but I can't understand why or what's happening. My heart stumbles. Pauses. Takes another stuttering beat. I fall forward, fingers slipping from Kieran's—

Somebody catches me at the same time as a hand, covered in a hard, cold metallic glove, covers mine over Kieran's, keeping them connected. Out of nowhere, an avalanche of energy releases inside of me, a burst of power so strong my spine bows backward.

"We got you," says a voice, sounding the slightest bit mechanical. "Everybody, *now*!"

Somebody touches my shoulder with a heavy, cold hand. Another metallic-feeling hand holds onto my other shoulder. My arm. My back. My legs. And that energy… it cranks it up.

"Everybody, move, move! Make room, come on, people!" Chase? Was that Chase? His voice was so close—

A little, tiny spark of light dances in front of my inner eye. Another one. One more. Another hand touches me, on my lower back—and this time it's obvious, even to me in my half-lucid state. Not even a half second after its contact, the sensation of falling apart lessens some more and I feel… less dead.

As if somebody had injected adrenaline into it, my heart jumpstarts into a faster rhythm, regular, strong, not skipping any beats. I suck in a long, deep breath. Forcing myself out of that darkness, that mental void and resting place, is a victory of epic proportions. Vision comes back like somebody had dialed up that dimmer. Awareness, too, likely body and mind were being patched up, stitch by stitch.

A gasp breaks free when the extent of the help we're receiving becomes clear to me.

Kieran and I are surrounded by Essken. Dozens and dozens of Essken stand, crouch or stretch around us, all one arm extended and one hand either touching Kieran or myself. Behind them, even more Essken do the same to their brethren, with more behind them supporting them. Overall, there must be close to a hundred, as many as will fit into this small, mostly fallen-apart space, and the chaos around us calms wherever they stand.

All the others—Mom, Grazer, Chase, Zio, Magona, Sheridan, the judge, even the FBTI-agents—are somewhere in the middle of the pack, eyes wide, chests heaving up and down, some of them swaying, their movements still blurred and sluggish.

Kieran's grip on my hand tightens and I suck in a deep breath, for the first time in minutes feeling it carries oxygen. The tiniest smile possible brings a corner of my lip to curl. Tinn got it. He got it, and it's working! The Essken are stabilizing us, knitting together our insides where they'd been torn apart by the K'Zees. It's exactly what we needed.

The coils wiggling free from the edges of reality keep on shooting into Kieran at true lightning speed, giving him an otherworldly glow. The amount of coil energy coming in from him to me is insane, but not as bad as I would've expected, not as bad as it should've been—thanks to the Essken's power boost.

Focusing all my available energy, I use it to flex my First Sense, like a muscle. My stomach tightens as the swirl of energy inside comes close to overwhelming me, but I won't let it.

If we fail, everything dies. The bracelet is gone, but the rift can still destroy reality as we know it, but with the Esskens' support we stand a fighting chance.

No time to lose. None of the humans and Magellans look much

better than we do under the attack of the coils. Mom is beyond pale, dark circles under her eyes, as she is holding on to an Essken. Chase's eyes roll back. Zio sways so hard, I expect him to fall any second.

No, there's indeed no time to lose.

With a roar, I welcome the energy inside my body and will my First Sense to weave it together. The stream of temporal energy shooting from my left hand thickens, swirling and glittering, as it enters the rift.

One of the agents faints.

Another one.

Mom sinks to her knees, eyes squeezed shut, face scrunched into a mask of agony.

The beam of energy stutters, but I keep it steady.

And it's working.

The edges of the rift sparkle and move closer together, closer, closer—

With a bang and flash of light, they reunite, and everything turns dark.

# Chapter Twenty –

# Change of Perspective

Hearing comes back first.

Harsh, heavy and fast breath sounds fill the air. Gasps. A few whispered curses. Fragments of sentences.

"They're alive. Incredible." Zio? Somebody else chokes on a chopped inhale. Chase?

Next, sensation comes back online. The ground beneath me is hard and cold, and *ow*, my whole body stings and burns, like I was hit by lightning.

*Izola. The temporal cleft. The timelines being destroyed—*

With a gasp I open my eyes and look straight up into Chase's strikingly blue ones.

"Hey there, savior of time as we know it." Could be my blurry vision, but despite the grin on his face, his eyes look teary. "Zio tells me all your cellular decay is reversed and you're as good as new, even though you don't look it right now, no offense." He grimaces. "How 'ya feeling?"

How am I feeling? "Fried," I mumble. Everything burns and stings, throbs and cramps, redirecting ninety percent of my mental functions to pain control—so much, I almost don't feel the twitch of fingers in my hand. Almost. Some ingrained sense of prioritization, of recognition, overrides the pain, especially when the twitch happens again.

I look to the side fast as I can and get rewarded by a wave of sharp stings and dizziness, but also by a sight so beautiful, it strips the constricting bands of sorrow off my soul and gives it wings instead. Lying next to me, his chest heaving up and down in irregular choppy breaths, is Kieran, unfocused eyes barely open, his hair disheveled and a mess.

That sight… Despite my thoughts being fuzzy and my body sore as—well, badly, understanding dawns that it's over. That we made it, against all odds.

Kieran blinks, his gaze sharpening and finding mine. A slow smile tugs on his lips. "Hey," he whispers.

I roll onto my side, like he is. "Hi."

So many emotions reflect in his eyes, probably the same as for me. Surprise. Wonder. Love.

"We're still here." The apple in his throat moves up and down. "We're still here." He glides his thumb across the back of my hand.

"We are. Thanks to the Essken," I whisper back. Without their help, their support, we wouldn't have survived, we might not even have closed the rift. Even if we did, we wouldn't have survived to tell the tale. Whatever they did—and I'm sure Zio is going to be all over that research—it saved us and fixed us.

I have no idea who moves first. Heck, I don't even know if I can move—but from one moment to the next, Kieran's arms are around me, and mine around him. Never has he felt more wonderful than right in this very moment. His wide shoulders, the bit of his scent reaching me over the ozone-y smell of the room. The way his chest moves with each rough breath, or his heart hammers against his rib cage so hard, it's bruising mine. Kieran nuzzles his nose close to the little hollow behind my ear.

"It's over," I whisper into his neck. The Temporal War, the threat of total destruction of reality. It's over.

Kieran holds on to me so tight, I can barely breathe. "It's over," he says, emotion choking his words.

It's over.

It's really over.

And we're alive.

*Alive.*

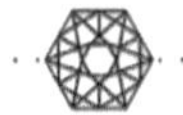

## Confederation Headquarters, 2399

It takes us a good while to let go of each other. Expecting to die and then surviving brings a whole new level of appreciation for the little things, like holding somebody close, feeling their heart beat in their chest, or their embrace. I'm pretty sure time has been restored to its normal flow, but for Kieran and me, it could've stopped for all we know. All that matters is us, is having survived the unsurvivable.

After what could be minutes or hours, Chase comes back to us. No idea where he went after we woke up, but obviously, he gave us some privacy. He lays one hand on Kieran's shoulder, one on mine.

"Ready to face the aftermath?" He nods at the large group of people, all mingling in the fully restored courtroom: at least a hundred Essken, the judge, our people, Sheridan, the agents from before. Everybody is chatting in an animated way, the relief and joy palpable in the air. My gaze is drawn to my mom in a lively discussion with the judge, gesticulating and drawing in the air. That could be me. We have the same gestures—which is so weird, considering I didn't have a chance to learn or copy her behaviors.

Kieran sighs, the sound bringing me back to the matters at hand.

"Do we have to brace for complications?" He releases me from the best embrace I've ever gotten, but keeps holding on to my hand.

"I don't think so, considering you guys just saved not only the world, but… every world, if we understand what happened correctly. There's still the matter of the previous accusation in this timeline, but I feel like the judge is your newest fan at this point."

"Glad we could help her make up her mind. Go big or go home." Kieran works himself to standing, helping me up. "Actually, in our case, go big *and* go home. Because we *are* going home, right?" He looks at me, one eyebrow raised.

I nod. "We're so going home. And with our minds unaltered, thank you very much. I doubt that or keeping us here would be on the table now." It better not be.

Mom looks over to us, a wide, elated smile crossing her face when she sees me up and standing. Touching Judge Alberti by the shoulder, she says something to her, then nods in my direction. With a few long strides, she hurries over to us and wraps me in a tight embrace.

"You are the most amazing person I have ever met, and I can't wait to spend more time with you."

A jolt of happiness shoots through me, such an unusual sensation after what we just went through, it takes me a split second to recognize it as such. Then though… then I bask in it. I beam at my mom. "I can't wait to tell Dad you're alive. He—"

I let my voice trail off as Mom's smile falls and morphs into something else: guilt.

No way. No way in the name of the universe. "He knows," I whisper. "Are you kidding me? He knows?" He knew all these years, and all I got was a sentence about my mom here and there that I basically had to beg for?

Cheeks flushing, Mom rubs my upper arms. "I'm sorry. Yes, yes, he knew, but… it's complicated. I was a secret, as you know. We—" She stops herself. "Actually, that's your dad's story to tell. I just want you to know that I'm sorry, more than sorry, we didn't get to spend those years together. And I hope…" Tears shine in her eyes. "I hope you won't let the fact we had to keep secrets ruin it."

I open my mouth and snap it shut. Old me might've been deadly offended and hurt, but this new me, the one who accepted dying for the greater good, but who regretted not having spent more time with the people she loved, is more mature.

Like, way more.

I give myself the time it takes to draw in a long breath, then release it. "I'm not stupid enough to do that. Doesn't mean I'm not going to have a stern talk with Dad."

Mom chuckles, her relief palpable. "You won't believe how happy it makes me to hear that, but something tells me I wouldn't want to be in your father's skin when you talk to him."

I chuckle back at her. "No, probably not." Although… I'm not mad-mad at Dad, just… regular mad. Disappointed. Like I was an accessory in this family, and not part of it. But again, mature-me will deal with it and live for the future, not the past.

One of the Essken talking to Zio gives a slight bow and comes over to us. It's close to impossible telling them apart by looks only, but I feel this Essken moves differently from Koll, although I couldn't be sure.

"Advisor Okata. Captain Wildason, Lieutenant Thorburn." He bows just like he did with Zio. "I'm happy to see you alive and well. And I'm happy I could bring help."

Tinn. Without hesitation, I step forward and wrap my arms around him. His armor feels cool against my skin, but also soft, which is unexpected. "Thank you, Tinn." A lump forms in my throat, a rough one, coming with a whole bunch of emotions.

I swallow hard to get rid of it, then clear my throat for good measure. Still, my voice breaks with the first few words. "Thank you for understanding what I meant, what I needed, and for bringing us help." *The Essken.* I needed not just one, but many of them. And he delivered.

I let go of a deep breath. "We couldn't have done it without you." I was about to die, I know that. That sensation… Losing awareness of my body, of what makes me me… I don't ever want to experience that again. I know I will eventually, nobody lives forever, but I wouldn't mind putting several decades between this event and the next.

Tinn returns the hug, which I guess makes me the first human of my generations to hug an Essken. "It truly was our pleasure, although I don't quite understand what happened."

A short laugh bursts from my throat, and boy, it feels heavenly. "Neither do I, at least not completely, but I have a theory." All those Essken, touching me, touching Kieran, giving us strength. Stabilizing us. Keeping us from falling apart.

"What theory?" My mom widens the circle, as the judge, Zio, and Taro Magona join us. "Always interested in theories." She smiles at me and winks, laying one hand on my shoulder.

I release Tinn from my hug before it becomes awkward. "A theory why the Essken were able to help me stop the rift."

Mom whistles. "I'm all ears."

I shrug and stuff my hands into my pockets. "Well, I connected two things—three, actually. Before the Taro's men took us from the *Hope*'s conference room to here, remember how I said when we were in the Realm and one of those episodes hit, Koll put his hand on me and… it fixed things? I felt better in an instant and the coils went away." Not that I understood at that moment what happened, but, as always, hindsight is 20/20. I should really put that on a shirt or something.

I lift up two fingers, getting to my second point of logical deduction. "And as I said then, before we were so rudely interrupted by the Taro's agents, when we saw the temporal cleft, the Realm wasn't affected by it. At all. It actually repelled the cleft." The darkness racing up toward us, It bounced off the Realm. Didn't bother it at all, even though it was deleting everything else.

"Possibly because, despite being attached to your universe and physics, we are still non-linear by nature, and so is our home," Tinn says. "I could imagine that being the reason why we're not affected. That's what I noticed as your world was falling apart. The chaos calmed down, wherever I went. It appeared that the temporal decay simply didn't apply to me as an Essken, which made me assume more of us could help."

"That was exactly my point number three," I count off my fingers. "Today, you were the calm in the eye of the storm. The world—our world—was falling apart and it didn't phase you. It didn't touch you."

"So, you added one and one and figured the Essken might be able to stabilize you and help you realign the temporal shards," Mom says.

Kieran raises an eyebrow at her. "Temporal shards."

Mom points at him, then me. "That's what I hypothesize they were, the things that needed you to get to Nonie, the loosened fragments of time. I wonder if you're specifically attuned to them, Kieran, maybe because you spent a long time in the Realm. I would also theorize you provided the perfect combination of attraction and stability to the loosened temporal fragments, since they couldn't enter Nonie directly."

"Loosened temporal fragments," Tinn says, wonder swaying in his words. "Time is such a fascinating dimension... We completely underestimated it."

"And I underestimated what a First Sense can do," Mom says. "I don't think we as a people knew it could realign temporal shards."

*Realign temporal shards*—when she says that, it sounds like I took a class somewhere and tried to put my knowledge into action. In truth, everything I did happened on an instinctual level. All I could do was step on the gas or brakes, but the rest was my body's work.

Zio shifts his weight, leaning his upper body forward, attentive. "An interesting theory indeed, Keel. You're postulating those temporal fragments recognized Nonie's temporal sensitivity."

"Correct. I mean, the verdict is still out and I have lots of data to examine, but I might come up with a few new temporal rules." She taps the ring she wears on her right thumb. Then, she shrugs in a sheepish way. "Until we became aware of the threat from the future, I always assumed my research would be published as I worked on it, until somebody smarter than me came up with a better understanding of time. Never did I imagine an assault on the timeline and having to hide myself and my research." She narrows her eyes and gives the judge a questioning look. "You do understand that you-slash-we are not the main timeline, correct?"

"I do understand that now," Alberti answers. "We already are an alteration to the original strand, hard as it is to believe. Another change brought on by Taro Izola that directly influenced our here and now." She shakes her head. "Actually, I should not call him Taro anymore. He will be stripped of that title and brought to justice for the unimaginable crimes he committed, all to get into power. It will take us years to unravel every change he made and every bit of ripple effect coming with it."

"For starters, we have a pretty good overview," Kieran says, still not letting go of my hand. "We're happy to debrief you before we leave to return to our time." The last words are spoken in the same friendly tone as the first, but with a little undertone of a challenge, and the judge reads them correctly.

"That would be much appreciated. I imagine you can't wait to return home and put this behind you. My sincerest apologies for taking you from your native time, accusing you, and even considering altering your minds. We... have a great many things to reevaluate."

Realizing you got a problem is the first step to resolving said problem.

The judge shakes her head, her cheeks pale as the wall. "What he planned, what he used you for... going back and resetting or undoing events..."

Ah, I see the judge has been brought up to speed and detail while Kieran and I were recovering.

She wrinkles her nose. "What he did is nothing short of murder. Attempted genocide when it comes to the Essken."

And all without the slightest bit of remorse, which is the part that shocks me the most. Almost. When I had thought my actions killed a planet full of Quaneez... Yeah. I had issues with that, and I'm happy I did, even though we considered the Quaneez enemies at that point.

I cross my arms in front of my chest. "Isn't it ironic that Izola wanted to kill the Essken people, and without them, *we* would've been the ones to be killed, and all because of his actions? Without the Essken's help, we might not have succeeded. We all would have been gone, while their realm would've been fine." What an advantage when linear time doesn't affect you.

"Proves that fate really has a sense of humor," Zio responds. Taro Magona looks up at him, the hint of a smile tugging on a corner of her lips, if I'm not mistaken.

The judge swallows hard. "And that people and their dedication are more important than technology. That being said, that bracelet of his was quite the powerful piece of technology."

"You should've seen it in action," I say. "He controlled the timelines with it like he was a puppeteer. Lined them up for inspection." To find one he could manipulate easier? Or where he could get better tech?

Horizontal wrinkles appear on Mom's forehead. "They responded to it?"

"Like first-year academy students to their drill sergeant. Until something went wrong and the—the *temporal shards* broke off. That's what started the whole downward spiral to the chasm and near-total destruction. Before that he was quite happy his bracelet was letting him jump without rejection." Sorry not sorry to see his plans fail.

Huffing once, Chase looks at the broken and partially melted piece of metal in his hand. "I'll of course have to defer to the experts, but I think now I understand your theory about staying in the same, altered timeline. Best way for the Taro to live off the outcome of the changes he carried out. Bet this bracelet does it all, control the timelines, keep him tethered to the altered version… Similar to that disk we examined."

Zio tilts his head. "Considering you're claiming time travel gives you headaches, that was a surprisingly insightful comment, and—"

"Thanks, I guess." Chase rolls his eyes, the hint of a smile tugging on his lips.

"… and you are correct, that theory would align with what we found out about the disk that Izola used to help him fulfill his deeds. Both anchored themselves to the newly split-off timeline for which the changes applied," Zio finishes his thought.

"But then, if he transitioned into the timeline he changed, what happened to the other Izola who should've been there?" Chase looks from one of us to the other.

"I don't know." Mom shrugs. "Theoretically, his continued presence could have deleted the timeline's native Izola from existence, but I'll have to have a closer look at what's left from that bracelet to come up with a more sophisticated answer."

"I still cannot understand how he invented the technology for any of this," the judge says, rubbing both hands over her upper arms absentmindedly. "Everything we do is under direct AI- and bio-observation. The amount of research needed…" She shakes her head in disbelief.

I lift and drop one shoulder. "You know the Magellan proverb, *time will teach you*? Well, we think he took that a bit too literally."

Kieran huffs in disgust. "Izola stole what he needed from another timeline. He's smart, but not smart enough to come up with that kind of tech, so he stole it." He gives a quick summary for the judge. "Not that you need my advice for handling him, but I'd recommend focusing on what he stole where. You don't need a surprise visit or attack from the affected timelines."

Yikes. You reap what you sow, and our timeline's Taro didn't exactly leave the best impression with others, I'd say. Coming to think about it, maybe Blue Nonie's idea of a timeline task force is only half bad. Which reminds me. I tap the bone behind my ear. "You also might want to reevaluate these. The only place we saw those temporal blockers was in that exact timeline where Izola was Praetor and the Essken were extinct. Maybe we don't want to go down the same path in any way." Especially with what I assume is stolen tech from that timeline.

The judge's eyes widen. "I will discuss it. It seems we need new laws and an update on our Temporal Rules."

Mom smiles. "I'll leave you a copy. I never go anywhere without them. My invention." She taps her ring, her wedding band—the same design as Dad's, only thinner, throwing a glance at Magona. "And no worries, Taro. Everything on here is triple secured."

"Uh-huh," Magona harrumphs. "It seems to me you have been using employment time for other… projects than direct temporal research." She keeps her face straight, but her tone lacks bite.

Mom shrugs with a smile. "I might have. Happens when you have too much time on your hands without your family."

"Touché," Magona murmurs, her stance a bit odd with her hands loose by her sides. I tilt my head. Am I seeing things or are Zio's and her hands touching? I blink, and Zio has moved his hands behind his back. Yeah, I'm seeing things. After all, I almost died a few minutes ago.

Mom points down to the floor. "Also, at this point, this here is not our future, not our timeline anymore. In ours, we will keep our Izola from becoming a murderous temporal assassin. Correct? Chase?"

Chase lifts both hands. "Not that I'm the authority when it comes to these kinds of decisions, but I would assume we allow the young Izola his normal development without revealing too much of what another version of him did or that we're actually keeping him—and his family, by the way—under observation."

"Spoken like a true defender of peace and freedom." Kieran claps his friend's shoulder. "Another reason I'm glad to be going back home, no offense, Judge."

"None taken, Captain. As I said, we have a lot to re-evaluate."

"And speaking of." I stand straighter, or rather, as straight as I can at the moment. "If we're done here, I'd like to take my team home now." Home sounds fantastic. An eleven on a scale to ten.

"Of course." The judge looks around. "But…"

But? My muscles tighten, as if my body readied itself for a fight out of reflex,

"…but if I could ask you to visit us in a few months of your time maybe? Maybe once the advisor has gained some more knowledge about the bracelet? Since our two timelines will now be split, I don't think we'd be receiving the outcome of the investigation otherwise."

I force my body to relax. A reasonable request, one that I understand and am willing to honor. "From my point of view, I'll be happy to give you an update, unless my temporal advisor," I nod at my mom, "tells me it's against the rules."

Mom squeezes two sides of her wedding band until a small green square is projected into the air about thirty centimeters above it. She pinches it with her fingers and throws it over to the judge, who catches it with the back of her wrist. For a second it lights her skin up green before it… well, before it seeps in. I raise my eyebrows. Okay, that was cool. Maybe PADs and wristPADs are all obsolete a century in the future. Kaytee projected her ID from the back of her hand as well.

Dropping her hand, Mom shakes her head. "This connection between our two times—and as of now, our two timelines—is already present. If you want, the contamination has already happened, in either direction. I don't think a future collaboration and exchange of updates is a problem."

"Then it's settled," I say. "Just please give us a nicer welcome the next time." I look at Sheridan, who blushes.

"Lesson learned," he murmurs, his cheeks reddening under the bruises Kieran gave him.

Alberti brushes over her wrist and flicks something over to Mom with two fingers. "You help us, we help you. I think we all will be more careful from now on. In many aspects."

And in the end, isn't that all we want? Lessons learned, peace upheld, and the bad guy paying the price for his actions.

I for one have no problem to live with that. Emphasis on *live*.

# Chapter Twenty-One -
# Change of Time, Change of Mind

**USEF Hope, Native Time**

The moment I land us back on the *Hope* a weight the size of a boulder falls off me. Not that I was worried-worried, but jumping alone or with one person is one thing, keeping a group of newbies together, another. Not the most difficult jump I've ever done, considering there was no shuttle to jump, like I did twice before. Coming to think about it, no idea how I took the whole *Odysseus* with me on my first and very much accidental jump into the past. Guess I got some mad skills I need to find out more about.

Still, I need to work on giving myself more credit in general. I just brought everybody back into our now, I landed us at the correct time, the correct location *and* standing up, all after almost dying. I should be at least a wee bit impressed with myself. "Mom, Taro, Admiral Grazer, Zio, Chase, Kieran—everybody accounted for." I swipe a drop of sweat from my forehead.

"That was... quite something." Grazer, way paler than normal, tucks his uniform shirt straight at the same second as the *Hope's* internal sensors have picked up on the Setayashi-radiation.

*"Code Magenta. All non-essential personnel return to your quarters. Keep hallways clear. Do not linger in locations other than your post or your quarters. Code Magenta. All non-essential personnel—"*

"It gets better with time," Kieran reassures the admiral. "Not that I'm suggesting you try it."

The older man chuckles. "Thank you, I'll stay clear of anything related to time-jumps. That's your guys' specialty. I'll stick to D-Two." And with that, he lays a hand on Kieran's shoulder. "I'll see you at debrief." He nods at everybody, then exits the conference room as a team of security officers come down the hallway, weapons drawn.

"Good to see the team is prepared," Chase says.

The first security officers scan Grazer, then salute and let him pass. They do the same for us, like a swarm of bees checking us out, and then deciding we're not interesting enough, leaving us in peace.

Chase taps his Hablamate. "Conolly to Bridge."

*"Herron here."*

"You can call off the cavalry, Herron. It's the same people who went missing—" He gives me a questioning glance.

"About an hour ago," I supply in a whisper. I think I timed it pretty well.

"About an hour ago. Your team scanned us. We're good?"

A short pause hovers before Herron confirms, most likely after checking in with his security team. *"That you are, sir. Glad you're back."*

"So are we. What's our status?"

*"About the same. President Thorburn is on his way and will arrive shortly."*

"Understood. Let's set a debrief for us for in three hours right here, in the conference room. Conolly out."

*"Understood, and out."*

Chase taps his Hablamate once more, then gives our group a curt nod. "Adjourned until the debrief. Get some rest, people. Kelia, Taro, we have more than enough guest quarters, I'll have somebody—"

"I will show both of them to their respective quarters," Zio says.

A wicked gleam lights up in Chase's eyes, but he snaps his mouth shut and clears his throat. "Thank you, Zee, that would be fantastic and so very helpful."

"Much appreciated, Admiral." Magona gives a slight bow toward Zio. How she can still look so calm like nothing happened is an absolute mystery to me. My clothes are dirty and torn in several places. I haven't seen my hair, but when I rake my fingers through it, all I feel are knots and chaos. Magona could've missed out on the whole experience and she wouldn't look any different.

Mom lays one arm around my shoulder and squeezes. "I'm so proud of you. You used your First Sense better than anybody I've ever seen, not that I've seen many people knit together the fabric of time. Have you developed Touch yet?"

I tilt my head. "Touch?"

"Some Magellans can get an impression of what the future might bring for an individual by touching them. Like... a foreshadowing. It works best between Magellans. I don't have it, but Zio does."

Zio does—Of course! I even remember him doing it, back at the academy, like after I failed my final drill, the one to rescue Kieran from the Essken bunker, touching me and saying *next time she'll do better* in his prophet-voice. Not an encouragement. A foreshadowing. I—

Oh, holy Sun and Stars, sometimes I'm surprisingly slow. "I do have it," I whisper. "I touched Sheridan, twice, and the first time... it felt like doom, the second, more like confusion." Guess I *really* have some more mad skills to discover.

Another proud look settles on Mom's face. "That's how it starts. Talk to Zio, he can help you control it. I'm so excited to see what other abilities you'll develop. And I'm excited to be part of it, finally," she says, and kisses my temple. I blame the spike of sudden overwhelming feelings for my inability to come up with an adequate—or any—reply. I'm not used to motherly affection, what can I say. By the time I've snapped my mouth closed again, everybody besides Kieran and me is gone.

He takes my hand and weaves his fingers through mine. "You know what sounds good right now?"

"A whole lot of things." I step closer, keeping the hand with our entwined fingers between our chests, but curl the other around his waist as I cuddle into him. "Like, making sense of what just happened? Not having to worry about Sheridan? Or, for that matter, the Temporal War? Destruction of the world and life as we know it?"

His deep chuckle reverberates through his chest and right into my heart. "That for sure, but I was thinking about smaller stuff. Take a shower. Fresh clothing. Food. Uninterrupted, calm sleep."

I smile up at him. "That sounds nice, too."

Lowering his head, he rubs his nose against mine. "Glad you like it, but I wasn't even done with my suggestions."

"No? What was missing?"

"Details, Nonie." He kisses the tip of my nose, then the corner of my mouth. His breath dances over my cheek with his next words, bringing goosebumps to a rise. "Very important details. Obviously, you and I are going to share said shower."

This time, the wave of emotions rushing me doesn't make me speechless. It makes me daring and excited. I glide my hand from his back down to his butt. "I like the way you think."

Kieran gasps when my hand squeezes his rear. "It's, uhh, all about saving water."

"Of course." I press myself harder into him, enjoying the feel of his body against mine.

He swallows audibly. "I think we should rather hurry up."

The laugh that escapes me is light and easy. I think we might actually have a shot at happiness. I place one teasing kiss on his lips, with the slightest bit of tongue, then step away from him, but holding on to his hand. "Then let's not waste any time."

Because we all know even though we can tweak it, we never have enough of it.

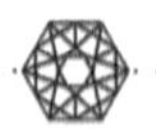

# TIMED OUT



Kieran cups my cheeks with both hands and kisses me. His lips dance over mine as if he was committing their feel to eternal memory. This kiss is different from the ones we shared over the last… how long has it even been? An hour? Two? No idea. Still, this kiss is different. First, Kieran is half dressed in USEF leisure pants, but without a shirt, and I'm only wrapped in my bath towel, my hair still wet. Second, it's not the almost hectic, passionate kiss from before, but more a languid, calm, self-assured version of it. One that says we're going to be around to do that again. A lot.

I glide my palm over his naked chest, circling a finger around the scar under his right clavicle, the one we share. Other people have tattoos to think of one another. We have this. Bit morbid, but I wouldn't change it for the world. It's how I met Kieran. It's how I saved Kieran. Fair to say that without this scar, my life and his would've gone very much differently.

And currently I'm very happy how our lives are going.

A contented sigh breaks from Kieran's throat as he presses his mouth against mine in another soft kiss, again, and then again. When he pulls back, he rests his forehead against mine, keeping my face in his hands. "If I don't let go now, we'll still be here tomorrow. And then there'll be questions and it's going to be very awkward with Chase and Zio."

A grin spreads over my face, together with a blush. "We wouldn't want that," I whisper against his lips. Too parental.

The doorbell rings, and Kieran sighs. "Speaking of the devils. Bet it's Zee or Trip. Can't give a man some peace and quiet." He drops a quick kiss on my forehead and grabs a fresh shirt from the uniform dispenser. "Take your time. I'll be shielding you from their jokes and overprotectiveness for as long as I can." And, with a wink and a smile on his face, he's slipped out of the bathroom, leaving the doors slightly open on air flow mode.

I look after him, a warm, fuzzy feeling in my core. Not only the kiss was different, but so is Kieran. Everything about him felt lighter, more alive. More like *before*. And it makes me a very, very happy camper.

I reach for my standard-issue grey underwear while allowing myself a moment to enjoy this sensation of inner peace and happiness. Of being in the moment.

The doorbell rings again. "Come in," Kieran calls, and the doors swoosh open. "I'll have to get used to you being so polite— Oh."

*Oh?* A jolt of adrenaline shoots through me. The last time we were in our quarters and *oh* happened, Sheridan abducted us—

"That is… unexpected," my dad's voice comes through the gap in the door. "These are Nonie's quarters, are they not?"

*Oh,* indeed.

"Crap," I whisper under my breath. Dad. Of course. Can I fault him for coming here to see me right away? No, not at all, and yes, it makes me happy I'm high on his list of priorities, but man, his timing is awful. And to think a moment ago I considered Zio and Chase too parental. Dad is worse, way worse!

There's a beat of hesitation before Kieran answers. "Well, we decided we'd share."

Pause.

"You're shirtless." Dad says it as if he had just discovered the Earth was indeed flat, with an air of absolute disbelief.

I hear the rustling of fabric as Kieran slides into his shirt as fast as I'm dropping my towel to don my undies and bra, but Dad's tone doesn't sound any more appeased than before, no matter Kieran put on his shirt.

"Where's Nonie?"

"Still in the bathroom. Sir," he says, and boy, is that awkward for about a million different reasons.

"I see," Dad says, reminding me so very much of Blue Nonie's dad when he was in protective mode. I cringe and pull my leisure uniform pants up as fast as I can. Got to rescue Kieran from my dad.

"I must say I'm quite shocked at what seems to have been going on behind my back—"

What? Oh, no. No, no! No way we're going down that route! I abort trying to slip into my shirt, throw it over my shoulder and burst out of the door into the living area before Dad goes all paternal on Kieran. "Excuse me, Dad? Would you mind repeating that?" I stomp over and stop right between the two men and in front of Dad, hands on my hips, glaring at him. The audacity! Hypocrisy! Ugh!

Dad flinches and averts his eyes. "Nonie! You—"

I roll my eyes. "Oh come on! You've seen me in a swimsuit or a bra before, and guess what, so has Kieran!"

Both men squirm, albeit for different reasons. Dad's brows slam down. "Excuse m—"

Enough of that! I'm not beating around the bush anymore, my tolerance for games has been used up thanks to the last months of being a pawn in a war that should never have happened.

I throw up both hands. "Dad, what did you expect? We're bonded!"

"What?" Dad's mouth pops open, just like his eyes. He choke-coughs, then looks over to Kieran. "You're *bonded*?"

I roll my eyes *again*. "Do you need Kieran to confirm what your daughter, clearly the expert in this matter, being a half-Magellan, is saying?"

Dad snaps his mouth shut. "N-no. I'm just..." He sighs and grimaces. "Surprised. Quite surprised. Is that... is that a recent development?"

I keep my hands on my hips and my chin high. "That depends on the point of view. It happened forty years ago, if that's what you want to know. If you're asking if we were bonded already when I saw you last, that's also a yes." Or when I saw him after coming back from the *Pioneer* for the first time, only then I had no idea what that tearing, raw feeling inside my chest meant. It's not like somebody had explained Magellan bonding one-on-one to me at that point, or that it could happen instantaneously, like for Kieran and me. One touch on his bare skin as I was trying my best to keep him safe from the Essken's weapon fire, and *boom.* I wonder if something similar happened to the other Nonies and Kierans, the ones who didn't travel back. Our lives show so many parallels and we, Kieran and me, seem to be such a constant, it could be possible. And life would be so much harder for them, especially in the timeline where Kieran was my mentor.

A shudder runs down my back. Don't even want to think about it.

Dad rubs his scrunched-up forehead, then drops his hand. "You could've said something, Nonie. I'm your *dad*. I feel like I haven't been told the whole story."

Oh, really? Don't I know that feeling! "Neither have I. I guess we both had secrets we were keeping, me about being bonded, you about Mom being alive."

*Zing!*

Dad twitches. That comment hit its target.

For the longest time I don't think Dad takes even a single breath, frozen as he looks. Then, he blinks quickly and slowly turns his head toward me again. "You... you know?"

Giving him *the look,* I nod. "Clearly you haven't been briefed yet, or you would know that Mom is on the *Hope*."

The smallest smile tugs on his lips, almost sheepish. "Honey, I felt that two jumps away from here. I just didn't know that she was officially out." He lays a hand on his chest and taps it.

Of course. Of freakin' course. The Bond. So many things make sense now, knowing that Mom is still alive and their Bond intact. I facepalm myself. "That's why you look so good," I whisper. And he does. Dad's dark circles under his eyes usually make him look like a raccoon after a bar fight. The lines around his mouth tend to be canyons, but today... he looks like he does when he comes back from a trip to Mag-2. I always assumed he got to sleep more away from his regular duties on Earth, but I didn't see what was right in front of my eyes. "And that's why you looked so rested every time you visited Mag-Two." I shake my head as all the puzzle pieces align. "You saw Mom then, didn't you? You saw her every time you went." It hurts saying that, because it happened behind my back. I didn't know Mom was alive. Dad did, and he saw her. He visited her. While I thought she was dead.

Dad deflates. "Yes. I saw her every time. All in secret of course—" He halts. "Do you... do you know what she does?"

I want to come up with a snarky reply, but surprisingly maturity wins. "Yes, I do."

Kieran tugs the shirt off my shoulder and hands it to me. I take the hint, and the shirt, and slip into it, snapping my gaze right back to my dad after pulling it over my head.

"Then you know more than I did for most of our marriage. I only recently got briefed on the full extent of her importance." He blinks and blows out a puff of air. "I should've known that when the Taro mentioned the FBTI recruited you that Kelia would be a part of it, but I guess it didn't click for me. All I knew for the longest time was that her work was beyond secret and we couldn't risk her being seen by anybody. I was on orders not to talk about anything regarding her. Nobody had clearance to know, Nonie. Magona and me, that was it."

Kieran whistles through his teeth, the sound bringing home what Dad *really* said. He literally couldn't talk about her. Whenever I asked about Mom and he said he couldn't talk to me, I assumed it was because it hurt too much. And while I felt for him, it also made me mad. As an adult, he should've been able to get to a point where he could tell me about my mom—and yet he never did.

Now I know why.

I swallow hard. "But you still saw her every time you went." Even if he couldn't talk about it.

"Yes, every time I was on Mag-Two, your mom and I met. Those were the highlights of my trip." Something warm and wholesome lights up in his eyes as his cheeks turn the slightest pink. It's such a boyish look on him... I can't be mad any longer. Not when I know how it feels to be separated from somebody you love, not just because you love them, but because of the stretch or disruption of the Bond. Not when his blush gives away how very much he loved and still loves Mom.

I suck in my lower lip and nod. "I get that. I just..." I shrug and dip my gaze to the floor. "I just would've loved to know she was alive. I kept all our other secrets, Dad. I would've kept this one." Like that I wore a genetic masker, not that I knew the true reason behind it at the time, but I never told anybody. Well, until Kieran, Chase, and Zio. But still. That counts as trustworthy.

"I know you would have, honey, but this… It was bigger than you and I. Than us and her. The only reason I was in on it was because I was luckier than Zio, who wasn't allowed on Mag-Two. But as the ambassador to the Magellan people, I would be on Mag-Two and would've felt her presence. And believe me, Taro Magona was not happy I was in on it. Took her years to relax around me."

I chuckle softly. "I can imagine. And I understand, Dad, it's just… I guess I feel left out. You had years of Mom before me, then met her behind my back, and I… had nothing." I hate that I sound whiny and needy, but my whole childhood and adolescence I hungered for information on my mom. We didn't even have pictures of her—of course now it makes sense, all part of the secrecy, not all *lost in a fire*. No wonder I clung to every little piece of information I could and treasured it beyond belief, even with as little as Dad was willing to tell me.

"Nonie," he says softly. "We both missed you so much every time we met. It felt like we were cheating on you. I wanted to tell you about Mom—"

A sting of sorrow pierces my heart. "And yet you never did." Again: trustworthy, right here.

"But I was going to, I had gotten clearance. Probably Magona foreseeing you becoming a member of the FBTI. Remember a few months ago, before you left on that mission Mashaule put you on, to retrieve the plants to cure the Reptilian Flu?"

Before I was thrown in the past and met Kieran? "Uhh, yeah?"

"And remember I told you I brought you something from Mag-Two? That little box?"

*Fresh import from Mag-Two. Special order for you, Nonie.*

Holy Universe, yes, I do! "That was—"

He nods. "In there was a data chip, coded for your eyes only."

I swallow hard. My mouth is dry, for whatever reason. "What was on it?"

Dad smiles his proud-smile. "The exact same thing I carry with me every single day." He lifts his left hand and touches his wedding band with his thumb and index finger. "Display file alpha-one, authorization Thorburn tango-tango-beta-fifty-five."

Without any acoustic acknowledgement, a projection pops up about thirty centimeters above the ring, displaying a picture of Dad and my mom, both quite a bit younger. Mom actually looks kind of exhausted with circles under her eyes, a bit sweaty, and hair plastered to her forehead. Kieran makes a soft aww-ing sound, and only then do I realize what the true biggie in this picture is: the baby in Mom's arms, umbilical cord cut and clamped off, face more purple than pink, but staring into the camera with wide eyes.

My jaw drops. "That's... that's me!" That's me, right after birth! What a monumental picture for somebody who was told their mom died during childbirth.

A nostalgic look crosses his face. "That's itsy-bitsy you. But that's literally only the beginning of what I wanted to show you." Dad winks and squeezes the ring once more. "Run file."

The baby holo gets replaced by another one with Mom and Dad, heads leaned against another, a holo-emitter between them, and...

"Me. That's... also me," I say, blinking. "Baby-me." Not much older than a few months or so, and the way the holo-emitter is positioned, it looks like I'm in Mom's arms. Had I seen this picture a mere few days ago, I would have needed to check if I ended up in a different timeline.

Dad smiles. "Correct."

The next one pops up, Mom and Dad on a couch I don't recognize, both looking down on the ground, where holo-me in a horrible green onesie is trying her best at crawling.

The next one: Mom, Dad, both with a proud smile. Plus a holo of me, walking, an even greater look of pure pride on my face.

Next: Mom and Dad at a dinner table, Mom holding a spoon with orange puree just like the one around holo-me's mouth.

Then, Dad running behind Mom, and Mom behind holo-me on a tricycle, her arms stretched out wide as if she wanted to catch me.

Emotion clogs my throat. Holo after holo the same pattern repeats, only that in each picture the me displayed is a tad older than in the one before. Seeing us all together... it does something to me. I never expected to know my mom. And when I found out she was alive, I felt deceived, somehow. Left out. But maybe that's not the whole story. Maybe they felt left out, too. Mom didn't get to meet me either and only had Dad's holos and stories to go by. Dad could never tell me about Mom. Truth is, we all missed out.

All those happy family pictures Blue Nonie had in her home come back to me. That's what we didn't have. Time together. Building memories and stories together.

Another holo pops up, this one with Mom and Dad making the same silly face that holo-me is pulling off, and that's when my self-control breaks. I was wrong. They were building memories, just in a different way—the only way possible.

A sobbing laugh breaks from my throat. "Dad...! That's..." I sniffle, then sob-laugh again. "I don't know what to say. You guys took family pictures."

"Every time I went," Dad says in a quiet, almost reverent voice. "We couldn't do it the traditional way, so..." He shrugs, his voice dropping to a whisper. "It was all we got, and I knew you were missing out, Nonie. I felt guilty for seeing your mom when you had no idea she was alive. She felt horrible. This, taking pictures quote-unquote together at least made us feel like we were planning for a future with you, and not only living our lives parallel to yours. And... we wanted you to have something from those years, something to look at, to feel included by."

Ignoring the next holo—me sticking my tongue out through the gap of my missing front teeth and Dad carrying Mom in his arms like a bride—I burst forward and wrap my arms around my dad's torso.

"Thank you, Dad. I love it." It makes me feel like part of a family of three I never knew I had. No, we don't have Blue Nonie's wall of family photos, but maybe mine are even better, because they show what our family is made of. Fate pushed you apart? Screw that, we're still a family, against all odds.

I like that very much.

Dad wraps his arms around me and rests his chin on top of my head. "Ah, daughter of mine. I wanted to prepare you and not throw your mom's existence at you as a surprise. I wish I had been there when you two met for the first time." His chest heaves up and down heavily.

I lift my head off his chest. The time for secrets is over, I guess. "Technically speaking, you were."

"No, I was still on Earth—"

Pulling away from him, I step back. "Well… This wasn't the first time we met." There, I said it, and I'm not even counting the hut on Alpha Rubrum, because while I saw them, they didn't see me.

Dad's eyes widen. He squeezes the ring to stop the projection, as if he couldn't deal with the distraction at the moment. "You— What?"

I give Kieran a look and a nod. He gets what I mean right away, reaching over the couch and retrieving the hat Mom gave him back at the Gemini-Colony.

"I believe this belongs to you. It traveled through time and universes a bit, so I apologize it's not in as good a condition as when I received it, but at least it made it back." He hands the hat to Dad, who takes it with a look of disbelief on his face.

"My old academy debate team hat," he whispers, turning the hat and looking inside. "With my initials on it. I thought I lost it. It's truly mine. How— When—?" He looks up at Kieran. "*How?*"

"The Golden Star of Combat on the Gemini-Colony. You and Kelia went. And well, so did we."

"Actually, I went there twice," I throw in, just for good measure and fun to see the look of confusion grow on Dad's face.

"You— Oh. *Oh.* You both travelled back there when—?"

I nod. "Yes. When Sheridan was chasing us. I jumped us to a time and location I had time-traveled before to hide our temporal signature."

"Right." Dad takes a deep, controlled inhale as Kieran points at the hat again.

"Kelia was there and gave me your hat to help hide my identity, given that I also was on stage and accepting the medal at that time. She said she had felt us thanks to her First Sense."

Slowly nodding, Dad turns the hat in his hands, a look of wonder on his face. "That's why she snatched my hat. Should've listened to my gut when she tried to blame me. That was my favorite hat, I couldn't believe I lost it."

Kieran grins. "Pleasure to bring it back. Sir." That tagged-on *sir* holds the same awkwardness like before, and this time even Dad picks up on it—now that he isn't quite so enraged to find Kieran in my quarters, that is.

He stills his hands, then looks up at Kieran. "I behaved a bit like a cliché father when I came in, didn't I?"

Kieran opens, then closes his mouth before he takes a deep breath. "Sir—"

Dad waves a hand. "Let's stop that right here and now. You don't need to call me sir. You don't need to address me as Admiral either. I'd be surprised if they didn't promote you up the food chain anyway, but either way… half the time, I still want to call *you* sir. All my life in active duty you were either my superior, or I remembered you as such. And now you're back and younger than me, which is quite confusing to align with my perception of your rank in relation to mine." A small smile plays around his lips. "But to be honest, that's not the most confusing thing to align with my perception." His glance dances over to me. "You're still my baby. My little one. I know you're an adult woman and graduate of the Academy, but in my mind you're still this little thing needing my protection. Especially after everything you've been through."

I cringe. Let's not go all the way into even more I territory, please. "Dad—"

"No, let me. Please. Long story short, I was caught off-guard. I didn't expect to find a man in my daughter's quarters, especially my first captain and the man I owe so much to. But that's not all that caught me off-guard. The whole last year did, more or less. I thought knowing that Nonie would be able to travel through time would prepare me, but it only gave me a false sense of security, as if I knew what would happen."

He huffs. "I displayed a level of naivety unbecoming of an admiral, and that applies to this situation as well. I was unprepared, and it showed. I felt like I was late to a party everybody else—" He pauses, then cocks his head. "Who knew of the two of you? Zio? Chase?"

We exchange a glance, and it's enough for Dad.

"Oh, great," he groans, "so I was the only one out of the loop."

I chuckle. "Actually, Dad, they were the only two *in* the loop."

Dad sighs theatrically. "As if that'd make me feel better. I've had hundreds of conversations with them, and never did they even hint at what I was unaware of."

"Which shows you how trustworthy they are." Right?

Dad nods slowly, then lays both hands on my shoulders. "Very true. So, let me correct what I botched when I came in. Nonie, I'm so happy you're back in one piece. I haven't heard the full report yet—obviously—but I know that without you we wouldn't be here. Pride doesn't even come close to what I'm feeling. I want to say you got all this talent from me, but we both would know it's a lie." He winks and rubs both hands over my shoulders before he turns to Kieran.

"And the same goes for you. Without you, we wouldn't be here. You saved the universe, but most importantly, you watched out for my baby girl—who doesn't need to be watched over, I know," he adds quickly when he sees me take a deep breath in. He knows me well.

"So, let's make this official." He holds out his hand. "I'm Tom."

Kieran takes it without the slightest moment of hesitation, a wide smile on his face. "Kieran."

As they shake, something passes between them, something more than between future father- and son-in-law, something speaking of years of service together, of loss, of sacrifice, of hurt, but also of something more positive, like overcoming, new beginnings, and, most importantly, hope.

Dad looks at me, then Kieran, as if for the first time he didn't have a weight pressing down on his soul. Light. Open. Accepting. "Welcome to the family, Kieran."

# Chapter Twenty-Two -

# Epilogue

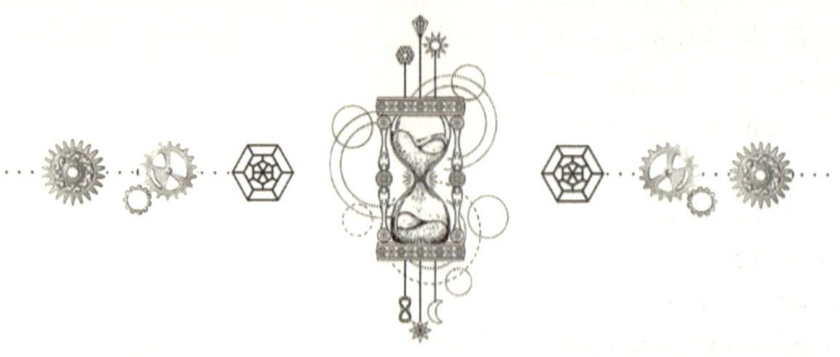



". . . because like you I have lost friends and family to the war," Kieran says, the directional microphone picking up on every word with precision, despite him straying away from the podium and walking back and forth across the stage, engaging the audience and making eye contact wherever he can.

And that's a lot of eyes to connect with.

I've been to the USEF Headquarters once, with Dad, when I was little, but at that point everything seemed big. Now I know how big translates into numbers. This auditorium, funnily enough named the Wildason Auditorium, seats five thousand people. It should've been named the Wildason Stadium, if they asked me. Usually, special graduation or medal ceremonies are held in here. If the *Pioneer* hadn't been so deep in space, Kieran would've gotten his Golden Star of

Combat in this very auditorium, and not on Gemini. It's the perfect location for any big, transmitted event, like for today's address to all of Earth: fantastic sound system, lights, and automated cameras to follow his every move. Helps to have holo-projections of Kieran throughout the auditorium, so that everybody can see him well—see the sincerity in his expression, feel he means what he's saying. The better this audience reacts, the better his ideas and opinion will stick with the people of Earth watching on their devices at home, or wherever they might be, Dad said, and right he is. We want to set a good mood, an excited, positive atmosphere, not one of doubt, fear, or impending doom.

We've been there, done that.

Halting in the center of the stage, Kieran pauses, and a smile grows on my face. Can you tell he's done this before? Pausing for emphasis and to give the remote camera operators time to zoom in on him? Check.

He takes a deep, slow breath. "I told you my story of forty years in the Realm with the Essken. I've told you about my despair and how long it took me to understand what was going on, how they were trying to communicate with me, just like we were looking for a way to speak to them."

Well. Some of us. Others were more trigger-happy, but details-shmetails, I get what he's going for.

"What I haven't told you yet, is why I'm thankful for those forty years in the Realm, and no, it's not just because I kept my youthful look, for whatever scientifically impossible reason. Not bad for a guy in his sixties." He rakes a hand through his hair and winks, getting exactly the laughs from the audience he was going for without having to go into the details of the nature of the Essken Realm. Some secrets are better kept, well, secret.

"Joking aside, I'm truly thankful for those years, no matter my personal losses. I now have the opportunity to be the ambassador between our two people and to help you understand the Essken want peace, just like we do." He begins to pace again. "Our two people are different in almost every aspect. How we are built, how we communicate, where we live. But we are the very same when it comes to core values. We love our families. We want to live in peace."

Throughout the room, a holo-projection of the day fated to make history pops up: Kieran, shaking the hand of an Essken. That alone is momentous enough for obvious reasons, but I tend to think the combined impact of all the little details in this picture makes me break out in goosebumps every time I see it.

First, the look of peace and joy on Kieran's face. It speaks of a level of comfort interacting with the Essken humans didn't think possible up to now.

Second, the three humans and four Essken standing in a semi-circle around the two handshakers. Chase, Zio, and my dad are wearing the same relieved and hopeful smile Kieran is, and even though nobody in the assembled audience today can read the Essken very well yet, they'll understand on a subconscious level they too look relaxed. It's something about their body posture translating into non-aggression. It works for us humans.

Third, the whole scene is serene and calming as only a sunrise on K55 can be. Helps to have a double-star and an atmosphere rich of fluctuating gasses reacting to those double-sun beams. Everybody looks as if they were surrounded by fine golden glitter, and it makes for a magical photo.

I must say, I did well when I took it.

A small grin tugs on the corners of my lips. Kind of funny how a day loaded with the pressure of settling a decades-long war between two people turned out to be the easiest task in a while. Compared to our wild chase through time and timelines without having a clue what we were doing, talking to the Essken was easy. After all, both Kieran and I had done it before. Also, while I'm sure there are timelines where something went wrong, it still helped to know the odds of us succeeding in bringing peace were on our side.

Now all we need is USEF confirming it.

Kieran pauses for a moment, looking at the image displayed throughout the room, then back at the audience. "My job description as captain of the *Pioneer* has always been to seek out new allies, to find new species and make new friends, so that we could grow with and from them and build a better society with input from many sources. Diversity makes us stronger. I couldn't do so without Admiral Zio Upinga, my best friend before I entered the Realm, and still the voice of reason in my ear, forty years and many changes later. The Essken can be friends to the human race, like the Magellans, like everybody else we have encountered. We only need to give them a chance. We need to give *us* a chance."

Coming to a standstill in the center of the stage, he looks straight into the audience, hands crossed behind his back, shoulders straight. Oh boy. I know which picture of today is going to make it into the history books, and not because I've been checking out the future, because I haven't. I'm behaving. Somewhat, at least.

"Before the vote on how to proceed with the Essken, I want to clarify one thing. I'm not asking you to forgive. I'm not asking you to forget. What I am asking of you is to look beyond the loss and the hurt to a future of understanding and peace. I'm asking you to give our future a chance. Thank you."

Thunderous applause booms through the room, whistles, yells— people jump up, clapping their hands and stomping their feet like after a rock concert.

Even here, behind the stage, people are applauding with the widest grins and proudest looks on their faces, just like me.

For at least five minutes, Kieran bows and waves to the audience, shaking hands with people reaching up from the first rows or coming down the aisles. Eventually, he retreats back, still bowing and waving until he's slipped behind the blackout curtain at the wings of the stage.

At least five people want to storm him right there and then, two admirals, my dad, the stage manager, and some other lady I don't know, but Kieran ignores them all by turning to me.

"You think that was enough? You think it worked?" He wraps his arms around me and pulls me close, nuzzling his face into his favorite spot, the crook of my neck, exhaling for what feels like an eternity.

And that would be the pressure of expectation, of assuring peace, leaving his body.

Holding him tight, I nod into his embrace. "It was, and it did. If that doesn't convince the skeptics, I don't know what will. They will vote yes for the Peace Accords. Pretty impressive last sentence." *I'm asking you to give our future a chance.* Even heavier in meaning knowing what we know about the future.

"I improvised." He shrugs and pulls away from me. "I felt it needed to be said."

"Agreed." Completely. I don't get why people want to know the future. It's a burden most of the time. Knowing what could go wrong, how not making peace with the Essken could turn out… It's a pressure weighing heavily on Kieran and me, and therefore on this very speech, the perfect definition of a Divergence Point.

Our future hinges on the vote cast tomorrow.

Kieran lets go of me, but keeps on holding on to my hand, no matter the admirals, my dad, and other people swarming him. Once they all have congratulated him, slapped his shoulders, made enough jokes, they let him be, and we can finally leave.

Exiting through the backstage door into the hallway, we turn left toward the nearest Demat area. Most people have left already, thanks to the many newly installed mass-Demat stations all over the facility. They get up to a hundred people in one transition to different locations, which is pretty impressive.

We haven't even made it around the first bend when fast steps approach us from behind. "Captain!"

Kieran jerks to a halt and turns on his heels, tension in his body.

An older, grey-haired man approaches us, dressed in a USEF gala uniform, fleet admiral's pips on his collar. That in and by itself isn't unexpected, after all, ninety percent of USEF's high brass were present today, but that specific person… definitely unexpected.

Kieran's grip on my hand tightens. "Chocho… Fleet Admiral Chocho."

Chocho extends a hand. "Good to see you again, sir." A genuine smile lights up his face as they shake hands. "I heard the speech you gave. You haven't lost your talent, if I may say so. It's good to have you back. It's good to see you happy." He gives me a nod, then lowers his voice to barely audible as his smile widens, true warmth in it. "It's good to see you, too. You haven't changed a bit."

I keep my face blank. "I don't know what you're talking about, sir. I don't think we've met at the academy." The hint of a smile crosses my face, enough for him to know what I mean.

He chuckles. "My bad then, apologies. You reminded me of somebody I knew."

We both grin at each other, in on the secret. That reminds me though to have somebody, probably Chase, re-emphasize with the former bridge crew of the *Pioneer* that I'm still top secret.

Chocho focuses on Kieran again. "I couldn't believe my eyes and my ears when you spoke to the fleet a few weeks ago. Just like the last years hadn't happened." He realizes what he said and flinches. "Apologies, sir. I understand those decades weren't easy for you."

"No offense taken, and I don't think you need to call me sir, Fleet Admiral."

"And you definitely don't need to address me by my title, Captain. You used to call me Leonardo, I don't see a reason to change that. Old habits die hard. You're my first captain. Your actions influenced my career like nobody else's. My life. Heck, you officiated my and Suzie's wedding."

Only because I know Kieran so well do I pick up on the subtle shift in his body language, how his shoulders slump forward the slightest bit.

Suzie.

Chocho's wife dying during a Quaneez attack has been weighing heavily on Kieran. It might've been a big factor contributing to his depression before he went into the nebula—that and hearing the Essken voices in his dreams, courtesy of the quote-unquote Quaneez mind torture and attempt at communication.

"I also was the one who gave the order for the attack that got Suzie killed," Kieran says, straightening up as if he was willing to bracing himself for Chocho's response.

A faint look of longing crosses over the older man's face. "Ah, Suzie," he says, nodding to himself. "It's been what, forty years? I've lived my life." He pauses. "You know, I never understood how heavy the responsibility of every life on board a USEF vessel weighs on the captain until I got my own command. And when I had to tell the parents of the very first ensign we—I—lost during the war, I kept on thinking back to when you brought me the news."

Kieran closes his eyes for one long second, throat working on a hard swallow.

Chocho's gaze lifts off to somewhere behind us, or rather, to forty years behind us. "How I freaked out when I understood, when I truly understood what you said. How I yelled and screamed and ended up on the floor, bawling. And do you know what I remember most?" His gaze finds Kieran's.

"No," he whispers.

"I remember you being there for me, like a rock. My life was crumbling and falling apart, but you were there to catch me. You didn't leave me alone for hours. You listened when I talked about her, our dreams. You listened when I cried. You let me rage when I had to rage. You helped me process the unimaginable." Stepping forward, he lays a hand on Kieran's upper arm. "And now that I'm older than you, I can say with a hundred percent conviction that I wouldn't have become the captain I was without your compassion, without you showing me how to not lose human touch despite the war, despite the deaths. I have you to thank for that."

Kieran nods once, clearing his throat. "I... I still would have preferred for you to never have to learn that lesson."

"Me, too, but it happened." He lets go of Kieran's arm, his gaze taking on a distant quality. "And maybe... I don't know, but it's something I tell myself to feel better—maybe she's still alive somewhere. Maybe there's a place where Suzie never died." A small, embarrassed smile crosses his face before he drops his gaze and shrugs. "The imagination of an old, sentimental man."

I open my mouth and close it again. Does he... does he know? No, he can't. He knows I travelled through time, but not about other timelines. Mom hasn't published the multiple-universe theory yet, she's going to wait until we have more political stability before she drops that bomb.

Kieran catches my attention and raises an eyebrow, placing his other hand above his stomach, his way of checking what my First Sense says.

Why would he—*Oh.* Of course.

I focus and call on my First Sense, which is so much easier than ever before. Comparing to when I was thrown back to the *Pioneer* and had no idea what those tugging sensations meant or that I even had a First Sense, I've become a pro. And who knows, maybe my development isn't done yet, given that I somehow started late and my sensitivity to time is still increasing. Potential new mad skills, coming right up.

Looking up at Kieran I give him a tiny nod. He's good, my First Sense is all relaxed about what he's going to say and share.

Observing our silent interaction, Chocho narrows his eyes. "What am I missing here?"

Now Kieran clasps the other man's shoulder. "Nothing at all. I just wanted to say that I wouldn't call it the imagination of an old, sentimental man, but maybe the idea of a visionary. And that we agree with you. Somewhere, Suzie is alive, married to you, and you're both living the lives you envisioned for yourselves."

When I had accidentally landed in Other Nonie's timeline and jumped behind the couch to hide from her Kieran, the admiral, coming in, I overheard him talking about Chocho. *If he ever stopped swooning about that wife of his long enough...* It doesn't make up for losing Suzie for himself in his reality, but maybe it gives Chocho some peace.

The admiral tilts his head and regards us for a silent two or three seconds, before he lowers his chin in a slow, controlled nod. "I... I understand, I think. And that's all I'll need to know." He holds out his hand to Kieran, and they shake, something passing between them, speaking of understanding and mutual support.

"I'm looking forward to following your career," Chocho says, "both of yours." And with that and a nod he pulls his uniform jacket straight and strides past us.

Kieran looks after him, a content expression on his face, one of peace. Maybe Chocho needed to hear about Suzie, but Kieran also needed to hear Chocho is doing fine.

After five or six meters, the admiral halts and turns around to us. "By the way, in case that was ever in question, you've got my vote for the peace accords, Captain. I can't wait to see what the future will bring."

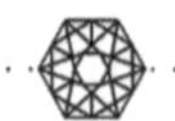

### USEF Star Hopper, March 8th, 2296, 1830hrs

"Lieutenant Elrabat, the *Exploration* is hailing us." Chetty, manning the comm for his colleague Reed, who delivered a beautiful baby boy yesterday—the first on the *Star Hopper*—turns toward the young officer in the captain's chair.

Kaitlyn Elrabat gestures at me. "That's for you, Commander."

Getting up from my chair at my station I nod. "I guess so. Put them through, Chetty."

"Would you like me to tie the captain in, Commander?" Chetty holds one hand hovering over his display.

"No, thank you, the captain would like to not be disturbed right now. Just put them through."

"Aye, Ma'am."

"*Good evening,* Star Hopper. *Commander.*" A holo of Chase in his office pops up a few meters in front of me, spiffy in his uniform as always. I swear he has them tailored, nobody's uniform fits that well.

"Admiral. Good to see you."

"*Likewise, I must say. It's been too long. Are you ready for us?*"

"Happy to demat you over and welcome you on board, sir. I'm sure you've seen the *Pioneer* arrived about an hour ago—"

He rolls his eyes. "*Have I? Well, Admiral Upinga has dematted over*" *to them the second the jump to this location was completed, so yes, I know."* Only because we're on an official channel with all my bridge crew listening in does Chase not say what he's thinking, but I've got a pretty good idea about that.

Which is why I'm keeping that grin tucked away and safe. "Well, sir, then come and join us, the captain has been preparing intensely for our meeting and is very much looking forward to it."

A grin spreads across Chase's face. He understands. And I guess he's hungry.

*"I'll see you in five, Commander."*

And with that, he cuts the connection, and I nod at Elrabat. "I'll be at the meeting," I say, making eye contact with Kaitlyn. She's been on the *Wanderer* before, earning her lieutenant's pips when she led the crew through a complete systems' failure which had disconnected the bridge and its officers from the rest of the ship—while cutting off oxygen and life-support. Her taking charge and finding a solution to override the malfunction probably saved the whole crew's lives.

"I got it, Commander." Kaitlyn gives a quick salute before she slides deeper into the center chair, looks around the bridge. "Easy routine, right?" She winks, and Chetty groans.

"You know, this jinxing thing is real, right?"

The bridge crew breaks out into a mix of excited squeals and worried groans, but before we have a repeat of the, uhh, *animated discussion* they had when the chef had tried to take a vote whether to implement Taco Tuesdays or Sushi Sundays, I lift both palms and everybody stops talking like I muted them. It's kind of freaky.

Guess I'm still not used to the impact I have on others. Or maybe I'm thinking and hoping they'll see me as a normal person who just handled the cards dealt to her and came out lucky, but so far that hasn't happened yet. That being said, I get it. I broke two of Kieran's records when it comes to promotions, jumping from cadet to lieutenant faster than Kieran, just like Grazer had said when he gave me those pips, and then topping it off making commander right after the peace with the Essken.

As soon as the accords were signed, Dad and Grazer talked, and a few days later parts of my mission to bring back the plants as the cure for the Reptilian flu were made public. Obviously not the parts that dealt with time travel, but the ones where I accepted a possible suicide mission into Essken space to give humanity a chance for survival.

People went crazy when they heard it, so crazy, I now understand why Kieran never liked the hype surrounding the Hotshot Trio. I got fan mail, still do. People ask me for autographs, which is so weird.

But alas, it's that mission and that fame that got me where I am today, promoted to commander and assigned to the *USEF Star Hopper* as special advisor to the captain. Of course, having been the one who brought back Captain Wildason from the Essken Realm and part of the team making peace with the Essken half the crew thinks I really work for D-2, which is quite hilarious, I find.

Either way, while Elrabat is in command right now, the crew is looking to me. I let my hands sink down. "There's no jinxing. While yes, surprises in unexplored space happen, everything looks calm right now. And if that changes, either you handle it, or you let the captain and me know." I don't expect it though, luckily, and I really appreciate the decrease in urgency. Since I was thrown back to the *Pioneer*, everything was about extinction. Either humanity from either the flu virus, or by the Quaneez-slash-Essken, or them by Izola's planned genocide. I don't mind the downgrade to our common, normal, close-to-boring problems, like a new species we met being offended we made contact with them *after* building a relationship with their neighbors. That's a problem we can solve with communication and understanding their point of view, and we'll get it done. I'm quite proud how USEF, under my dad's direction, has changed. We're no longer so arrogant to keep to ourselves.

Kaitlyn lowers her chin in a quick nod. "Exactly, Commander. *Star Hopper* is home to the best." That statement gets her agreeing murmurs from everybody, and I smile.

"That's why the captain chose each and every one of you." I nod to Kaitlyn. "I'll be at the meeting."

"Aye, Commander."

I resist to look back and check the crew one more time as I exit the bridge. Like I said, they are the best, but after a temporal war and feeling like I was always a step behind, Kieran I have control issues.

Which I'm working on letting go.

That being said, it helps to know that we could get to the bridge in no time—even at my leisurely pace down the hallway, it takes me no more than thirty seconds to get to our quarters.

Ah, the luxury of rank.

Our doors recognize me and open, releasing an aroma of herbs and roasted meat from the inside. Stepping in quickly so the doors can close, I hope not too much of that scent has made it into the hallway, or our cover of a serious meeting will be blown in no time.

Oh, well. Who cares? The captain can do whatever he wants. If I thought I was famous, it's still nothing against Kieran's reputation. Ninety percent of the crew still get starstruck whenever he addresses them by name, and we've been on this mission for close to five months at this point.

I inhale a lungful of the deliciousness Kieran has been preparing, a little jolt of happiness shooting through me. My soul is full of warm and fuzzy emotions, so full, it might spill over.

What a good problem to have.

"Honey, I'm home," I call out, and earn a chuckle from Kieran.

"And dinner is almost ready, as it should be after a long day of work." He looks up from whatever he's mixing together—ah, a salad. "Everything go well on the bridge?"

I kick off my shoes and hold my hands under the UV sanitizer next to the door. "Business-wise, yes. Chetty still asked to call you though when Chase hailed."

"He just likes me more than you." Kieran wiggles his eyebrows, and while a year or two ago, I would've felt the same, I don't anymore. I'm not the odd one out anymore, being Admiral Thorburn's daughter. Not the odd one out being a *Mag Lover*. Not the *maggot* anymore. Nobody's been bullying me since I left the academy—and again, not because I outrank them or because they're starstruck, but because I work with good people, and people in general have seen the light. Since Kieran's speech, diversity has been the new rage. Peace has. I'm one of the team, accepted for who I am and what I did *and* despite my age, which is such an odd feeling to get used to, but quite exhilarating.

So, I just give Kieran a shrug, unconcerned. "Maybe he likes you more, but I'm thinking he was just fishing for information about where you've been the last three hours."

"And you told him…?"

"That you're busy, preparing for the meeting with the admirals. Which, you are." I gesture at the set table and the appetizers already on it. Cheeses, a charcuterie board, crackers… "I wasn't lying, was I?"

"Definitely not. This took a while." He leaves the salad tongs in the bowl and wipes his hand on his apron. "When everybody's here—"

The doors open without a ring or announcement, and Chase steps in, greeting us as soon as the doors closed behind him. "Evening, my favorite time traveling couple."

Kieran raises a brow at him. "Politeness is out the window again?"

Chase raises the close to gallon-sized bottle of Lubbeck's before he puts it on the dining table. "Nah, not in general, but I figured I just spoke to Nonie five minutes ago, and if I need to knock after five minutes…" He cringes. "I don't even want my mind to go there."

Kieran throws a balled-up kitchen towel at him. "Don't make me regret giving Zee and you full access to our quarters."

Catching the towel and throwing it back, Chase grins. "Oh, I surely will, but you'll also love it. So, suck it up." He turns to me and winks, purposefully ignoring Kieran's extra-deep sigh.

"All right then, you're here, make yourself useful. We both need an update on Project Behave."

Chase chuckles. "Still the best project name ever assigned."

"Why, thank you." I lower my head in a mock royal bow, after all, it was me who came up with that name—my first official FBTI-project, and named after my suggestion. But what could be a better name if it's about ensuring the future doesn't turn out like what we saw?

I sit down and reach for the Lubbeck's. Somehow it does taste better when it's from the bottle compared to from the synth.

"What about the information the judge gave Kelia? Did it help? Anything good in it?" Kieran makes a pinching motion over the back of his hand and flicks his wrist away from his body in reference to what Judge Alberti did, when she sent the file, a true cornucopia of history, to my mom.

Chase pulls out a chair from the same spot he always takes, no matter on which ship we eat together. Old habits die hard. "It was a gold mine, actually. Not that we're acting on everything, but it helped tie together some loose ends. Plus, from a certain point of view, it's interesting to see history unfold when it hasn't happened yet. The progression is truly fascinating to follow. Humanity First was in its infancy and somewhat innocent when we were young and still on the *Pioneer*—don't get me wrong, they were already annoying back then, but not to their recent levels. Then, during our now, they're already infiltrated by Izola's family, which is still so crazy, I never would've considered it."

"Hiding in plain sight," Kieran comments, taking a seat at the table with us. "Right up my dad's alley of paranoia."

"That for sure. Founding and supporting an anti-Magellan group and using it to support and build xenophobia, so that eventually, in a few years, humanity would be okay defending itself with total genocide and kill the Essken people only to then put the one inventing that technology in charge. The self-made rise of a murderous tyrant."

"Cut short and prevented by the evidence presented by Admiral Niall Wildason. Not that we're going to tell that to anybody besides the people in the know." I glance over at Kieran. The slightest blush colors his cheek, together with a proud smile on his face. The Wildasons, separated by time, still united to save the universe. Poetic, given the nature of the Temporal War.

Pointing his index finger at Kieran, Chase clicks his tongue. "Which is a pity, because your dad's intel was quite something. Your *dad* was quite something, Kieran. I can only imagine how long it took him to connect all the dots and find proof, or how deep he had to dig. Heck, we're only scratching the surface when it comes to figuring out how Izola got all his chess pieces in place, using Humanity First. Remind me to tell you more about that when the others are here. But my point is, having Nonie kidnapped, blackmailing Addi into shooting you, Kieran…" He huffs. "Your dad knew it before anybody else did."

Kieran flinches, then sighs. "Yeah, Dad was on a roll. I'd be lying if I said his evidence didn't help me come to terms with what she did." Slowly, at least. Kieran loved Addi. In a different universe, they would've been friends—or even family—forever, like in the Zeroverse. When she shot him, it didn't only leave physical wounds, but large, gaping psychological ones. "Her suicide after she shot me is yet another death Humanity First is responsible for."

"And we've added it to their tab." Chase helps himself to some cheese. "You know, I've never seen Bas happier than when he arrested Travis Roodt with the evidence brought up against Humanity First."

That I believe without a doubt. And while that makes me very happy, I'm not stupid enough to think the problem is solved by cutting off the head of the snake. These kinds of beasts regrow them. "There are still too many people out there who believe what he preached."

Chase nods. "Way too many. But showing them the ugly truth helps for them not to see him as a martyr and idolize him. Maybe we de-radicalized Humanity First, and if so, I'd count that as a victory. They have a right to their opinion. Not my fault it's the wrong one." He sticks out his tongue and takes a sip of Lubbeck's before the corners of his lips pull down. "I just wish your dad knew how everything turned out, Kieran. He'd have deserved some clarity and peace of mind. Especially after the way you had to leave last time."

Kieran stands up so quickly, his chair topples over. "Whoops, forgot the bread in the oven, let me check." With two quick strides, he gets around the kitchen island and opens the oven, moving the bread from right to left, the protective heat shield giving his hand a slight yellow glow.

Chase narrows his eyes, then tilts his head slowly. "Your poor father must have lived his last years in agony."

"Uh-huh," Kieran says, his back still facing Chase.

"And desperate to know if you were alive."

"Uh-huh."

"A very hard fate for a man who loved his son so very dearly." He looks at me, but I'm quite busy with my napkin at the moment.

For a long few seconds, nobody says anything. Then Chase groans. "You did it. You guys went back. You talked to Niall."

Kieran closes the oven door, his shoulders heaving up and down in a big sigh before he turns around, face blank. "I don't know what you're talking about. Would I have liked to see my dad again and make sure he doesn't worry for the rest of his life? Of course."

I look up at Chase. "But of course, we don't just jump through time for personal gain."

"Never." Kieran shakes his head. "But if we did, I would've made sure he knew the outcome and that I was happy where and when I was. I'd tell him about you all and how you are still my backbone. Maybe I'd tell him I got a new ship and a new mission, he would like to hear that."

"I'm sure he would." Chase looks positively tortured. "Good thing this is all hypothetical."

Nodding twice, I hold up a finger. "Exactly. And hypothetically speaking, if we had done this, only one of two events would've happened: either Niall being in the know would not change the flow of time, or, if he changed his behavior because of it in a drastic manner causing big impact on the timeline, a new one would've split off. We wouldn't be affected. Rule three, Temporal Deviations." I tap my brand new, pink PADdy, courtesy of Chase. For a split second I thought about refusing his gift, then gladly accepted it: one, buzzword Lubbeck's, and two, the information and tech he put on my old PADdy saved my butt more than once. At this point, I consider a PAD from him a good luck charm.

Chase grunts. "Don't quote temporal rules at me."

I *tsk* at him and grin. "But I have a handbook. And believe me, I love that I do." Okay, granted, I came up with most of the rules myself, being the only inter-dimensional time-traveler we have, but still. Mom supplied the theories, me the experience, so this is a family-project at this point. "And if—I'm saying *if*—we had talked to Niall, we would've checked afterward for the integrity of the timeline, and it would've been pristine." Because Niall is good. That man lives USEF through and through. Finding out his theory helped stop the Temporal War and save his son was the best gift we could've given him. Well, that and coming back. Kieran and I talked it through for a while, with a sound block in place, by the way. Not that anybody could stop me or check what I did when I jump, but I'd like to not give off too big of a renegade-vibe.

With a good couple of years between our encounter in the Wildason's backyard and Niall's eventual death, Kieran felt it would be nice to come by at somewhat regular intervals to see his dad. Just like other kids visit their parents, only we'd do it not only from a different place, but from a different time and place. And the kicker is, we're going to visit him every couple of years from our vantage point, so he gets to see his son grow older, in a slightly accelerated way. For that I did cheat a tad more, to be honest. I followed Kieran's and my signature futural in our timeline, just to make sure we'd be there to stick to our plan. Working for USEF can have unintended consequences, as we both know. Seems like we will at least reach retirement age—after that I stopped looking. I don't want to know when we die, or who dies first. Even the knowledge that we'll make it to a certain age could influence my decision making, but here's one thing I learned: It's okay.

If that piece of knowledge changes the course of my life in a significant way, a new timeline will develop. New paths will be opened. Nothing is lost, not the past, not the future. Time is forgiving in that sense.

Laying his forehead down on the table, Chase holds up a hand. "I don't want to talk about hypothetical rule-breaking anymore. It's only going to get me into trouble with Zee. Although…" He lifts his head. "Hypothetically, if you ever did such a thing, you'd know to say hi from me and that I still miss his guidance?"

That's when Kieran grins from ear to ear. "Of course, we would do that. Hypothetically."

They share a long glance, then Chase chuckles. "You two…!" Shaking his head, he occupies himself with more Lubbeck's and some crackers.

"Well, anyway. When is Zio coming?" Kieran asks, rubbing his hands together, a tad too eager to switch the topic.

Rolling his eyes, Chase takes another sip of his drink before he replies. "Whenever he and Magona can take their hands off each other."

"Eww." I wrinkle my face. "TMI, Chase."

He gives me a look that says, really? "Imagine how I feel when I'm near them. Wasn't expecting the whole love-bird experience at our age."

"To be fair, Zio has some catching up to do." Kieran wipes down the counter with a kitchen towel. "And the Taro and him always seemed to click."

"Yeah, yeah, I'm happy for him and everything." Chase waves a hand. "But anyway. Where's Tom? Kelia?" He counts the number of plates on the table. "You guys, Zee, me, Magona, Tom, Kelia—Bas?"

"No Bas," Kieran says. "*Star Hopper*, display message received from Admiral Grazer at 0900 hours this morning."

A holo of Grazer appears in the middle of the room. *Star Hopper*, as the newest of the fleet's ships, has flexible holo emitters to display messages where they're needed. The system takes the number of people in the room into account, which is why Grazer is visible for everybody.

*"Captain Wildason,"* Grazer says with a bow of his head. *"Unfortunately, me and Saria won't be able to make it today. Hopefully, next time it'll work out better. Please give my regards to everybody. Grazer ou"*—

A tall, Magellan woman steps into the recording, about Grazer's age. I recognize her immediately: she's the woman I saw him with on Alpha Rubrum, when Kieran surprised them!

She waves at us, the widest smile on her face as she hooks her arm around Grazer's. *"Thank you again for what you said during your speech, Captain. It didn't only make humans think, but also Magellans. Without it, the Magellan people would still keep themselves closed off to others, but thanks to you, life has changed. My nephew is applying to the USEF Academy to go into engineering, and a friend of mine is now serving on a USEF ship. Gone are the restrictions humans put on us, or that we put on ourselves. All of a sudden, we have options. And, of course, when I say options, I mean other options as well."* She places a kiss on Grazer's cheek, and Grazer... Holy Universe, Grazer blushes! He *blushes!*

*"Thank you, Captain. You're always welcome at our home."* She waves again and steps out of the recording zone.

Grazer's mouth opens, then closes, before he shakes his head and sighs. *"Well, there goes my authority in front of the commander, if she sees this message. Anyway. We'll hope to be there next time. Grazer out."*

The projection stops and Chase shakes his head. "Whatever I said the last couple of decades, I take it all back. He actually looks... happy." He huffs, in a disbelieving way. "Never thought I'd see the man smile or blush—or be nice to a Magellan. Zio can tell stories about what he said."

"Add it to the list of things Mashaule messed up," I say. Quite sad Grazer had to go polar-opposite of what he believed to keep Mashaule happy, his job secured—and me safe. I'm glad Dad was never blackmailed because of Mom or me. Coming to think about it, partially thanks to Grazer, who knew, but didn't tell, which deserves respect.

"Oh, I got news on that despicable individual as well." Swirling his Lubbeck's in his glass Chase raises it. "Here's to Mashey never getting out of prison again, not that that comes as a surprise."

"No, it doesn't. Still makes me feel better though." I wrap my fingers around my glass as if it could provide some added stability. "He's caused too much trouble, and that over decades."

"But you know what? I guess at this point, now that Izola's gameplay has failed, Mashey is quite forthcoming with information. It bought him a bit of leeway for his end-of-life prison stay, not that I like that, but I appreciate the confirmation. What you told us about..." He crunches up his face. "... Blue Nonie, you called her, I think? The dystopian version of our reality, with the military government and Mashaule's Law? That's exactly what Izola promised him. Power, control, Earth in control of other species, and I mean that in a dominating way. It played right into his racism, oh, and savior complex, of course. Saving the world from destruction by killing you while ridding the world of other species and keeping Earth pure was the perfect allure for Mashey."

"Magellans don't count?" Kieran looks over his shoulder while reaching for the olive oil in the cabinet. "Because, in my book Izola, a Magellan, would still have been the one truly in charge."

Chase raises and drops his shoulders. "The smaller evil? No idea what he was thinking."

The doorbell rings. Good. I don't want to give Mashaule any more brain space than he has already occupied over the last year. It's time to feed my soul, not having it sucked dry by *that* guy.

I catch Kieran's gaze. *My parents*, I mouth. Although, could be Zio. He's the more polite one between him and Chase, he might actually announce his arrival.

"Come in," Kieran calls out.

The doors open to my mom's laughter and Dad's chuckle. "Zio, your sense of humor is fantastic," he says, walking into the room first. "Good evening, everybody."

Mom follows him, holding on to his hand. "Sorry we're late."

Zio, looking confused, is last to enter. "I wasn't aware that I was joking," he says, but his protest is drowned out in all of us getting up and hugging everybody.

It still feels like a gift every time I wrap my arms around my mom.

"Hi, sweetie," she says and holds me a second longer than hugs usually last. I guess we're both still making up for lost time, even though our research on temporal physics has us working together a lot, sometimes remotely, sometimes in person, depending on the *Star Hopper*'s route and Mom's availability. Needless to say I've cherished each and every moment.

"Have a seat, please." Kieran withdraws from his manly embrace with my dad—still an odd sight to behold—and gestures at the table. "Have some nibbles. Dinner is almost ready."

"It smells delicious." Mom beams at him as she takes a seat.

"Don't get your hopes up, Kelia. His concoctions are usually barely edible." Chase gives an exaggerated shudder. "But at least he isn't poisoning us."

"Changing my mind about that in your case right now," Kieran calls out from the stove.

"Kidding." Holding both hands up Chase grins, then drops his voice. "But I do so very much enjoy teasing him."

Zio gives him a skeptical glance. "Have you spoken to your physician about your deep-rooted need to dominate others verbally? It might be the sign of a small ego."

Mom and Dad hide a chuckle behind their hands.

Chase opens his mouth and closes it, a fish out of water. "Well," he eventually draws out, "interesting theory, although I can promise you it's wrong. But you know, I shall bring it up with my physician—but oh wait, I can't. He's been *busy* lately." He puts the word in air quotes. "Busy in the morning. Busy at noon. Busy until late in the evening. Scandalously late, actually."

Zio blushes. "I—"

Before it can get even more awkward, Mom comes to her brother's rescue. "By the way—sorry for the interruption, but I, uhh, didn't want to forget this—the feedback is in."

That gets everybody's attention.

I sit up straighter. "And?"

"And my theories have been discussed, checked, and counter-checked by every science committee on Earth and on all the colonies *and* by all species we're in contact with, including the Essken."

"And?" I repeat, more urgency in my voice. That was the plan, publish her multiple timeline theory and open up the discussion, see where it takes us.

Mom beams ear to ear. "Everybody is beyond excited. They're calling it a breakthrough in temporal mechanics—"

"Which it is," Dad cuts in, pride in his voice.

"Which it is, but I'm still relieved it was received that well."

Chase pours Lubbeck's into everybody's glass. "That deserves a toast! To Kelia and her theories building us a safe and healthy future."

"Hear, hear!" We all raise our glasses and take a sip.

Amazing how much I've learned, how much we've all learned about temporal mechanics in the last months. Mom is literally writing the book on it and has already overhauled the complete curriculum of the Academy's Temporal Mechanics class. Future cadets will definitely have to study harder to pass than I did, but for a good reason. I could've saved myself all the headache, sorrow, and worry over the last year if I had come out of the Academy knowing half of what I do now. Ignorance isn't always bliss.

I take another sip of Lubbeck's, then put my glass down and smack my lips. "Have you made any headway with Izola's bracelet, Mom? Not that it's urgent, but I do want to update the judge at one point." Plus, once we're there, we've got to say hi to Kaytee too—even though technically speaking the two of us will not be her great-grandparents, but the Nonie-Kieran couple in her timeline. Makes interacting with her somehow less awkward, at least from my point of view, even though it's a technicality. And no matter that, I still want to catch up with her though. In a different world, she would've been our relative, and I want to make sure her future turns out well just as I want to make sure ours turns out... well, better than hers did so far. *Cough-cough bubble-prison,* etc.

Mom turns her glass in her hands. "Actually, yes, the bracelet—"

"Oh, when you speak to the judge, I want to get an update on Izola," Chase says, not picking up on my mom rolling her eyes at the interruption. "Because I really, really don't want that guy to ever be free again. Mass-murderer."

"Neither do I," Kieran calls out from the kitchen. He lifts the casserole dish out of the oven and sets it down harder than strictly necessary, the only hint at the depth of despair Izola's game brought him to. Kieran has been doing much better with my help and the help of a therapist. Still, not that I think he should, but I don't think he'll ever forgive Izola. *He made me think it was better for the timeline to get myself killed,* he told me shortly after we'd been assigned to the Star Hopper, *and that's a feeling I will need some time to get over.* But Kieran is resilient, and the moments where everything catches up with him are becoming rarer. So are the nightmares, although he'd have all the reasons to suffer from them—temporal cleft and near-death experience, anybody?—he hasn't had any for months.

Mom wags her head left to right and waves dismissively. "As I was trying to say, I was able to restore some data from the bracelet, but I also need to be careful to not restore it to a degree that it could be replicated."

"Yes, please don't." Chase downs the contents of his glass before he sets it back onto the table. "Too much trouble. I like to keep reality off the self-destruction mechanism for a while. That reminds me though. I wanted to update y'all on what I've lovingly named the *Gordian Knot of timelines and headaches.*" He reaches for the half-empty gallon of Lubbeck's. "And the reason why I've named it that is the sheer complexity of Izola's interventions throughout his life. Together with Bas and D-2 we've been able to paint a pretty good picture, and when I say good, I mean bad."

Kieran snorts. "I don't think any adjective mentioned together with Izola's name should be a positive one."

"Agreed." Chase pours his glass to the brim with Lubbeck's. "Anyway, I'll give you the short version, and most of it is as we suspected to one degree or another. Tala Torona, Izola's grandmother— remember, she's the specialist in temporal mechanics—had the idea to get Magellans to travel through time again. She started the research, passed it on to her daughter, Izola's mom, who then passed it down to him. When Izola tried it out, it malfunctioned and accidentally threw him into the dystopian timeline, the one with Praetor Izola. So, of course our Izola did what you did, Nonie and Kieran, and looked at the differences between our universes. That's how and where he learned there were multiple timelines and how the future could be shaped if he took out the Essken."

Dad brushes both palms over the napkin in his lap, straightening it.

"Do we know how that timeline knew about tau-bombs?"

"Not yet." Chase shakes his head. "Smarter people than me tell me the difference might've been years in their past. After all, they seem technologically more advanced than we are. Maybe they had smarter scientists than we did, or maybe a specific scientist died in our world and not in theirs." He shrugs. "Point is, Izola planned to kill his counterpart in that timeline so he could take over, but temporal rejection set in before he could set his plan in motion."

I snap my fingers. "Blue Nonie knew it before we did. Or rather, her mom did." The whole *trans-universal and futural jumps lead to disruptions in the nucleotide bases of our DNA and ultimately, death*-thing is quite the bummer, not only for Izola, but for me, too. Puts a damper on future trans-universal jumps, I must say.

"Sounds like me," Mom says, a twinkle in her eye. "I tend to be right a lot of times. And it would make sense. Looking at our medical records and scans from before Izola took us to the future to right after, there also were some cellular changes to all of us, but most to you and Kieran, Nonie, the two people who'd been in the future and different timelines the longest. The damage resolved on its own, but I imagine that the longer one stays in the future or a different timeline, the more severe the rejection will become and eventually be deadly."

"So, we're not bringing people from the past to our time," Dad says. "We should make that a law."

"No, we're not bringing people from the past or other timelines to ours now, unless we'd want them to die. And yes, besides that, it's still common sense to not mess with fate and time, it should be a law. I'll add it to our list." Mom nods at me, and I give her a small salute in acknowledgement. The handbook is gaining substance.

Chase claps his hands twice. "And to get that story over with, because I really want to eat and not have my appetite taken by Izola's ugly deeds: since our Izola had to leave the Praetor's timeline, he stole himself some tech he then used to come up with that disk you all know and love. From there on, Izola tried to change the past so that it would turn out as the Praetor's did."

I shudder. "Not a life goal one should have, but that's why that man has issues."

"Indeed. So, here the headache usually sets in for me, since we're talking about Izola trying to alter the past several times throughout his life. And let's just remember that without that bracelet keeping him tethered to the new, altered timeline, he wouldn't have gotten to enjoy any of the changes. Anyway. First, he travelled back himself and recruited family. His grandmother, who did the dirty work for him through Humanity First. She's also the one who blackmailed Addi to shoot Kieran and who got the engineers to sabotage the *Journey*'s jump drive." As a form of acknowledgement, Chase points over Kieran's shoulder at the picture of Niall on Kieran's desk.

"When that didn't work out, he changed his approach and tried to get Nonie killed. No Nonie, nobody to rescue Kieran from the Mind Crucification. Luckily for her and us those two idiots apparently drew a line at killing a child and decided to instead sufficiently traumatize her, physically and mentally, to never make it into USEF." He closes his eyes for a short moment, muscles in his jaw tight. "Disgusting. But to continue, the two kidnappers were also blackmailed by grandma Torona. Not yet sure what dirt she had on them or where they vanished to from the USEF prison, but we're working on it. Once our Izola refined the disk, he then used it to get Mashaule to change the course of time at Alpha Rubrum—that's when he could project a solid hologram, by the way, quite advanced."

"Why did he make it so complicated?" Dad asks. "If I ever wanted to change the past to become the one in power, I feel I would start... I don't know, somewhere bigger. Throw a tau-bomb on the Essken Realm, maybe. Make it clear I'm superior, and that would include altering the past myself. The error rate of having other people do the job for you..." He shakes his head.

Chase points at Dad. "Great minds. I asked the same thing. Turns out he tried to kill the Essken with a tau-bomb, at least he claims he did."

Everybody looks at me.

I lift my palms. "Hey, just because I can jump through timelines doesn't mean I've been to all of them. No idea if what he's claiming is true."

"Our forensic psychologist seems to think so. And Izola's story does make sense. Apparently, we haven't given Nonie enough credit and it's difficult to jump and bring somebody or objects with you."

"It takes practice to be awesome." I blow on my cuticles and rub them over my shirt. But to be fair, I had no idea how I had brought the shuttle with me the first time—or second time—I jumped. Once I jumped and didn't have my weapon anymore, so there you go. Only now do I feel I got a pretty good grasp, literally, on jumping with passengers or items.

"More than practice, Nonie. Izola doesn't have your genes or skills, so no, he luckily couldn't just take a tau-bomb with him and get the job done." Chase grimaces and shudders. "So, he tried to convince the people of Earth they should build one and do it. But alas, my faith in people is somewhat restored, since that didn't work either. Imagine what it would take for us to sign off on genocide. We were close to it, and while that was years in the making it would still have needed approval from many different authorities. Izola's reach didn't go far enough when he traveled back. He simply didn't have enough pull, and he had no patience to insert himself into time and age through it while strengthening his position. So, he changed his tactics to tweaking the past in a way that would benefit him once he was born, using people who were in a position of advantage for his plans already, like Addi. For him to get to the same position would've required a lot more planning, and well, time. And," Chase lifts a finger, "that role fits the image he has of himself as an orchestrator and savior of humanity. He's full of grandeur. Only reasons why he had Sheridan do the jumps were his fear of temporal rejection—better Sheridan than him, right?—and that doing the dirty work himself didn't and doesn't fit the picture he has of himself. Simply put, he wants to save humanity from the evil Essken and be celebrated as the savior. He wants to be the good guy."

"Obviously that worked out well," Kieran deadpans.

"Right. In neither universe, by the way," Chase says, eyeing his plate with a hung expression. "Since, to carry on with that story, he went back to the Praetor's timeline to steal more tech when he didn't get the results he needed. Bad boy."

"Very bad boy. That's when he injured Blue Nonie's mom," I add. While I can distance myself from Izola and what he's done to me, that little tidbit makes it personal somehow.

"I'm pretty sure my counterpart would feel better if she knew he failed, even after stealing their tech. And since you asked earlier and I didn't get to tell you because *someone*"—she throws a glance at Chase— "couldn't let me finish a sentence, here's the update on the bracelet he needed said tech for. As I suspected, every time it was activated it wore down the fabric of time." Mom makes a stretching motion with her hands. "And because he designed the bracelet to keep himself in the new, split-off universe it added an unnatural stress on time, which started the episodes you and Kieran were experiencing. Whenever he activated it, temporal shards broke off from random innocent timelines due to the stress—and then the two of you got assaulted by those K'Zees when they recognized Nonie's First Sense could put them back together. And, when you did, you fixed what Izola's bracelet had caused. At least until he had added more features to the bracelet. Like, the ability to control the timelines as you saw in the Maelstrom, Nonie, and that it would've protected him from rejection had he jumped to a different timeline."

"Completely abhorrent," Chase says. "That kind of power is too much for anybody."

"And for the fabric of time." Mom sighs. "When he activated the bracelet this very last time, those alterations were the reasons it ripped time apart." She makes a tearing motion with her hands, then pops a piece of cheese into her mouth with a challenging look at Chase. "And that's my update."

Dad reaches over to squeeze her hand on the table. "Quite scary imagining the potential of the technology he stole from that Praetor's timeline. But thinking as the USEF president, what does that mean for us? Do we need to worry about that timeline?" He looks at me, one eyebrow raised.

I swallow the olives in my mouth. "I'll check in with Blue Nonie once we've figured out how long I can stay in a different timeline without damaging my DNA, thank you very much, but to answer your question, I don't think so. They sounded like they were ready to defend themselves, but not considering attacking others." I hope. Or else we really need to come up with a temporal task force, and to be honest, that's not a direction I want our future to go in.

"We'll plan that together with Taro Magona once Bas and your mom have gotten us the intel and research to guarantee your safety," Chase says, nodding, before he makes a slicing gesture. "And that's it. Done. I want to start my appetizers and not to think about Izola for the next couple of hours. That man has occupied way too much of my brain space."

Everybody murmurs in agreement. For a good ten or twenty seconds, silence hovers as we all pick from the selection of appetizers. Chase groans when he takes the first bite of a cheese dip Kieran made.

"That's the sound of Trip enjoying my *barely edible concoction*," Kieran comments drily.

"It'sh not too b'd t'day," Chase says, his reply muffled by the cheesy goodness and cracker in his mouth.

Zio gives his friend a slightly exasperated glance, then pats his mouth with his napkin and clears his throat. "An update from the Taro: She sends her regards to everybody and will be here in about an hour. Nonie, she would also like you to check in with her in the next few days regarding the jump back to the Diversion Points you discussed."

I crack my fingers. Perfect, and about time. Those jumps I can do without any risk, and I've been waiting for the Taro to contact me. I love that I'm able to be on somewhat normal duty on board the *Star Hopper* until the FBTI calls. I love even more that we're part of OUTREACH and get to work with Chase and Zio, and so does the press. Granted, they left me out because I didn't fit the narrative—*boo* for that—but I very much enjoyed to read about the reunited Hotshot Trio, and so did many, many others, if the amount of fan mail all three are getting is any indication. No idea what Zio and Chase do with theirs, but I learned how to handle fan mail from Kieran: his goes straight to his secretary for a somewhat personalized, but standardized reply. He never cared about the fame; that hasn't changed from forty years ago. Kieran working with OUTREACH is doing what he always dreamed of doing: discovering new species, making first contact, and finding new friends.

Thank you, fate, for that wish fulfillment. Even though we complained about you along the way, in the end we all owe you one. It hasn't passed me by that ultimately, even my two mentors got what they wanted, me joining their division. But then, so did I, pulling off my dream of also working for the very same division that sent the operative who saved me from my kidnappers, i.e, me.

Gotta love the little quirks of time travel.

"Taro Magona said Diversion Points? Plural?" Dad takes the napkin from the table and lays it across his lap.

Nodding, I get up and walk over to the kitchen to help Kieran serve the main course. "Yes. First, I've got to be the medic saving young Kieran—"

Kieran grimaces. "Yes, please do, I'd appreciate that."

"It will be my pleasure." I add a slightly awkward bow. "And then I can't forget to give myself-from-a-few-months-ago the data disk while I'm at the Raspberry farm, but then I also have to jump back as Star Hopper, get nine-year-old me out of the kidnapper's grasp, and have a talk with my dad about little Nonie's future in the Academy." I should start keeping better track of my footprints along the timeline. It's getting complicated, especially considering me saving myself might've been a new timeline split-off. Actually, I'm pretty sure it was. Is. Either way, it needs to happen. I won't let myself be stranded in time, not with everything that depends on me—and Kieran—being in the correct location at the correct time.

Dad groans. "Don't enjoy taking my temporal innocence too much, please."

Grabbing the side salad, I grin at Dad. "Let me have this. I feel like

I've been paying for that one moment for the next couple of years, so at least let me appreciate the look on your face when it clicks for you."

Dad rolls his eyes and takes the salad bowl I hand him. "Don't hold against me whatever I said. I was still in shock from my daughter having been kidnapped—"

"But hey, at least not killed," I add. Still gives me goosebumps thinking Izola was about to jump back and get the job done himself. And lately I've been wondering… How and when did I first travel back to save myself? I have so many questions. Like, what happened to that other me, how damaged was she, and why did she decide to jump to that specific point to save herself? Did she know she was splitting off a new timeline, or did she just not care that she was changing the past?

I cringe as a shudder runs down my back. Don't want to imagine what would've needed to happen to me to not care about temporal integrity anymore.

Maybe I'll look for the timeline in which older me makes the decision to go to the past and save her younger self. Seriously, she must know she's changing her timeline's path at that point, not that I'm complaining. I can only imagine what other cruel plans my kidnappers might have had. If I hadn't saved myself I doubt I would've gotten out of there as quickly or with only one destroyed leg.

Dad gives me *the* look with his brows pulled into a critical V. "Yes, but I would've preferred for none of it to happen. Either way, not only was I recovering from that, but you," he points at me, "also turned my world upside down on that day. Cut me some slack when you explain time travel to me, will you?"

I pat his shoulder. "No problem, Dad. I'll be gentle."

He huffs and serves himself some salad, handing the bowl to Mom.

Zio pours himself some water. "Let me know when you will jump, and I will have the cocktail ready for you." He nods at Kieran, then at me. "For you both. In fact, I developed a small, discrete auto-injector for you to wear." He wraps two fingers around his wrist, like a bracelet. "It contains analytic functions and will be able to tell when the Bond is broken. At that point it will inject the medication—or, if you want to manually trigger it, you can do so as well. Either way, neither of you should be suffering from the effects of a broken Bond anymore."

"Hallelujah," Kieran says, carrying the roasted veggies over on a large serving platter.

Hallelujah indeed. And now I know why future-me wasn't doubled over from the interruption of the Bond like I was. She popped up in that cave like it was no big deal, while me... Yeah. I didn't like that transition at all.

We all serve ourselves, and for a good thirty seconds, silence hovers.

"Smells delicious, Kieran," my mom says, rubbing her hands together, and she's right. The roasted veggies, the synth-meat in its gravy, the fresh baked bread... My stomach grumbles as I dig in. It's been a long day.

After a few minutes of back and forth small talk, Kieran puts down his fork. "I'm thinking we should introduce the idea of an alliance soon." He taps his fingers onto the table. "Your multiple timeline theories have been well-received, Kelia. Maybe people's mental walls and preconceptions are crumbling. It strikes me as a good point in time to talk about the future of humanity, which isn't in dominance or solitude, but in peaceful cooperation."

"I agree with you." Dad wipes his mouth with his napkin, then drapes it back over his lap. "The time is right. Old concepts have been shaken loose, xenophobia is at an all-time low, people are on an emotional high from the peace treaty, and the Essken have just developed the first mental-audio translator. Founding the UWO now would give us a very high percentage of approval—"

"And once it's founded and going well, no reason to undo it. Voila, we have a peaceful cooperation of peoples to support each other and learn from." Chase points his loaded fork at Kieran. "Are you done getting yourself into the history books then?"

Kieran snorts. "From my point of view, I didn't need to be in them at all. But since that got me to where I am and ultimately to this command..." He raises his glass. "To the future. To other timelines. But mainly, to all of you, because there's no timeline I'd rather be in than in this one. Cheers." He holds his glass out to the center of the table with one hand while searching for mine under the table with his other, squeezing it when he laces his fingers between mine and brushes his thumb over the rainbow ring.

"Cheers!" Everybody responds as we clink our glasses.

"Hear, hear," Dad says.

Most of us only take a sip of our beverages, while Chase downs his Lubbeck's to the last drop.

"You just added another hour in the gym to your fitness regimen," Zio says, shooting a criticizing glance at the empty glass.

"So worth it." Chase pours himself another glass. "Sometimes you gotta know how to celebrate, Zee."

"I—"

"Trip is right, you need to loosen up, Zee." Mom bumps her shoulder into her brother's.

"Excuse me," Zio scuffs. "You haven't seen me for close to twenty years, and you're taking his side?"

Mom laughs. "I've heard stories." She winks at Zio and nods her chin at Dad.

"Hey, leave me out of it, I didn't say anything—"

"Much," Mom mumbles under her breath.

"And yet you realized *I* am the misunderstood person here, not Zio. Thank you, Kelia." Chase fake-bows in place, the most content smile on his face.

Zio huffs. "While my sister's intellect when it comes to temporal theory is clearly above average, her common sense and judgement of your Lubbeck's consumption is surprisingly off. I wouldn't—"

"Hey!" Mom elbows her brother into his side. "Watch what you're saying, you might be older, but—"

As they bicker back and forth, a rare sensation of peacefulness wraps over me, like a soft, secure blanket. I look around the table over my friends—my *family*, because neither Chase nor Zio are simply friends anymore. They're family, literally in Zio's case, but even though I'm not related to Chase, he's family, period. I look from one to the next, so incredibly thankful we're here together. We're alive. Thriving. In a good place, all of us.

It's way more than I expected over the last weeks. Who knows what new problems are going to await us, but we've survived the almost-destruction of reality, how bad can it be?

Right now, my First Sense is calm, quiet, and happy, just like my soul. *I'm* happy.

Kieran turns his head to look at me. Our gazes meet, and he must've seen something in mine, because he lowers his fork and cups my face with both hands, then leans his forehead against mine.

The bickering becomes background noise, so does the teasing and the loving get-a-room jokes, but they still fill us up, they still recharge our batteries.

This is what we wanted. What we longed for, what we hoped for.

Family.

Us.

We have what we thought was never in the cards: a future, and it's ours to shape.

**THE END.**

# About the Author

Micky O'Brady is a pediatrician-turned-writer living in beautiful, dry Southern California with her husband and two critters (one son, one dog). Micky loves to write YA thrillers and sci-fi with a romantic twist, mainly because she wishes her life had been such an awesome mix of action and cute guys when she was a teen.

When she isn't up at around 3 a.m. (with a cup of tea, Earl Grey, hot) drafting stories she can't get out of her head, she can be found at a martial arts dojo, though maybe not at 3 a.m. She holds a first degree black belt in Krav Maga and a second degree black belt in Judo, and is convinced every girl should know how to kick some butt.

Micky also is a firm believer in the healing powers of Nutella eaten straight from the glass and in the magic that can happen on a rainy day, as long as there are fuzzy socks and a cup of hot tea involved.

Her previous publications include a doctoral thesis and several medical articles as well as a medical book about emergency communication. None of them are as fun to read as her YA novels though. Her first YA-novel, THE PRESIDENT'S DAUGHTER, and its sequel TRIAL BY ICE, are published by Curiosity Quills and available through all major retailers, such as Amazon, B&N, Kobo, and Smashwords.

Through Snowy Wings Publishing Micky is the author of the YA-sci-fi romance BETWEEN WORLDS, a super-cool contemporary romance-slash-pro-wrestling-story PLAYING WITH #FIRE, as well as another sci-fi romance, TIME WARPED, and its sequels TIME BOUND and TIMED OUT.

www.ingramcontent.com/pod-product-compliance
Lightning Source LLC
Chambersburg PA
CBHW030952190726
48285CB00004BB/1310